STONY
RIVER

ALSO BY TRICIA DOWER

Silent Girl

TRICIA DOWER

Tricia Dower

STONY RIVER

PENGUIN

an imprint of Penguin Canada

Published by the Penguin Group
Penguin Group (Canada), 90 Eglinton Avenue East, Suite 700, Toronto, Ontario, Canada M4P 2Y3
(a division of Pearson Canada Inc.)

Penguin Group (USA) Inc., 375 Hudson Street, New York, New York 10014, U.S.A.
Penguin Books Ltd, 80 Strand, London WC2R 0RL, England
Penguin Ireland, 25 St Stephen's Green, Dublin 2, Ireland (a division of Penguin Books Ltd)
Penguin Group (Australia), 250 Camberwell Road, Camberwell, Victoria 3124, Australia
(a division of Pearson Australia Group Pty Ltd)
Penguin Books India Pvt Ltd, 11 Community Centre, Panchsheel Park, New Delhi – 110 017, India
Penguin Group (NZ), 67 Apollo Drive, Rosedale, Auckland 0632, New Zealand
(a division of Pearson New Zealand Ltd)
Penguin Books (South Africa) (Pty) Ltd, 24 Sturdee Avenue, Rosebank, Johannesburg 2196, South Africa

Penguin Books Ltd, Registered Offices: 80 Strand, London WC2R 0RL, England

First published 2012

1 2 3 4 5 6 7 8 9 10 (WEB)

Copyright © Tricia Dower, 2012
Map created by Patricia Geernaert

Author representation: Westwood Creative Artists, 94 Harbord Street, Toronto, Ontario M5S 1G6

Several scenes in *Stony River* first appeared in story form in *Silent Girl* (Inanna, 2008) and *The Malahat Review* (2010).
Parts of *Stony River* were inspired by the crimes of Robert Zarinsky, as documented by Robin Gaby Fisher and
Judith Lucas in *Deadly Secrets* (*Newark Star-Ledger*, 2008).

Page 348 is an extension of this copyright page.

Manufactured in Canada.

Library and Archives Canada Cataloguing in Publication data available upon request to the publisher.

ISBN: 978-0-14-318247-4

Visit the Penguin Canada website at **www.penguin.ca**

Special and corporate bulk purchase rates available; please see
www.penguin.ca/corporatesales or call 1-800-810-3104, ext. 2477.

ALWAYS LEARNING   PEARSON

FOR MY SISTER

We're home, Lillian.

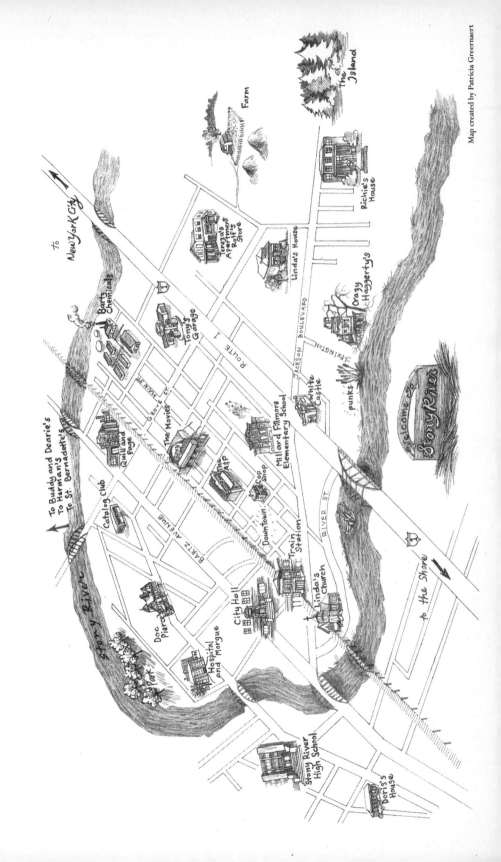

Map created by Patricia Greernaert

How brilliant to have come by this house at road's end.

Only the river's liquid eyes on us.

—JAMES HAGGERTY, MAY 12, 1944

✿ ONE ✿

JUNE 22, 1955. The river crooked its finger at her.

Linda Wise crabwalked down the squishy bank, taking care not to slip. She didn't dare show up at home with mud on her behind. Even the call of a tree frog or a fluttering swallowtail made her jump. Strides ahead, her new friend Tereza Dobra—a regular Marco Polo—carved a path through tall, hairy milkweed.

The Stony River meandered for miles through a dozen New Jersey towns like Linda's. Her geography teacher said the river passed through woodlands and wetlands, salt marshes and tidal flats, and once upon a time had harbored creatures with astonishing names like diamondback terrapin, alewife and cormorant. Now you were more likely to find rusty car fenders and stinky chemical foam.

Daddy told of swimming in the river when he was a boy, of the whole town turning out for canoe races past bridges decorated with paper lanterns. Mother told of lying awake at night after Pearl Harbor, sick with worry that the Japanese would skulk up the river, signaling each other with jars of lightning bugs. She also told of two boys who'd drowned when Linda was a baby, the ice breaking as they slid across the river, their frozen bodies found with sad little arms outstretched. Linda was forbidden to go anywhere near the river.

Honor thy father and thy mother. If caught, she'd be banished to her room without dinner. And there'd be one more black mark against her on Judgment Day. Nonetheless, on that hot, sticky afternoon, when Tereza said "Let's go smoke punks at the river, it'll be cooler there," Linda had said "Sure."

It wasn't fair. Tereza seemed to do whatever she wanted. Maybe because she was thirteen and Linda two months shy of twelve. Or maybe because, as Mother said, "There's more than a little gypsy in that girl." All Linda knew of gypsies was that they got to play tambourines and trek around exotic lands in painted wagons strung with pots and pans. Tereza's family had rumbled into the neighbor-hood two weeks ago in a rusting blue truck chock-a-block with boxes, mattresses, a bicycle and furniture odds and sods. They'd lugged it all into the ground-floor apartment of a two-story building across the street and two doors down from Linda. The corner of the building held a store to which Mother sent Linda when they ran out of bread and milk. Mother didn't like going there herself because it was "seedy." Daddy said it had just been neglected. Linda tried not to feel superior to Tereza for living in a tidy bungalow with green siding and its own yard. *Judge not, that ye be not judged.*

What Tereza called punks were cattail flowers that looked like fat cigars. To get to where they grew, the girls had scampered down a narrow road past Crazy Haggerty's house, the biggest and creepiest in the neighborhood, its once white paint weathered to gray. It sat high above the water with no other houses around. The drapes were drawn tight, not a window open to catch a breeze. Linda wondered if Haggerty was in there watching. She'd only ever seen him on her way home from school; he'd be heading toward town, weaving back and forth, always wearing the same red shoes and satiny black suit with sequins. He'd scowl if you gawked, tell you to get lost. Mother had said to steer clear of him. Daddy said the poor man seemed "tortured."

Reaching the river's edge without a tumble, Linda released a breath and lifted her gaze from her feet to brown water as sluggish as the air. Globs of bright green slime lazed on the surface. She couldn't picture Daddy swimming in that.

Tereza held her nose. "Smells like sweaty socks, don't it?"

When the wind was right, Linda would catch whiffs of the river on her way to school. The sometimes sweet, sometimes rotten smell of mystery lurked behind houses grander than hers with plush green backyards leading to wooden docks and rowboats. But this close to the water, she found the smell almost indecent, more like soiled underpants than sweaty socks.

Tereza pulled a penknife from her pocket and cut a couple of punks, leaving short stems. She produced a small box of wooden matches, too. The punks weren't dry enough to flame up and she wasted a couple of matches before they caught and smoldered. "Mmm," she said, waving her punk under her nose, "I'd walk a mile for a Camel."

Linda hid herself behind a bush and held her punk down by her knees so the smoke wouldn't give her away. She stuck the thin, hard stem in her mouth and *puh-puh-puhed* as she'd seen Daddy do to get his pipe going. The stem tasted like potato peel.

Tereza snorted. "Ain't nothing to inhale, genius. This your first punk?"

So what if it was? "Of course not. It's just more fun this way."

Tereza tried *puh-puh-puhing,* too, and then sucked on the stem so hard her eyes crossed. "No it ain't." She plopped on the ground without a care for the mud.

Linda kept crouching, though her knees and thighs had started to burn. "What should we do this summer?" she asked. Tereza was the only girl even close to her age on the "right" side of the highway Linda wasn't allowed to cross alone. Tereza moving in was like finding an extra gift under the Christmas tree.

"I don't know. Hang out. Play baseball. I seen a couple of cute guys at the store."

Hoods. Rude boys who made Linda feel ashamed even when she hadn't done anything.

Tereza was first to spot the police car as it crept down the street. "Shit." She snuffed out her punk and spidered up the riverbank.

Linda was right behind her. Both girls wore pedal pushers, but Tereza looked better in hers. Her skin was the color of a root beer float and her body wasn't lumpy. Linda squinted; she'd left her ugly glasses at home, but she could still make out two shapes in uniform emerging from the car. They scaled the hilly lawn to Crazy Haggerty's and took the steps to the wraparound porch. One was stout enough to be the crotchety officer who gave talks at school on what to do if someone tried to force you into a car. All Linda could ever remember was: scratch the license plate number in the dirt with a stick. What if there was no dirt, no stick?

"Somebody must've got bumped off."

"No one gets murdered in this boring town," Linda said.

THE DOG HAS ABANDONED his post at the foot of the lad's bed.

He bounds down the once fine staircase to the shadowy front entrance where Miranda stands awash in her own fear. His growl is a deep rumble she feels through her bare feet. Nicholas wouldn't be growling if the footsteps belonged to James. And James wouldn't be coming in the front. He'd be shuffling through the back where Miranda has looked for him off and on since last sunset, slipping up and down the stairs stealthy as a shadow, risking more than one furtive glance under the back-door window shade. She's had to keep the lad amused on her own and cope with Nicholas doing his business all over the house.

James never leaves her overnight. And they've not been apart before on Summer Sun Standing: the day of the year when the sun stands still before retracing his steps down the sky; when night holds her breath, beguiling you for a moment into believing mortal life can exist without death. James should be here, dancing with her on the summer king's tomb.

Nicholas's growls become short sharp barks as one pair of feet and then another reach the porch: Miranda's Veranda, as James named it when she was learning to rhyme. He tells her she trod on its boards when they crossed the threshold. She doesn't remember. She was only three.

Strangers knock from time to time. Most leave quickly after hearing the dog. Not these. Nicholas hurls himself against the ponderous oak door so violently it shudders. The impact throws him to the floor. Miranda winces, feeling his pain in her shoulder and hip.

"Police!" A clean, hard voice, not breathy and musical like James's. "Anyone home?"

Nicholas's nails click against the pegged wood floor as he scrambles up, readying himself for a second assault. If James were here, he'd be retrieving his shotgun from the closet and making sure she and the lad were hidden.

The doorknob rattles. She ponders the lock and the long black key she's never turned.

Should they appear one day when I'm away, James said, welcome them a thousand times over but deny all knowledge. She closes her eyes and summons the memory, hoping to extract more guidance from his words, but the memory gets lost in the dog's barking and the mewling of the lad upstairs who has woken to find Nicholas gone.

Is there still time to hide?

The door shudders again, this time from pounding on the outside. "Anyone in there?" Louder now. "Don't make us break the door down and shoot the dog."

Miranda drops to the floor next to Nicholas and wraps her arms around his quivering body. He smells of decay. His heart thumps so hard she fears it will burst.

"Breathe my air," she whispers.

He licks her face, his tongue hot and frantic. He's already lapped up more than his measure of years, but she can't bear the thought of anyone shooting him.

"Open up!"

One arm about the dog, Miranda drags him with her as she sidles on knees to the keyhole. She pinches and turns the key with thumb and forefinger until she hears the click. Stands and grips Nicholas by the ruff. She pulls open the door enough to detect two bodies, one near enough to touch. Muggy air infiltrates the entryway.

"Good day," she says, summoning the courage of Alice facing the Queen. But her voice comes out as thick as cold treacle and her legs go weak. Nicholas howls and a gun materializes in the closer man's hand. Miranda presses her free hand against the wall to steady herself.

"Silence," she hisses. Nicholas obeys.

"This Mr. James Haggerty's home?" asks the man with the gun.

"Aye." In twelve years she has spoken only to James, the lad and Nicholas. She knows not how much or how little to say.

"This your home, too, Miss?"

"Aye."

He inhales sharply and says to the other man, "Thought they said he lived alone." He turns back to her. "We have news. Are you able to control the dog?"

She points and says firmly, "Nicholas, go."

He backs up through the dining room into the kitchen and, with an extravagant sigh, slumps to the floor by the wood stove, in eyeshot of the door.

Miranda's arm shakes as she opens the door a smidgen wider and blinks into unfamiliar daylight. The one who spoke is tall and wiry, younger than James but clearly a man, a beautiful one, garbed in black trousers and a white short-sleeved shirt bearing a shiny metal emblem. Miranda would like to stroke the light brown hairs covering his arms. Although she means to admit only him, the second one, dressed the same, slides in behind. He's older and potato-shaped, a gun belt hanging low under his belly.

"Should we wait while you cover up?" that one asks. She shakes her head. On sweltering days she always wears her mother's white cotton petticoat if she wears anything at all.

The men remove their hats, revealing hair damp with per-spiration. They exchange looks she cannot decipher. "It's dark in here," the tall one says. The house is illuminated only by sunlight splintered through gaps in the midnight-blue drapes drawn full across the windows. The older man flicks a switch on the wall up and down.

"Power out?"

"We use candles." She doesn't offer to squander any so early in the day. She anxiously follows the tall one's gaze to the room on his right with the mahogany table where they eat and she does her sums, and then to the library, on the opposite side of the entryway, where she and James play the wind-up phonograph and he reads to her of "a time before time." She sees nothing a spy could report. Our way of knowing isn't wrong, James says, but others fear it and therein lies the danger for us.

The tall one's ears stick out like handles and she stares at them frankly. Curiosity instructs, James likes to say, and a sense of wonder is a gift. Is it wonder or dread making her draw a jagged breath? The house has shrunk with the men in it; they've swallowed all the air.

The tall one dips his head, smiles and says, "Officer Nolan, Miss. Don't be afraid. We won't bite." He shows her a thin black billfold with his photograph and name. "My partner here's Officer Dunn. That a baby crying?"

"Cian!" The lad's old enough to climb from his cot, but he's never tried. James says it's a sign of Cian's advanced trust in the universe to provide for his needs. She starts toward the staircase.

"I'll go with you," Dunn says.

Miranda turns back and searches his face, round and pale as the moon but with small, cold eyes. It looks as if the man's spirit has been nearly pinched out of him, which is what James says about his own spirit on days he can't bear to be human anymore.

"You'll vex him," she says.

"Where're you from?" Dunn asks. "The way you talk is strange."

How to answer? She speaks like James. The officers are the strange-sounding ones. *Dawg. Tawk.*

"How 'bout you radio the station, Frank?" Nolan nods toward the door. "Let 'em know what's up." Officer Dunn leaves.

Miranda climbs the stairs and hurries down the hallway to Cian, who's rattling the bars of his cot and bleating.

"Mandy!" he cries, his mouth pitifully distorted. He stands in his cot, hiccuping little sobs. A sodden nappy rings his ankles. Ammonia from it and others in a nearby bucket stings Miranda's eyes. Cian's fair hair is sweaty, his wee organ an angry red from rash. When James left yesterday, he said he'd return with the ingredients for a healing salve.

"Mandy's here, poor biscuit."

If she had the lad's trusting nature she'd chance opening a window in hopes of a cooling breeze. If she didn't fear exhausting the drinking water, she'd bathe Cian and launder his nappies. Fear is the mortal's curse, James says. Look at me, so dreadfully afraid of losing you. She lifts the slight child, shaking the wet nappy from his feet. She carries him down the stairs.

Nolan peers up from a notepad. His eyebrows lift. In surprise? Dismay? For a moment Miranda forgets to wonder why he's here. Perhaps he isn't. It's easy to imagine herself, James and Cian as the only souls alive.

She heads for the burgundy horsehair sofa in the library. As she sits, dust motes rise in a slow dance and drift back down. She drapes

Cian across her lap and wriggles one arm free of the petticoat. He clamps his mouth on her breast and wraps a spindly arm about her waist. His head is warm and damp in the crook of her arm.

Nolan remains in the entryway. To see him, Miranda would have to wrench her head around. "So the child is yours?" he asks. "You look too young."

In three years, when she's eighteen, nobody can wrest her from James. She will stand beside him under a ceiling of stars while he invokes the mighty ones. When she's eighteen, she'll venture out on her own for Cian's earthly needs. James won't have to bring her lilacs each spring. She'll seek them where they grow and drown her nose in their drunken scent. She'll lie on soft grass, garbed in gossamer and sunlight. She will climb Merlin's oak tree and Heidi's mountain, row a boat down the enchanted river behind the house, tread on hot sand and sing as boldly as she wants without worrying someone will hear. She and Nicholas will lope over carpets of dandelions as they do in her dreams. *Lope* is a word she likes to say out loud for the way her tongue starts it off before disappearing behind her lips.

"You say you have news?"

"Yes."

She hears him inhale deeply, hears his belt jangle as he shifts weight from one foot to the other. "Mr. Haggerty died on the three-forty-two from Penn Station yesterday," he says.

"What's a three-forty-two?"

"You serious?" When she doesn't answer, he says, "A train."

"Did he jump?"

"Why would you even think that?" He jangles again.

"Anna Karenina did."

"Who?"

"A woman in a book." The longest she's ever read, one James challenged her to get through, hoping to seduce her from the youthful fantasies she prefers. "*But truly, truly, it's not my fault, or only my fault a little bit,*" she says aloud, trying to say it daintily like Anna.

Nolan releases a short, tuneless whistle and says, "Jeez, it's stifling in here. How can you breathe?" His shoes squeak behind her as he goes to the window and pulls back the drapes. He grunts with the effort of hoisting a sash that's not been lifted since the lad was born for fear his cries would be heard. Panic rises in her throat, a reflex. She tenses, ready to flee upstairs with Cian, until she remembers it's too late to avoid detection.

"Okay if I take a seat?" He's at the chair on her left.

She nods and he sits, his face in profile, his gaze averted. She runs an imaginary finger over the small bump on his long nose as he hangs his hat on one knee. World scents cling to him, as they do to James when he's been out. She likes to guess at them, surprising James with her accuracy. Nolan smells of leather and smoke.

"Several passengers witnessed him collapse and die. The coroner determined it was a heart attack. He won't order an autopsy unless the family insists."

Miranda focuses on the far wall near the fireplace where the floral wallpaper is peeling. She envisions an angry heart with arms and legs leaping from James's chest and stabbing him with a fork. Her own chest begins to ache. Pain is an illusion, James says; float above it. She stares at the dangling wallpaper strip and floats as far as the anchor of Cian's rhythmic sucking on her nipple allows.

Nolan glances at her then quickly looks down. "You okay?"

"Aye."

It will storm tonight. She can tell from the weight of the air pressing in through the open window. Thunder will prowl the sky and Nicholas, the house. Lightning will crackle outside the room she shares with Cian and they'll both cry out for James.

Later, Bill Nolan will tell his wife that the girl's composure was unnerving. No sign of grief as she sat brazenly nursing that naked, emaciated, shrunken-headed child on a couch with lion-clawed feet. He will file a report that says Miranda Haggerty is disturbingly detached and possibly slow-witted.

"Has he started walking yet?"

"Oh, aye."

"I ask because he seems weak."

She unhooks Cian from her breast and sits him up on the couch. "Will you walk for the man, then?" The lad widens his hazel eyes at the officer then hides his face in Miranda's shoulder. "He's not seen the likes of you before," she says.

"The uniform, I suppose. You take him out, right? The park, the doctor's?"

Why doesn't the officer leave, now that he's delivered his news? She pulls the strap back over her shoulder, tucks in her breast and lifts her hair from her perspiring neck. She doesn't lie but she's learned to remain silent when it suits her.

Nolan stares at her straight on, his cheeks flushing, his Nicholas-brown eyes intense. "I've got a three-year-old daughter and my wife's expecting again. We're hoping for a boy."

"Why is that, now?"

"I don't know." He laughs self-consciously and rubs the back of his neck. "Don't most men want sons to carry on their names?" He clears his throat and straightens his spine. "Who's your boy's father?"

Some mysteries cannot be expressed in words to the unready, James says, for they will not be understood. She is sworn to secrecy for the child's sake. She peers down at Cian clinging to her and softly sings his favorite song: "There was an old man called Michael Finnigan, he grew whiskers on his chinnigan."

Cian lays a finger on her mouth and says, "Mandy."

She sucks in the finger and he laughs, a deep chuckle that threatens to loosen her fragile hold on the tears pooling behind her eyes. Without James, who will guide Cian to his calling? Who will brush her hair?

Nolan pulls his notepad from his shirt pocket. "That your name? Mandy?"

"Only to the lad."

He slaps the notepad on his open palm, an angry sound that jolts her. "I'm trying not to push you but I need more to go on here, Miss Whoever You Are, more than you're giving me."

James flashed with impatience, too, yesterday morning when she asked would he bring back strawberries. "I cannot cover the sun with my finger, can I?" he said.

Well, she too can be stroppy. "How are you knowing the dead man is James?"

"He had a library card with him." Nolan glances at the bookshelves lining two walls. "Seems he liked to read."

The card was for her benefit. Most books on the shelves were published before Miranda was born; they don't hold all James wants her to learn.

"I mean to see him," she says. The dead man might have stolen that card. James could be in a public house right now, performing card tricks for drinks.

"I can arrange that, provided you're next of kin."

Nolan's words call up a line from a book forgotten until now: *It is understood that the next of kin is Mr. Henry Baskerville.*

"James is my father," she says, thinking how deficient a word is *father*. "My mother passed over years ago and there's no one else." She thinks on her mother's parents, brothers and sisters all perishing in their summer cottage when it was swept out to sea by a fierce storm two years before Miranda was born. James spoke of it only once because Miranda trembled and cried for days afterward, imagining herself tossed about and pelted by flying crockery. If there be family alive in Ireland she doesn't know of them.

Nolan is quiet for a moment. Then, "That's rough. I'm sorry." He reaches over and pats her knee, sending a shiver of longing through her. "There a priest or minister I can call for you?"

She shakes her head. James says a soul's journey needs no priest, no mediator.

"An unusual name, that—Key-uhn. How's it spelled?"

She tells him and, sensing the need to offer more, adds, "It means ancient one."

"You and the boy can't stay here by yourself," he says, putting words to the terrible truth creeping into her mind: only James knows where the money tree grows, how to find food, bless the well, chop wood.

"And where shall we go?"

"Children's Aid will find you a family, might take a day or so." He spins his hat around in his long-fingered hands. "You can stay at my house tonight, at least."

She cannot recall being anywhere but here.

"I don't suppose you have a telephone," he says.

"We do not." Or anything else that would allow a tradesman access to the house.

"Did your father have an employer we should contact?"

"He did not."

"Will you be okay if I leave you a few minutes to radio the station? I should let my wife know you're coming."

She nods and stands with him. She follows him to the door and watches it close behind him. With both men outside now, she considers locking it. The family they found for Jane Eyre treated her badly: *You ought to beg, and not to live here with gentlemen's children like us.*

She's never tried to leave their house before, though she could have easily. James locked the back from the outside when he made his forays into the World, but he always left the key inside the front door.

Finding her gone would have shattered him after all he'd forfeited for her: a professorship, old mates, his mother's wake. She could never be that ungrateful.

Her mind flies through each room of the house. The windows facing the back are shuttered from the outside. The small window on the back door at the bottom of the kitchen stairs isn't. She'd have to smash it, drag a chair down the stairs to the landing, stand on it and crawl out. Push Cian through first and drop him to the ground. Would the officers hear? Would Cian get hurt? And Nicholas, how could she leave Nicholas? Her mind is surveying the upstairs when Cian lets out a high-pitched cry. She turns to see him toddling toward her, clutching his groin and dribbling urine. His face twists in pain. She scoops him up, rocks him in her arms and softly finishes the verse: "The wind blew up and blew them in again. Poor old Michael Finnigan." He smiles up at her with such love and trust she can no longer dam her tears. She carries him into the kitchen and crumples to the floor next to Nicholas who licks her salty face.

There's naught to deliberate. She must accept Nolan's help.

He and Dunn return with two sweaty-faced men and contraptions for which she has no words. To catch and contain Nicholas, they explain, so they can transport him by truck. He can't ride with her and the child, they say in response to her question. Not enough room. No, the cage isn't cruel. It will prevent him from being thrown about the truck and getting hurt. Miranda doesn't know how else to resist.

The net isn't needed. Head down, tail drooping, Nicholas meekly enters the cage when Miranda directs him to. "Anon," she tells this creature she has loved from the time they stood nose to nose. He refuses to meet her gaze.

Nolan suggests she dress the child and clothe herself in something "more suitable." She remembers a worn valise in James's room and tiptoes in to get it, half expecting him to be there and scold her for entering his private space. She chooses a dress her mother once wore and packs two others, along with rags and cotton drawers for her bleeding times, the petticoat, three handkerchiefs, heavy stockings, flannel pajamas, a woolen jumper, clean nappies and the clothing bits James has managed to acquire for Cian. She dresses the lad for the heat, in a white cotton singlet and nappy.

"Sure we never needed them," she explains, when Nolan inquires about coats. He frowns and scribbles in his notebook. The lad has no shoes but she manages to squeeze into the open-toed high heels of her mother's she wore when she was smaller to play glass slipper.

Dunn asks about birth and death certificates, wills, the deed to the house and other "relevant documents." If any exist, they're in the locked desk in James's room, a possibility Miranda doesn't mention, partly because Dunn is gruff and presumptuous but also because she doesn't know what else might be there that James wouldn't want them seeing.

No room for the books, the phonograph and records, they tell her. Someone will collect them for her later. After having lived in this house so long with the days stretched out before her, she's rushed now into leaving. She packs Cian's Peter Rabbit bowl and the small flannel blanket he sucks on at night, her most recent journal, a pencil, a lump of moonstone, a white candle and matches, her hairbrush and a drawing James made of the goddess Ethleen holding the moon—a milky-skinned, dark-haired woman wearing a gown of starlight. For as long as Miranda can remember, the drawing has hung over her bed as proxy for her mother. She says anon to the walls, floors and ceilings and all who lodge within them, wondering who will hear their scratches and whispers in the night until she returns.

TEREZA'S ASS was sweating. She'd rather have been puffing cigs with the guys who hung out at the corner store in her building, but they weren't around. She was stuck with a kid who looked like Tiny Tears with those blonde curls and chubby gut. The only cool thing about Linda—sandals with laces that crisscrossed her ankles like a Roman soldier's—was also the only cool thing about a Jesus movie Tereza had gotten rooked into seeing by a dumb girl the last place she'd lived. When Tereza became a star, she'd say uh-uh to movies that made you feel like you had to be "saved" from yourself. She liked sci-fi thrillers where the entire Earth had to be saved from total destruction. She wasn't keen on most girls, either. They didn't know as much as guys about things that mattered. Take Linda: she didn't know shit about the river even though she'd lived only blocks from it her whole life. And she was scared of too much to be any fun.

Tereza would have split by now if the cop car hadn't shown up. She'd almost crapped her pants when it did, thinking Jimmy had gotten home early and sicced the cops on her for leaving her eight-year-old brother Allen alone while Ma was out looking for work. Then it occurred to her that the last person Jimmy would want to see was a cop.

A Charlie Chan mystery was going on at Crazy Haggerty's. Two cops had clomped into the house, come out one at a time and parked themselves in their car for a while. Then dogcatchers showed up in a white truck, went in with the cops and came out with a black German shepherd. Tereza would've liked that dog. Jimmy wouldn't be so fast to smack her with Rin Tin Tin at her side.

It was ages before the short cop waddled out the front door carrying a small tan suitcase. The tall one followed, holding the elbow of a girl with cocker spaniel hair down to her waist. The girl wore high heels and a navy blue dress with white polka dots. On her hip she held a puny kid with a freak-show-small head. The girl looked like she might know a thing or two.

"Who's that?" Tereza asked real low.

"Somebody visiting Crazy Haggerty, I guess," Linda whispered.

"What's wrong with the kid?"

"How would I know?"

The girl turned and stared straight out to where Tereza and Linda were hiding. It made Tereza shudder. The kid looked starved. Maybe the cops were taking the girl to jail because of that. Jimmy used to threaten her with jail before she figured out she could scare him worse with it. He told her the cops would pull her fingernails out with pliers and parade her around naked.

A sudden dread for the girl brought her to her feet. "I'm gonna find out what's going on."

"No!" Linda yanked the back of Tereza's pants and pulled her back down. "They might tell on us. I'll get in trouble."

"With the cops?"

"No. My folks."

"What's the worst they can do to you?"

"You can't imagine."

Tereza hadn't spotted a single scab or bruise on those rubber doll arms and legs, but maybe Linda's old man and lady weren't as harmless as they looked.

Tereza dropped back to the ground. "My brother's a big chicken, too."

Linda's face collapsed like a squashed Dixie cup. Tough gazzobbies. Tereza couldn't babysit everybody's feelings.

FOR TWELVE YEARS Miranda has viewed the World through the attic's streaky half-moon window, seeing half a tree, half a street and only the birds and clouds that passed by her scrap of sky. Being at one with nature is our birthright, James said. Depriving her of that pained him. Daylight makes her eyes water. And the smells! She feels dizzy.

Focus, James would say. Imagine yourself the circus tightrope walker he described seeing as a child—taking slow, deliberate steps, placing one foot carefully before the other.

She wants to touch the tree whose branches scratch the roof. She wants to hug the earth. But Nolan leads her steadily to a black car with two white doors. *Car* is from the Celtic word for wagon, James says, but then James believes you can trace anything to the Celts. Believed. James believed.

Miranda balks as Nolan opens a door for her. Is the car any less a cage than that holding Nicholas? Then she recalls the professor's nephew who was afraid to enter the volcano at first, nearly missing out on that incredible journey to Earth's core. She ducks her head inside. Cian squeals when the engine erupts but bounces excitedly on her lap as they pull away. Twisting to see through the rear window, Miranda watches the home she hasn't seen from the outside since she was three shrink and grow faint.

TEREZA HACKED OFF two more punks and handed one to Linda. "If you smoke it down to the end," she said, "sap will fizz up into your mouth."

Linda screwed up her nose as if Tereza had farted. "Revolting," she said.

Tereza turned away and studied the old house with new eyes. No sign of Crazy Haggerty. Plus the dog was gone. If the house turned out vacant for sure she'd come back and prop a window open in case she needed to get in someday. She was feeling better and better about Stony River. One of the first things she always did in a new town was suss out possible hidey-holes. Bordering the neighborhood were the river, a farm and the highway her family had taken all the way from their last place in Florida. In the middle were houses, empty lots and trees. The farm had a haystack big enough to hide a girl, but a vacant house would be better when the weather turned cold. Across the highway were a zillion other possibilities. Right now, though, Crazy Haggerty's house was boss. She'd sneak back to it after dark.

❧ T W O ❧

AS THE CAR GATHERS SPEED, a hot breeze from the open windows lifts the ends of Miranda's hair and slides under her dress. Curious wonders pass by so quickly they become blurs of color: so many shades of green, yellow, brown, blue and red. Cian, frightened and delighted at once, clings to her neck with one arm. He points with the other and babbles, attempting to name all he sees. Each dog is "Nicko." Closing her eyes when sights overwhelm her makes Miranda queasy. Fixing her gaze on the back of Nolan's head helps, but even so she's nauseated and disoriented by the time they arrive at a building Nolan informs her is the hospital.

Dunn deposits them at the entrance. Carrying Miranda's valise, Nolan leads them through a door made of glass (imagine!) into a large room with sofas, chairs and illuminated ceilings. Someone approaches them. A woman, Miranda realizes with a thrill. A woman who rises on the toes of her flat black shoes and kisses Nolan on the cheek.

"Thanks for being here," he says to her. "Where's Carolyn?"

"With Mom. She'll keep her as long as we need."

"Ah, she's a peach." Turning to Miranda, he says, "My wife, Doris."

Doris has tightly curled black hair and a swollen stomach under a long white shirt: a mother goddess at full moon. Her black trousers stop mid-calf. Doris captures Miranda's free hand with her two small ones. Her smooth hands are pink against Miranda's candle-white skin, her pursed lips painted the color of fresh blood.

"I am so sorry for your loss," she says.

Panic flaps its wings inside Miranda's chest as Nolan excuses himself to check on arrangements for viewing James's body. She no longer wants to see a corpse. About her come and go more people than she's ever seen. Voices from nowhere say words she can't decipher and invisible chimes go *bing-bing*. She misses the slow, predictable rhythm of the house, wants to chase after Nolan and ask would he take her home. But Doris, smelling like dried wildflowers, steps even closer and shines a smile on Cian.

"What's your name, little guy?"

Miranda answers for him. *Cian* isn't one of the five words he can say.

Doris mispronounces it as a single, reverent syllable: "Keen. That's a new one on me. How old is he?"

"One year and four months."

"I would have guessed younger."

Miranda lays a hand on Doris's melon-hard stomach.

Doris quicksteps back then seems to catch herself. She smiles. "Three more months." She extracts a red tubular object from a large blue-and-white-checked cloth bag. "Say, Keen, do you like kaleidoscopes?" The lad frowns and sniffs it, puts his tongue on it. She laughs. "No, no. Look into the eyehole. Here, let me show you." Softly, almost mouthing the words, she asks Miranda, "Can he understand?"

"And why wouldn't he?"

"Well, I wasn't sure, given his condition."

"There's no want in him," she says, just as James answered her when she wondered if the lad was like other children. James said naught about a condition.

Doris succeeds in getting Cian to peer into the tube and hold it by himself. "Nifty, isn't it?" She sets her bag on the floor and opens it wide. "I have more toys. Want to see?"

"See," Cian says. Miranda sets his bare feet on the floor. He toddles to the bag and reaches in as though he's done it forever. He pulls out a block with the letter Y.

Nolan returns and says to Miranda, "Whenever you're ready."

Doris bends her head to touch Miranda's: a silent benediction. "Go on," she says, her voice as soft as dusk. "He'll be fine with me."

THEIR FOOTSTEPS RESOUND as Nolan leads Miranda through double doors and down a hallway smelling like pinecones. At the end, a blue door opens to a narrow windowless room with a red floor and a yellow chair beside a gurney. Her toes in the open shoes recoil at the cold. The rest of her body shudders. *All the dark was cold and strange.*

"It's called the cooler," Nolan says. Another word for her journal.

They move from doorway to gurney. Tightrope walking again, a thunderous pounding in her head. She stares, unseeing, at the white tiled wall before her. Nolan says, "Jeez, they usually clean them up." He guides her to a spot in front of the chair. Asks for "a positive eye-dee."

She slowly lowers her gaze and sucks in a breath. The body on the gurney is rigid, its face and neck the color of moldy bread, the mouth frozen into an O, the eyes open as in surprise. The carapace of a life reborn in the Other Life.

So this is what death looks like.

She finds the frigid chair with the back of her legs, sits herself down and says, "Aye, 'tis James." She knows that shiny black suit with the satin lapels and frayed cuffs, the theatrical red shoes. His Mad King Sweeney outfit, he called it.

He'd make his hair and eyes wild and say, "Tell me, is this a look that would sour cream?" He wanted people to think he was gone in the head so they'd stay away from him and not find out about her.

"We are the gods' hidden children," he'd say, his voice defiant and proud.

The suit is wet in spots, as though he's leaking. His cheeks have sunk into his face. Terrible strange flecks lodge in his moustache and beard. She studies his chest, half-expecting its rise and fall. Sees her child self crawl into his lap and fall asleep to his thumping heart.

Nolan says, "I'll be right outside." The door closes on the silent cold.

She reaches out and lightly touches a hand, bloodless on top, deep purple where it rests on the gurney. The fingers are curled under as though they died scratching the earth. His skin is as alien as the chrysalis he once carried home to demonstrate that life follows death as surely as morning, night. "One day I will shuck this shell," he said that day, "and emerge on the other side fluttering and swooping among flowers so beautiful they forbid themselves to grow here."

She wept at that, unable to imagine life without him. Being human is incomplete, he explained, disappointed she couldn't see that. He could leave his body at will, but a craving for whiskey held him back.

Until now.

She swallows a deep breath, holds and releases it, trying to channel his energy. She drinks more air, holds and releases it. She listens with ears and heart.

She never matched his concentration, never lifted the physical veil. Someday she'd summon the will to let the power enter her, he said. When she did she'd be ready to accept the legacy of her grandmother and great-grandmother, who taught him to call forth summer and winter on the harp he was to have played for her this day of Summer Sun Standing.

She rises from the chair and sniffs the length of him. Unwashed hair, stale sweat, urine and feces: the smell of a body abandoned and a vow forsaken. He's left her alone to care for the child; she and the lad were no longer enough to tether him to the World.

"Could you not wait?" she cries out. She hugs herself to stop her arms from shoving him off the gurney and squeezes until she feels the pulse beneath her fingertips. She empties herself of tears then leans over him until her swollen eyes are level with his deflated ones.

He isn't in there.

She whispers what he had her say each morning: "I am the same and not the same as I was before."

"As tonight's moon will not return tomorrow," he'd say, "you will emerge altered after each night's sleep, after each book you read, after each moment you experience."

She tugs out a strand of his ginger hair for herself and removes the red shoes for Cian. Gives thanks for the hallway's warmth and Nolan leaning against the wall.

"Shouldn't he be buried in those?"

"A butterfly won't be needing shoes."

In a small room with a narrow table and two chairs Nolan records her answers on a Death Information Form. James Michael Haggerty: born March 3, 1907, County Meath, Ireland. Spouse Eileen Reagan Haggerty: born October 10, 1918, Milford, Massachusetts, deceased January 7, 1943, Providence, Rhode Island. Miranda knows these places only on maps, but their names, along with the dates, are bound into her memory from a page in a book James kept, inscribed with his flourishes, his script more beautiful than hers despite all her practice. Providence is where James said he met Eileen. He was a visiting professor at the university for which she organized collections of scholarly books and papers.

The Form demands the deceased's children's names and birthdates.

"Miranda Brighid Haggerty," she says, "May 12, 1940, Providence, Rhode Island." She was named after Prospero's daughter and a Celtic

goddess. Nolan writes the goddess's name as it's pronounced—
Breege—and she doesn't correct him. He waits a moment. "And
Cian?"

On a mattress with James saying "Float, float" as Danú possessed her womb.
"Miranda will suffice."

James catching Cian. The pulsating cord, the bloody placenta.

A tight-lipped smile. "We'll have to talk about that eventually.
Father have insurance?"

"Sure I don't know."

"No matter. The city will bury him." He hands her a large, bulky
brown envelope. "Some items he had with him."

Inside are James's brown leather billfold, cracked at the fold, his
playing cards and two small paper bags. Inside the billfold: the library
card and a dollar bill. She'll wait to open the bags when Nolan isn't
watching.

She inquires about Nicholas. Nolan says he's in a place called
Quarantine. He can't say when Miranda will see him again.

She asks, "Why did yourself come if you thought James lived
alone?"

"It's my job to doubt what others tell me."

DADDY WAS HOME. His briefcase met the floor with a soft plunk and a
hanger scraped the rod as he hung up his jacket. Linda waited for him
to call out in the voice she pictured rising from a deep, black well.

"James Haggerty died yesterday. A heart attack, apparently. I
stopped in at Tony's for a new wiper and he told me." Daddy often did
that when he got home: started talking without checking if anyone
was around to listen, spilling his news at once as if he'd forget if
he didn't. His shoes rattled the furnace grate as he crossed into the
dining room where Linda stood behind her chair on the waxed wood

floor, starving, as usual, counting the purple fleurs-de-lis on the wall-paper to distract her mind from her stomach.

Steam rose from the green beans Mother carried out from the kitchen. "I didn't think he was that old," she said. She always got gussied up before Daddy came home, putting on nylons and makeup, fixing her hair. If Daddy noticed, he never let on. That evening Mother was in a full-skirted baby blue dress with a wide white belt and her usual black heels. When Linda ate at Tereza's the week before—the Dobras had called it supper—Mrs. Dobra was barefoot. Her nipples showed under her scoop-necked blouse and her legs through a thin wraparound skirt.

"Late forties, according to Tony." Daddy took his position behind Mother's chair, ready to hold it out. His white shirt was damp under the arms, his round face flushed from heat.

"Must've been the drink, then," Mother said.

"Did he die in his house?" Linda asked.

"Hello, kiddo!" Daddy said. "I forgot to give you a hug."

Linda stepped into the brick warmth of his open arms. He smelled of starch and underarms. "Did he die in that big house?" she said into his chest.

"No, on the Pennsy from New York. He'd gone into the city for some reason. Had bags of strange stuff in his pockets, so they say."

Linda had ridden the fifteen miles into New York City on the train once with Mother and Daddy. She pictured the man she knew only as Crazy Haggerty sitting on a slippery brown seat, his shoulders swaying with the motion of the train. "What kind of strange stuff?"

"I think that's everything," Mother said, surveying the table, leaving Linda's words to hover in the air like dragonflies. Daddy pulled out Mother's chair. She sat and smoothed the tablecloth, brushing away invisible crumbs. Daddy took his place opposite her and Linda hers between them. They bowed their heads.

Daddy said, "For what we are about to receive we are truly grateful."

They removed the linen napkins from under their forks. Custom-made pads and a white linen cloth protected the ski-legged cherry wood table Daddy had bought Mother last year for their fifteenth anniversary.

At Tereza's, Mrs. Dobra had taken two pans right off the stove and set them on the bare wooden table without the slightest concern about scorch marks. "Dig in," she'd said: to canned corn and stewed tomatoes and hot dog pieces, like chopped up worms, swimming in baked beans. Eight-year-old Allen had stuck his hand in a huge bowl of potato chips. No one said grace. The table wasn't quite big enough for five people. Tereza's stepfather, Jimmy, straddled the chair between Allen and Linda, his thigh pressing against hers. He was slighter than Daddy but the muscles on his arms stood out more. A construction worker, Tereza had said. They moved whenever he ran out of work.

"What kind of strange stuff?" Linda asked again.

Mother put a thin slice of roast chicken, a small mound of mashed potatoes and a spoonful of green beans on Linda's plate. A canned peach-half waiting in a small dish on the sideboard would be her dessert. Since Linda had inherited her father's build, Mother said, she'd have to watch what she ate for the rest of her life. Linda's ash-blonde hair came from her mother, which was lucky, Mother said, because the gray would blend in when Linda got old and be hardly noticeable. Tereza's black hair was "a regular rat's nest," according to Mother, who set Linda's hair in tidy pincurls every Saturday night.

"Apparently he had a child," Daddy said, unbuttoning his cuffs. "Possibly two." He rolled up his sleeves. "Tony had quite a bit to say about that."

"Really." Linda recognized the look Mother gave Daddy as a warning. When she was younger, they'd spoken in pig Latin. *Eally-ray.*

"What did you do today, Linda?" Daddy asked.

"Hung around with Tereza."

"Interesting expression, that. Can you be more specific?" To Daddy, slang exposed an indolent mind and profanity a dearth of imagination. A single new word in your vocabulary, he claimed, could help you see the world differently. Each month, Linda memorized the words in *Reader's Digest*'s "It Pays to Increase Your Word Power." Daddy might have been impressed if she'd said *confabulated*, but it wouldn't have expressed the joy, the shivering bliss, of having a friend who wanted to spend the whole day with you.

"I don't know. We just talked and stuff." She didn't let on that she and Tereza had been in eyeshot of Crazy Haggerty's spooky old house. "How old's his child? Boy or girl?"

"That's not open for discussion," Mother said.

"Why not?"

"Don't argue with your mother. Did you help around the house?"

"She peeled potatoes and set the table."

"Good. He had a teenaged daughter and there's a little boy who might be hers."

"Roger!"

Dinner at Tereza's had ended badly, too, after Jimmy asked Linda if she'd ever eaten wild boar and she said no sir, and he said it tasted like polar bear and Tereza made a rude noise and said how would he know. Jimmy asked if Tereza was looking for trouble and Mrs. Dobra rushed in to explain that, after the war, before she and Jimmy met, he had worked in the North. Jimmy said he could tell his own stories. He'd waggled his fork at Tereza and said it was in Thunder Bay, Miss Smartass, that's in Canada, in case you haven't learnt that yet, I'm not the dumb fuck you think I am. Nobody spoke after that, just applied themselves to getting the meal over and done with, Linda pretending she hadn't heard Jimmy's dearth of imagination.

After dinner, her parents sat in the backyard while Linda did the dishes, a chore she rarely objected to because it let her pick at the leftovers. Tonight it also allowed her to eavesdrop through the window over the sink, her ears on full alert to the rasp of Daddy's match as he lit his pipe. Their voices were as faint as fly hums at first, but soon came a buzzing and a hornet-like crossness that was loud enough for Linda to pick out words.

"He should have been shot."

"No point poking a stick in his dead eye, Betty."

"Why are you defending him?"

"I'm not. I don't know enough about it to blame or defend. Neither do you."

"A teenager with a baby and nobody knew she existed. Isn't that enough?"

Their voices dropped again and then tapered off. Linda wondered why "a teenager with a baby and nobody knew" meant Crazy Haggerty should have been shot. But Mother said no more. She came in and went up to bed—her *modus operandi,* as Nancy Drew would have said, when she was peeved. She'd have a headache tomorrow and not come down for breakfast. Linda finished the dishes, thinking about the baffling girl who'd emerged from Crazy Haggerty's house, the child's arms around her neck, the sway of her hips as she stepped toward the police car. Something about her had seemed older than teenaged, something that made Linda squirm.

Daddy stayed outside for a while, smoking his pipe. Later, Linda sat on his lap, as she did most nights when they watched TV. His lap never objected to her build.

"BILL HAS TO CLEAN UP some paperwork," Doris explains as she leads Miranda to a grape-green automobile longer and lower than the

police car. "We'll see him at home later." She places Miranda's valise
on the back seat. Miranda gets to sit in the front, holding Cian on her
lap. His hair smells like Doris.

"I can't imagine how you must be feeling," Doris says.

Like a tree drained of its sap. Miranda wants to be in her bed,
sleeping this bizarre dream away. Even the air is drowsy.

"If you want to talk, my ears are wide open. I don't suppose you
felt like saying much to those two galoots." Doris waves at Nolan and
Dunn as the cars part ways.

James said every word generates its own force and every action
its own unique consequences. Miranda wouldn't be in Doris's car if
that last morning had gone differently. James built a fire on the stove
and set water on to boil as he did each morning. He took the chamber
pots out the back door, as usual, Nicholas in his wake. Miranda nursed
Cian and bathed him in the sink, mixing cold water from a bucket
and hot water from the stove. James returned, kissed Cian's head and
recited the line from Joyce he always quoted when he came upon her
bathing the lad: *Why, when I was a nipper every morning of my life I had a
cold bath, winter and summer.*

"See how light it still is and already seven," Doris says, her unborn
babe's chrysalis nudging the steering wheel. "The longest day of the
year. We should eat outside."

Miranda and James usually prepared breakfast together, she
stirring the porridge, he slicing the bread. They'd eat in silence,
James hunched in his chair, concentrating on his food. Conversation
came later in the day over tea, after her lessons or following the evening's "reading from the gospel," as James jokingly called it, the gospel
being the sometimes tragic *Ulster Cycle* tales or myths of the Tuatha
Dé Danann who arrived in Ireland in dark clouds that blotted out
the sun for three days and nights. Sometimes he read in unfamiliar
tongues, but she liked his voice in any language. It saturated her
mind, crowding out her own muddled thoughts.

"What should we make for dinner?" Doris asks, as if she and Miranda do so every day.

"Colcannon," Miranda says, surprised at her own spontaneity.

"Aha! The accent I couldn't quite place," Doris says, glancing over with a smile. "You must be Irish. Bill loves colcannon. Never heard of it before I met him."

"Sure I'm not as Irish as James."

"Your father?"

"Aye."

"I wouldn't have the nerve to call my father by his first name."

"He wanted me to. I'm supposing he was not like most fathers."

Doris's laugh is a song.

Miranda thinks on her father. Was it only yesterday he said, "Well, then, if I'm to get in a good day's work, I best be off." His usual jest. His only work was foraging for their food and other supplies, made easier when the money tree was in bloom. She said, "Strawberries would be lovely if you can manage them." That's when he wheeled around sharply and said, "I can't cover the sun with my finger, can I?" That had to be it: the only thing not as usual, not as always. If she hadn't asked for strawberries, James would still be alive. The back door would have opened that night and Nicholas would have skidded across the floor to greet him.

Doris turns onto a wide street with a ribbon of trees down its middle. She nods to a building on the right. "Good old Stony River High. Did you go there before the baby?"

"I did not."

"Private school?"

"Nor that." How fortunate she was, James said, to be free of the distraction of school and friends. They would only draw her away from her spiritual path. She would advance more under his tutelage because most classrooms moved only as fast as their slowest pupils. And Miranda had too fine a mind to queue up for an education she could easily get from him. Not the true reason, of course—if she were to place even one foot in a school "they" would take her away from James—but his argument made her envy less the young people she saw from the attic window ambling toward the river she pictured shimmering with faeries and moonlight.

"Did you *ever* go to school?"

"No."

Doris presses her lips together for a long, silent moment before humming under her breath: a joyless, ominous hum. Miranda wants to say more and, at the same time, nothing. She doesn't know if she can trust Doris.

Doris rounds another corner. "Has Keen had his shots?"

"And what might those be?"

"Inoculations. Needles to prevent a whole nightmare of things that could kill him: smallpox, whooping cough, diphtheria, tetanus."

"I think not."

"Do you have a doctor?"

"We do not." James kept them well with infusions, poultices, teas and tonics of ginger, yarrow, nettles, mullein, lavender, evening primrose, meadowsweet, lemon balm, bergamot, milk thistle, sage and more. The recipes were in a book handed down from his mother and grandmother, a leather-bound notebook of spells, magic charms and potions he called a *grimoire*. He'd added to it with his own brews using plants that grew wild in the area and ones he cultivated behind their house.

"Honey, he's got to have his shots. I'll phone Carolyn's pediatrician tomorrow."

Miranda hugs Cian tighter. This brave new World is a dangerous place.

AT TWENTY-SIX, Doris was behind schedule for the six kids she and Bill wanted. It had taken two years of doing it every which way before she got pregnant with Carolyn. All the while she'd been working for Children's Aid, typing up case studies about parents who didn't deserve the precious babies they'd been given. It broke her heart to come across a neglected child she could have been sheltering. And now two were in her car, although Miranda was old enough to be more sister than daughter. If not for the missing side tooth and morbidly pale complexion, she'd have been a looker, with her Teresa Brewer nose and wide-set green eyes. Doris wanted to take a brush to that gorgeous but tangled red-gold hair. The boy was another matter. It had taken all the restraint she could muster not to gasp at his stunted head and narrow, receding forehead.

"Welcome to Nolan Manor," she said, trying to lighten things up as she pulled into the carport beside the modest red-brick ranch house.

The desk sergeant who phoned had said only that Bill needed help with a toddler and a teenager whose father had died. He wanted to put them up for a night or two if that was okay with Doris. Of course it was: whatever Bill's job demanded came first. She'd learned the practical wisdom of that perspective from her army Wife-with-a-capital-W mother. The sixty-four-thousand-dollar question was Who fathered Miranda's baby? While Doris dreaded what she might learn, she was drawn to the mystery as to a locked diary. The whole drive she'd been yakking like an old gossip, trying to loosen the girl's tongue.

They entered through the side door. Doris set the girl's suitcase on the faux marble linoleum Bill had installed last year for their fifth anniversary. With the boy on her hip, Miranda spun around slowly, googly-eyed, as though she'd never seen a kitchen. She walked her fingers along the turquoise tabletop and matching counters, the paper-towel rack above the sink. "What's this?" she asked, opening the refrigerator without the slightest do-you-mind. She lifted the wall phone receiver, listened and smiled. Flicked the ceiling light switch up and down. Turned on the tap and let perfectly good water escape down the drain.

"Looks like you're thirsty," Doris said, slipping a glass under the tap. She filled Carolyn's Tommie Tippee for Cian and held it up to his mouth. He stuck his tongue in it and lapped. "Adorable," she said, because he was—like any frail creature needing protection. "We'd better feed him soon. He wolfed down the cookie I gave him at the hospital."

Miranda pulled out a kitchen chair and unbuttoned the dress that looked like a USO hostess hand-me-down with its shoulder pads and Peter Pan collar. Her small, blue-veined breasts were braless. On the shopping list she kept by the fridge, Doris wrote *Bra for M—nursing/other?*

"Carolyn stopped nursing at nine months."

"Sometimes this is all he'll take," Miranda said with a challenging lift to her chin.

"Well, sure, if you keep indulging him." Doris immediately regretted her words. Bill complained that she was quick to judge and sometimes he was right. "Will he eat a banana?"

"Sure I don't know. We never have them. They're too dear."

"Let's give it a go." Doris held out her arms and Miranda uncoupled Cian from her breast. He whined as Doris lowered Carolyn's high chair tray over his head. Settled down as she sliced a banana onto it. When he stuffed all the slices into his mouth at once, Doris laughed, nearly missing Miranda slipping into the hallway. She lifted Cian from the chair and hurried after.

"I must relieve myself," Miranda said. Doris directed her to the bathroom. Miranda asked Doris to go with her and insisted the door stay open. Doris made a mental note to add panties to the shopping list. And more appropriate shoes. She would have liked to throttle someone. After Doris showed her how to flush, Miranda remained, watching the swirling water.

Doris handed Cian to Miranda, desperately needing to pee herself. When she came out, Miranda was in Doris and Bill's bedroom, as though no one had taught her manners, studying a Blessed Virgin postcard Doris kept tucked in the frame of her dressing table mirror.

"And who's this?" Miranda asked softly.

"Mary, our Blessed Mother." Doris wasn't surprised the girl hadn't had proper religious instruction.

Miranda stared at a framed photograph of Carolyn on Bill's shoulders, taken last month at Surprise Lake, and then, like a breeze, deserted the room with Cian on her hip. Doris followed her to the living room. Miranda pushed back the sheers covering the picture window and pressed her face against the glass, leaving marks.

"Would you like to go outside?"

Miranda didn't reply. She plopped herself onto the dark green Hide-A-Bed and, moments later, bounced up to try one wingback chair and then the other. She stood, picked up a newspaper from the maple coffee table and read out, "'A hundred and forty-nine confirmed polio cases among children receiving Salk vaccine.' What's polio, then?"

"You can read!"

"Aye." She glanced about. "Where are your books?" She turned away, not waiting for an answer. Her hand caressed the wooden console TV. "What is this for?"

"I'll show you later," Doris said. "Bring Keen into the kitchen, please. It's time to cook dinner." She was done letting this flippy girl call the shots.

MIRANDA IS BEWITCHED by Doris's house, especially the kitchen with its white box that keeps food cold and the counters and tabletop the color she imagines the ocean to be, the glittery specks in them like the sparkle of sunlight. Knowing from James that water flowed from other people's pipes doesn't make witnessing it any less thrilling. And the long-legged chair! Cian is in it, his hands and mouth happily occupied with tiny animal-shaped biscuits. Doris has given him a clean nappy—she calls it a diaper—and smeared thick white cream on his rash. Doris is so clever, Miranda wonders if she has invented her along with all else that's happened today.

Doris chops a cabbage she's taken from the cold box and has Miranda wash her hands before peeling the potatoes. Warm water over her fingers makes Miranda giggle. Doris opens a cabinet filled with pots and pans. What bounty. Miranda and James had only what they needed. Whenever she asked for more of anything, James would say she was indulging in wishful jam-on-your-egg thinking.

"I add onion. Do you?" Doris asks.

"When we have it, aye."

They boil the potatoes in one pan, the cabbage and onion in another. Miranda marvels at the blue flame Doris can force higher or lower simply by twisting a knob. Living here could be as fine as living with James, perhaps finer. If he were here right now, Miranda would be worrying she hadn't done her lessons correctly or meditated long enough. She'd be watching his eyes and the set of his mouth for what they might mean to the evening ahead.

Doris mashes the potatoes with butter, seasonings (the true art of the dish, according to James) and real milk from a bottle, not the powdered kind. She mixes it all with the cabbage and onion. "Want a bath while it's in the oven?" she asks. "I'll keep an eye on Keen."

Doris fills the tub with water and bubbles so sweet-smelling they make Miranda laugh and cry at once. At home, she had a tub bath once a month after her bleeding ended. The water had to be heated on the stove. Not enough to cover her chest and never, ever, bubbles.

Doris brings her a spare nightgown and tells her that Bill phoned to say they shouldn't hold up dinner for him.

Since it has started to rain they eat at the kitchen table, an electric fan blowing on them with the breath of a dozen snow angels. Doris touches her forehead, chest and shoulders with two fingers and mumbles something. Miranda touches her forehead, chest and shoulders and mumbles, "Thank you, Mother, for sending Doris."

Miranda and Cian will sleep in the small, square unborn babe's room. Its yellow walls close around Miranda like a hug. "The crib is Carolyn's old one," Doris says. So a cot is called a crib. A nappy a diaper. Biscuits: cookies or crackers. Miranda has grown new eyes and ears.

Doris plugs a tiny light bulb into an outlet, pulls the sheet over Miranda's shoulders and kisses her forehead. Crouching by Cian's cot, she recites, "Angel of God, my guardian dear, to whom His love commits me here. Ever this day be at my side, to light and guard, to rule and guide. Amen." Miranda would have said "Angel of god and goddess," but that would have spoiled the rhythm of the prayer that has lulled Cian into closing his eyes.

Doris leaves the room and returns with a white plastic figurine: a woman in a hooded robe, no taller than Miranda's hand. Like the picture in Doris's mirror, it could easily be Ethleen. "Our Blessed Mother will watch over you tonight and light your dreams," Doris says, placing the figurine on the dresser near Miranda's bed. She closes the door.

There's too much daylight for sleep, even with the curtains pulled. Miranda retrieves the valise from under the bed. With an expectant breath, she withdraws the two parcels James had with him when he died. Inside: only packets of powders and dried plants. No strawberries that would speak of love and forgiveness. She removes the drawing of Ethleen and the chunk of moonstone from the valise. She places the drawing beside the figurine. Taking the translucent stone in her left hand, she whispers "I am one with the moon" three times. The ritual often yields the sense of a wise and caring presence that Miranda associates with her mother. Tonight, it's Doris.

Miranda tiptoes to Cian's cot and studies his sleeping face. Now that she's seen a picture of Doris's daughter Carolyn, she suspects something is amiss with the lad. James claimed Danú and Dagda brought forth nothing but geniuses. But wouldn't they give a genius a bigger head?

She returns to the bed and watches shadows skip along the ceiling. It's her first night here, yet she can almost believe this is the life she's always had. James would be proud she's forgotten to be afraid and allowed herself to trust. Tomorrow she will be the same and not the same as she is tonight. Tomorrow she will take Cian to a park and ask again about Nicholas.

As the longest day finally darkens, the Blessed Mother begins to glow.

⚘ THREE ⚘

JUNE 29, 1955. Another scorcher. Waiting for Tereza in the small woods she'd dubbed The Island, Linda closed her eyes and pretended the pines were palms and their cones coconuts. Last year Aunt Libby airmailed a coconut from a real island and Daddy smashed it open with a hammer. Aunt Libby was a buyer for a department store in Elizabeth. She wore Tabu perfume and suits with pleated skirts. Linda could still taste the bittersweet crunchy insides that Aunt Libby claimed would make Linda's complexion soft and creamy like hers. Mother had said it must be nice to gallivant around the world.

Linda sat on the old hollowed-out log, the ridges scratchy against her bare legs under Bermuda shorts. The log stowed props she and Tereza had stashed for Swiss Family Robinson: a bent spoon, acorns, some string, the silver foil from gum wrappers. Tereza saw uses for things Linda considered trash, like cigarette butts. She stripped them and collected the loose tobacco in a Wonder Bread bag. She said they could sell it for food when they escaped from The Island.

Escape to where?

Eyes still closed, Linda was listening to the ebb and flow of cars and trucks on Route 1 four blocks away, pretending it was the sound of the shipwrecking sea, when Tereza snuck up on her like an Indian scout and stomped on her foot. She laughed when Linda yelped in fright. Tereza's hair was wild, as if she'd just gotten out of bed. She wore red shorts tinier than Mother would have allowed and her arms were full of cattails.

"What are those for?" Linda didn't care how grouchy she sounded.

"If we let the punks dry out they'll be better smokes. When they turn to fluff we can make pillows. We can weave the leaves into sleeping mats."

Linda sighed and rolled her eyes. "The rule is we live on whatever we find on The Island," she said. "Punks don't grow here. Berries and acorns do."

"It's our game, right? We make the rules."

"It's my game. I played it a whole year before you came."

"Yeah, and what have you got to show for it? You didn't make a tree house. You didn't make nothin' we could sell when we get off The Island."

"What if I don't want to get off? What if I want to live here forever?"

"Why? Nothin' to do here, nobody to see. Might as well be Crazy Haggerty's kid, locked up in that house." It had been a week since they'd watched the teenager and her baby leave.

"Maybe she liked it there."

"Not a chance." Tereza stuffed the cattails in the log and sat next to Linda. "Jimmy said her old man must've parked his car in her garage."

"What's that supposed to mean?"

Tereza made a hand gesture Linda could tell was dirty. "I told Jimmy he tries that with me, I'll kick him in the balls. He backhanded me for that."

Linda sucked in a breath. You weren't supposed to say balls; at least *she* wasn't. Her cousin's dog was always licking his. She didn't like to think of fathers having them.

"Maybe Jimmy's wrong," Linda said hopefully. The way the girl walked out as though she wasn't in any hurry to leave had stuck in Linda's head. "Maybe Haggerty wasn't her father."

"Nope," Tereza said. "Ma found this." She pulled a newspaper clipping out from under her waistband and began reading aloud as slowly as a third grader, shaping each word with her lips as though tasting it. It made Linda's jaw ache.

She held out her hand. "Here, let me."

James Michael Haggerty, 48, of 2 Lexington Street, passed away June 21 of natural causes. Predeceased by his wife Eileen. Survived by his daughter Miranda. He will be buried in the potter's field section of Stony River Cemetery.

Seeing the girl's name in print gave Linda a thrill, as though she'd discovered the secret in Nancy Drew's old clock. "It doesn't say anything about the child," she said.

"They don't want nobody knowing that crazy coot knocked her up. My mom got knocked up with me, you know."

"Did it hurt?"

Tereza laughed so hard Linda wanted to punch her. She stood and said, "I'm leaving."

"No, wait. Go with me to Crazy Haggerty's. You gotta see something."

Linda didn't want Tereza to call her a chicken again and she itched to learn more about the girl who now had a name. "As long as you don't tell your folks so they can't tell mine."

Not that Mother was likely to seek out the Dobras. At dinner one night she'd said, "Just because she's the only girl your age this side of the highway doesn't mean you have to play with her; we don't know anything about them." Daddy suggested Mother walk over there and welcome them to the neighborhood, poke around in their garbage can. Mother didn't, of course.

Tereza pulled a rusty crowbar from the log.

"How'd that get there?" Linda didn't like the idea of Tereza visiting The Island on her own and putting stuff in the log without her agreement.

"I found it back of my house, hiding in the grass."

Tereza lived in an apartment building and what she called grass was more like weeds, but Linda didn't correct her.

They crept along the riverbank, approaching Crazy Haggerty's from the back, stepping around mounds of dog poop. "I never saw him walk that dog," Linda said.

A small stack of firewood rested against a wall by the back door. "The door's locked," Tereza said. "I tried it already. I could've busted in but I waited for you." Padlocked shutters covered the windows on the outside. "I can smash 'em open, easy."

"If you do, I'm not staying. I won't tell, but I won't stay."

"Look up there," Tereza said. She pointed to a small window close to the corner of the house too high to reach without a ladder; its shutter hanging by a hinge. "I broke that shutter because it's harder for the cops to spot. I jimmied the window and propped it open with a rock."

"When?"

"Last week, at night. It was too dark to see inside." She monkeyed up the drainpipe, leaned so far over Linda thought she'd fall and peered inside the window.

Linda's heart thumped at the fear of getting caught, but she was too curious to leave.

"The kitchen," Tereza said when she got back down. "Nothing in it except a wood stove. No table, no chairs."

"They must have eaten in the dining room."

"Or not at all. They could be zombies from outer space."

Linda sighed in exasperation. "Zombies are already dead. Crazy Haggerty wouldn't have died of natural causes if he was a zombie." Then she noticed two small basement windows barred but not shuttered. Kneeling on a piece of wood so she wouldn't get her knees dirty, she peered into one. The light was dim but she could make out two white pillars with black drapes hanging between them.

"I see a robe on a hook," Tereza called out from the other window.

Linda scooted over to look.

"The guys at the store say Crazy Haggerty worshiped the devil," Tereza said. "They say he had snake fangs, rat tails and porcupine quills in his pockets when he died. I think the old man kept her as a slave, and sicced the dog on her if she didn't do everything he wanted. Too bad I didn't move here sooner. I would've sprung her."

"How?"

"I would've figured a way."

"Maybe Miranda was a lunatic that Haggerty saved from the horrors of an asylum," Linda said. "They tie you up and turn hoses on you, you know, attach wires to your head and cook your brain." She'd learned about asylums from a comic book passed around the school playground. She wanted to believe Haggerty had been protecting Miranda from that or something worse.

Tereza snorted. "The *horrors*? La-di-dah, Miss Dictionary."

Linda stomped home alone.

At dinner, she asked, "Did Mr. Haggerty's daughter have a garage?"

"What an interesting question," Daddy said.

Linda related what Tereza had said.

Mother looked at her plate.

Daddy said, "You and your mother need to have a chat."

That night a huge black bug climbed onto Linda's back. It was so big and heavy she couldn't breathe. She must have screamed because Mother came into her room and rubbed her back. "Hush, angel," she said. "It was only a dream."

SIX WEEKS LATER Mother disappeared into the hospital for what Daddy called a *female thing*. "Take care of your father," she said. "He has no idea what to do with a stove."

Linda rummaged in her brain for everything she knew about being a wife: keep your hands out of the wringer washer; start with the collar of the shirt when you iron, then the yoke, then the sleeves; skim the cream off the top of the milk for his coffee; make sure all evidence of your housework is out of sight by the time he gets home.

Tereza was no help. She didn't want to help dust or vacuum or wash floors. "I'm never getting married," she said. "If I have to clean somebody's house I'd better get paid for it." When Linda was stuck at home cooking and cleaning, she suspected Tereza was with the greasy-haired boys who prowled the neighborhood in a pack.

Sometimes women from church dropped off a meatloaf, cabbage rolls or even a chocolate cake, but you couldn't count on it. Linda could scramble eggs and dissolve Jell-O. She could open cans of soup: Daddy's favorite was Manhattan clam chowder. She'd sit outside with him after dinner while he talked about his secretary, his boss and the vital role of the cost accountant at Bartz Chemicals. He'd help her with the dishes before their nightly hospital visits. While he was at work, she ate jars of expensive Queen Anne cherries Mother had hidden in the pantry behind a broken toaster. She sat at Mother's mahogany dressing table and smeared her face with Pond's—as cool and creamy as junket pudding. She licked two fingers as she'd seen Mother do and moistened the tiny brush before dipping it into the little red mascara box. She washed her hair by herself for the first time and needed every bobby pin in the house to set it. Without a mother, did Miranda know to brush her hair a hundred strokes a night?

Driving with Daddy to the hospital a week after Mother went in, Linda asked, "How come nobody knew Mr. Haggerty had a daughter?" She was in the front where Mother usually sat and got to watch Daddy shift gears. The seat cushion still held Mother's lemony scent.

"People were scared of him. Your mother went over there once to collect for the Red Cross and he greeted her on the porch with a shotgun."

"Do you suppose his daughter went to school somewhere?"

"I doubt it."

Poor Miranda. Linda liked almost everything about school: getting escorted across the highway by a police officer, waiting on the playground for the bell to ring, learning about the solar system, using the pencil sharpener. "Why wouldn't her father have let her go?"

"No idea." He reached over and patted Linda's leg. "If only we'd known. Everybody just thought he was eccentric. We left him alone."

"Where did he work?"

"He didn't as far as anybody knew. If you asked, he'd tell you he had a 'condition' and 'scraped by' on his 'ma's meager charity.' I had an inkling he was smarter than he let on. During the war he did his bit patrolling the neighborhood. After that, he kept to himself." Daddy slowly shook his head. "How long ago that was. To think of a little girl in there all that time."

Daddy had never talked to Linda so confidentially. The regret in his voice emboldened her to confess in a quiet voice, "I used to call him Crazy Haggerty."

"You weren't the only one."

"Daddy?"

"Yes?"

"You said he had strange stuff in his pockets when he died on the train."

"Did I? Why are you so interested in Mr. Haggerty?"

"I want to know, that's all."

"Well, kiddo, there are some things we're just not meant to know."

AUGUST 24, 1955: Linda's twelfth birthday and Mother wouldn't be home from the hospital. Linda was trying to be grown up about it. Daddy said he'd take care of dinner and the three of them would celebrate later that night at the hospital, wouldn't that be fun? But Daddy didn't know how to make Baked Alaska. Linda considered trying it on her own, but the effort it took on Mother's part was what she liked best.

"Forget housework," Daddy said at breakfast. "Spend the day with your little friend."

Tereza showed up at The Island wearing dungarees that didn't fit. "Somebody gave 'em to Allen but they ain't his size."

"They're too big in the waist for you."

"Yeah, and they cut into my crotch. I feel sorry for guys. Ever seen a dick?"

"A what?"

"A penis. A guy's pee-pee."

Linda's face got hot. "I don't think so."

"Some are stubby like punks. Others are kinda worm-like."

"How many have you seen?"

"Well, my brother's, natch, but that don't count. Let's see ..." She added on her fingers: "Richie, Vinnie, Paul, Vlad"—the greasy-haired boys who blocked the sidewalk and said "all that meat and no potatoes" whenever Linda tried to walk by.

"They smoke cigs," Tereza said, "and they let me take drags if I kiss 'em."

Linda was horrified. "Kiss their penises?"

"No, genius, their mouths."

"Can you taste what they've been eating?"

"Natch."

"How nauseating." *Nauseating* was Linda's favorite new word, but Daddy wouldn't allow her to say it at the dinner table. "Don't your folks mind you going with them?"

"They don't ask and I don't tell."

Linda didn't want to hear any more about the greasy-haired boys. She suggested they play Swiss Family Robinson. Tereza said she wasn't going to pretend anymore until she became a Broadway or

Hollywood star. Linda thought about mentioning it was her birthday, but she didn't want Tereza to play out of pity. She went home and looked up penis in *Webster's Unabridged* and then the words in the definition she didn't understand. Eventually she got to "intercourse" and "impregnate" and began to think about Miranda and Crazy Haggerty.

It made her stomach hurt.

She paged through medical books in the house she'd had no interest in before, searching for the rules of intercourse—reassurance that what happened to Miranda was out of the ordinary, something she didn't have to be afraid of. From Mother's bottom bureau drawer she retrieved a booklet called *Growing Up and Liking It*. Earlier that year the school nurse had sent the sixth-grade girls home with it along with a sanitary napkin, a belt and instructions to discuss it with their mothers. Mother had said, "We won't need this for at least another year." The booklet was silent on the subject of intercourse. Maybe the child wasn't Crazy Haggerty's. Maybe he'd kept Miranda inside that house because she was like Tereza, wandering off whenever she wanted, kissing boys and looking at their penises.

Daddy brought home a pizza and let Linda have as much as she wanted. At the hospital, Mother held out her arms and said "Here's my birthday girl," but she didn't look in a party mood. Leaning over to hug her, Linda caught a whiff of talcum.

"We were together twelve years ago in this very hospital," Mother said in a way that made Linda sad. "The windows were blacked out because of the war."

Daddy patted Mother's hand. "I remember." Then to Linda, "Here you go, kiddo, open your present." He'd brought it in a shopping bag. "Madge wrapped it." Madge Bryson was Daddy's secretary. Linda had seen her only the one time she'd ever been in Daddy's office. To Linda, Madge was heavily rouged cheeks and a smile that made you feel special. She had used pink paper sprinkled with black polka dots for Linda's present. Underneath the paper: a Brownie Hawkeye camera with a flash attachment and a box of bulbs.

Linda had asked for a portable radio.

"It's all loaded up, ready to go," Daddy said.

Linda made a show of looking through the instruction manual. "It's swell."

Mother said, "Don't take my picture, I look a fright." Linda hadn't intended to.

Madge had sent along three cupcakes with chocolate icing, paper plates, napkins, plastic forks and three candles. Daddy set the plates and cupcakes on Mother's dinner tray, placed the tray on the bed and lit the candles. He and Mother sang Happy Birthday in a whisper so they wouldn't disturb the other sick people. Linda forced herself to think about all the orphans in the world with nobody to sing to them; she thought about Miranda.

"My cupcake is dry," Mother said.

Daddy laughed and said, "It would be, wouldn't it?" He pulled up the only chair beside Mother's bed, sat and patted his knee for Linda. She pictured his boxer shorts holding something worm-like and said, "I think I'll go down to the maternity ward and look at the babies."

FOUR

OCTOBER 28, 1955. The moon was out by the time Chevy Man dumped Tereza back at Tony's Garage at the corner of Route 1 and Grove, a block from her apartment building. She hustled down the sidewalk, pimply cold in tight white shorts and a Dubble Bubble–pink sweater. She was too busy cooking up the story she'd give Ma and Jimmy to notice Linda on her front stoop across the street. Linda called out but Tereza didn't slow down.

Linda stumbled after her. "Hey, wait up!"

"Beat it!" Tereza hurled the words over her shoulder. Miss Goody Two-Shoes probably wanted to brag about having her weekend homework done already. Tereza should've been in eighth grade, not seventh with Linda, but she'd missed too much. Whenever a school snooped into her injuries, Jimmy would find different work and they'd move.

"What were you doing at Tony's?"

Tereza turned just short of her porch steps. "You seen me?"

"Yeah, after school, getting into a car."

"You rat on me, I swear I'll kill you."

"Rat on you about what?"

In work pants and undershirt, Jimmy exploded onto the porch, a long belt wound around his hand. "Get up here, you little whore. I know what you been doing."

Tereza backed up and Jimmy ran down the stairs. Tereza shoved Linda out of the way as Jimmy let loose with the belt, flicking it like a whip.

"Go ahead, you piece of shit," Tereza said, dancing around. "The worst you can do is kill me. Do it and make me happy. I dare you."

Linda dashed back to her house, screaming "Daddy!"

Tereza led Jimmy in circles down the middle of the street. He lashed the pavement with the belt, looking more and more pathetic as she zigged and zagged out of his reach.

"Ooh, big brave man," she taunted. "Takin' on a *girl*."

Linda's old man appeared at his front door and stood like a mummy. Linda ran into the street, waving her chubby arms, yelling at Jimmy to stop. It distracted him long enough for Tereza to scuttle to the end of the street, turn left and run like spit along the edge of the highway. Jimmy wouldn't hurt Linda. Even so, Tereza owed her one.

The ground burned under Tereza's thin-soled shoes and her lungs nearly blasted through her ribs but she didn't look behind her until she made it to the White Castle a few blocks away. Jimmy hadn't followed. Winded or too lazy, she didn't care which. She bent over and clutched her knees, panting. Waited to catch her breath before opening the door to the smell of cigs and steamed onions. Richie, the beanpole, and blubbery Vlad perched on stools at the counter with a new guy, coffee cups and a choked ashtray spread out before them.

"Hey, Teeze," Vlad said, moving his hand like he was jerking off. "Here to suck my dick?"

"Got five bucks?" she asked, still breathing hard. That was what Chevy Man had given her. Enough for fifty Castle burgers.

Vlad and Richie laughed like they thought she was joking.

"You're nibbing out," Richie said, copping a feel of her left tit as she slid onto the stool beside him. He had a pencil behind his ear, as usual. A doodler: spaceships and ray guns mostly, sometimes the Green Giant with a hard-on.

"Asshole," she said, slapping his hand away, but she wasn't cheesed off at him. Vlad either. Talking dirty was their way of showing they liked her. She only ever let them stick their tongues in her mouth and flash their dicks at her. Guys were so impressed with their dicks.

"My cousin Buddy from Linden," Richie said, nodding toward the new guy, two stools away, next to Vlad. "His grandma is my mom's aunt." Buddy spun slowly toward her and nodded. Pouty lower lip, sleepy eyes, slicked-back hair blonder than Richie's. Under his black leather jacket, a white T-shirt strained against his muscles.

"You a bodybuilder?" Tereza asked.

Buddy smiled at her with half a mouth and cracked his knuckles.

Richie smirked. "The next Charles Atlas."

Buddy spun off his stool and swaggered toward Tereza, his pointy-toed black boots scraping the floor and his shiny black pants squeezing his thighs. He shrugged off his jacket and draped it around her shoulders. "Turning frosty out there," he said, not letting his gaze slide down to her chest like most guys.

Something stirred between her legs. "Thanks," she said, slipping her arms into the sleeves still warm from his body. The jacket weighed her shoulders down. "The name's Tereza, not Teeze."

"Pleased to meet you, Tereza," Buddy said. He cupped one of her hands in both of his, as you might a wounded bird. He released it seconds later, turned his small, high ass to her and strutted back to his seat.

"What's with your eyes, Ter-eese-a?" Richie asked. "Your old man try to punch your lights out again?"

She fished around in her pocketbook and pulled out a small mirror. "Mascara," she said, licking a finger and swiping at the black streaks. Her eyes must have leaked doing Chevy Man. She lifted Richie's cig from the ashtray and took a long drag that went to her head. "He's not my old man," she said. "My real father speaks three languages." She paused to pick tobacco off her tongue. "Jimmy only speaks caveman. Ugga, ugga."

Richie slapped his thigh and hooted. Vlad's laugh was more like a wheeze.

"He tried to belt-whip me but I got away."

"Want me to take care of him?" Buddy asked.

She snorted. Who *was* this guy?

"Don't laugh, Teeze," Richie said. "He can rip a phone book in half and hold me over his head with one arm. Show her, Buddy."

Buddy's face flushed. "Later, Rich."

"I'll take a rain check," Tereza said, although she liked the idea of Buddy hoisting Jimmy off his feet with one hand and flattening his pointy nose with the other.

Buddy stood abruptly. "Time to cruise town. Coming along, m'lady?"

"He's got a cool car, Teeze."

"What are you, his pimp?" she said. Richie looked hurt. Tough gazzobbies. "Can't," she said to Buddy. Ma would be having a cow by now, assuming Jimmy had told her what happened. She shook one arm out of the jacket but Buddy held up his hand.

"Keep it until you get home." He pulled the pencil from behind Richie's ear and wrote his phone number on a napkin. "Call me. I'll come pick it up."

Richie and Vlad stood to leave.

"See you on the flip side," Vlad said. He tried to be cool but slobbered when he spoke and lived with his Russian immigrant mother. Some people said they were spies.

The three guys filed out. Tereza stayed on her stool, chewing over Buddy's offer. Why'd she keep taking Jimmy's shit? And why didn't Ma make him stop?

"Hey, Buddy!" she called out. "You got a flashlight in that car?"

"Yes, ma'am."

With Buddy's phone number and flashlight in her pocketbook, she ordered an orange soda and, for a buck, a sack of the little square burgers you could down in three bites. She liked having her own money, spending it how she wanted.

Allen would be in bed already. If she were home, she'd be skulking into the room they shared and undressing in the dark. Instead she headed for the woods where she and Linda had played that lame shipwrecked game in the summer. It was just plain dumb that Linda wanted to live there forever. And it was just plain dumb for Tereza to wait to be rescued from Jimmy.

Buddy's flashlight beamed the way four blocks to the hollowed-out log and the crowbar, then to Crazy Haggerty's house. It loomed like a ghost ship in the night sea. Sounds stood out in the quiet dark—a truck downshifting on the highway, a dog's whiny yelps. Each left a shivery silence when it died. Buddy's jacket swished and crunched as she walked, keeping half of her warm at least. Her toes were numb in the ballerinas Linda claimed would ruin her arches.

Tereza hadn't been back to Haggerty's since she'd climbed the drainpipe in June. (In gym, she could shinny up a rope like nobody's business. In gym, nobody called her dumb.) Every window and door was boarded up now, including the one she'd propped open with a rock. She crowbarred the nails from the plywood covering the back door—whoever put it up had done a half-assed job—then stood aside and shoved the board over the steps. It fell with a loud thud. Shit. She slunk around the side and waited. When it felt safe she crept back, forced the lock and counted to ten before pushing open the door.

Not more than a foot away stood Crazy Haggerty.

Tereza screamed and nearly pissed her pants before realizing she was looking at a coat and a hat on a hook at the bottom of some steps. Recovering, she climbed the steps and called out, "Yoo hoo, is anybody?"—the only funny line in that hokey show Ma loved. Her shaky voice tumbled out huge in the high-ceilinged room.

She waved the flashlight around, lighting up cupboards, a bucket in the sink, a pan on the wood stove. The air reeked like the Creature from the Black Lagoon had sloshed through. The flashlight landed on a light switch. A dud. She ventured deeper into the room, whipping around each time a floorboard squeaked. Stumbled over an empty dog dish, making it rattle.

In a room off the kitchen sat six chairs and a fancy table even bigger than Linda's. Beyond that, a circular staircase split the house. She shot a beam up to the landing. The darkness closed around the beam like a fist. Tomorrow, in better light, she'd climb the stairs. The flashlight guided her to a room as big as her family's whole apartment. A picture window, shuttered from outside, reflected the flashlight. The lumpy dark furniture could've been Dracula's. The air was cold and the radiators silent. At home they'd be banging out heat, Ma moaning because only the super could control them.

She tried another light switch. Crap. It wasn't too late to go home. Ma and Jimmy would be drinking beer and sitting on the floor watching TV because they didn't have a couch. Jimmy might have had enough beer to forget he was mad at her. She was pretty sure he was bluffing about knowing what she was doing at Tony's.

She'd been sneaking into men's cars a couple times a week after school for over a month. The idea had come to her after she found out Linda's old man dropped off their turd-brown Nash at Tony's Garage in the morning when it needed work and walked to his job. Linda's ma didn't drive. Once the car was fixed, it would sit behind the garage with the others, where the mechanics couldn't see, until Linda's old man returned. Tereza cut school one day to check it out for herself. Most men leaving cars wore suits and hats and carried briefcases. They looked well off. And safe.

Tereza chose newer cars with full ashtrays. She'd have the Wonder Bread bag of tobacco in her pocketbook as she hid in the back, turning herself into a ball on the floor behind the driver's seat. Sometimes she had to wait a leg-cramping hour or more, but wondering who might turn up gave her a charge—like buying Cracker Jacks not knowing the prize you'd get.

After a man drove a short distance away, she'd edge onto the back seat and make little waking-up sounds, scaring the bejesus out of him. He'd pull over and she'd apologize, handing him a story about not getting any shuteye because she didn't want to disturb her dying mama lying in the only bed in the teeny room they rented. She'd tell him she was selling tobacco to pay for the doctor. She'd practiced her naive, pitiful come-on look in the bathroom mirror for days before the first time. Some men went apeshit and ordered her out. A few forked over a couple bucks and a lecture. But there were others. She'd taken in forty-three bucks so far, none from tobacco. But if Jimmy knew now because Tony had found out, she was screwed.

Heavy dark drapes covered the two living-room windows. Tereza yanked on one set until rod and all crashed in a dusty, coughing cloud. She blanketed herself in the drapes and sat on a couch, hugging the flashlight as a weapon to her chest, her sharp ears listening to the house stretch and yawn, burp and fart. She dragged three chairs from the dining room and stacked them against the back door. Anyone trying to get in would make a racket and warn her.

Back on the couch, she closed her eyes and saw the dead-giveaway plywood she'd left on the ground. To the kitchen again, to unblock the back door. No sign of other earthlings. She stepped outside, dragged the board into the kitchen, dropped it on the floor and blocked the door again. Maybe now she could sleep.

She shrugged off her shoes, made a pillow of Buddy's spicy-smelling jacket and stretched out sideways on the scratchy couch. She drew her legs to her chest and rubbed her toes back to life. Remembering a mouse in Ma's slipper two houses ago, she tucked her shoes next to her pocketbook under her blanket of drapes.

It must have been swell when there was only her and her mother, Reenie. Just Tez, as Ma called her, and Reenie. She wasn't quite four when Jimmy came along; she didn't remember having Ma to herself but it must have been heaven. Ma looked younger than thirty-three and, with makeup, Tez looked older than thirteen. But they had the same curly black hair and brown eyes. If not for Jimmy, they could almost have lived as sisters. She closed her eyes and sank into that warm thought.

"TER-EEEEEZ-A!"

She woke to a room as cold and gloomy as the night before, shot up and listened, but the voice didn't call again. She must've dreamt it. Splinters of light peered from the edges of the plywood covering the window. She wouldn't have known it was already nine if not for the glow-in-the-dark watch Ma had gotten her with Green Stamps so she'd be on time once in a while.

Allen would be having Sugar Pops and grape juice in the Howdy Doody glass that used to be hers; Ma, a boiled egg and rye toast; Jimmy, three basted eggs, six bacon strips and four pancakes. Tereza did the breakfast dishes on Saturdays and, later, took Allen to the movies so Ma and Jimmy could screw. They didn't say they were going to, but when Tereza and Allen returned, that telltale fishy odor would be in the air and Ma's voice would be throatier.

On Saturdays Jimmy was nicer to Tereza, probably afraid she'd crap out on babysitting. She hated the full-of-himself way he doled out the money: only enough for two tickets and a puny box of Dots to share, like nothing was theirs unless he gave it to them and what Ma made was his, too. Ma acted like Saturday's Jimmy was the real one. Embarrassed to own up to marrying a jerk, probably, because what would that make her?

"Give him credit once in a while," Ma would say, "and you'll see how sweet he can be."

She might as well have told Tereza to balance on one finger. Jimmy hardly ever smacked Ma and Allen. He never hit their jaws so hard they practically amputated their tongues with their teeth. That time, he'd been scared shitless the hospital would call the cops. He bought her a Dale Evans lamp and didn't raise a hand to her for months. That was when she was eleven and keener on Dale Evans.

She played the flashlight around the room: cobwebs, purple old-lady flowers on the wallpaper, a pink and beige rug clumped with dog hair, a fireplace she'd use if she wasn't afraid the smoke would give her away, half a dozen candles on holders as tall as her ringing the room, a wind-up phonograph and stack of records on a small dark table, bookshelves so high even Haggerty would've had to stand on tiptoe to reach the top shelf.

She couldn't have gotten through that many books if she gave her life to it. The kids at school rolled their eyes when she read aloud. Nobody believed that the words bounced around like Mexican jumping beans and gave her a headache; her eyes tested perfect. Teachers said she didn't apply herself; that she only wanted to clown around and distract the class. She couldn't help it if she was funny as hell. She could belch the alphabet from A to K. Do a great Elmer Fudd, Desi Arnaz, Imogene Coca.

She had to pee. "If I was a john, I'd be upstairs," she said out loud, but she wasn't ready to chance it. She'd heard skittering above her head during the night. Probably mice, but it could've been rats or foot-long radioactive tarantulas. She peed into a pan that had been left on the stove—the inside was furry. *Nauseating*, Linda would've said. She emptied it down the sink and turned on the tap to rinse the pan. Nothing came out. What a crock. She'd suss out the backyard pump later, under cover of night. The thought of no water until then made her mouth go dry.

How long did it take to die of thirst?

Searching for something to drink, she happened upon the gassy lagoon smell: a bag of oozing potatoes. "Them! Them!" she screamed, like the stunned kid in the movie smelling the giant mutant ants. If Richie were here, he'd be splitting a gut.

She found dishes, oatmeal, crackers, powdered milk and—cowabunga!—cans of baked beans, corn, peas, stewed tomatoes, green beans and Spam. Jimmy hated Spam because that was all the navy fed them during the war. She rooted around for a can opener and spoon. Sat at the high mucky-muck end of the dining-room table, spooning baked beans from the can and washing them down with stewed tomatoes. Miranda and Haggerty must've eaten by candlelight. Two brass holders with white candles stood on the table, one candle melted down more than the other.

A candlelight meal with Tereza's father had snookered Ma. She'd met him in a tavern on a sleety January night two days before his army unit was to go overseas, exactly where he wasn't allowed to say. He asked her out for supper the next night and she said yes. Not much else to the story, Ma would say whenever Tereza pestered. She didn't know if he made it back alive. Tereza was frosted Ma hadn't asked for a picture.

"He gave me you. Who needs a picture?" But two years ago she brought home a poster of John Derek in *Rogues of Sherwood Forest* and said, "Your father looked like this except darker."

Although Tereza couldn't find a speck of John Derek in her face, she saw all his movies after that. Her favorite was *The Adventures of Hajji Baba*. He played a lowly barber who rescued a beautiful princess as mouthy as Tereza. "Complaints flow from your lips like water from a spring," the barber told the princess, or something like that.

She wasn't finished eating before the beans and last night's burgers began churning up her guts, making them hot. She fled up the hallway stairs, not caring who or what might be hiding there. After a false turn, she found the crapper in time but had to wipe herself with her skivvies. She tossed them into the claw-foot tub and pulled her shorts over her bare ass. Forgetting about the water, she tried to flush. Swore. Haggerty's house was bad news.

In the small scratched mirror over the waste-of-time sink, she looked clown-faced from yesterday's makeup. Her coarse black hair pointed every which way and she'd sprouted half a dozen new zits. She fingered the lump of bone where her jaw had healed and imagined the shellacking she'd get if she went home now. Ma standing with her back against the wall, her hand on her throat whimpering "Oh, Jimmy" and Allen hiding under the bed. Tereza could take the blows. Worse would be looking up at that King Tut expression on his face after he decked her. Ma said Tereza was too stubborn for her own good, but sometimes stubborn was all you had.

To the left of the john was a room with nothing in it except a mattress on the floor with dark stains reaching out like bloody fingers. It gave her the shivers. Across from that room was another with a four-poster bed still made up. Against one wall stood an antique desk with a bookcase and four big drawers. The desk and bookcase were locked. She could've busted into them easy but Linda would've said that whoever boarded up the place left everything inside because Miranda was coming back and deserved better than busted stuff.

Hanging in a tall, dark, sour-smelling wardrobe were a bathrobe, workpants and shirt, so worn out she could see Haggerty's shape in them. On shelves: underwear, snot rags and socks. Wearing a dead geezer's clothes gave her the creeps, but warmth was warmth. The green plaid shirt came below her knees and the maroon robe fell to the floor, its sleeves flopping over her hands like Dopey's. Something in the pocket bumped her leg: a silver flask etched with a harp. She unscrewed it. Sniffed. Took a swig. It burned her throat in a good way and tasted like smoke.

Lighter and bolder, she heigh-hoed down the hall and came to a room with a rumpled bed and a tall, narrow dresser. Off the room was an alcove with a crib and a pail of stiff, moldy diapers. Beside Miranda's bed—it had to be hers—was a pot of turds. Linda would've shrieked in disgust. Tereza took another nip from the flask; the heat the house had sucked from her was returning.

A door off the alcove led to narrow stairs. Up she climbed, one hand beaming the flashlight, the other on the wall, feeling the way. A long, unfinished room with a half-moon window waited at the top of the stairs. The window wasn't boarded. Bands of light from it stained the wooden floor. Tereza knelt by the window, lifted her face to the stingy warmth of the autumn sun then looked down. From this perch Miranda could have eyeballed her and Linda on their way to smoke punks.

She looked for chains. Why Miranda hadn't escaped bamboozled her. Maybe Haggerty *had* worshiped the devil. It would be swell if she and Miranda could live here together someday, close to Ma but safe from Jimmy. They'd tear down the plywood and shutters, push the drapes aside and let sun, like melted butter, pour into every room.

2:00 PM. Had Allen gotten to the movies? *Abbott and Costello Meet the Mummy* was supposed to be on. He loved Abbott and Costello. After Tereza brought Allen back from the movies she'd usually hook up with Richie, Vlad, Vinnie and whoever else was at the White Castle, maybe play ball with them in the empty lot beside Vinnie's house. It was October now and ball was over. She tipped the flask back.

3:40 PM. Downstairs again, carrying a blanket from Miranda's room for later. In a closet under the staircase, hard to see in the dim light, she found a gun nearly as tall as her, with a long, skinny nose and a polished wood butt padded in red rubber. She managed to heft its weight and rest the rubber pad against her shoulder. Pretending Jimmy was at the front door, she aimed and said, "Bang, bang, you're dead."

6:10 PM. Dark enough to risk stepping outside. She unblocked the back door, took the bucket from the sink and dashed to the Ma and Pa Kettle pump in the sharp cold air. The handle squeaked when she lifted it. She pumped hard and fast until water gushed and splashed her feet. She lugged the full bucket inside, dipped a cup into it, took a drink and waited to croak or at least double over in agony. When she didn't, she filled every glass and cup in the house for later. She washed herself with the rest, toted the dirty water up to the bathroom and flushed away the reeking evidence of herself. Then back down the stairs to hurl the oozing potatoes toward the river and refill the bucket.

The booze had worn a hungry hole in her stomach. She opened the green beans and peas and set the cans on the coffee table in Dracula's room. Lit the candles on the tall holders with wooden matches from a tin box on the mantel. Spectacular! A movie set, with candles as spotlights. In the dim mirror of the picture window she watched herself eat, then cross the room in that dumbass outfit to check out the records beside the old phonograph. She cranked up the machine and put a record on the turntable. It wobbled slightly as a man sang "Yes, we have no bananas" like he was in a tunnel. She mugged it up for the spotlights, turning her hand into a megaphone and *wah-wahing* to the tune through her nose. She pretended Miranda was watching, laughing and saying, "You fracture me, Tez."

Tereza sang and drank from the flask until the room did a dance, her insides swayed and her ears felt full of water. She sat down heavily on the couch and stared at the drunken flickers of candlelight until her head fell onto Buddy's jacket. She pulled Miranda's blanket over her and drew her legs up to her chest like the babies in jars at the State Fair last year. Embryos that didn't make it, Ma had said when Tereza got agitated, not poor little bastards nobody wanted.

EARLY THE NEXT MORNING Tereza was dreaming about a TV wedding. When the preacher said "forsaking all others," the realization that Ma had been forsaking her for Jimmy since she was four years old smacked her clear across the face. She woke to a throbbing head and a mouth crusted with drool. Her whole body felt pissed off as she trudged to the kitchen. She couldn't stand this cold, dark prison any longer. If she had a boat, she'd row down the river all the way to the ocean and let herself get swallowed by a whale.

Leaning against the sink, chugging glass after glass of water with shaky hands, she spotted a door on the landing at the bottom of the kitchen stairs, hidden behind the coat and hat she'd thought was Crazy Haggerty. She pushed the coat aside and turned the knob.

Locked.

She got the crowbar. Linda wouldn't have approved but Linda wasn't there. So what if there was something behind the door that could kill her? She didn't exactly have great plans for the future.

She broke open the door, fired up the flashlight and started down another set of stairs, swiping at cobwebs. The air smelled like a wet mop. A mouse scurried in front of her and disappeared into shadows. The basement was long and narrow, one half filled with crap, the other set up for some kind of meeting. On the crap side, dried-up plants hung from a clothesline strung beside a boiler. The boiler looked like a dead bug with four pipe legs reaching up into nowhere. She'd check out the boxes of junk cluttering the floor later. The other half of the room was squawking for attention.

A harp, like the one on the flask, leaned against a black-draped table in front of the black curtain and white pillars she and Linda had seen. The black hooded robe still dangled from a hook. Pinned to the curtain was a hand-drawn picture that looked like the one-celled creature Mr. Boynton had shown them under a microscope. Weird objects sat on the table just so: a metal goblet wearing a necklace of acorns and seashells, a creepy animal horn, a tall white candle, a wooden stick, a long piece of knotted yarn, a black-handled knife and three jingle bells on a string. The stick, polished and tapered at the end, looked like a wand. Tereza picked it up, tapped the air and said "Bibbidy bobbidi boo," but she was still there, still pond-scum ugly.

She lifted the knife and blew the dust off it. Its double-edged blade was six or seven inches long, but it would fit in her pocketbook.

Ma claimed Tereza had ESP because she always knew when it was safe to come home. What if Miranda and Tereza were tuned to the same frequency? It would explain why Miranda had looked across to where Linda and Tereza were hiding the day the cops took her away and why Tereza had known she'd hole up in this house one day. The voice calling her yesterday could've been Miranda's, the objects on the table a coded message.

Tereza had to break into the desk now. Miranda would want her to.

☙ FIVE ❧

OCTOBER 30, 1955. In a chapel cool and dim with rafters high and dark, Miranda prays: "I confess to Almighty God, to blessed Mary ever Virgin, to blessed Michael the Archangel, to blessed John the Baptist, to the holy Apostles Peter and Paul and to all the saints ..."

Mass is over but she remains, knees pressing into the unforgiving bench she can feel even through her mother's rose-patterned dress. Lingering as well is smoke from burning incense—"the petitions of the faithful drifting up to Heaven," Father Shandley calls it. The pungently sweet smell tugs at her: a longing for James and the sacred ground of their altar, their place apart from the World and protected.

"... that I have sinned exceedingly in thought, word and deed, through my fault, through my fault, through my most grievous fault."

The musicality, not the meaning, of the words renders the Confiteor Miranda's favorite prayer. She recites it first in English, and then, not sure she's pronouncing it correctly, in the Latin she memorized from the short, squat missal Doris gave her when she was baptized. Once she's able to attend high school, like the inmates who get to wear uniforms, she means to study Latin properly. Miranda has spent half of the four months she's been at St. Bernadette's in religious instruction. The nuns are amazed at how much she's absorbed. She finds it easy to grasp and strangely familiar: the saints in heaven have the same great power as the gods and goddesses to intercede for mortals. At *mea culpa, mea culpa, mea maxima culpa* she strikes her chest with her fist three times, a gesture of sorrow for sin. The words and the gesture reach far down to the faceless place where the Voice of James lives curled up inside her. It tells her she has no need for sorrow, that the concept of sin is a fallacy. Some days she believes the Voice; other days, the nuns and Father Shandley.

Worshipers file out in the aisles on either side—the girls, like her, with mandatory white lace doilies on their head; the nuns all in black, swooping like the war goddess Morrígan in her scald-crow-of-battle guise. And those from the hunched-together houses and tenements surrounding St. Bernadette's Orphan Asylum and Convent: bowed old women in long, dark dresses whose bones crack as they kneel; parents who supply the chapel with altar boys; rough-looking men rumored to sleep on the ground outside the gates.

The girls will proceed to the dining room on the same floor as the chapel. They'll pass the laundry where Miranda works two hours each day after school, ironing sheets the nuns take in from hospitals and nursing homes.

"Do they pay you?" Doris asked. "You should insist they pay you."

They don't.

It's fair play for the food Miranda eats and has not to prepare. She doesn't tell Doris that the nuns dole out additional hours in the laundry as punishment. She's partial to the smell of hot iron on bleached sheets and enjoys the power she has to make wrinkles disappear. She likes ironing better than building wood fires or laundering nappies.

Miranda will join the lunch queue once she finishes her prayers. It doesn't bother her to be last. She doesn't care with whom she sits. Others will push their way into the room, tripping over each other to secure their favorite places at the long wooden tables and benches. Sisters Elaine and Monica, the prickly-voiced twin goddesses of the dining room, will threaten to banish them, *right this minute*, if they don't slow down. Miranda will think about nothing except holding Cian after lunch, kissing his soft cheek, hoping this time he won't cry when he sees her.

He eats in the nursery with the children who aren't yet school-aged. He's gained six pounds since they arrived. If not adopted by age five, boys are sent to a different orphanage; girls move to the dormi-tory. Miranda means to be free of St. Bernadette's before Cian is five and return with him to their house until his calling is clear. He will cling to her, not Sister Joseph, when he's sleepy or hungry. She, not Sister Cameron, will be first to hear his latest word.

She'll collect him today before Doris arrives, as she does every second Sunday after the midday meal. Sometimes it seems as if Doris exists for Miranda alone. It's surprising when she materializes suddenly, like a rainbow, where others can see her, too.

Miranda squeezes her eyes shut to concentrate. Distraction from prayer is a sin.

"Therefore, I beseech blessed Mary ever Virgin, blessed Michael the Archangel, blessed John the Baptist, the holy Apostles Peter and Paul, and all the saints, to pray to the Lord our God for me." The repetition and the symmetry reassure Miranda that order exists outside her often chaotic mind. Whenever prayer leads her into a dreamlike state, the Voice whispers encouragement. *The words matter less than the surrendering*, it says; *ritual's purpose is to distract the conscious mind and let the subconscious take over.* Whatever sadness Miranda's conscious mind may be feeling when she enters the chapel recedes with the magical chill of holy water from the font, the ritual crossing of herself and the hush that allows James's voice to come through and make each next day possible.

To the right of the sanctuary is a stone angel robed in a cloud, wings spread, poised for flight. It brings to mind James's tales of invisible beings, some winged, some not, some benevolent, some not. Pure energy they are, James told her, shaped from beliefs and memories. He often encountered them on his journeys between this world and *an saol eile,* the Other Life, where everything is more intense and nothing is hidden. She says six Our Fathers, six Hail Marys and six Glory Be to the Fathers in case James is stuck between this world and *an saol eile*—the place the catechism calls Purgatory.

Miranda marvels at how the individually mute fragments of brilliant glass in the windows speak as one to tell stories she'd never heard before coming to the orphanage: Gabriel advising Mary she'll bear a child; the Last Supper; Mary appearing to Bernadette when she was as young as Miranda. Light from the World illuminates them. The Voice claims that the light's source deserves to be honored more than a god that forbids eating from a knowledge tree.

The sun, the glorious sun, was ablaze the afternoon Miranda arrived at St. Bernadette's, in the city called Newark, a twenty-minute car ride from Doris and Bill Nolan's house. Bulgy-eyed Sister Bonita escorted her and Cian directly to the infirmary. Past the chapel, up two flights, along a queer-smelling hallway hung with photographs of solemn children, their huge eyes wary, past dormitories and the sisters' sleeping quarters. Except for the wee ones in the nursery, the children and most nuns were away at summer camp. The only sounds were the rustle of Sister Bonita's long, heavy black tunic and the *tip-tap* of her black shoes on the linoleum floor. The infirmary door opened to a long corridor of closed doors reminiscent of the morgue in Stony River. From Miranda's suitcase, Sister Bonita confiscated the "unholy" drawing of Ethleen holding the moon, the "dangerous" candle, matches and moonstone and Cian's "unhealthy" blanket. Miranda and Cian were to be quarantined until the sharp-chinned nurse, Sister Marie Claire, pronounced them free of communicable disease.

Miranda's heart quickened at the possibility of finding Nicholas in Quarantine. But Sister Nurse said St. Bernadette's had no animals except for stray cats that hung about the kitchen door due to Sister

Ernestine's soft spot. Not the same type of soft spot the visiting doctor asked about when he measured Cian's head and said he was micro-cephalic, a word Miranda wrote in the journal Sister Bonita allowed her to keep because it was educational. At eighteen pounds, Cian was no heavier than an eight-month-old, the doctor said. Miranda couldn't say what the lad weighed at birth. And she couldn't report anything unusual about her pregnancy.

"Did you try to escape?" he asked.

"From what?"

The doctor said Cian wouldn't live to an old age and, most likely, would be retarded.

Sister Bonita said it was God's will.

The Voice of James said: *Hogwash*.

Sister Nurse said she'd seen a man with a very small head sing and dance at the circus once when she was a little girl. He looked happy, had seemed to enjoy the attention.

In the infirmary room Cian and Miranda shared, the shades were always up. Sunlight caressed Miranda's face each morning, making her weep for the years it had not. She sleeps now in a dormitory with thirty-nine others, her steel-frame bed in the row nearest the door, farthest from the sun. Some mornings, when she awakens before the chimes and the subsequent sound of forty sets of knees dropping for Hail Marys, she lies abed imagining herself as the goddess Eri, to whom a man in a silver boat floats down on a shimmering sunray. The man is always James.

She sees Cian once a day before bedtime and weekend after-noons. She assumed she'd continue to feed and bathe him, but Sister Cameron said it was best if he began to detach from her. Like the lambs of Lughnasadh James spoke of, abruptly weaned from their sheared and washed ewes. Sister Joseph said Cian would respond better to toilet training and learn to use a spoon and fork if Miranda weren't around catering to him. Sister Nurse bound Miranda's breasts until the milk dried up. Occasionally, it leaks out when a cry from the nursery reaches her ears.

The chapel is empty now except for her and Father Shandley, who has returned from seeing the outsiders off. He's moving items about the altar under the big cross on which Jesus suffers night and day. Miranda likes the father-bird way the priest deposits Christ's body on her tongue. How he places wine and water into the chalice as James placed salt and water into theirs. The way Latin spills from his mouth as Gaeilge did from James's.

He could be older than James or younger; Miranda's not yet a good judge of age. His hair is as dark as Nicholas's, neatly parted on the side and slippery looking. She lifts her doily and smoothes her own hair, the same ginger-spice shade as James's, the waves ending just below her ears. Sister Nurse keeps the inmates' hair shorn so that lice will find no haven there.

"That gorgeous mane gone," Doris said, nearly crying, the first time she visited.

Miranda doesn't mind. It's easier to brush. And when she glimpses herself in the mirror above the row of lavatory sinks, it pleases her to look more like James.

A whiff of onion floats by. Miranda pictures one hundred and twenty bowls of soup waiting obediently. Even from the chapel she can faintly hear the warning chimes. *Bing-bong, bing-bong:* ten minutes to lunch. Chimes announce when to get up, when to go to meals, to Mass and to school. Some inmates complain they feel like dogs ordered about by a whistle—the same girls who put sweaters on backwards, as if they were straitjackets, and say "Look at me, I'm in an asylum," daring Sister Bonita to emerge from her room with the strap to remind them that asylum means refuge, asylum means home.

Being ordered about doesn't bother Miranda. She likes not having to decide what to do next. She likes knowing when to worship: Mass every day and twice on Sunday, prayers upon rising and before falling asleep, the rosary in the afternoon. Around the sisters' waists hang heavy wooden rosaries that nearly brush the floor. Miranda's is shorter and has blue glass beads, a silver crucifix and a silver medallion with Mary's face. She received it for winning a spelling bee. She's the best reader and speller in Sister Celine's fifth-grade class and excels at religious studies; she'd be in a higher grade if she knew more about such things as the Pilgrims and the Gold Rush. When she works the beads, relishing the smoothness of them under her fingertips, she imagines James's hands moving along the cord of knots. She hears the chant he repeated at each knot and sees him slipping into a trance.

Quick as a morning shadow, Miranda crosses the aisle and slides into a pew closer to the stained-glass windows for a better view of Mary's halo—a radiant aura, like that ringing the moon. Sometimes the light breaking through the windows is so bright it bleaches the edges of all around it. Today it lights up a strip of wooden floor, making it shiny, like honey on porridge.

Father Shandley turns sharply as though just noticing her then lifts his hand in greeting. Embarrassed to be caught watching him, she quickly bows her head and whispers, "Hail Mary, full of grace. Our Lord is with thee. Blessed art thou amongst women and blessed is the fruit of thy womb, Jesus." Miranda has learned much about Mary in the past four months and feels a kinship with her. It is as if the Blessed Mother and Danú are one and the same. She asks them both to cast an invisible net of safety over Cian each morning, as James once asked Lugh to do for her. She wonders if Mary felt the Holy Ghost enter her to conceive Jesus, as Miranda felt the Wise Father god Dagda enter her.

But Mary kept all these things and pondered them in her heart.

Like Mary, Miranda must suffer in silence the knowledge of how Cian came to be. The catechism says that Jesus had no human father. Neither does Cian, despite what the nuns and Father Shandley want her to confess.

The catechism also says there is but one God, a He. The Voice says: *The book is wrong. There are many gods and many goddesses; remember our altar, one side for Her, the other for Him?* But increasingly Miranda remembers only bits of James's lessons. Isolated words and phrases, like shards of stained glass no longer able to form a tableau. *Hold onto them,* the Voice urges, *if not for yourself then for the lad.*

Being a good Catholic is easier. The catechism has answers for everything and the answers are full of certainty. We know God made the World because He says so. To be confirmed, Miranda had to profess faith in Christ. The Voice reminds her that the Christ story is oft told: the mythical sacred king who must be sacrificed for the seasons to be born and die, like the summer and winter kings whose births and deaths James and Miranda celebrated each year. *You need honor naught but the sun and moon, water and air, day and night, sea and land,* it tells her. Softly, under her breath, she reminds it she's never been to the sea. It pleases her to be one of *them,* now. No longer, as Sister Bonita branded her, the devil's child who lay on the wrong side of the sheets.

Father Shandley ascends the slanted nave from the sanctuary to Miranda's pew. A flush rises through her as he kneels beside her. She wants to touch his arm but Sister Bonita says Miranda's habit of touching people is sinful. That and the way she stares.

Father Shandley lives alone in a small house behind the orphanage. Some inmates think he looks sad; they speculate that he's lonely. Miranda envies him. She would like to not hear the night sounds of thirty-nine others and to be able to cry in private.

Father Shandley's presence fills more space than his slight frame requires. He crosses himself with his blunt-ended fingers, silently moves his thin lips and, when done, lifts himself onto the creaky pew. She follows as though drawn by a magnet. He leans into her and asks in his confessional voice, gentler than the one he uses for his impassioned homilies, "Shouldn't you be at lunch? I wouldn't want you in trouble with the sisters." So like James in his concern for her.

His face is close enough for her to smell Christ's blood on his breath. She thinks of the biscuit-eating girl who said at dinner, "Yum, like Jesus with no bloody aftertaste." Not seeing the humor in it, Miranda didn't laugh, but was punished for being at the table with those who did. They had to kneel and hold their arms straight out to the side until they wept in pain to appreciate what Jesus endured for them. If communion wafers taste like anything, it is tears.

"I can't go to lunch until I say more prayers to release my father from Purgatory."

"Was he truly penitent before he died, worthy of Purgatory's fires?"

"And for what would he need be penitent?"

Father Shandley sighs as though the air has been punctured out of him. He stares out toward the giant crucifix hanging above the altar and waits. He's good at that. His silence behind the confessional grille often feels like an invisible hand reaching out to seize her secrets. He asks her, every time, to tell God how Cian came to be. Every time she responds that, if God is all-seeing, he already knows. He tells her she's young; God will forgive her for having been seduced into sin if she is contrite. She says she wasn't seduced. He asks on how many occasions she and her father sinned. Each time she assures him that she and James did not sin.

Today he smiles. "The sisters claim that if Saint Peter bars you from the pearly gates, Mary will let you in the back. Maybe your prayers will open Heaven's back door for your father."

Miranda realizes he's joking—she's getting better at that—and a tiny smile inside her expands. She pictures Heaven's gates as the tall wrought-iron ones Doris and Nolan's car passed through the day they delivered her and Cian to St. Bernadette's. She imagines James going round to the kitchen door with the stray cats, petitioning Sister Ernestine.

"On Wednesday," Father Shandley says, "I will say three Masses in honor of the dead, including those who, it is said, still 'groan' in Purgatory. If you make a full confession"—he gives her a pointed look—"and take Holy Communion at All Saints Mass the day before, you might gain an indulgence for your father's soul. In fact, I guarantee it."

It's more than coincidence that the dark half of a new year begins soon. At the precise moment when the Dark Moon of Samhain blocks starlight, time will belong to neither the old year nor the new and the dead will find it easier to wander among the living. On Samhain Eve—Doris calls it Halloween—she and James left plates of food for departed souls and built a fire in the hearth to warm them. She thought she could will her mother to rise out of the flames simply by wanting it badly enough. James said it would require years more study and practice before she was open for communing with the dead. And even then, it might not happen. His mother and grandmother bled through each year, but never Eileen. Miranda wonders now if her mother was trapped between worlds with no one to pray for her.

"Will you wear black?" she asks.

"I will." He laughs. "You ask the most ... Remind me which saint you chose for your confirmation name."

"Maura."

"Ah, yes. You ask the most interesting questions, Miranda Breege Maura Haggerty."

"Sister Bonita thinks not. She says curiosity wastes God's time." Miranda doesn't tell him that some girls laugh at her questions about things they take for granted: hissing radiators, the walking and talking photographs of television, water in fountains bubbling up like tiny dancing balls. *Say goodnight, Gracie,* they croon.

"Does she? Well, you can waste my time. Nobody's mistaken me for God yet." He stands and extends a hand to help her up. With a warm thumb, he traces a firm sign of the cross on her forehead. "Now, to lunch, please. If need be, tell the sisters I kept you."

Miranda feels a quiver of hope, then fear. She will invite James to the Mass of the dead, but what must she confess to deliver him there?

1:35 PM. Haggerty's desk was pocked with cubbyholes stuffed with boring shit: mostly papers, some with date stamps and fancy seals. Only a moron wouldn't have known that the two removable compartments shaped like books were fake. The one on the right held a bunch of sealed envelopes. The heavier and harder-to-slide-out one on the left was stuffed with rubber-banded rolls of bills. She thought they were Russian until she unwrapped a roll and recognized the ones, fives and tens. She'd never seen a twenty or a fifty before. She dumped the rolls onto the bed, pulled off the rubber bands and started counting. When she lost track, she made piles of a hundred bucks each. They took up so much of the bed she made piles of five hundred, then a thousand. Nine piles. Enough to buy nine thousand sacks of White Castle burgers? She must've goofed. She started over and ended up with the same number.

Plopping down hard on the bed, she gawked at the money and told her heart to take it easy. She'd figured Haggerty was poor. Everybody had. The rundown house, the scruffy clothes. People had seen him sift through garbage cans, beg scraps at the fish market and greengrocer. Just goes to show, Ma would've said.

With nine thousand bucks, she and Ma could get away from Jimmy. Except he'd never give up the Chosen One, the fair-haired, fair-skinned copy of himself who read better than Tereza but couldn't lie worth shit; Allen was doomed to do whatever he was told. Even if they *could* take him, Ma was too soft to leave Jimmy. "You don't know how it was with no husband and a kid. I couldn't support you proper. Jimmy was the only man who'd take us on."

Besides, the money was Miranda's. No getting around that. No finders, keepers. If Tereza left it in the desk, somebody else would come across it and gyp Miranda out of it. Would it be so awful if she used a little and found a way to repay it someday? Enough for a ticket somewhere far away, some food and clothes?

Whatever she did, nothing would be the same as it was before. In the basement, her idea had been to head downtown on Halloween dressed as a monk in the black robe and buy undies and dungarees with cash already in her pocketbook. After that, she'd ditch the robe and hitchhike on Route 1. Blow guys for meals and places to sleep. She'd charge big bucks to the first to pop her cherry. Vinnie said his cousin in Roselle paid for a week down the shore by auctioning hers off. If Tereza borrowed Miranda's money, she wouldn't have to hitch-hike and she wouldn't need any guy.

She thought about how Miranda had led her to this moment, and at some point the voices in her head stopped scrapping over whether to take the money. She'd made the decision to leave home for good before she found it. Had already chosen to save herself. She rolled up ninety wads of a hundred bucks each and stuffed them into the four black socks from the wardrobe. "Ho, ho, ho," she said, her voice bouncing off Haggerty's ceiling. An early Christmas: stockings sagging with dough instead of oranges and walnuts.

"MIRANDA!" Doris sounds out of breath as she crests the stairs to the hallway on St. Bernadette's second floor. Miranda stands outside the visitors' lounge, trying to quell the panic that has transformed her legs into rooted trees, not sure how they carried her from the nursery, where Sister Cameron said, "Someone was to have told you."

Doris points to her watch, then holds her palms out in a gesture of helplessness. She unbuttons her black-and-white-checked coat, yanks a white kerchief off her unfazed tight black curls and hurries across the floor to where Miranda has stood for ten minutes on the same beige linoleum square murmuring over and over catechism words that still the clamor in her head and help her breathe without gasping: "How shall we know the things we are to believe?"

She considered going to Sister Celine, who sits behind the visitor registration table in the lounge. But what if Sister was supposed to have told her? Of all the nuns, she's the most encouraging and understanding, treating Miranda practically as a teacher's aide in deference to her age, praising her progress in subjects James didn't assign. "If you ever want to talk to me about anything, know that you can," she said one day, taking Miranda aside after school and looking at her hard, as if she could see into the girl's heart.

Doris, smelling of baby and cold air, kisses Miranda's cheek. "I'm late, I know. Bill was called out this morning and I had to wait for him to get back." She laughs. "Leaving the kids with him is such a production. Gotta be sure Mickey's diaper is dry—Bill sure as heck won't change him—pump out four ounces of milk, leave a list of snacks Carolyn can have, the TV shows it's okay for her to watch."

A tear escapes and dribbles down Miranda's cheek. Doris wipes it away with her thumb. "Oh, sweetie, listen to me whine. Showing off how important I am. I wouldn't miss visiting day for the world. You know that, don't you?"

"Cian's gone."

Doris's smile freezes. "What do you mean?"

"He's been fostered out, he has."

Doris slumps against the wall and closes her eyes for a second. "When?"

"Today. I went to collect him for your visit and he wasn't there."

"You didn't meet the people? You didn't give your approval?"

"I did not."

Once a month couples visit the orphanage to consider children they might want to foster or adopt. They cluster in the lounge, perched on couch and chair edges, as inmates march past them. Their faces betray no emotion. Sister Celine assured Miranda that, if she kept Cian in her arms, prospective parents would know they were to go together. How often did Miranda parade, unaware, in front of the people who took Cian? A doctor and his wife, according to Sister Cameron: "Good Catholics with a weakness for babies in need of healing love."

Doris takes long strides into the lounge and right up to Sister Celine. Miranda stops just inside the entrance to the big room that throbs with inmate and visitor conversations. Any other day, she would be at Doris's heels. But entering now, without Cian, she's self-conscious, as if everyone in the room knows of her loss. Did Father Shandley know all the while he sat with her?

"How can a child be fostered out without his mother's permission?" Doris demands.

Sister Celine glances up at Doris, over at Miranda and then pointedly around the crowded room. In that low, first-warning voice she uses when someone in class misbehaves, she says, "This is not the time or place for such a discussion."

"When is and where?" Doris's voice is loud and shrill. Conversations stop. She leans toward Sister Celine, speaking as if she and the nun were equals or, even more astounding, as if Doris were superior. It took Miranda weeks to recognize that the twelve identically garbed sisters are not mirror images of each other. To see that Sister Celine has one blue eye and one brown, Sister Joseph a hairy mole on her chin and Sister Cameron a flat nose. Yet they are as one in their authority over her, their word not to be doubted, their orders not to be questioned.

Sister Celine strokes the silver crucifix over her heart and mutters too softly for Miranda to hear. Doris nods and backs away. Sister pushes herself from the table as smoothly as if the rigid wooden chair were on wheels. Doris crosses to Miranda and gives her a quick hug.

"She's escorting me to Mother Superior," she whispers, then laughs softly. "Pray for me."

Sister Celine, smelling of soap and starch, leans into Miranda. "Would you mind sitting at the desk until I get back?" A kindness. Inmates ordinarily aren't allowed in the lounge without a visitor. Some girls never have visitors, even those who are at St. Bernadette's because their parents are unable to care for them. Sister Bonita says their parents don't visit because the girls are bad. Sister Celine says it's because the parents feel ashamed and guilty.

Miranda sits in Sister Celine's chair and feels the warmth she left behind. She peers out into the room where conversations have resumed in hushed voices. Dice hit boards as inmates and visitors return to games of Monopoly, Parcheesi and Snakes and Ladders. She and Doris have played checkers with Cian, letting him move the pieces wherever he wants. Will he recall that if he never sees her again? Of her own mother she retains only the scent of tangerines.

The visitors are better dressed than the inmates, who select their clothes for the week from freshly laundered garments dumped onto a bed each Saturday. Inmates aren't allowed to own anything that might make them proud and vain. They push and shove to avoid ending up with a too-long skirt or a too-tight blouse. Miranda's mother's dresses don't fit most girls. Some say they wouldn't be "caught dead" in them anyway, so she can usually count on them for herself.

She spots a dormitory mate, the crinkly-haired, fat-cheeked Rosalee, a bed-wetter. Sister Bonita forces Rosalee to march about with soiled sheets on her head. Public shame teaches humility, Sister Bonita claims, makes you more Christ-like. She will welcome Miranda's shame over losing her child. And shame it is coursing through her now, along with shock and grief.

"Where did I go wrong, James?" she whispers, and waits in vain for the rush of warm air that will tell her he has heard.

Rosalee appears to whisper into the ear of a woman in a pale blue suit and matching hat with delicate veil. The woman glances over. Rosalee is one of the girls who follow Miranda around the playground at recess like flies, buzzing with questions: what's it like to give birth, what does a penis feel like inside you? In the lavatory, they ask to see the hair between her legs. They want to compare their nascent breasts with hers as though their bodies were in competition. In Miranda's dormitory room of fifth and sixth graders, she's the only one who bleeds each month, something the others are anxious to experience, despite Sister Bonita's telling them it's a curse upon women for Eve's mortal sin.

Miranda is torn between keeping her promise to James and sharing what she knows with the inquisitive girls whose acceptance she craves. But it's unlikely they will one day lie naked, intoxicated from wine and chanting, while spirits possess their bodies.

The Holy Ghost shall come upon thee, the angel said to Mary.

It wasn't lust, she wants to shout at Sister Bonita and Father Shandley.

Some girls claim that the day they inhaled their first breath of St. Bernadette's was the worst of their lives. Miranda's mind hid in the giant sycamore inside the gates, her senses trembling like its leaves, as she watched herself carry Cian up the stone steps to the cold-faced red-brick building. That same day, however, was the first she stood under a night sky after Sister Nurse took pity on her. Miranda had cried until her eyes were nearly swollen shut because the moon did not appear in the infirmary windows and Sister Bonita had confiscated the only other way she could say goodnight to her mother: the picture of Ethleen. After midnight, Sister Nurse, in white skullcap and long white nightgown, led her down the two flights of stairs and out a side door, tiptoeing all the way. At the sight of a crescent moon floating amid no end of stars, Miranda fell to the ground and lay on damp grass, overwhelmed by the sensation of being sucked up into the black sky. She felt part of something vast and whole. Asked then, she might have declared it the best day of her life.

Joy and grief mingled in the cup, she thinks of it now.

From Sister Celine's chair, she can see a bank of four windows. Out there, as vast as that starry night, lies the World into which Cian has vanished like an Eloi taken by Morlocks. Miranda is the Time Traveler, catapulted into an alien future she never imagined.

3:30 PM. Tereza decided to take the knife from the basement, in case anyone tried to mess with her, and the shell necklace as a souvenir. But when she put them in her pocketbook, their shapes remained on the dusty, faded black tablecloth. On the chance that somebody might enter the house after she split and notice that, she buried the cloth, animal's horn, candle, jingle bells, wand, knotted yarn and goblet in boxes of old clothes. She took down the black drapes and the hand-drawn picture and packed them in a box with dolls, an old telephone and a radio. Shoved the table, pillars and harp in a corner so that they looked like just more old crap stored away.

Her stomach was griping. She hadn't eaten all day, afraid she'd upchuck the booze. She sliced the Spam onto a plate, sprinkled canned corn like confetti over it and lit the candles on the table. "To the last night of my old life," she said.

The hours turtled by. She'd never stayed away this long. Ma might be worried by now. Jimmy wouldn't care. He'd be lost in his Sunday blahs. Ma said Tereza should try to understand that poison from the war kept seeping out of him and not make things worse by being so difficult. If he couldn't help it, did it matter what Tereza did? She thought about Haggerty's shotgun and how powerful she'd felt with its weight on her shoulder.

Just as well it was too big to take.

She might shoot Ma instead of Jimmy.

WHEN DORIS AND SISTER CELINE return, Miranda stands quickly.

"No visitors, Sister," she says, searching her teacher's eyes for reassurance but seeing only pity. Doris's face looks scrubbed of emotion.

Doris and Miranda find a vacant couch and sit thigh to thigh. Doris seems uncomfortable, twisting her head this way and that as though she's never been in the lounge before. "Mother Alfreda has a tiny office," she says.

"Does it matter?" Miranda says, wondering whether the day James died could have been worse than this one. But if something happens that makes you want to stop living, does it matter if it's better or worse than something else that made you feel the same?

Doris says, "No, of course not. I was surprised, that's all. You can bet the Pope doesn't work in a closet." She leans forward and straightens the magazines on the low wooden table in front of them. Turns to face Miranda. "I'm very angry right now. Mother Alfreda showed me papers that make it perfectly legal for St. Bernadette's to foster or adopt you and Cian out.

"Sister Cameron said I mustn't be selfish. If the foster parents like Cian, they might adopt him. She says it could be his only chance for a real family."

Doris's eyebrows shoot up. "Baloney. I will not let strangers adopt him. I promise you." She pulls Miranda to her and smoothes her hair. Miranda closes her eyes to stop her tears from spilling over and imagines herself and Cian in Doris's house. Doris knows so much about the World. How will Miranda ever catch up?

"I nearly forgot," Doris says. She opens her pocketbook. "I brought you and Cian treats for Halloween tomorrow." She gives a rueful laugh. "I guess they're both for you, now." She pulls out two brightly wrapped candy bars named Baby Ruth.

"I won't be allowed to keep them," Miranda says softly, stealing a glance at Sister Celine.

"Then we'll have to eat them here."

Miranda's never tasted a candy bar. She sucks it until the chocolate coating dissolves and drips down her chin. Doris laughs and hands her a tissue. Wipes her own mouth with another.

Miranda says, "Sister Bonita would say I'm adding to Christ's sorrows right now."

Doris laughs again, a howl that silences the room for a few seconds. "You're gonna be okay, sweetie. You've got a scrappy soul, like me." They sit and hold hands without speaking until visiting time is over. Doris's hands are warm and soft, her long fingernails painted red—so different from Sister Celine's serviceable hands with their bald nails clipped short and square.

Miranda doubts anyone laughs at how Doris speaks. She wouldn't permit it. Beginning tomorrow, Miranda won't either. And she'll demand to see Cian. James used to say Samhain Eve was a night for letting go as well as for grieving, a time for starting over.

When Doris goes, she leaves behind a red lipstick smear on a tissue and a timid stirring of greediness for life in Miranda.

❧ SIX ❧

OCTOBER 31, 1955. In white cotton nightie, black lace bed jacket and mantilla, the Spanish Princess hopped over pavement seams, hurrying to school without her once-upon-a-time friend at her side. Tereza would have looked more authentic in the costume with her coloring, even though Daddy said you could find blondes in Spain, just not many. What about fat blondes, Linda asked. He'd shaken his head and given her a fierce hug. That was before Friday night when she told him she hated him.

He'd objected to her leaving this morning without a proper breakfast—"Your brain needs more fuel than cold leftover potatoes"—but she wanted to reach school early enough to catch Mr. Boynton alone. She didn't care what Mr. Roger-not-so-Wise said right now anyway. Just as he could be disappointed in her, wounding her heart whenever he said so, she could be disappointed in him. If the Good Samaritan's daughter had asked him to help a friend whose stepfather was about to lash her with a belt, the Good Samaritan wouldn't have said, "Not our business."

She'd tell Mr. Boynton not to expect Tereza in school today, possibly never again. She would tell what she knew even if she got in serious trouble, which she hadn't been in since kindergarten, when she spent more time in the naughty chair than anyone else. For no good reason! Miss Glannore had written "Linda is inclined to be heedless" on her report card, making Linda's mother sick with humiliation. Linda tried harder to please Mother after that, bringing home cards that reported: "Linda is a joy to teach; Linda is a bright, helpful child; Linda will go far." Although she'd figured out how to avoid trouble at school, the rules at home kept changing. But she was more afraid of not doing right than of breaking a rule because God would have worse things to say in Heaven than her parents could on Earth.

Tereza was the heedless one, if you wanted to know. She didn't play by the rules and didn't listen to anyone. She often showed up with raw welts on her arms and legs, due to her getting "mouthy," she'd say, like you might explain away a rash from too many tomatoes. Tereza seemed to accept the cost of doing what she pleased. Linda wanted to admire her for that, for being true to her beliefs like a Christian facing lions, but she doubted Tereza's beliefs fit into the same category.

Linda had done the right thing Friday night, despite what Daddy said. After he said "Not our business" she'd run into the street, yelling at Jimmy to stop. (It was hard to think of him as Mr. Dobra.) He'd glanced at her long enough for Tereza to scurry away. When he pulled back the belt as though to whip Linda, Daddy came to life, like Superman getting over a dose of kryptonite. He stepped between her and Jimmy, put a hand on Jimmy's chest and said, "That'll be enough of that." Jimmy's cheeks went splotchy with anger and he straightened to his full height, as if ready to sock Daddy. But then he seemed to lose air. He slapped Daddy's hand down and strode away.

"Such a foolish thing you did," her father said as he ushered her into their house. "You could have gotten hurt."

That's when Linda had shouted "I hate you," fled to her room and locked the door.

The next morning she'd found her mother out of bed for the first time in ages, in a quilted blue robe that stopped above puffy knees on pasty, wobbly legs. Her cheeks looked dented. She was dropping pancake batter into a sizzling pan, stinking up the kitchen with Crisco fumes. "Tuna casserole and rice pudding tonight," she said. "What do you think about that?"

"Is it okay for you to be up, Mother?"

Daddy, who sat at the kitchen table with his coffee and crossword as if last night hadn't happened, looked up at Linda and shrugged helplessly. "I couldn't talk her out of it."

Even if Mr. Boynton hadn't been Linda and Tereza's homeroom teacher Linda would have gone to him. He was the only seventh-grade teacher gutsy enough to do something about Tereza. On the first day of school he told them they would receive one pencil for the year and that was it, too bad if they lost it. Linda was outraged at the injustice at first, but when Mr. Boynton explained he was tough-ening them up for eighth grade where the teachers would be even stricter, she realized he was brilliant.

Mr. Boynton's nubby wool jacket hung over a chair. He was at the other end of the room, briskly erasing Friday's homework from the board. Fluorescent light ricocheted off his bald spot. Linda coughed. He whipped around.

"Linda! Or should I say, Señorita? You look radiant."

She flushed with pleasure. Occasionally, when he called on her in class, she sensed he saw through her hideous plaid eyeglass frames to someone he could love if she were older and thinner. Now his olive eyes, magnified by perfectly round tortoiseshell glasses, gazed at her unblinkingly as she told him that Tereza had fled from her stepfather's belt Friday night and hadn't been seen since. He swallowed hard, making his bow tie wiggle, as Linda explained how she'd looked for Tereza everywhere she could think of. And how Mrs. Dobra searched the neighborhood, too, calling as if Tereza were the Lost Sheep. Linda didn't admit she'd been too cowardly to check out Crazy Haggerty's. But neither did she brag about marching into the White Castle where she'd nearly died of mortification asking those hoods Tereza hung around with if they knew where she was.

"Have her parents reported her missing?" Mr. Boynton asked.

"No."

"Why not?"

"I think only one of them wants to."

Mr. Boynton's eyebrows shot up, pushing little folds into his shiny forehead.

Linda had gone to Tereza's apartment building after breakfast Saturday morning. Mrs. Dobra answered on the second knock, cigarette between two fingers, purple shadows under her eyes. "Linda!" she said, as if she were starving and Linda a peanut butter and jelly sandwich. "Did Tereza bunk with you last night?"

From the door, Linda could see Jimmy at the kitchen table and feel his mean eyes on her. "Quit going on," he called out. "You know she always comes home."

Mrs. Dobra ushered Linda to the porch so they could talk. She looked scared. "I was out this morning before Jimmy was awake. Up and down every damn street this side of the highway and all along the smelly river, calling for her. Jimmy might be right she'll be back but I don't know. This time feels different." The soft, husky voice, so intimate and trusting, drew Linda in. She couldn't picture Mother traipsing around the neighborhood for her.

Later, Linda's mother had said, "She lets her get away with murder. What did she expect?" Mother didn't approve of women working outside the home, leaving their kids to "run hog-wild."

"What do you think we should do, Linda?" Mr. Boynton asked.

"Call the police."

Mr. Boynton stood and went for his jacket. "Let's go see Mrs. Warren," he said.

Linda was no stranger to the principal's office. She went often to mimeo tests or deliver messages to teachers. Only students bright enough to miss classroom time were chosen. Linda tried not to act smug when she was called because, as had been impressed upon her in Sunday school, "Pride goeth before a fall." (It was so hard to wait for the rewards of the meek.)

This morning, while the principal and Mr. Boynton conferred, Linda waited on the hard pine bench outside Mrs. Warren's office, watching the school secretary type, admiring the speed at which she made the carriage move across the page—*clackety, clackety, ding!* Linda wondered if she liked working for Vinegar Lips, as some kids called Mrs. Warren because of her sour expression. Linda's stomach flip-flopped, imagining what the principal and Mr. Boynton were saying about her, but she was determined not to waver.

Mr. Boynton had to return to his classroom. When Officer Nolan came, he interviewed Linda in Mrs. Warren's office. His voice was kind and lines radiated from the corners of his eyes like pencil-drawn sunbeams. He might have been one of the policemen she and Tereza saw at Crazy Haggerty's, but she couldn't be sure because she wore her glasses only when she had to.

Mrs. Warren told Officer Nolan about Tereza's stepfather chasing her with the belt. The officer asked Linda if she knew why. She wasn't allowed to say *whore* and she didn't know for sure why Jimmy was mad, so she repeated only his ungrammatical "I know where you been" and said she thought he would have hurt Tereza badly if he'd been able to catch up with her. The officer took notes when Linda mentioned the number of marks on Tereza's arms and legs in the four months she'd known her. He took down Tereza's description and the direction in which she'd fled.

"Linda thinks Tereza might be hiding in a vacant house," Mrs. Warren said, her head helmeted in tight curls, dyed (everybody said) daffodil yellow.

"Which house?" he asked Linda.

"Mr. Haggerty's," she said. "The grand house on Lexington Street?"

"Oh, that one. It's boarded up. I ordered it myself."

"That wouldn't stop Tereza," Linda said.

"How come?"

She told him she'd checked the log where she and Tereza had hidden things and discovered the crowbar gone. She told him Tereza wasn't afraid of the house that sat all by its lonesome and might have broken in to stay warm; she hadn't exactly been bundled up when she ran away.

The officer asked Mrs. Warren if she'd called Tereza's parents.

"They don't have a telephone," she said, her elbows on the desk, her fingers forming *here's the church, here's the steeple.* "We don't usually send a truant officer around until a child misses three days in a row. They have a son in third grade. I checked and he's not here either."

"He was okay yesterday," Linda said, although that wasn't completely accurate. After church she'd gone over to see if the Dobras had heard from Tereza. Allen was keeping vigil by the front window, arms crossed, hands under armpits, a miserable look on his face.

"He don't believe Tereza ran away," Mrs. Dobra said, clutching Linda's hands so tightly it hurt. "Says she would've been back to take him to the movies if she could've. He's sure the bogeyman snatched her. I couldn't get him to sleep last night." She asked Linda to take him trick-or-treating the next day so she could stick around in case Tereza showed up. Since it wasn't fair to hold it against Allen for getting Jimmy's beaky nose and wingy ears, Linda agreed.

Officer Nolan asked for Tereza's address. "Think anyone's there with the boy?"

"Mrs. Dobra usually isn't home till four. Mr. Dobra later."

He took Linda's address, too. "I may need a statement from you and your father."

Linda's heart thumped. Daddy would scold her again for not minding her business. "Will you look for Tereza at the boarded-up house?"

"You bet," he said with the kind of head-patting smile she despised.

"That girl who lived there," she said, a bit crossly. "Miranda?"

His eyes widened. "You knew her?"

"No. Her name was in the newspaper."

"Oh, I suppose it was. What about her?"

"Where is she now?"

"With people who will take care of her."

So-called grown-ups never told you what you really wanted to know.

11:05 AM. Ma would've been at Catalog Club, in the north end of town, for hours by now. Her job was to fill baskets as they traveled down a conveyer. Like Lucy and Ethel with the chocolates, except Ma couldn't stuff the baskets in her mouth. Tereza headed out for the two-mile jaunt to downtown, disguised in Haggerty's hooded black robe, the bottom scissored off so it wouldn't drag on the ground. Buddy's jacket warmed her underneath. She'd stitched the stuffed socks together into a fat, lumpy belt and pinned the belt to her shorts, using a needle, thread and diaper pins from a sewing box she'd found on a bathroom shelf. The belt cinched her waist like a too-small swimming tube. She'd kept out two rolls of bills, now in the pocketbook on her shoulder under the robe.

The world outside felt bigger. She turned for a last look at the blind plywood eyes and yawning mouth of the house. She felt released, like a balloon slipping from a kid's hand, floating up to get lost in the clouds. She zigzagged to town, avoiding the school and the highway crossing where she knew a cop would be on duty. She wouldn't go to school ever again if she could help it. She'd never understood what she was supposed to be learning anyway, couldn't see what difference it would make to how her life turned out.

The closer to downtown she walked, the tighter her heart got. The nearly bare trees lining the street looked like twisted old men ready to pounce and steal her money. She folded her arms across her middle and clutched the money tube gripping her waist.

She'd gone to town lots in the summer, usually with the guys and mostly to places that let you horse around: the diner, the soda shop, the five-and-dime. Today she braved a luggage and gift shop where anything noisier than the rustle of tissue paper was probably against the law. A briefcase in the window said twelve bucks. A present for her father, she told the perfumy saleswoman who smiled and whispered, "A lucky man." She didn't say boo about Tereza's costume, maybe because she was wearing a witch's hat herself. The briefcase came with a lock. In the shop's bathroom, Tereza tucked the rolls of cash into it and abandoned the socks in a wastebasket. She locked up the necklace, knife and flashlight in the briefcase, too.

She carried the locked case across the street to the only department store in town and headed to the women's section for something grown-up looking. She took three suits off a rack and peered around for blouses. A nearly chinless woman in a pleated plaid skirt and red sweater set appeared from nowhere at her side, took the suits from Tereza and returned them to the rack.

"Hey! I wanted to try them on."

"The children's department is in the back." The woman didn't even look at her.

Tereza hadn't anticipated needing a story. What she came up with on the spot—that she had the Grace Kelly part of the wife who almost gets bumped off in a school production of *Dial M for Murder* and needed the right costume—wasn't her best.

Chinless scowled at her then, with eyes the color of mold. Tereza produced her pocketbook from beneath the robe and fished out some bills. "I got cash."

Chinless suggested that Grace Kelly would choose a slim black-and-white tweed suit (extra small for Tereza), a white blouse, a gunmetal gray double-breasted wool coat with big round buttons and fake pearl earrings. "A wig would be the crowning touch, pardon the pun," she said, "but with your coloring, something more Dolores del Rio than Grace Kelly."

Tereza didn't know any Dolores, but a wig was a boss idea. She opted for a black one with Ava Gardner waves, then picked out gloves, bra, skivvies, garter belt and nylons. A hundred and six bucks for the whole shebang.

Chinless helped her do her makeup, going easy on the eye shadow. "You look good," she said, "and older in that outfit. If I didn't know better, I'd think you were a young wife out for the day." Tereza could tell she wasn't bullshitting.

She had Chinless bag up Haggerty's robe, Buddy's jacket, her old bra, shorts and sweater. Told her she'd wear the new clothes out of the store to begin getting in character.

"Grace Kelly would not wear ballerina slippers with that outfit," Chinless said.

Tereza admired her for continuing to play along. She exited a shoe store, inches taller, in what the salesman called "an amazing pump." Black. $10.95. Matching pocketbook: $3.50. The first roll was gone and the second shrinking.

The amazing pumps took her to the train station three blocks away. Her plan was to take the Pennsy to Linden, first, to return Buddy's flashlight and jacket. She'd have him meet her at a fancy hotel to show she didn't need his help.

"There a nice hotel in Linden?" she asked the old ticket seller with a missing middle finger.

"I wouldn't think so," he said.

"What about Elizabeth?" The stop after Linden.

"Oh sure."

On the twenty-minute ride Tereza envisioned a bath hot enough to steam up a mirror and, later, a soft bed. After seeing Buddy, she'd get back on the Pennsy and get off in New York City. Finally see the Rockettes, the Empire State Building and the Automat. She wouldn't tell him where she was going in case he blabbed to Richie. The realization that she could do whatever she wanted from now on gurgled up into her throat. She wanted to hug everyone on the train.

The conductor pointed her to a hotel a five-minute stroll from the station. On a canopy over a carpeted entrance, the hotel's name was lit up in fancy script Tereza couldn't read. Green-and-white-striped awnings hung over every window of the eight floors. Linda would've said it was *grand*. A man in a jacket the same green as the awnings stood at attention behind a wood-paneled counter holding a jack-o-lantern. He flashed her an Ipana-white smile.

"A room, please," Tereza said, dropping her voice to sound older. "A single." She'd seen people check into hotels in movies.

"For how many nights?"

"Two." In case she couldn't get hold of Buddy tomorrow.

"American Plan or à la carte?"

"American Plan." She was feeling patriotic.

"The rate is six dollars a night. Are you comfortable with that?"

"Yeah, no sweat."

He handed her a card and a pen. "I'll need name, address and telephone number."

Tereza stared at the card, her heart pounding against her ribs. She set the briefcase and shopping bag beside her feet and slowly picked up the pen, buying time while her mind conjured up a phony name and address. Stop watching me, she wanted to yell as she gripped the pen in her fist and printed ugly letters that strayed off the line. His

X-ray eyes burned through her new clothes to the dumb old Tereza underneath. She looked up at him. "Don't got no phone."

He took the card from her and read it quickly. "May I see some identification, Miss Derek?" When she didn't respond, he said, "A driver's license or social security card will do."

"I got money in case you're worried." She opened the new pocketbook and pulled out what remained of the second roll.

He lifted his eyebrows and smiled flatly. "Excuse me a moment." He ducked through a doorway behind the desk.

She snatched up the briefcase and shopping bag and left.

REENIE OPENED the door just a wedge, so the cop couldn't see inside. He stood feet apart, hand on holster. He flashed his badge and gave his name but her head was too full of noise to take it in. "Tereza Dobra's mother?" Her legs went spongy. They've found her, she thought, face down in the river or run over. "Call me Reenie," she said, her voice coming from someplace else. She squeezed out a smile to cover the fear seizing her lungs. "Anything wrong?" "Your children weren't at school today, Reenie, and the principal's concerned. They home now?" "My boy is. The school send the cops every time a kid don't show up? That must keep you busy." "Mind if I come in and talk about it?" She didn't want a cop in the house. Didn't want Allen hearing whatever he might say. "My husband ain't here." "Would it be better if we spoke outside on the porch?" A gentleman cop; that made a change. "Yeah, it would, thanks, just a minute, lemme turn off the stove." She shut the door, leaving him in the hallway. Allen was sprawled on the floor watching *The Mickey Mouse Club,* the first show in days to drag him away from the window. "Stay here," she told him. She grabbed her coat off the hook, her Winstons and matches from the counter. The cop tested the porch railing before half-sitting on it. "I heard there was trouble between your husband and daughter Friday night, an incident involving a belt. I understand your daughter ran away afterward and hasn't been seen since." "Who told you that?" "Is it true?" Reenie drew a cigarette from the pack and handed him her matches. He flinched like she'd stepped on his toe but recovered and offered her a light. She took a deep drag and watched her icy breath fuse with the smoke. Linda, she thought, it had to be Linda who told. "I don't know nothing about a belt. Tereza was late coming home, my husband seen her coming down the street and went out to meet her, to make sure she come in, you know? He said she yelled at him and ran away." "Did he say why she yelled at him?" This cop was good-looking but so tall you'd have to kiss him on the stairs, him a couple steps below. Reenie pursed her lips and shook her head. Sometimes the truth was nobody else's business. Tereza thought that too, and it drove Jimmy nuts. "What have you done about finding your daughter?" "I called around the neighborhood all weekend. Stayed home from work today—pissing off the shift boss; Tereza's got no idea the trouble she's making. Anyway, I stayed here because my boy was too upset to go to school but also because I thought Tereza might sneak back to get some clothes. My husband's out right now checking places she might be at." Doing penance, she thought but didn't say. Jimmy always felt like crap after a row with Tereza. "Why would she have to *sneak* home?" "She don't, of course, just that when she gets a bee in her ..." Reenie didn't finish because Allen's worried little face was pressed against the window. She turned her back so he couldn't read her lips. "She's stubborn is all, thinks nobody but her is ever right." "Why do *you* think she hasn't come home, Reenie?" "I got no idea." "Sure you do." Reenie shivered and hugged herself. She studied the peeling paint on the porch, the same baby-shit color of the last building they'd lived in. She hated having to leave places just when they started to feel like home. *Hated* having to choose between being a good wife and a good mother. "Has Tereza run away before?" "Not here, but yeah, last place we lived. She always

came home after she cooled off." "Does your husband hit her?" Reenie
took a last drag and tossed the butt over the railing. "Why'd you ask
that?" Her teeth clicked like castanets; it was goddamned cold out.
"Because Tereza has been observed with marks on her arms and legs."
Ah, only four months in Stony River and already time to move on.
Well, this apartment was nothing special and she'd need a lobotomy
to do that job at the Catalog Club much longer. "She's a tomboy is
all," she told the cop, "always taking a tumble, scraping or breaking
something." He nodded slowly, looked straight at her and said, like a
punch in the gut, "Does he hurt you and the boy, too?" If Jimmy went
to jail, how would Reenie take care of Allen? It might be better if
Tereza didn't come back; she'd be leaving in a few years anyway, and
Jimmy was calmer when she wasn't around. She stared right back into
the mirror of the cop's brown eyes. "You bring me any news about my
girl? If not, I gotta go feed my boy." She could tell he didn't like that.
He slid off the porch rail and stood like he had a rod up his behind. "I
inspected a vacant house a few blocks from here. Someone's been in it
recently. It might have been your daughter. We'll keep an eye on it in
case she returns. Also, I put in calls to the county hospitals and police
stations this afternoon. No unidentified young females found. I'd like a
recent photograph of Tereza to show around." Imagining her baby in a
morgue, no one to claim her, Reenie teared up. She thought about that
lump of bone where Tereza's jaw had healed. "Don't have no picture,
no camera." "When will your husband be home?" "Seven, maybe." "I'll
be back then." Inside, Reenie took Allen's chin in her hand. "Don't tell
nobody about that cop being here, understand? And I'll be the one lets
Pop-Pop know."

A COLD and windless night. Trick-or-treaters filled the sidewalks and
spilled onto the streets.

"What if she don't got food or water?" Allen asked. He and Linda were traveling house to house, holding pillowcases out for treats. He'd never said more than a few words to her before. He was supposed to be Sailor Jack from Cracker Jacks in Jimmy's old flat white hat and navy middy. Even over a jacket, the middy came down to his ankles.

"Tereza wouldn't let herself starve," Linda said.

"But what if she's tied up?"

"I don't think she's tied up."

"Ma calls her Tez," Allen said. "That rhymes with Pez. I used to like Dots, but Pez is gooder. I have Mickey Mouse and Santa Claus. Maybe somebody'll give me a Popeye dispenser tonight."

Fat chance: too expensive. Linda's house was handing out candy corn in yellow napkin pouches—a Tootsie Pop, head down, sticking out of each. Daddy said they looked like "festive plumber's helpers." That had dragged a laugh out of Mother, making Linda relieved but jealous. Lately, the most she got from her mother was a smile so slight it seemed to have been squeezed from her. Linda had assembled fifty pouches, counting ten pieces of candy corn for each, to be fair. Mother fretted that fifty might not be enough (Daddy had done the shopping). She said she'd rather die than tell a child she'd run out of treats. So just do it, Linda thought, immediately sending up a frantic plea for God's forgiveness. She and Daddy had been doing just fine until Mother got up and interfered. Linda promised to drop back partway through to empty her pillowcase.

She kept her eyes open for a camouflaged Tereza sneaking up to surprise Allen. That's what she would have done if her little brother were so worried about her he couldn't sleep. She would've had a brother too, if she hadn't killed him. She hadn't meant to. She didn't even remember doing it. She'd been three, and Mother six months pregnant, when she crawled into her parents' bed after a nightmare. Once back to sleep, she kicked Mother in the stomach, making her lose the almost-boy they named Robert. "He was the length of a ruler," Mother would say reverently. She told the story whenever people asked, "Only one child?" Always adding, "Of course, it wasn't her fault."

No chance of a brother now. Daddy had finally confided that mother's operation in August was to remove her uterus, which, it turned out, wasn't diseased after all. *Growing Up and Liking It* had a sketch of a uterus. Ugly as a bagpipe. Linda couldn't imagine having one inside her.

Mother had returned from the hospital right before Labor Day and slipped into a funk the doctor couldn't explain. She'd be in bed when Linda left for school and in bed when she returned. Linda brought her ginger ale and toast every afternoon, but it didn't help. "Is your father home yet?" was all she'd say.

It seemed she saved her voice for Daddy. "She says she feels too heavy to move," he'd report. Or, "She says she can't see colors anymore." He'd look at Linda as if she could make everything hunky-dory in the few hours she had after school.

For two months Linda had wished, "star light star bright," that Mother would get well so Linda could win Tereza back from the boys she'd started hanging around with after Linda took over the house-work. And now that it was too late, Mother had arisen from her bed like Lazarus to make Linda's favorite dishes and hand out Halloween treats. Her sudden recovery had something to do with Friday night, Linda was sure, and if Mother ended up back in the room that smelled of unwashed hair and stale sheets, it would be one more thing that would and wouldn't, at the same time, be Linda's fault.

BEHIND THE WHEEL of Doris's '53 Ford—sea foam, not a color he'd choose—Bill Nolan felt the colossal moon tracking him, its features clearly defined, each crater seemingly illuminated from within. It was the first full moon on a Halloween since before he was born: an alien yet benevolent presence that wouldn't let him come to harm. Doris hadn't wanted him to leave his revolver at home, but sometimes it was a barrier for people to get past when you needed their confidence. The gun, the uniform, the cuffs, the badge and the billy club gave him an unearned superiority, transformed *him* into an alien presence people rarely found benevolent.

Tonight he was in cords, last year's Christmas sweater from Doris and his dad's old fishing jacket. He'd decided against the panda car to spare the Dobras additional gossip. The neighbors would have been speculating already about his afternoon visit. While he knew Reenie Dobra hadn't been straight with him, he didn't want to add to her troubles. Her unschooled speech and bravado made him want to protect her. From what, he didn't know yet.

He'd formed a mental picture of her husband: overweight, belligerent, as dark as she was. Hard to reconcile with the thin, fair, sharp-featured fellow at the kitchen table submissively clasping callused hands before him. He didn't look like he belonged with Reenie. Bill could see her in some Egyptian get-up. He'd never been to Egypt; it was just a feeling. Judging from the sparsely furnished apartment, Dobra wasn't a great provider. But with an honest-to-Pete tear in his eye, he said he loved his stepdaughter and wanted her back. "I'm strict, won't lie about that, but only because I don't want her going bad. Don't expect no medal for taking care of her. Seeing her grow up right will be enough."

Their boy was trick-or-treating, Reenie said in her tobacco-lusty voice, and she wanted to settle whatever they had to before he got back.

Doris had taken Carolyn in her ballerina costume to a few houses in the afternoon, along with their month-old baby in the carriage. Bill couldn't get over it: a son, Michael David, the goofs at the station dubbing him Mickey D, like some little mobster. He couldn't conceive

of doing anything that would make his kids want to run away. It irked
Doris that he dropped by the house or telephoned several times a day
to check on them; made her feel he didn't trust her. Not at all, he'd
explained, hoping she'd understand that, when you see what a cop
sees day after day, you can't pretend nothing bad could ever happen
to those you love.

Reenie had brewed coffee. She served it in cups with thick rims.
Bill scalded his tongue on the first bitter sip. For a while that afternoon he'd thought she was flirting with him, but she was preoccupied
tonight, lighting her own cigarettes, tapping them into a Cinzano
ashtray. Considering the heat blasting from the radiators, she was
appropriately dressed in a summery white blouse and red cotton
skirt. Dobra was stripped down to workpants and a sleeveless undershirt that revealed an anchor tattooed on a ropy arm.

"Don't let them hoodwink you," Doris had warned him over
dinner. "You wouldn't believe the lies some parents tell." Sure he
would. He'd heard a few in his six years on the force, but Doris,
having worked for Children's Aid before Carolyn was born, assumed
the mantle of expert in their home when it came to such matters.
She'd given him heck for not knowing what had been going on in
the Haggerty house, had actually wanted to keep those kids. She'd
returned from a visit with the girl yesterday steamed at him about it
all over again. Bill's mission for tonight, she said, was to collect any
evidence that the Dobra kids were in danger and report back to her
for further consultation. She wasn't concerned about the wife. "She's
a big girl." That was Doris for you.

Bill brought out his notebook and a handkerchief to wipe his
forehead, considered peeling off the sweater. "What happened Friday
night, Mr. Dobra?"

"After work, I stopped in at Rolf's for smokes."

"The corner store?"

"That's right. Rolf tells me there's a story going 'round about

Tereza. That she gets into cars at the garage down the street. Rolf says he thinks I should know."

"Tony Tomasso's garage?"

"If you say so. Anyways, the story is she does things with men in those cars, things I don't want to talk about in front of her mother."

Reenie lit another cigarette.

"Did you ask Tereza if the story was true?"

"Didn't need to. It added up. The slutty way she'd started dressing, not staying with her brother until her ma got home like she was supposed to. When I saw her coming home late again, sashaying down the street like the Queen of Sheba, I blew up."

"A witness saw you threaten her with a belt. Did you?"

"I didn't hit her."

"She ran away before you could?"

"If you say so."

Dobra's habit of lobbing questions back was annoying. "Taking a belt to a child could be considered assault, you aware of that?"

"Were you in the war, son?" Dobra asked. A locker-room challenge. A rutting elk looking to lock antlers. For a moment, Bill regretted not having worn his uniform.

"No. It was all over by the time I was old enough. You?"

Dobra narrowed his eyes, as though wringing out the memory. "A troop ship in the Pacific. At dawn, we'd throw cargo nets over the side, watch the troops climb down, swaying and cussing, stepping on each other's hands. They'd drop into LCAs and take off and we'd still be watching as the Japs blew them all to Hades. You do that enough, it gets to be routine, you know, body parts in the water, the sea turned to blood, you get to thinking, today wasn't so bad, not so many as yesterday. If a girl lies and whores enough it gets to be routine for her, you know what I'm saying? And it gets around. When Tereza gives me lip, says what's the big deal, I can't see nothing in my mind but her busted-up body in a puddle of blood."

A prickle rose from Bill's tailbone to his scalp. His mind groped for mollifying words. "My father-in-law's a retired officer," he said. "Not navy, but I could ask him if he knows someone you could talk to about what you went through in the war."

Jimmy's torso snapped to attention. "What the fuck you talking about?" The muscle beneath his anchor started to twitch.

Bill's long legs slowly pushed his chair from the table. Foolish to have come without Frank.

"Jimmy," Reenie said quietly, putting her hand on Dobra's arm.

He shrugged her off. Got up and turned on a stove burner, bent down and lit a cigarette. He took a long drag and let it out, his eyes wild and unfocused for a moment. Then he came back into himself. Said, "Let's talk about finding Tereza."

Bill asked to see the girl's room. He thought it might offer a clue.

"It ain't cleaned up," Reenie said. "Allen insisted everything stay like when she left."

A blanket over a rope divided the room. On what Reenie said was Tereza's side: a narrow bed with rumpled sheets, a movie poster tacked on the wall, an old dresser and a lamp with cowgirls on the shade that made Bill's eyes sting with sudden emotion. Schoolbooks had been dumped on the bed, a dresser drawer left open. No games or stuffed animals, no bedspread or curtains. Not much to come home to. He peeked over the rope to the boy's side. Just as bleak.

He agreed to visit Tony's Garage the next morning and to keep checking the vacant house and the police reports. He asked them to confirm the description he'd gotten from Tereza's friend and the school principal. "If we suspect foul play, we'll assemble a search team, get the newspapers involved, even drag the river if it comes to that. But teenagers run away all the time. Most come home."

"That's what I told her," Dobra said, flipping a thumb at Reenie.

When Bill asked if Tereza had any birthmarks or scars, Reenie's shoulders started to shake.

LINDA TOOK ALLEN one block down and two over to newer houses boasting bigger yards and front doors with wrought-iron flamingos. Those houses gave out better treats, sometimes a Hershey bar or a package of Chuckles. A Pez was a long shot, but for some reason— maybe to show she was "gooder" than Tereza—she wanted Allen to get his wish. Tereza's friend Richie was sitting on the steps outside his house in dungarees and high-school jacket, cigarette smoke settling on his pompadour like a cloud.

Allen said, "Hi, Richie."

"Hey, squirt, neato costume."

A colony of kids swarmed in. Allen ascended with them to Richie's house. Linda hung back, suddenly self-conscious about chanting "Anything for Halloween" with a pack of juveniles.

"His mother asked me to take him around," she told Richie.

"Tereza still missing?" he asked.

"Yeah. You haven't heard from her?"

"Nah." He drew on his cigarette, leaned his head back and blew gray rings into the black air.

"Not with your friends tonight?" Linda said, hoping she wasn't breaking any rules about what you could ask a high-school boy.

"Later," he said, "after the little goblins go in. We'll smash a few pumpkins is all." He took another drag and said, "Linda, right?"

"Yeah."

"You look nice."

She searched his face. He didn't seem to be mocking her. Mother had let her wear lipstick, "just this once." Maybe it made her look older like Tereza. She smiled and said, "Thanks."

Richie ground his cigarette out with his black loafer, setting off tiny fireworks of sparks. He stood and moved so close she had to take quick, shallow breaths against his Old Spice. His voice was soft and secretive. "There's something I didn't tell you when you came to the Castle on Saturday."

Allen thundered down the steps with the others. "Let's do the rest of the street."

"Go ahead," Linda said. "I'll catch up."

Richie watched Allen's disappearing back then turned to Linda. "Don't ask me how, but I happen to know Tereza was giving blow jobs to guys she picked up at Tony's. Old guys who left their cars to be fixed. She might've gone away with one."

"What's a blow job?"

He barked out a laugh. "You shitting me? You don't know?"

She shook her head.

"C'mere," he said, gesturing for her to follow him up the steps. "I need more light." He pulled a small notebook from a back pocket and a pencil from behind one ear. "I'm gonna be famous someday," he said, his right hand making sharp, quick strokes. "You read the funnies?"

"Sure."

"It's more than telling a good story," he said. "Most people don't appreciate the artistic skill you need. The guy that does *Steve Canyon*? His brushwork and knowledge of anatomy are phenomenal. I'm saving up for art school."

Linda was amazed Richie knew the word *phenomenal*.

He finished the drawing and held it under the front-door light so she could see: a cartoon girl with pointy breasts, on her knees in front of a cartoon man with his pants down. Without thinking, she let out an encouraging "Ooh," anxious to let him know she appreciated art. Then she noticed It sticking out of the cartoon pants as straight as a dishtowel rack and the girl's fish-like mouth opening to

It. Linda's face got hot and her throat tight. Tereza had said she only kissed mouths.

"Liar!" she said, batting the paper from his hand. She fled down the steps to find Allen.

THE MAN BEHIND THE DESK at a hotel that billed itself as "Your Home Away from Home" didn't care who Tereza was as long as she paid in advance.

"Six bits a night, four bucks a week," he said, squinting into his own cigarette smoke. He had a thick neck and dandruff-speckled shoulders.

Tereza bought two nights. He led her down a hallway of grimy black-and-white linoleum squares arranged in a checkerboard pattern. Her windowless room, lit by a blinking fluorescent tube, was no bigger than a jail cell. The bed stuck out of the wall like a shelf. On it, a thin mattress and blanket and a pillow without a case. A chair held a towel and washcloth, the floor an ashtray. She'd have to get her own lock for the footlocker, the man said. He nodded toward her briefcase. "You in some sort of business?"

Tereza couldn't answer. Her voice was with her gut in a deep hole between her feet.

"Well, none of my beeswax," he said. "We don't get many ladies here. Mostly men on benders. When they get drinking good they stay in their rooms, but I can't guarantee it. If I was you, I'd push that locker up against the door when you're in here."

"The bathroom?" she whispered.

"Down the hall. There's a lock on the door."

After he left, she bolted the door and dragged the footlocker over to it. She hung her coat on a hook, sat on the bed and hugged the briefcase to her chest. Stared at the nicotine-stained wall, refusing to cry. She hadn't run away to be shipwrecked someplace worse than she'd left.

She retrieved the napkin with Buddy's number from her pocketbook, opened the briefcase and took out the knife and flashlight. Set them beside her.

9:15 PM. They'd be watching *I Love Lucy* at home right now.

❧ SEVEN ❧

NOVEMBER 1, 1955. How dare Richie think she'd want to see that drawing? If a girl had to do that when she got older, Linda would stop having birthdays. Fear and disgust, thick and sour as vomit, had congealed in her throat overnight. She couldn't bring herself to smile at the breakfast table and swatted Daddy's hand away when he tried making the "little bird" sit on her lip.

"I'm not a child," she said.

"Whoa ho," he said.

She grabbed her books and stomped from the house, not expecting Allen on her front stoop, sucking his lips in, his forehead lost in a too-big hat with earflaps. "Can I walk to school with you?" he asked. "The bogeyman won't get me if I'm with you."

"The bogeyman didn't take Tereza," Linda said. "She doesn't want to come back." Linda was too full of outrage to care about Allen's quivering lower lip. She took big steps, hoping he'd disappear, but he kept pace with her while bouncing a ball, a feat she'd have admired if her heart hadn't become a knotted fist.

"I can't play with this in the house no more," he said. "I drive Pop-Pop bananas."

"You're driving me bananas, too. Walk with your friends." Allen had never tagged along with Linda and Tereza; he'd always trailed behind them with a pack of other little boys.

Allen stopped bouncing the ball. Head down like an old man, he hurried along, occasionally stumbling in his attempt to keep up. One of his shoelaces dragged but Linda didn't stop to let him tie it. She didn't care if meanness doomed her to Hell. She belonged there. If she hadn't become Tereza's friend, she wouldn't be scouring her memory to recall if Daddy was late coming home any time he left their car at Tony's. He wouldn't have had occasion to say "I like Tereza; she has spunk," leaving Linda to wonder now what he meant.

She didn't return the smile of the policeman who helped them cross the highway.

She slogged through the school day, hunched and angry, ignoring Mr. Boynton's questioning looks and, at recess, the gangly new girl Connie Boyle's invitation to double Dutch. Such a baby game. At the final bell, she dashed away before Allen could trail her down to the river's edge near Haggerty's boarded-up house. The river was foamy and smelled like rotting lettuce. The cattail leaves were dead and the punks gone to fluffy white seed. Tereza had sworn you could live on nothing but cattails in the spring, eating the shoots and the male part of the punk while it was still green. She said it was easy to tell the male because it was always on top. Linda's cheeks stung at the recollection; Tereza must have been laughing inside at her ignorance. Richie, too.

Had Officer Nolan found any trace of Tereza at Haggerty's? Linda inched along the river toward the house, screwing up the courage to look for herself then losing it again.

She left the river and trod purposefully to The Island, keeping her eyes straight ahead as she walked past Richie's. The hollowed-out log was creased with shadows, a dirty secret now. Linda yanked out everything she and Tereza had collected for Swiss Family Robinson. She screamed as if her clothes were on fire. She stomped on the tinfoil, acorns, string, sticks and withered punks, trying to make a Rumpelstiltskin crack in the earth big enough to disappear into forever. Were the Wonder Bread bag not already gone, she would've let the wind blow Tereza's precious tobacco to Mars.

"LOOK AT THIS HEADLINE," Daddy said over breakfast the next day. "Fear Missing Boy K-i-d-d-n-a-p-e-d. Next thing you know, everyone will be spelling it that way. Newspapers used to take their responsibility for literacy more seriously."

"Can I see?" Linda asked.

Daddy peered over the page. "Well, well, glad whatever was bothering you is over. Welcome back to the family. And it's *may* I, *may* I see." He folded the paper to the article and handed it to her.

The newspaper said a Long Island woman had gone into a store to buy bread and left her two-year-old son outside, beside a stroller holding his seven-month-old sister. The girl in her stroller turned up a few blocks away but the boy was gone. Under a picture of men fording tall grass, it said that more than two thousand people were searching for the boy. Two thousand!

Why weren't thousands looking for Tereza? She could be in as much trouble as that little boy, especially if Richie was right and she'd gone off with a stranger. On the other hand, she might be playing the Prodigal Daughter, living it up in a distant land before coming to her senses and returning home. Linda could not see Jimmy killing a fatted calf for her.

The article had a second picture: the young mother, tight hands in her apron, eyes like a spooked kitten's. Allen's eyes, yesterday. He was waiting for her again this morning. This time, she let him trot beside her. "Pop-Pop says I gotta stop having nightmares," he said.

"What are they about?"

"Somebody chasing me, sometimes monsters, I don't remember good."

"How does he know you have nightmares?"

"I wake up screaming. He comes in my room, all mad."

"When I was little and woke up from a bad dream, instead of yelling, I spelled my name with tummy breaths. My mother taught me that." Linda sometimes forgot the ways Mother had cared for her before she got sick. She missed that mother.

She showed Allen how to put his hand on his tummy and spell out his name letter by letter between breaths.

"Can I do Tereza?" he asked.

She spelled it with him all the way to school and, with each breath, grew hungrier to find Tereza. She wondered why the police hadn't organized a search and how Mr. and Mrs. Dobra could go to work every day as if Tereza's absence was as normal as nightfall.

LINDA AND ALLEN would have been having lunch by the time Tereza woke up, lost and panicky. She groped for the knife until she remembered locking it in the briefcase with Miranda's money and necklace. So where was the briefcase and how had she ended up in a clammy room wearing only a bra and skivvies under a blanket that smelled like mothballs? She sat up so fast she got dizzy. Had to lie back down so she wouldn't puke. Her eyes took in the cheesy wood paneling and the Anheuser-Busch sign on the bar with relief: she was in Buddy's basement. She threw off the blanket, got down on all fours on the cold linoleum floor and felt under the sagging convertible couch. The briefcase was there where she'd put it. The pocketbook she'd slept with between her knees had crept its way to the bottom of the couch. The key was still in it. She opened the briefcase and counted the money. It was all there except for what she'd spent.

She let out a noisy breath and shook her head at how easily she'd let Buddy rescue her.

She'd planned to return his jacket and flashlight yesterday then head off on the train to New York. Try her luck at finding a decent place to stay, maybe audition for a show. She started calling at nine, practicing in her head how she'd say, all cool as cream, "Hi, remember me?" when he got on the phone. Her calls rang on and on until the afternoon when a high-pitched, quivery female voice told her to call around nine-thirty that night after Buddy's shift at the A&P. By the time Tereza reached him, all she could manage was a whiny "I need you." It shamed her to be such a chicken but she couldn't stand a second night in "Your Home Away from Home," listening to banging doors and hollering voices, scared sleepless she'd be raped or murdered.

"I'll be there in two shakes, fair damsel," he'd said, like some lame Prince Valiant.

"There" was the diner she'd hung out in all day, eating, using the john and the pay phone, leaving only to buy new duds, including dungarees she wore out of the store with the pink sweater she'd had on the night she met Buddy. She wanted to be sure he recognized her despite the purple shadows below her eyes and the greasy Brillo pad her hair had become under the wig. From the booth where she sat nursing a root beer, she watched him enter and cast about before spotting her. His shoulders seemed even wider than she remembered, his pants tighter. He slid in beside her, so close his thigh pressed against hers. She handed him the flashlight and his jacket.

"I thought about it holding you," he said, his milky-smelling breath tickling her face. "Imagined it was me."

He didn't seem to notice the briefcase she'd slipped into the shopping bag with her new clothes. And he said "Of course" when she asked him not to tell Richie he'd seen her. He took her to a tall, narrow, banana-colored house, let her in through the back porch and made up the convertible couch for her. The basement had a small bathroom, with toilet, sink and mildewy shower. She washed off two days of slime and came out in new undies thinking he'd expect a thank-you hand job, at least. But he had one foot on the basement steps. "Thank you for letting me help you," he said, like he was giving a speech. "You're very brave, but fragile, like an African violet."

Tereza would've said something smartass but a zombie look she'd seen too often in Jimmy's eyes warned her off. "I'll put a note on my grandmother's door so she won't be surprised when she sees you," Buddy said. He left her wondering what happened to the guy who'd imagined himself as his jacket around her.

Her watch showed nearly noon. She stepped into the dungarees she'd left on the bathroom floor and pulled a new sweater over her head—purple, Ma's favorite color. She climbed the basement steps and heard, "In here! In the kitchen." Following the smell of coffee, she found a saggy-boobed old lady seated at a small wooden table. Her red-and-yellow-striped housecoat fought something awful with the bright pink hair swirling round her scalp like cotton candy. The woman peered up from her newspaper over wire-rimmed specs and smiled with her whole wrinkly face, as if Tereza's being there was the most normal thing in the world.

"Just reading the funnies," she said. "Have a seat. Buddy's long gone to school. You staying awhile?"

Tereza pulled out a chair, turned it around and straddled it. "Nope. Heading to New York to become an actress."

"That so? You got a stage name?"

Tereza didn't but one came to her right away. "Ladonna Lange." Her own middle name and Ma's last before she married Jimmy.

The old lady took a swallow of coffee. "It suits you. My birth"— it sounded like *boith*—"certificate says Mina, but the day I came out, my three-year-old brother stuck his head in my cradle and said, 'She's a dearie.' Nobody's called me nothing else ever since. You hungry?"

"Wouldn't mind a cup of joe."

Dearie had a boss cackle. "Hear that, Alfie? Your words exactly."
She got up and shuffled over to a cupboard in fuzzy blue slippers.
Thick orange hose stopped at her knees. "Cream and sugar?"

"Uh-uh. Who's Alfie?" A radiator beside the table hissed out
warmth and, off the kitchen, a glassed-in porch trapped sun. Ma
would've been fanning herself like crazy.

"My husband. Dead five years now. A Fuller Brush Man all his
working life and proud of it. I was seventeen, him thirty-two, the
Saturday he knocked on our door with a free pastry brush. I told
him I liked what he was selling. He didn't have a chance." She poured
coffee from a percolator on the stove and set a cup and saucer in
front of Tereza. "Buddy left me a note. Said you need looking after.
Why's that?"

Tereza shrugged. "I don't, really."

"Your ma okay with you going to New York?"

"She don't know."

"How long you been gone?"

"Couple days."

"I wouldn't want the cops coming 'round looking for you."

"They won't. Only you and Buddy know I'm here. Ma would
get in trouble with Jimmy if she called the cops and he sure as hell
won't."

"Who's Jimmy?"

"Wish I didn't know." Tereza went on to say more than she
probably should have about her stepfather and the shit he'd done but
the coffee was going down warm and Dearie's eyes, not at all sleepy
like Buddy's, seemed to yank the words right out of her.

Dearie ran her fingers softly over the lump on Tereza's jaw. Her
eyes got damp behind her specs. "Nobody should have to live where
it ain't safe. Where's your real dad?"

Tereza shrugged again. "I don't even know his name. Ma's folks
sent her away to have me. When she got back they made up a story for

neighbors about how she married a G.I. who got shipped overseas; later they said he got snuffed in the war."

Dearie squeezed her hand. "Girlies used to get sent to unwed moms' homes all the time. It says a bunch about her that she didn't give you away." Dearie took her specs off and wiped them on her housecoat. "You old enough to quit school?"

"Don't matter if I ain't. I'm never going back." For some reason Allen tumbled into Tereza's head. She could see the twerp lining up for school on the playground that last day, as though time had stopped and she could step right back into the scene.

"I always wanted my high-school diploma," Dearie said. "Had to leave after eighth grade to help support the family. I worked as a seamstress until I married Alfie. Buddy's almost finished eleventh. I'm darn proud of him."

"I don't need a diploma to be an actress."

"How you gonna pay for a room and eats in New York?"

"I got money. Been saving for years."

Dearie raised her eyebrows at that. "I grew up across the river in Jersey City. New York's big and expensive. It can swallow a piggy bank fast. You ain't old enough to get an honest job. You should call your ma. I'd turn into one big puddle if I lost Buddy."

"She don't have a phone."

Dearie got up and poured more coffee. "Tell you what. Take the train into the city and look around as many days as you need. Come back here to sleep every night till you find something. The deal's off, though, if the cops start snooping."

A chance to see Buddy more. "Why you being so nice to me?"

"Why wouldn't I be? You can stay as long as there's no hanky-panky. That's my rule."

"Does Buddy bring girls home a lot?"

Dearie cackled again. "You're the first"—it sounded like *foist*—"but I just think it's a good rule. If you stay, I could use some help with the lace coitans. It takes two people and Buddy's been too busy. They're filthy from the winders being open all summer."

Tereza didn't know what coitans were, but she said "I don't mind." Copping a safe place to sleep until she landed an acting job didn't make her lazy or chicken.

Dearie gave Tereza what she called the fifty-cent tour of the main floor: parlor, dining room, bathroom and her bedroom. Pipsqueak glass frogs sat on shelves, tables and windowsills everywhere. They were holding footballs and baseball bats; fishing, dancing, smoking cigars; squatting on lily pads and tree logs; playing drums, banjos, guitars. Dearie said that Alfie had given her the entire collection. "All it took was me saying he was my frog prince."

That afternoon, between school and work, Buddy hauled down wooden frames from the attic room opposite his bedroom and set them on chairs on the back porch. They looked like torture racks with hundreds of little spikes all around. Tereza stood on a step-ladder and removed the lace curtains from the parlor windows. She washed and rinsed them in the pink bathtub while Dearie sat on the toilet lid telling her how. Together they stretched the wet curtains so they could dry on the frames, Tereza pulling the bottoms, Dearie the tops, until each outside loop of the lace fit over a spike. You would've thought the World Series was at stake the way Dearie kept at Tereza to do it right, not miss a loop. Tereza felt an unfamiliar flush of pride when Dearie said she couldn't have done it without her.

That night, when Dearie and Buddy were both at work, Tereza palmed one of the frogs and stuffed it in a box in the basement, under a pile of Fuller Brush receipts. She wondered how many she could pinch before Dearie hated her too and kicked her out.

Elizabeth Daily Journal, Saturday edition
Balloons Search for Missing Stony River Teen
BY JUNE MACOMBER

STONY RIVER, NOVEMBER 12. For this reporter, there was something stirring about a sky of white balloons as far as the eye could see in the softening sun. Like white words shimmering on blue pages: "Tereza Dobra, please come home. Call Fulton 8-6898."

Yesterday, at school day's end, the 655 students of Millard Fillmore Elementary School on Jackson Boulevard released over a thousand balloons into the sky above the school's front lawn, each balloon bearing a tag at the end of a string with the plea to thirteen-year-old Tereza Dobra who hasn't been seen or heard from since the evening of October 28th. Miss Dobra's eight-year-old brother, Allen, gave the signal for the balloon release. The students were silent as the balloons left their mittened hands but cheered as the wind spirited them away.

According to Police Chief Lawrence Durmer, the Stony River Police are aware Miss Dobra is missing and are monitoring the situation. Foul play is not suspected. The teen was reported to have run away after an altercation with her stepfather.

The balloon release was the inspiration of Miss Linda Wise, a twelve-year-old Millard Fillmore student. "I read about all the people searching for the missing boy in Long Island," she said, "and felt bad for Tereza. Everybody's acting like she's just away on vacation or something. I hope with all my heart a balloon finds her and she calls me."

The school's principal, Mrs. Anita Warren, donated the balloons. "I was enormously moved by Linda's devotion to her friend," Mrs. Warren said. "At Millard Fillmore, we encourage our students to look after each other."

The sixty-two seventh graders, classmates of Miss Dobra and Miss Wise, hand-printed the tags and blew up the balloons, under the supervision of seventh-grade math and science teacher Mr. Henry Boynton, who said, "We all miss Tereza and pray for her safe return."

THE PAPER, folded to the story, was on Linda's chair when she came down to breakfast. A photo she'd taken of Tereza on the log leered at her. Across the table, her parents sat side by side, looking like they'd sucked lemons. They said nothing until she'd read the article and glanced up, her eyes stinging.

"That was a caring, Christian act," Daddy said, lifting a forkful of trembling egg. He swallowed, set his fork down, reached over and squeezed her hand. "Jesus would be proud of you." He cleared his throat. "Heck, I'm proud of you. I'm only sorry you didn't feel you could confide in us."

"We've had two calls already," Mother said. "One man said we raised a good daughter." A fleeting smile. "I thanked him. The other, a boy, wanted to speak with you. He said he'd call back."

Daddy cleared his throat again. "Now, as much as we applaud what you did for Tereza, we can't condone telegraphing our phone number to the world. Did you ask your mother if she minded taking calls from strangers while you're in school?"

Linda shook her head. She was ashamed for another reason. The article made her look too good. The real reason she wanted to find Tereza was to ask if she'd ever gotten in Daddy's car.

"All acts have consequences, even those committed with good intentions," Daddy said. "We expect you to stay by the phone this weekend. When you're in school, we'll leave it off the hook until we can get the number changed."

Linda swallowed hard. If they changed the number, Tereza wouldn't get through. "I'll stay home and answer the phone."

Daddy gave her a smile full of pity and shook his head.

Mother spent the rest of the day in her room with a headache. Linda sat on a cushion on the kitchen floor under the wall phone. Before noon, she had answered twelve calls, most from members of the church, a few from people simply curious to find out who would answer, one from a giggly young voice that asked, "Got any soup?"

Richie called, too. She half-expected him to taunt her for running away on Halloween, but he said, "That was a cool thing to do, the balloons. You're okay, you know."

She didn't feel okay.

At noon, Daddy told her Mrs. Dobra was at the door. "I asked her in but she wants to speak with you outside."

Linda glanced at the phone.

"It's okay. I'll take over for a while." He squeezed her shoulder. "Put your coat on."

Like a falling iris in her purple coat, Mrs. Dobra was leaning against the telephone pole near the curb, smoking a cigarette. Linda closed the front door and descended the few steps to the sidewalk.

Mrs. Dobra straightened. "You seen the article in the newspaper?"

Linda nodded.

"Rolf showed me it when I stopped in the store for cigs this morning. Allen didn't say nothing about the balloons, but I see now why he slept better last night." She took a drag. "Jimmy's upset." She laughed. "What else is new? He says the paper makes him look bad." She finished her cigarette, snuffed it on the sidewalk and put the stub in her pocket. "Can't stay but I wanted to come over and give you a hug. That okay with you?"

Linda didn't feel deserving of a hug, but she wanted one more than anything. She leaned into the woman's soft chest, wound her arms around the small frame and closed her eyes. The crisp air embraced Mrs. Dobra's musky-smelling warmth.

Tereza's mother pulled away first. "Gotta go," she said, holding Linda out at arm's length. "Just wanted you to know I'm glad you was Tereza's friend, even if only for a little while."

Linda watched her walk away, thinking how, from the back, it could have been Tereza. She went in the house for a spare balloon tag, took it to Tony's and asked him to tack it to his office wall.

❧

"THIS FRUSTRATES the heck out of me," Bill said, handing the news-paper to Doris. He was still in his robe, his legs stretched under the length of the kitchen table. "The girl's mother told me she didn't have a photograph. How'd the newspaper get one?"

Doris had been up for hours. She'd given Mickey his six and nine AM feedings and put him back in his crib. Fogged up the kitchen windows cooking Carolyn a bowl of Wheatena. She'd plunked the three-year-old in front of the TV for the Farmer Gray cartoon show and made waffles for Bill. Warmed the syrup the way he liked, hoping they could have a pleasant breakfast together and dispel the tension that had been hanging around them for two weeks like a bad smell. But he sounded weary and discouraged.

She took the paper and quickly scanned the article. "This the runaway you think broke into Miranda's house? She's a scrawny thing."

She saw his face shut down at Miranda's name, imagined him thinking, *Don't start again.*

"James Haggerty's house, you mean. It was in his name." Bill had searched for legal documents before he boarded up the place. He'd found the deed to the property and the girl's birth certificate. Not the boy's.

"It'll be hers when she's eighteen," Doris said. "I checked the inheritance laws."

"Did you, now? Well, if she doesn't pay the taxes before then the county will take it over. Or hoodlums will. I wouldn't be surprised if somebody torches it." He tapped the paper with his knife. "This girl, this Tereza, worries me more. Frank and I have been tailing the parents. The principal's watching, too, to see if the boy comes to school with any signs of abuse. But I don't think they did her in. Durmer should've told me about the balloons. He knows it's my case. I'll get a copy of this photo and show it around town."

Doris picked up the paper again. Poor Miranda had never had a friend who would miss her. "This Linda has a point," she said. "Why no search party, like the one for the Long Island boy?"

Bill looked up at her with a tired frown that almost broke her heart. He worked so hard and here she was suggesting he hadn't done enough. "Different situation. According to her mother, Tereza Dobra has run away before. No reason to think she didn't this time. No reason to drag the river or stomp through tall grass."

"What if it were Carolyn?"

"Well, it isn't."

As if on cue, Carolyn, in quilted robe and Princess Summerfall Winterspring slippers, padded in and climbed up onto Bill's lap. "Kiss-kiss, Daddy?"

That brought a smile and an easing of Bill's shoulders. Doris had been afraid he'd lose interest in Carolyn once he had a son, but not a chance. She was the one he called for when he walked in the door. He loved that she could put a sentence together and pedal a tricycle; that she was full of wonder, something he said he'd lost along the way. He was a good man. Doris knew he could find room in his heart for Cian and Miranda if he took the time to get to know them.

She'd come home in a state after learning Cian had gone to a foster family and there was nothing Miranda could do about it. "What did you expect?" Bill had said. "You worked at Children's Aid, you know how legal guardianships work." Yes, and she knew how perverts and other abusers sometimes made it through foster and adoptive parent screening. She'd expected him to understand why she was upset. She'd wanted to adopt those kids the day he rescued them, but he'd have none of it. He said they were damaged and, while he wasn't unsympathetic, he wouldn't expose Carolyn and Mickey to the effects of who knew what had gone on in that house.

Carolyn leaned into Bill's plate and said, "Smells like more."

Bill laughed and stabbed a piece of waffle on his fork for her.

"You want your own waffle?" Doris asked her.

"And appleboss."

Doris spooned batter into the waffle iron and bent over it, savoring the sweet smell that steamed out when she first closed the lid. Keeping her voice casual, she said, "I spoke to the mother superior about putting the Haggerty house up for sale."

"You saw her again?"

"Yeah, on Thursday." Doris's mom had watched the kids. "She's willing to petition the court for permission. If we can sell it, St. Bernadette's gets cash for Miranda and Cian's support until Miranda is eighteen. The balance will be put in trust for her until then." She took a jar of applesauce out of the fridge. "Mother Alfreda says if their room and board are covered, she'll make sure they aren't fostered out or adopted." She opened the jar and stuck a spoon in it. Specifically, Mother Alfreda had agreed to not farm the kids out to strangers; she'd consider the Nolans if Doris were able to persuade Bill.

"What do you mean, if *we* can sell it? The orphanage should hire an agent."

"Oh sure, they will. I meant somebody's got to clean out the place, decide what to save for Miranda." Somebody who would stand in for this forgotten child, she thought, and not callously discard everything she'd grown up with. "You said she'd wanted to take her books and records, didn't you?" The red light went out on the iron. "Carolyn, your waffle's ready."

Bill swung Carolyn off his lap and into her booster chair. "You're in your element with those orphans, aren't you?"

Doris considered a sharp comeback, but she didn't want to spoil the morning. She spooned applesauce onto the waffle and set it in front of Carolyn, took a calming breath and said, "The only orphan is

Miranda. Cian *has* a mother. I promised her I wouldn't let strangers adopt him."

Bill started to cut Carolyn's waffle, but she pushed his hand away. "Me do it!"

"Who else but strangers *could* adopt him?" Bill said. "The girl's too young to be a mother and her boy is obviously backward. He's better off with people who can deal with that."

"Who says she can't? I don't know what I'd do if someone took my children from me."

"There's something not right about that girl. How could there not be?"

"She's bright as can be. She's read the entire Daily Missal—over a thousand pages—and memorized the prayers. Gone from fifth to sixth grade in only two months since she started school."

"So she says."

"So says Mother Alfreda, too. She's a good Catholic girl already, Bill."

"We've talked about this enough. I'm on call tonight. I'd like to relax today."

Doris felt her chest catch. "Sorry," she said. She came up behind him, leaned over and kissed his head where the hair was starting to thin. "I'm being pushy again like Mom, aren't I?"

He turned and caught her hands; kissed them. "Maybe we can hang onto the books and music for her. She was pretty torn up about leaving them behind. I might even have promised to get them to her. But we don't have room to store everything in that house. She probably wouldn't want it, anyway. You haven't been there yet. The furniture's nothing to write home about."

Doris sent up a silent prayer of thanks to the Blessed Virgin.

SIX DAYS LATER. "Check the terlet after each girly's done," Dearie told Tereza as she pushed opened the ladies' john door. "Some's too drunk or lazy to flush."

Dearie was breaking Tereza in at Herman's Place, a swanky Newark restaurant where she'd been a washroom attendant from the time Buddy entered first grade. She'd dragged him with her the nights Alfie was on the road. Had raised him since he was three, after the war took her son and her floozy of a daughter-in-law ran off with another man. She told Tereza the whole story one afternoon, trying to explain why Buddy sometimes disappeared behind his own eyes.

"Herman's is pricey," Dearie said, "but lucky for us, people have more money than sense. It's always packed. On weekends they line up down the street. Herman don't take reservations."

Holy shit but Linda would've flipped over the john! The swinging door opened to a red-carpeted, velvety red–papered room with a long white couch, two plush white armchairs and two small dark wood tables with glass ashtrays as big as bowls. A mirrored wall at the far end made the room feel like an echo. The crappers were behind another door, out of sight.

Dearie set her shopping bag on the floor next to a white ottoman by one of the tables. "We'll take turns taking a load off here. Your dogs'll be barking by closing, seeing as you ain't wearing sensible shoes like mine." Fat-heeled white leather lace-ups swallowed Dearie's feet clear to the ankle knobs. Tereza sank down into an armchair.

They'd taken two buses to get there, eating meatloaf sandwiches on the way, saving thermoses of tomato soup for later. They wouldn't get away until two in the morning. Most nights the restaurant closed at ten, but on Fridays and Saturdays Herman brought musicians in and rolled back the carpet to make a dance floor. Herman would drive them both home tonight, as he did Dearie every Friday and Saturday, because the buses weren't dependable or safe after midnight. Buddy came for Dearie the other nights, but "Charles Atlas don't like him staying up past midnight."

"He worships the guy, don't he?" Tereza said. "I seen his lesson book. Lot of pictures of a beefy guy in leopard-skin skivvies."

Dearie snorted. "That's him. Buddy saw the ad in a comic book. Imagine spending a week's pay so a fella in a Tarzan suit can tell you to wash your privates in ice water."

Tereza threw her head back and laughed. "Go on."

"Honest injun. And Tarzan tells him to exercise naked and keep his winder open all the time. He's gonna catch his death up there."

Buddy kept his converted attic room locked. Tereza had tried the door a couple times when she was alone in the house. How could he think freezing his balls off would make him manlier? Either Atlas was a con man or guys were stupid. *I was a ninety-seven-pound weakling* sounded like something she might've come up with herself.

Dearie lifted a white porcelain teacup from her shopping bag and set it on the table next to the ottoman. She dropped two quarters from her change purse into the cup. "I don't let it get too full in case my ladies think I don't need no more." She poked Tereza's arm. "G'head, admire yourself whiles you got the chance."

Tereza had been stealing glances at herself in the mirrored wall.

"I was the cat's meow too, once," Dearie said. She grabbed her skirt at the hem, pulled it tight around her ass and strutted across the room. "Dresses were longer then. We had to hold our skirts so's we didn't trip. Pretended we didn't know how it made our heinies look."

Tereza stood and checked herself out, front, back and sides. From Haggerty's robe, Dearie had made Tereza a uniform like her own except that Dearie's was the same bright pink as her hair and looser fitting to slip over her corset. Tereza wished Buddy had been home to see her all done up. She'd never worn so much black, including fishnet nylons Dearie had dug up somewhere and the pumps and wig Tereza had bought in Stony River. The only color came from her

Hot Tomato lipstick and the gold hoop earrings Dearie said had been taking up space in her dresser.

"Ava Gardner as the Waitress Vampira," Tereza said, baring her fangs.

"Your skin's too dark for that. More vampy than vampire."

"I zink you're right, dahlink," Tereza said, extending a limp-wristed arm.

Dearie bowed at the waist and kissed her hand. "Now you're talking. Put on an accent. Get the ladies buzzing." She pulled a key from her pocket. "A reporter wrote about me once. He called me the Pink Lady, like the cocktail, and it caught on. You'd be surprised how many girlies know about me before they come in. Some ask for my autograph." Dearie unlocked the door to a closet stocked with towels, little soap bars, toilet paper and cleaning crap. She pulled a stack of white towels off a shelf. "Every Saturday night after closing, Manny at the bar says, 'Make you a Pink Lady?' and I say, 'Twist my arm.' It's nice having a drink with them that stays around after closing. Buddy wants me to retire. We'd manage with Alfie's pension and what Buddy makes, but he ain't home much and I enjoy being with others."

Dearie was right about Buddy not being around much, what with going to school and working at the Linden A&P all day Saturday and five to nine every night except Friday. After school he had time only for homework before changing into black pants, white shirt and clip-on bow tie. On Fridays he went out who knew where. On Sundays he waxed his car and did chores for Dearie. If Tereza didn't get up with him in the morning, she'd hardly see him at all.

She liked the way he smelled from the shower, his freshly slicked hair. Liked watching him fix himself eggs, toast (always brown), bacon, oatmeal and juice. "You slay me," she said the first time she saw him drink milk, moving his mouth up and down like he was chewing it.

Coffee seemed to be against the Atlas religion, along with soda, sugar and a bunch of other stuff. Why Buddy had gone to the White Castle that night was beyond her; they didn't make anything he ate. He said Dearie couldn't keep his diet straight so he fixed his own meals except on Sundays. "She's getting on," he said. "I'm happy you're with her when I can't be."

Tereza couldn't recall ever being accused of making somebody happy.

Dearie took a soap bar from the closet. "Listen for the rattle of the lock in the stall and turn the tap on so's it's ready when she steps out. Hand her a new soap; be sure she sees you take the paper off. Turn the water off when she's done and hold out a towel."

Dearie had started coaching Tereza on the gray city bus as it farted its way down streets lined with row houses and stores, Tereza only half paying attention, imagining Buddy bagging groceries and thinking about her. Staying in during the day so a truant officer or cop wouldn't spot her was boring. Being stuck in the house when Dearie and Buddy were both at work was like being on a deserted movie set. Tereza would wander from room to room, imagining herself a character written out of a soap opera. She didn't want back in that story but didn't know how to get into a better one. She kept meaning to get on the train to New York but hadn't found a day yet when it felt right. Hadn't found a day when she wanted to be that far away from Ma.

Dearie had said that if Tereza was going to stick around she needed to pull her weight. Her boss, Herman Schottler, was okay with Tereza helping her out, as long as she understood he wasn't paying double. Dearie made seventy-five cents an hour plus tips. The roly-poly, shiny-skulled Herman had shaken Tereza's hand when they got there and said, "Welcome to my humble eatery." He didn't look humble at all in tuxedo and bow tie. He showed her around the dining room where other old guys in tuxes set tiny vases with rosebuds on tables.

A sudden image of Ma and John Derek at a table for two caught her by the throat.

The big room was quiet as air. Chandeliers dripped glass icicles and ornate, heavy mirrors covered the walls. The deep red of the tablecloths, flocked wallpaper and carpet sucked her in. It could've been a Hollywood set for a whale's belly or an Amazon's snatch. The restaurant held two fifty at a time. On a good night, Herman told Tereza, four hundred might come in for a meal and more, later, for drinks and a dance.

The deal was, Tereza and Dearie would split the tips which could be anywhere from a nickel to a dollar; on a good night Tereza's share could be as much as ten bucks. She thought about Linda cleaning house for nothing, about how many guys you'd have to jerk off for sixty dollars a week. Tereza could pay Dearie for room and board and not need to dip into more of Miranda's money until she moved on. She'd taken the money out of the briefcase and hidden it behind a loose cinder block near the furnace. No reason Buddy and Dearie had to know about it.

Tereza hustled all night, keeping up with Dearie's orders to check stalls, wipe sinks and countertops ("Tips don't crawl out of wet pocketbooks"), refill toilet paper holders, empty the towel basket and the ashtrays. Her legs went to jelly each time the door swung open. She didn't know a soul in Newark, much less anyone who'd come to such a ritzy place. But a spark of hope told her that Ma might want to find her bad enough to march through that door.

That night one woman puked. Someone else needed help washing blood out of her skirt. More than a few came in to light up and stare into space, their smokes growing into drooping worms of ash. Tereza didn't see anybody ask for Dearie's autograph, but some knew her name. Dearie received them like a queen on her ottoman, her cackle rising above the sound of flushing.

By the time Herman's closed that night, Tereza could size up women by the way they reacted when she handed them a towel: the cheapskates waved her off, the nervous ones had to be told it was okay to throw it in the wicker basket, the self-confident ones thanked her and the assholes took it without looking at her, not even grunting. They made her think of Jimmy, made her want to take off in shame. But she didn't. It was still better than sucking dicks.

Thanksgiving was next week. Herman's and A&P would be closed. She'd sweet-talk Buddy into driving past the apartment. Drop in and see if Ma had turned into a puddle.

NOVEMBER 21, 1955. Allen wasn't waiting for Linda and nobody answered the Dobras' door. Linda peered into their apartment through the window that overlooked the porch. Gone were their meager furnishings. An abandoned sneaker lay in the middle of the living-room floor.

Linda stopped in to see Rolf. He lived in a few dank rooms behind the store with his wife who was shrinking more each day from cancer, a constant smile stretched taut over her skeletal head. Tereza had claimed that Rolf was an escaped Nazi but Linda didn't care. She loved his accent and he'd loaned her *lederhosen* for fifth-grade Show and Tell.

"Zey must heff sneaked out in ze night," he said. "Gone tiptoe. Zey owed me money, ja? Maybe run out on ze rent, too."

Linda barely heard Rolf after "Gone tiptoe." Her ears had begun to ring with God's accusing voice: if she'd only kept her fat nose out of things Tereza would still have a home to return to.

$\varsheet$ EIGHT $\varsheet$

JANUARY 3, 1956. Linda's winter boots trampled the crusty snow as she trudged home from school, her body frozen with anger and shame. She'd considered faking a sore throat this morning but missing school would only have put off the inevitable.

She'd invited everybody in her seventh-grade homeroom to her first New Year's Eve party ever, the same kids who'd been at Kenny Ronson's party the night school let out for Christmas vacation. At Kenny's they'd had chips and soda. Danced. Played Spin-the-Bottle, Post Office and Flashlight. At Kenny's party, *his* mother hadn't come into the living room time after time during Flashlight, turning the lights back on and marching back out without a word. Why couldn't New Year's Eve have been one of Mother's sick nights? She'd gussied herself up in a scoop-necked maroon taffeta dress Linda had never seen before and greeted everyone at the door as if she was the hostess. Every time she came into the room to turn on the lights, the taffeta went *husha husha* against her nylons. Linda had wanted to die.

Linda had stuffed celery stalks with Cheez Whiz and made popcorn balls for midnight, but the kids didn't stick around until then. Mother acted surprised when everyone left, but Linda thought she'd probably planned it so she'd have the living room to herself to watch Guy Lombardo. Daddy made things worse when the kids were gone by lecturing Mother that kissing games gave "sexually

awakening adolescents a safe outlet for physical desires." Mother said
there would be no such awakening in her house. Linda had stormed
up to her room and not come down until noon the next day.

At school today the girls gave her pitying looks and the boys
made rude jokes. She'd suffered through the day, praying that a huge
sinkhole would open up beneath her desk. She was so full of misery
on the cold walk home she almost missed the FOR SALE sign at the
end of Lexington. She turned and tramped down the middle of
the unplowed road. Someone had shoveled a path to the house and
cleared the snow off the steps and porch. Linda trod right up to the
front door where another sign said BY APPOINTMENT ONLY.

The boards were off the windows and doors. Maybe Miranda
Haggerty was dead. Why else would they sell her house? Linda
imagined her own funeral and teared up. The kids would be sorry for
leaving her party early and her mother for putting the lights back on.

Unable to find the doorbell, she knocked on the heavy oak door.
She stomped her feet to warm her toes and announce herself, but no
one came.

She cupped her mittened hands around her glasses and peered
through a porch window into an empty room with a wall of shelves
rising clear to the ceiling. She knocked again then tried the door. It
opened. Maybe the real-estate agent was inside and would show Linda
around. She called "Hello" into the echoing hallway. Legs shaking, she
stepped inside onto a rubber mat—the only thing in the room—and
peered up at the grand stairwell, shrinking back reflexively as if she
expected Crazy Haggerty's ghost to float down it. The place smelled
like stale crackers. She wanted to explore where Miranda had lived,
but her conscience reminded her that an unlocked door wasn't an
engraved invitation.

Forgive us our trespasses.

She backed out and closed the door. Tereza would have called her
chicken, but honestly, Linda was merely respectful, not to mention

considerate of Mother and Daddy who would be mortified if she ended up at the police station. If Tereza had taken cover in Miranda's house, she probably tromped all over, rude as could be. But Linda was responsible. The sun was hanging low: Mother would be expecting her to get dinner started.

She reached Jackson Boulevard just as the high-school bus stopped a few feet away. Richie got off and waved. She hadn't spoken to him since he'd phoned about Tereza's balloons. "Hey there," he called. He pointed to the FOR SALE sign. "Buying Crazy Haggerty's?"

"Maybe," she said. "I have a dollar forty-seven in my pocket."

He laughed. "They'll jump at that." He wasn't wearing gloves and blew on his hands. "I'm heading to the Castle. Can I buy you a cup of coffee to warm you up?"

Mother said coffee was too stimulating for children, and she disapproved of the White Castle because she'd heard they used horse-meat during the war and passed it off as beef.

Linda took a big breath and said, "Why, thank you, sir."

He laughed again.

Her glasses steamed up as they entered the White Castle. Richie gently lifted them from her face, set them on the counter and helped her onto a stool. He winked at the guy behind the counter who was wearing a white paper hat. "The usual, barkeep," he said, "and the same for the little lady here."

Linda needed lots of cream and sugar to get the sharp-tasting coffee down. Richie told her his cousin had loaned Tereza a jacket in the Castle the very night she'd run away. She'd returned it to him a few days later, but his cousin didn't know where she was now. Richie didn't know either; Tereza hadn't gotten in touch with him. Linda wanted to learn more about what Tereza had been doing with the "old guys" Richie had mentioned on Halloween, but she didn't want to remind him of her ignorance and risk being humiliated again. She talked about a bunch of other things, but

couldn't remember what later, only that Richie listened as if she
had opinions worth hearing. She wondered if he was a better kisser
than the boys at Kenny's party had been during Flashlight. They
either slobbered all over you or pressed your lips so hard it made
your teeth hurt.

She didn't have dinner ready until a half hour later than usual that
night. Crossing her fingers behind her back, she told Daddy she'd
stayed at school to try out for a play. He told her she had a duty to
come home directly after school and take care of things. "Twenty
years from now," he said, "you won't remember if you were in a
school play or not."

"Twenty years from now," she said, her voice steadier than her
nerves, "you won't remember if you ate dinner at five-thirty or six."

Although he sent her to her room for being disrespectful,
his eyes betrayed the faint concession that she might have scored a
point.

WATER RUSHING through the pipes told her Buddy was up. Tereza
slipped into dungarees and her tight pink sweater and was in the
kitchen when he came in to make his breakfast. She said "Sure" when
he asked if she knew it was Leap Day and pretended she knew what
he meant about the Earth going around the sun and al-go-rhythms.
She sang *I got rhythm, I got music,* wishing he'd jump in with *I've got my
man,* which would have been hysterical, but he didn't.

From the dining-room window, she watched him back his car
down the drive into the dark morning, his right arm draped over
the front seat, his head turned to check over his right shoulder.
She pictured herself next to him, breathing in his English Leather,
twisting the heater to full blast to keep him warm.

She turned the basement shower on and stood under it screaming like Fay Wray, practicing for her future career in sci-fi thrillers; they'd be a snap compared to Broadway. Actresses in thrillers mostly just screamed and buried their heads in some guy's chest.

She folded the Castro convertible up into a couch so that the basement looked more like an apartment. Imagined a *Photoplay* interview in her Hollywood mansion, recalling when she'd rented some old pink-haired broad's basement, cracking up the reporter with her boss imitation of Dearie saying "terlet," "goily" and "Hoymin."

Water rushing through the pipes meant Dearie was up. Tereza followed her nose to the kitchen and the smoky coffee smell. Said, "Toast and joe, same as usual," when Dearie asked her to name her poison.

"A girly needs more than that if she's going to make a baby someday," Dearie said. Tereza flashed on Ma pregnant with Allen, one arm resting on her belly shelf like she'd grown it just for that. After breakfast, she screwed up her nose when Dearie cold-creamed her face and made her look at the crap that ended up on the tissue. Yelped when Dearie ripped a brush through her tangled hair and said she had to show her body that she cared more about it.

When the lady from next door ding-donged, Tereza ducked down to the basement. She and Dearie had cooked up the story that she was a friend's niece from Brazil and didn't speak English. The neighbors never demanded to see for themselves. Dearie could have been torturing Tereza with a hot iron for all they knew. It made her think about Miranda Haggerty. Best not to waste your hope on things like guardian angels, Saint Bernards and nosy neighbors.

It was safe to be outside for an hour when school kids trekked home for lunch. Wearing her Grace Kelly coat and the red-and-white striped stocking cap and matching mittens Dearie had knitted her for Christmas, Tereza took Dearie's shopping list (milk, Ex-Lax and Niagara starch) and hotfooted it four blocks over to a little store. Got back in time for spaghetti with meatballs and the radio announcer's chocolate pudding voice: *Once again,* Backstage Wife, *the story of Mary Noble, a little Iowa girl who married one of America's most handsome actors.* Dearie never missed that program. Tereza was going to *be* a star, not marry one.

After lunch, shuffling on her knees with Dearie as they dusted baseboards along the piss-colored carpet in the parlor, Tereza asked, "How come Buddy's so serious?"

"A real sad sack at times, ain't he? Should've seen when he was little, trying to drown himself in a pail of water once a week. He ain't put his fist through a wall since you came."

When Dearie took her nap, Tereza descended to the basement. She stepped into her white shorts and the amazing black pumps. Practiced cheesecake poses, lying on her back, legs in the air, or leaning against the bar, hands behind her ass. Even though her tits weren't as big as Marilyn Monroe's, she imagined Buddy going bonkers over them, never wanting to drown himself again. Count your luck, Ma used to say. Tereza eased out the cinder block and counted Miranda's money, adding five dollars from tips. Wouldn't take long to replace what she'd spent.

Water rushing through the pipe meant Dearie's nap was over. Tereza helped her make the supper they'd take on the bus. She got into her uniform, wig, coat and gloves, slipped on the galoshes she'd bought in December with tips and trekked with Dearie to the bus stop, leaning into the stinging wind. As the bus slogged from stop to stop, she watched her ghostlike reflection in the window eat a ham sandwich with mustard that nipped her tongue. Her real father could have been sitting behind her and she'd never know. She plotted the ways she'd get back at Ma and Jimmy if she knew where they were. Maybe being stuck with each other was punishment enough.

She handed out a bazillion towels and soap bars and thought about how the shitters and pissers would scream "It's her!" when she was famous. They'd be sorry they hadn't asked for her autograph instead of Dearie's.

When Buddy came to pick them up, she climbed in the back and thought about Thanksgiving, when she'd sat up front and ridden with him to her old apartment. He'd waited until she came back down the porch steps shaking like she had a fever. "What kind of mother moves away without her kid?" she'd asked him.

"One who gets a better offer," he said, his voice as hard as a fist. Tereza thought about the guts it would take to keep your head down in a pail of water.

The day after Tereza discovered her family had split from Stony River, Buddy had gone cruising with Richie, who told him about the balloons. When Buddy told Tereza, she'd laughed and said what a waste of good balloons. Truth was her throat got tight at the thought of a thousand of them sailing the sky looking for her.

She climbed into bed with her little notepad and marked off the day as she had the hundred and twenty-four others since she ran away: four strokes down, one across to make five. February 29 was just one more.

BEST TIME OF THE DAY was when Dearie could close her door and have a good long chat with Alfie without Ladonna rolling her eyes.

She hung up her uniform, freed her griping waist from the corset and pulled down the slip that had crept up her middle. She closed her eyes for a moment so that her ears could enjoy the sound of no toilets flushing. Opened them again to take in the soft colors that calmed her nerves. After Alfie died, she'd papered their bedroom in a pink and mint green pattern that looked like drizzled icing, hoping it would help her miss him less. Two pink-shaded lamps, one by the bed and the other on her dressing table, gave off a rosy light that blurred her wrinkles. Not that Alfie cared she was past her prime. She could be natural with him. Didn't have to pretend everything was jake, either, like she did with Buddy.

"Something was eating our little Mary Pickford tonight," she said aloud. "I probably shouldn't have told her about Buddy sticking his head in the pail. And he ain't put his fist through the wall all that often. But it's easy to lay it on with her—she acts like nobody ever took an interest in her before. I didn't mention the devil holding his head down. The doctors can say whatever they like. You and me both know the boy's always had a better imagination than most." She smiled at Alfie's urn over on the dresser. "Remember him seeing trees floating in the window and that teacher saying how precocious and sensitive he was?"

Dearie lowered her sore heinie onto the bench in front of her dressing table. Some girlies called it a vanity—a fitting name for something only good for looking at yourself. She rolled down her support hose and rubbed her cramped toes, then burrowed them into the thick pink carpet. She'd been on her dogs too long tonight and the pain got her thinking about turning a few shifts over to Ladonna if the girl didn't take off for New York like she kept saying she would.

"Ain't just me that's happy she's still around. The boy's been better since she came. He don't seem stuck on her—can't say I'm surprised—so I don't see no harm in her staying. And she's a lulu, makes me laugh. Didn't realize how little laughing goes on in this house till she came along. Oh, she's got her secrets down in the basement, all right, but so far they ain't spelled trouble."

Dearie picked up her tortoise-shell brush and ran its soft bristles carefully over her thinning hair. She used a stiffer brush on Ladonna's coiled-up mess. "You'd get a kick out of her, Alfie. 'I'll hire you as my personal blackhead and tangle remover when I'm a movie star,' she says. I'm thinking movie stars must have a terrible need to be loved."

Buddy must have seen that, too, with that sensitive side his teacher spoke of. It had surprised Dearie when that little girly with the brave face and scared eyes showed up. Buddy didn't usually have time for anything but exercising, school and the A&P. Got real upset if he thought he'd done less than his teachers, his boss or Charles Atlas expected. Until Ladonna, Dearie didn't know he'd even had any friends besides her grandnephew, Richard, who didn't count since he was family. She didn't want to discourage Buddy.

She took off her specs, slip and brassiere. Opened the jar of cream with the nice violet stink and smeared her face, the lizard skin on her neck and the rough patches on her elbows. She pulled her pink flannel nightgown over her head and settled into bed. The cool sheets were always a jolt at first. Even after all this time, she still half-expected Alfie's long warm toes to reach for her under the covers. "Abyssinia," they'd say to each other before drifting off to sleep.

She reached over and turned off the bedside table lamp.

"Abyssinia, you old patootie," she said into the darkness.

❧ NINE ❧

APRIL 9, 1956. The mass for the Annunciation of the Blessed Virgin Mary is over and the chapel nearly empty. Miranda remains, lost in wonder at being both within and outside herself. She can see her body kneeling in prayer before the altar even while she senses her spirit rising above it. *Don't be afraid,* the Voice tells her. She feels a powerful pulsing of love in her veins as Danú appears in the rafters, wearing a green and silver gown, a snake curled around her waist like a sash. *Blessed are you among women,* she says in a voice like night whispers. *You have been chosen to nurture my child to greatness.* As suddenly as she materialized, the goddess evaporates, leaving a rapturous pain in Miranda's womb. With sudden clarity, she views her body, now bathed in purple light, as the sacred vessel it is.

She sees Father Shandley slip into the pew in which she prays. He touches her arm, lifts her wrist and cries out. Sisters Diane Patrice and Celine are the only other ones in the chapel. Their skirts whoosh as they dash to Father Shandley's side. How dear they are to Miranda at this moment, their own vessels glowing yellow, orange and pink.

"She's cold as night," Father Shandley says. He pulls off his white chasuble and wraps it around her shoulders, clasps her body to his chest and rocks it roughly. Miranda falls back into her body with a gasp, an acidic taste rising from her throat to her mouth. She opens her eyes and speaks into the embroidered gold cross on the white linen amice atop Father Shandley's black shirt. "I saw her and felt his life enter my womb."

Sister Celine gently eases her from Father Shandley's grasp and briskly rubs Miranda's blue hands. "Whose life, dear?"

"Cian's." Warmth re-enters Miranda's body but she trembles at the realization that she's finally done it: turned off her rational mind as the Voice of James urged, gone back in time and experienced the precise moment the father god Dagda planted his seed.

"Whom did you see?" Father Shandley asks.

"The Mother Goddess." The goddess of rivers, of birth and beginning.

"The Blessed Virgin," Sister Diane Patrice says, crossing herself.

"Let's not rush to conclusions," Sister Celine says. "Sometimes a dream is only a dream."

"It wasn't a dream, Sister." Danú's appearance was sharp and unequivocal.

The rumor that Miranda has seen Mary spreads quickly among the nuns that afternoon as Sister Diane Patrice tells one, then another, "The Holy Ghost entered her. I knew right away."

Mother Alfreda sends for Miranda. Inmates summoned for discipline usually wait on a bench outside her office, but a sister ushers Miranda in directly to a hard-backed chair in front of a wide oak desk. A large brass crucifix commands the white wall behind the desk and a tall oak bookcase the adjoining wall. The desk holds a green blotter, writing pad, pen and inkwell, telephone and two framed pictures: one of St. Bernadette in peasant-like head scarf and shawl and the other of the Blessed Virgin Mary pointing to a glowing, flaming heart on her chest. The office does not seem as small as Doris described; Miranda senses power and authority in it. She stands when the mother superior enters, as she's been taught, and remains standing until the woman sits behind the desk and nods her permission.

Miranda dips her head and drops back into her chair. "Thank you, Reverend Mother."

Mother Alfreda is a tall, big-boned woman with flaring nostrils and fine skin, her face as hard as the four-inch onyx crucifix between her breasts she uses to rap the heads of misbehaving inmates. She calls to mind James's description of the winter goddess Cailleach who could freeze the ground with a glance. James said Cailleach was to be fed with a long-handled spoon.

"I've been following your progress, Daughter," Mother says. "The sisters tell me you cry for your son. That seeing him once a month is not enough for you."

"I pray each day for his return, Reverend Mother."

"Is he not doing well in fosterage? Not treated kindly?"

"Oh, aye, he seems content enough, but a child belongs with his mother." Miranda recalls James's tale of the god of light holding a festival in his foster mother's honor. Cian shows up each month with new clothes and new words. He seems happy to see her but just as happy when their hour together is over. Miranda has to swallow back her jealousy.

"I ask you to be patient. Trust that Jesus and the angels are watching over you and your boy." Mother Alfreda shifts in her chair, leans forward. "Now, tell me about your vision."

The Voice says: *Careful, now.*

Mother Alfreda's smile is inscrutable as Miranda, without uttering Danú's name, describes the woman she saw. She does not speak of reliving the moment Cian entered her womb. The reverend mother would never believe that Miranda and James lay together only once. Or that it was divinely ordained. There would be room for only one savior in her mind.

"The Blessed Mother appears in many guises," Mother Alfreda says. "Our own patron saint, Bernadette, saw the Virgin eighteen separate times without knowing who it was. You may have the potential for holiness, Daughter. We will have to watch you closely and see."

"Cian is the holy one," Miranda says. He sends her his presence each day as night gives birth to dawn; she feels his soft skin and smells his dough-like sweetness.

"Every child is a divine gift."

Mother Alfreda lays out orders: lest Miranda show a continued proclivity for losing a pulse, she will move to the infirmary where Sister Nurse can watch over her; she'll be excused from the classroom so that she won't be tainted by other inmates' cynicism and worldliness—Bernadette suffered much from people who didn't believe her; Sister Celine will guide Miranda's academic studies but Mother will personally nurture Miranda's spiritual growth with a future religious vocation in mind.

Miranda's mind is too muddled to ask if a woman with a child can have a religious vocation. She hopes her infirmary bed will be near a window and welcomes the prospect of lessons apart from girls who call her stupid and tell jokes she doesn't understand. She'll not miss the rows of desks with black metal legs or Red Rover Come Over. She has no talent for games.

A WEEK BEFORE Miranda's vision, Linda had sauntered home from school with her books pressed against her chest and her jacket over her arm, feeling as puffed up as a blowfish but with gladness, not poison. Sunday had been the most inspiring Easter ever, the first since she became eligible to join River Street Methodist. She'd spent three hours in church on Good Friday, staring at the rough wooden cross leaning against the altar. She'd had to work at grieving, to be honest, at pretending it was she who'd been betrayed and humiliated and left to die of thirst. Worship is meant to be hard work, Reverend

Judge had told the new member class. You can't pop in, sing a couple of hymns and think you're done. Much like playing the piano, you have to learn the notes and practice every day. Linda had taken piano lessons for a while before losing interest. She wanted to be more faithful now at, well, being faithful.

On Easter morning, she'd gotten up in the dark and sat in the chilly park with the rest of the youth choir for the sunrise service, praying Jesus would say to Mother, "Take up your bed and follow me." She prayed that Mother, who'd recently been in and out of the hospital with a suspected ulcer, would be dressed for church when Linda returned home. And she was! Later that morning the youth and adult choirs formed a procession and led the congregation in singing "Christ the Lord Is Risen Today." The triumph of that song after Good Friday's sorrow choked her voice and made her cry. Daddy said the Holy Ghost had entered her. More likely it was that her period had arrived. Thank goodness it hadn't ruined her new satiny-finish dress and her first nylons.

She would stop by Rolf's corner store in case Richie was waiting for help with his latest comic. He liked her quirky ideas for speech bubbles. At Rolf's he'd often sit on the ice-cream freezer chest and draw until his behind got cold. Linda didn't remember exactly when she'd started going in with him or the first time he'd let her help.

The bell over Rolf's door went *chadup-bing-bing*. She smiled in anticipation, but no Richie. Only Rolf, restocking the Dixie cups and Popsicles. He looked up, grinned and said, "Cold vork." He was a crinkly-old blob of beige skin and looked a hundred years old, but Linda supposed he was only half that. He'd been there as long as she could remember, a local celebrity due to the sheet cakes he made for birthdays and anniversaries—elaborate confections with icing roses and lemon filling. The store smelled different every day, depending on what he'd been cooking in his back rooms. Today, it smelled of coffee too long on the stove.

"Have a good Easter?" she asked.

He shrugged and gave her a tight smile. She remembered, then. His wife had died only a few months before. And he might not even be a Christian. She felt terrible. To mask her embarrassment she plucked a bottle of something called Silk Magic from a stack on the counter. "Is this new?"

He closed the freezer and came to where she was standing, assaulting her nose with his sharp vinegary smell. "Ja, for fine ladies like you." His gray teeth grinned at her. He took the bottle and pulled his glasses down to read the small print. "Says it vill double ze life of nylon hoze. Guaranteet."

"Really? I could use that." Mother had said Linda would have to buy her next pair of stockings with her allowance. A detergent that doubled their life would be a smart investment. Taking the bottle from Rolf, she moved to the back where glass jars of penny candy rested on their sides, their mouths wide open. She wanted to resist since she was finally getting a shape, but the Hershey kisses, wax lips, candy corn, licorice babies and banana chews cried out like orphaned children: Take *me*, take *me*. She didn't hear Rolf come up behind her. She jumped when he said, "Take vhat you like, no charch." He handed her a paper bag.

"I couldn't. I mean, I want to pay." She set the Silk Magic on the floor, took the bag and dropped in a few licorice babies, but she felt uneasy. She heard him breathing behind her.

He put a hand on her shoulder and squeezed. "You like me, Linda?"

"Well, sure," she said, standing frozen, staring ahead at the jeering mouths of the jars, praying for the bell over the door to ring and to hear Richie's "What's up, buttercup?"

"Den how about a kiss." Rolf gripped her shoulders, turned her to him and kissed her with hard dry lips.

She pulled away, her cheeks hot with shame.

"Ach, now you madt at me." He pouted like a little boy.

"No," she lied.

"Den kiss me again." He tapped his lips with a finger.

Linda shook her head.

He bent down and picked up the Silk Magic. Held it out. "Take it. Show you not madt."

It was wrong to hurt someone's feelings. She mumbled her thanks, set the bag of licorice on a jar and hurried out the door. She took refuge in her room, rehearsing what she'd say when Daddy got home. At dinner, she related what had happened.

"Did you say anything to encourage him?" Mother asked.

"No." Should she have said she *didn't* like him?

"Did he hurt you?" Daddy asked.

"Not really." His hands had dug into her shoulders.

"Well, then," Daddy said, "try to understand how lonely he's been since his wife died."

That night she took the bottle of Silk Magic and hid it deep in her closet.

APRIL 30, 1956. Miranda approaches Mother Alfreda's office, expecting another lesson in the distressing lives of Catholic mystics. Instead she finds Cian perched on the edge of the desk, the reverend mother's solid arm protectively around his waist. Heat deserts her body and her feet freeze to the office threshold. Cian is not scheduled for a visit. Has he been adopted and brought in for a last goodbye?

"Hurry," Mother Alfreda says. "I've forgotten how squirmy two-year-olds are."

Cian holds out his arms. "Mandy!" Miranda saw him only a few weeks ago, but he grows so quickly, he's a different child each visit.

His spine seems straighter today and his tummy less rounded. A little boy, not a baby, in green corduroy overalls and striped shirt.

She forces her throat to move. "Is something wrong?"

Mother Alfreda's mouth is stern but her narrow gray eyes look amused. "It depends on your point of view. The foster parents claim he's overly resistant to toilet training. They've returned him as they would a defective toaster."

A rush of warmth. The Voice of James saying, *There are no coincidences.*

"For good?" Miranda asks.

Mother smiles broadly now. "Yes, Daughter. Now please"— she nods toward Cian—"relieve me. No lesson today. I've told the nursery you'll be delivering him and likely spending the rest of the day there, helping him get reacquainted."

Miranda sweeps Cian up in her arms and buries her face in his sweet neck. The Voice reminds her that today is Bealtaine, the day April steps aside for May. The third anniversary of Cian's conception, a date deliberately chosen so that he might be born with the lambs on Oimelc in February, the same day Father Shandley calls Candlemas and wears violet. The Daily Missal says Mary and Joseph took Jesus to the temple that day because he, as their firstborn son, had to be offered up to God then bought back with five shekels. Miranda had only prayers and tears to buy back her child.

That must have been enough.

TEN

JUNE 6, 1956. Two months ago Miranda was overwhelmed by the sweeping changes Mother Alfreda wrought after Danú's appearance and felt like an exiled misfit. Now, she treasures her isolation and the grudging respect her novitiate-in-waiting status gets from some inmates. The nursery sisters seem to take her right to be with Cian more seriously since she was issued different clothes. Doris says the brown tunic and black tights make her look like Cinderella before the fairy godmother.

Once a week Mother Alfreda tries to guide Miranda into a trance state. Last week she had her gaze at a crucifix because, hundreds of years ago, Christ had visited mystic-turned-saint Margaret Mary with his hands and feet bloodied as if he'd just fallen off the cross. Today Miranda's eyes fix on a globe on Mother's big desk because a saint named Catherine saw Mary standing on top of the world. Miranda focuses on the tiny splat called Ireland, the place of James's birth, where time happens five hours before it does at St. Bernadette's. Mother Alfreda has instructed her to stare at the globe in hopes she'll go into a trance long enough to entertain another holy visitor or to glimpse, as Mechthild of Magdeburg did, the "Eternal Hatred" of Hell.

The prospect makes Miranda shudder. She has no desire to wear a girdle of thorns, drive nails into her hands or be put in chains and fed to wild beasts. She doubts she has ever once glowed "with a devout and holy love," as Saint Augustine said every good Catholic should. What if she's a fraud? Danú has come to her only the once. Perhaps it *was* only a dream.

A warm breeze ushers in the Voice of James. *Allow it could be. The globe has a story to tell. Become one with it to hear.*

Mother Alfreda's moldy smell wafts across the desk.

The Voice says: *To begin, explore every inch of the globe with your hands. Then close your eyes and see with your heart and your mind all your fingers have felt.*

Miranda caresses the globe, her fingertips climbing the Alps and crossing the equator. She closes her eyes.

"Inhale deeply for a count of six," Mother says, her voice an extension of James's, "then exhale for six. Repeat until your mind is lifted up and free."

The Voice says: *Repeat until your mind enlarges the globe enough to enter it.*

Miranda breathes in and out, over and over, until her body feels no more substantial than a hum and is oblivious to the stiff wooden chair holding it. She breathes in and out until the circle under the North Pole turns into quicksand and swallows her whole.

The globe is hollow and hot. Miranda stands in the center, balancing as though on a ball, her feet in constant motion. Her fingers traverse the inner shell, feeling the shape of the continents and seas. The world appears seamless, a wondrous notion she contemplates until her lungs constrict from lack of oxygen. She looks up; the North Pole is too high to touch. If she leaps toward it she may lose her balance. She stretches out her arms. Her hands scrabble for another exit and her breath quickens in mounting panic. Hearing muffled voices, she calls out for help, further depleting the air. Her tunic is soaked in sweat now and she feels woozy. The voices get louder. "Reanimate," says one. "Wiggle your fingers and toes," another. Miranda does and, with a loud crash, the globe rolls over the edge of the desk.

Later, after Sister Nurse pronounces Miranda's pulse and heartbeat back to normal, the reverend mother sits by Miranda's infirmary bed and asks her to describe what she saw, searching for clues that the mysterious voices might have been divine personages. She seems dejected that God did not forecast the end of times nor Mary appear with a message.

The Voice whispers: *Trying to meet the gods leads you to miss the message. You sensed the trapped and isolated feelings of the sister from whom Mother Alfreda borrowed the globe; you learned that objects retain the energy of those who own them and transfer knowledge to those sensitive enough to receive it.*

Miranda recoils at the possibility that she entered a sister's feelings uninvited. Is that not as rude as eavesdropping? *Not for the mother of a divine child,* the Voice responds. *To keep him safe you must read the world around him.*

Mother Alfreda stands and presses a hand on Miranda's forehead. "You don't seem feverish, but I'm uneasy with what I've observed today. You are not to enter another thing, if indeed you entered that globe as you claim. You must conserve your mystical energy for divine visitations. Keep yourself open to that and nothing else." She crosses herself and leaves.

THE VOICE TELLS MIRANDA she has the potential to surpass James's abilities—an irresistible challenge. When Sister Nurse is asleep, she practices on objects she can spirit away for a while: Sister Celine's fountain pen; a stamp pad Sister Theodore has handled. Because she sees only images of fractured tales she can't confirm, she brings Doris into her confidence and enters items Doris brings her. A skeptical Doris acknowledges that it is more than coincidence when Miranda "hears" a conversation she had with her mother and "sees" Carolyn fall off the backyard swing. She brings Miranda a newspaper story about a missing girl but Miranda detects no energy of the girl in it; that seems to suck the air out of Doris and disappoint her terribly.

AUGUST 8, 1956. Summer was boss. Tereza could go outside whenever she wanted without worrying about a truant officer nabbing her or Dearie bugging her about going back to school. She bought sunglasses with glow-in-the-dark orange frames and a white bathing suit to show off her naturally tan skin at the Linden pool. She could swim like a shark but preferred sauntering around the edge of the chlorine-stinky pool, attracting "Hi doll," "Hey baby" and "Ow, you're breaking my heart" from guys in plaid trunks with bulges. Their calls and whistles made her wonder why Buddy hadn't made a move on her when Dearie wasn't looking.

Summer was boss for him, too. He got to work the eight to four-thirty shift and had Wednesdays and Sundays off. At night he'd record stuff for her to practice reading during the day. Sunday mornings, after breakfast, he'd insist she read out loud. If she did well, he'd smile, making her heart open up like the little morning roses in Dearie's garden. If not, he'd ball up his fists, clench his jaw and stalk away. He could be such a prick, like on Wednesdays when he went to the shore without her, even though every Tuesday Dearie would say, "Take our little actress with you tomorrow; she needs some fun."

"She needs to stay home and practice her reading," he'd say.

It was Tereza's own fault. She'd given herself away on a Sunday morning at the end of May. She could still see it happening, still feel the shame stinging her face.

Dearie had been standing at the stove in that zip-up blue-and-white seersucker housedress, slicing bananas into pancake batter. Buddy and Tereza sat opposite each other at the kitchen table. "Look at them, Alfie," Dearie said. "Like baby birds waiting to be fed." She'd turned to Tereza then and said, "The funnies ain't funny anymore, but God's truth I'm hooked on 'em. What's old busybody Mary Worth up to today, Ladonna Madonna? Read her to me."

Tereza tried to fake it, coughing and sneezing between words, but it was obvious she couldn't read worth shit. She felt like a turd, but Buddy just narrowed his blue eyes at her like she was a broken carburetor and said, "I can fix that. What would you read if you could?"

"Photoplay, Movie Fan, Silver Screen." Her fork traced the black-and-white checkered pattern on the oilcloth. She bought the magazines mostly for the pictures.

Buddy stilled her fork with his hand. "Actresses have to read scripts, and fast."

She hadn't thought of that.

He asked what kind of movies she liked. It should've been obvious. She went to the show every Sunday afternoon, getting home in time for the supper Dearie insisted the three of them eat together since it was the only day both Herman's and A&P were closed. Over supper she'd act out the plots for them: humans replaced by zombie-like aliens, a giant H bomb–infected octopus terrorizing San Francisco, a woman turning into a cobra and killing with a single strike.

"Sci-fi thrillers," she reminded him.

"You like being scared?"

"I like how good it feels when it's over."

He cocked his head as if wanting more.

"Like going on a roller coaster," she said. "You know, after that slow climb to the top, when it tears to the bottom and you can't hear nothing but your own screaming—it's like you're this close to death. Sci-fi thrillers are like that, only safer. Plus, even if your life stinks like a backed-up toilet it'll never be as bad as a planet blowing up."

Buddy borrowed a Dictaphone from a typing teacher for the summer. At night he'd record articles from Tereza's fan magazines so she could listen while reading them alone. She held a ruler under each line, like he suggested, to make the words stop jumping all over the page. She found out that John Derek had a son and a daughter and that Grace Kelly's parents had given Prince Rainier two million bucks to marry her.

When she handed him a second batch of magazines to record, he said, "These are unworthy of you." She couldn't see how they were any less worthy than the magazines with bare-chested soldiers and sailors she'd seen on the floor in the back of his car.

He borrowed *Dracula* from the library and recorded it for her, a chapter a night. She'd never known it was a book. She found it boring: too much description and too many words she didn't under-stand. What the hell was a Carpathian and who cared? She tried to remember words to ask Buddy about later because she couldn't write them down fast enough and the library didn't like you making marks in the book. He loaned her his dictionary and showed her how to replay the Dictaphone for parts she didn't understand. His reading voice was the reason she kept listening: it was so dramatic ("The coffin was empty!") you'd swear he was a professional actor. His everyday voice was kind of flat. She wanted to learn more about him and read well enough so that he'd take her down the shore. She practiced every morning before Dearie got up and every afternoon when Dearie took her nap.

It must've paid off, because last night, driving home from Herman's, Buddy had said, "If you're going to the shore with me tomorrow, be ready at seven. I want to beat the traffic."

IT TOOK NEARLY AN HOUR and a half to get to Seaside Heights. Tereza loved the hot air on her face. Felt boss when they stopped at a traffic light and people sneaked peeks at them. She tried to make conversation but Buddy only grunted. He gripped the wheel with both hands like it might fly off. She wanted the radio on, but he said it was rude to force your music choices on others when the top was down.

They parked on a side street and hoofed the few blocks to the beach. Buddy toted a blanket and Tereza carried their suits wrapped in towels. She took in the salty air, the seagulls circling overhead crying like babies and the whoosh-slap of the ocean she couldn't see yet. The shore was another world, just a car ride away. Buddy gave her a dime for the ladies' change room and waited for her at the end of a tunnel of wet sand leading to the beach. He didn't look as freaky as Charles Atlas, but his thighs strained against white trunks and his leg and arm muscles stuck out. Beside him, Tereza felt as puny as a tick he could squash between two fingers.

She sat on the blanket and watched his cute ass strut across the sand to where you could rent an umbrella. Other heads turned and gave him the once-over. She wanted to shout, He's mine! Nobody'd know she'd goaded him into taking her; they'd think it was his idea.

Under the blue-and-white striped umbrella, they could've been the only ones on the beach. Hugging her knees, wishing she'd painted her toenails, she asked if he thought his ma was still alive. She couldn't picture her own too well anymore.

"No reason to think she isn't."

"You ever look for her?"

"She knows where to find me. I wasn't the one who left."

Had he said that to be mean?

They bounced up and down in the waves like jack-in-the-boxes. Lay on their backs afterward, wet arms touching. The sun-bleached hair on Buddy's arms and chest stood up on his goose bumps. He asked her to name the worst thing she'd ever done. Staring up at the umbrella ribs, she thought about what had happened behind Tony's Garage, but told him instead that she'd lifted a pack of cigs from Jimmy.

She could hear the frown in his voice when he said, "You smoke?"

He must not have remembered her taking a drag at White Castle.

"Not anymore."

"Bravo," he said. "Live clean, think clean."

"Something Atlas said?"

"Yes, ma'am."

He wanted to know if she'd enjoyed stealing the cigs, if it had made her want to do it again. She said she couldn't remember. That was honest in a way: even she wasn't dumb enough to take Jimmy's smokes. She *had* gotten a rush with the men at Tony's, a feeling that she had some secret power over them she didn't have over Buddy.

She went up on an elbow. "It's okay if you kiss me."

"Holding hands is better than kissing," he said. "Holding hands is magnetic."

They lay on their backs and held hands until Tereza's bathing suit felt so steamy against her skin she thought she'd melt. She ran into the ocean and pretended not to know he was sneaking up behind her. He grabbed her ankles, pulled her under and held her until she bit his hand. "Bastard," she said after she got her breath back and was struggling to stand with waves sucking the sand out from under her feet.

"Forgive me, m'lady!" he shouted. He lifted her up like a bride and carried her back to the blanket, the people around them cheering and clapping. She was pissed off at him for making her lungs want to burst, but proud that he'd carried her for everyone to see. She wanted him to kiss her, tell her he was so scared she might die it made him realize he loved her.

But he plopped himself on the blanket and lay with his hands behind his head as she gulped down lemonade, her mouth dry from salt and fear. She waited until her heart had stopped thumping before asking, "So what's the worst *you* ever done?"

"I got sent to juvie a few years ago. Dearie doesn't like anybody knowing, so I won't tell you why in case you let it slip. I don't remember much about it anyway, except seeing an Atlas ad for the first time. I couldn't afford the lessons then, but the ad itself started me down the right path. It said: 'With good health goes honesty and integrity.' Made me realize my body was full of poison and I was denying my true manly nature."

She turned on her side to face him. "What's 'integrity'?"

"Being who you are and not what you think others want you to be."

"What if integrity gets you a black eye or a busted jaw?"

"Then you need to keep somebody like me around." He sat up, puffed out his chest and flexed his arm muscles. "Try to open my fist."

Even with two hands she couldn't pry a single finger loose.

When the beach closed they changed their clothes and sauntered along the boardwalk. On the merry-go-round she rode a white horse with a golden saddle while he stood on the edge reaching for the brass ring, the two of them like planets, he said, orbiting around the booming calliope. Later she ate thick, salty fries from a white paper cone. She told him her favorite vegetable was beets because they made her pee turn red—always good for a scare until she remembered and then good for a laugh. He said one thing he liked about her was how uncomplicated she was.

She said, "What else?"

"I appreciate that you let me help you. I can teach you a lot more than how to read."

"Yeah, like what?"

He cracked his knuckles. "How to tell when the devil turns into a guy like me."

By the time they left Seaside, Tereza suspected Buddy was as screwed up as she was, but she wanted him to do more than protect or teach her. She wanted him to want her.

AUGUST 27, 1956. "Is a puzzlement,"Yul Brynner would have said.

How could Linda once have considered Richie a slimy lizard, like the other neighborhood guys Tereza had hung around with, and now want nothing more than to get this family trip to Kansas over with and spend more lazy afternoons with him? The answer came between Springfield, Illinois, and Hannibal, Missouri. She sprawled on the back seat in green shorts and a white blouse, the hot, dusty wind blowing her hair every which way while the motion of the car and the monotonous vista of corn, beet and bean fields hypnotized her.

God had sent her to watch over Richie. Not as a guardian angel— she wasn't virtuous enough for that. More like a flawed missionary who could be perfected if she cajoled Richie into spending more time with her and less with troublemakers. She could help him tell right from wrong, like when he wanted to use a crude word in a speech bubble.

She wouldn't have seen that so clearly had the old Nash not broken down three days ago on her thirteenth birthday for which Mother had planned a dinner at a fancy Springfield restaurant that served Baked Alaska. (She'd had Daddy telephone ahead to make sure.) "This year will be different," Mother had said, having felt guilty about being in the hospital on Linda's twelfth and then, three months ago, going in for an operation to remove what turned out to be a perfectly healthy appendix, just as the uterus had been. That annoyed Daddy because even with a good medical plan you didn't get away scot-free.

They had to be towed into Springfield—a real hoot because they got to stay in the car, staring at its nose in the air, their backs pressed against the seats. The tow truck had room for only the driver and his pimply son—younger than Richie, maybe fifteen, and so shy he could hardly look Linda in the eye long enough to say his name was Dwayne. His denim shirt and dungarees were oil-stained and he shook her hand with a sweaty palm. When he and his father hooked up the Nash and Linda and her parents were tipped back, ready to roll, Mother said, "He seems like a nice boy." Linda rolled her eyes at the back of Mother's head, imagining the sympathy she'd get at school if Mother died during one of her hospital stays and how tragically romantic she'd look to Richie in black.

By the time they bounced into Springfield every restaurant was closed, including the one with the Baked Alaska. The tow-truck driver also owned the auto repair shop. He got them a "good deal" on a room in a hotel close to his shop, within walking distance of the Lincoln museum, a place he said they might enjoy visiting. The desk clerk said, "We had a heap of rain past couple of days. You might spot a water bug or two in your room." Mother's face got that pre-headache look.

Linda and Daddy walked a couple of blocks in the warm night air to a small, smoky place named Vi's that was sold out of everything except beer and Danish. "Earth Angel" blasted from a jukebox, sending Linda all dreamy. Boys dressed like hoods were shooting pool. That started her wondering why she'd once seen Richie as just another hood, but now more like poor dead James Dean in *Rebel Without a Cause:* trying to fit in but confused as to how.

The hoods must have gotten Daddy thinking, too, because on the way back to the hotel he said maybe it was a good opportunity to express his concern over reports Linda had been seen more than once walking with Richard Sulo. Daddy said that he too had gone through a rebellious phase when he was younger and that Richard might be a fine person under all that pomade and bluster but didn't she think he was too old? She considered asking "for what?" but she knew he meant kissing, which she and Richie had never done, another reason she'd concluded that God was involved: according to Reverend Judge, Jesus had hung around with harlots—apparently it was okay to say that word—only because he had compassion and a wholesome love for anyone trapped in sin. Hoods weren't harlots, of course, but Linda thought the general principle applied.

Back at the hotel Mother said stale Danish was a poor excuse for a birthday dinner. Linda told her she'd rather go to the farmhouse restaurant near her grandparents' place for a belated celebration. It served country-fried chicken, mashed potatoes, biscuits and white gravy in family-sized bowls so that you could have seconds. "I don't need Baked Alaska," she said. "Blueberry pie would be swell." But Mother seemed to want to be miserable. Honestly, if you didn't laugh you'd cry at the impossibility of keeping her happy. She never told you what she expected until you failed to deliver it, and sometimes not even then. Linda and Daddy did most of the housework even when Mother was well because it eliminated at least one reason for her giving them the silent treatment. They sometimes turned their frustration with her silence into little jokes. Daddy might ask Linda, "Did you forget to do something you promised, like defeat communism?"

The next morning the hotel floor was carpeted in undulating water bugs. They made a crunchy sound under Linda's sneakers. Mother barely spoke as they trudged around wax figures and old documents at the Lincoln museum. The car needed a thingamajig that wouldn't come in until the next day, so Daddy said, "Let's make lemonade out of lemons and go out for the birthday dinner tonight." Once there, Mother stared at her food like *she* was a wax figure. It took forever for the Baked Alaska to arrive and it had vanilla ice cream inside, not Neapolitan. Sometimes it was a relief to have Mother in the hospital where you didn't have to see her sadness.

The car had been ready this afternoon, thank goodness. As boring as Kansas would be (nobody was allowed to stay up past nine-thirty because Grandpa, who hadn't farmed in decades, rose at five each morning to listen to the hog and grain report), Linda was relieved to be finally heading there. Daddy had just paid for the repairs when Dwayne, all stuttery and red-faced, asked Linda to a square dance that night, and didn't Mother finally open her mouth and say, "If you'd like to go, Linda, we can stay another night." Thank heavens

Daddy said, "Sorry, we have to be on our way." A few minutes later he said, "Sometimes you amaze me, Betty." Mother just stared out her window.

Linda was staring out her window now, too, thinking that Dwayne had reminded her of the boys she'd met at church camp last month. They acted all shy and innocent during services but tried to get the girls alone behind the chapel after dark. Richie hadn't once tried to hold her hand, even when she secretly wanted him to. God had kept her safe until she understood that her love for Richie was to be only compassionate and wholesome and that her mission was to ease his confusion about how to fit in.

❧ ELEVEN ❧

SEPTEMBER 12, 1956. Dawn, soft as a lullaby, creeps in on timid fingers and toes across the early sky. Miranda lies abed, picturing herself at both ends of a tug-of-war. Which side does she want to win: the one keeping her "grounded in the here and now," to use Sister Celine's words, or the one beckoning like a Siren? The Voice of James exhorts her to abide in three worlds at once: that of the physical, the soul and *an saol eile,* the Other Life. *Imagine yourself under a deep ocean, aloft in the sky and firmly on the ground all at the same time.* Oh, how she tries!

The closest she's gotten was the day Doris took her to a beach where people sunned themselves like tortoises. Wearing a bathing suit of Doris's that felt tight as a sausage casing, Miranda ventured into the ocean, clinging to the safety ropes strung between posts. The cold stung her legs but the inhaling and exhaling of the waves drew her in. Farther out she went. She closed her eyes and felt the water inside her body change first to ice and then to cloud and rain. She understood, then, Augustine's claim that God created the Earth in a single moment. But almost immediately a wave caught her unawares and she lost her grip on the rope. Flailing around in the surf, she was terrified of drowning. As terrified, it occurs to her now, as the dead must be in the fires of Purgatory.

She rises from her infirmary bed and removes her coarse woolen nightgown. She slips a tunic over tights and laces her black oxfords as morning enters the city beyond St. Bernadette's gates. James would have called it a soft old day. If she could, Miranda would spend all her days in meditation, trying to straddle the shores between worlds, but Sister Celine has impressed upon her the need to tether herself to the earth. She told Miranda of a mystic convent nun she once knew who was lost to the community when in rapture, leaving others to do her work, something that offended Sister Celine's sense of fairness. So that Miranda might develop a practical skill, Sister has her report to the library two hours a day to assist the librarian, Sister Theodore, a woman so tall and thin she appears stretched.

St. Bernadette's library is industrious, with school classes in and out during the day and inmates encouraged to borrow books for personal reading. Miranda marvels at the Dewey decimal system that allows you to find any book easily and restore it to its proper place. When she returns home she'll reorganize the books there. So many she never opened because they were too high on the shelf or she didn't know what they were about. She relied on James to tell her what to read. Now, at Sister Celine's urging, she selects books from the library at random.

In the past few months alone, she's read books on plant life cycles, elephants, opera, geysers, sedimentary rocks, planets and asteroids. Books about ancient philosophers, exotic countries, modern history and so many other things she was ignorant of when she lived in the protective cocoon James spun for her. He may have assigned her novels that spoke of hatred and brutality, but they were too beautifully written and set in places too far-flung to seem real. She feels foolish for not having questioned him more. The Voice is unapologetic. *You needed to know your inner world before you faced the outer.*

The library isn't only for inmates. Scholars from all over the world come to do research, using its collection of antique books about church history. Many cover the time in England when it was criminal to be Catholic. Speaking of that period makes Sister

Theodore emotional. "Being a priest was high treason," she said one day. "Harboring a priest could get you executed."

"How dreadful," Miranda said. The image of a sweaty priest crouching in a dark pantry darted across her mind. "My father told me that similar things happened to those who honored the gods and goddesses of the earth, water and sky."

"If you mean pagans and witches," Sister Theodore said, "then most terrible things absolutely should have happened. The Bible says thou shalt not suffer a witch to live."

Since arriving at St. Bernadette's Miranda has read most of the Bible several times. (She could endure the begats only once.) "Are not changing water into wine and casting demons into swine the magical acts of a witch?" she asked Mother Alfreda after Sister Theodore's reproof.

"Not when performed by God's son," Mother Alfreda replied. She doesn't get annoyed at Miranda's questions. In fact, she encourages her to arrive at her own beliefs through reason and the wisdom of St. Thomas Aquinas, St. Anselm and others whose dried-up words bounce off the walls of Miranda's brain as if it were a babe's rattle. Miranda dutifully writes in her journal words like *theophany, ontological, Mariology, apostasy, exemplar.* It's only when Mother Alfreda speaks with passion about desiring to find a transcendent and personal god that Miranda's emotions are inflamed. How accepted she felt when Danú visited her and, for days afterward, how transformed. How transported when the Voice of James guides her to a state outside of herself.

Sister Celine warns that what Miranda and Mother Alfreda are doing is dangerous: "You could die, you know, and the reverend mother would only say, 'She was ripe for Heaven.' She'd love to boast of a martyr under her roof." Sister Celine says Miranda needs to glimpse the world, not Hell. She is preparing Miranda already for the day she'll leave St. Bernadette's womb by instructing her about life on the outside. "You must face what you don't want to know about your father," she said. "That won't happen if you stay here."

Miranda doesn't mind dying if she can walk among the dead with James and Eileen. But such thoughts are selfish. *The children of Danú are light and order,* James once told her. *They are born to counter the children of darkness and chaos.* With him gone, Danú has charged Miranda with raising this child of light and guiding him to his mission. Sister Celine's instruction about bank accounts and budgets, jobs and apartments offers no clues as to how to do that. Nor does the book she gave Miranda by a Doctor Spock.

Miranda loops her rosary over her belt and leaves her room, patterning her walk after Sister Celine's fluid glide. Today will test her ability to stay in the physical world. She will spend it in the nursery helping Sisters Cameron and Joseph herd the children from place to place and keep them occupied. She heads there after breakfast. The children are watching *Romper Room,* their faces bathed in the television's flickering moonlight. Cian flaps his arms and makes a buzzing sound. He's doing the Do Bee dance. Registering her presence, he hesitates a moment then resumes with more energy, bubbling like porridge. She sits on the floor behind him, watching his two-and-a-half-year-old body move with abandon. When he's done dancing he crawls onto her lap, looks at her with his ancient eyes and pats her face.

Miranda asked Mother Alfreda one afternoon how Mary raised Jesus to be a savior. Mother said she supposed Mary simply loved him and let God do the rest.

✢ TWELVE ✢

DECEMBER 16, 1956. Buddy started going to Sunday matinees with Tereza when it was too cold to do much outside for Dearie. He went the first time because he wanted to see *Battle Cry* again—an "encore performance," the theater had called it, trying to put one over on them.

Tereza wasn't big on war movies but Buddy said they helped him understand what his father went through. He didn't call him his old man. Buddy was born the month the war started—a bad omen, he said. His father lived in a photo on a radiator cover in the parlor; a tall man with wide shoulders, standing hands behind back, army pants tucked into combat boots. Next to the picture was the Purple Heart he'd gotten for letting a shell fragment pierce his heart. He'd volunteered after Pearl Harbor, Buddy said. Had been in only four months before he got zapped. After Buddy told her why he liked watching war movies, Tereza didn't mind seeing them. She pictured her own father, not Jimmy, as one of the happy-go-lucky film soldiers who give speeches about what they plan to do when they get home, right before falling on a grenade to save a bunch of other kids' fathers.

They went to a theater in an Italian neighborhood—not much danger of running into anybody she knew there. The lobby stank of sausage as well as popcorn but the theater had a crystal chandelier and a Wurlitzer organ. They'd go early enough to nab two seats in the balcony. They were watching *Love Me Tender* when he first put the heel of his hand on her mound and curled his fingers under her crotch. She hardly breathed. The theater was packed with screaming girls, making Buddy's gutsy move even more impressive. She glanced over at him staring at the screen, chin thrust out all intense, as if that hand couldn't possibly belong to him. They sat across from each other at Sunday dinner that night like nothing had changed. But Tereza felt the way she had after scoring a home run on the empty lot beside Vinnie's house.

The next week Buddy did the same and the week after.

Never looking at her, not saying anything after.

She put her hand on his fly the first time during *The Mole People,* expecting he'd swell up under it. He didn't. The next time he covered her hand with his and pushed down on it so hard his balls had to be shrieking, but it did the trick. You'd never have known by his face, though. It reflected only the flickering screen. Tereza had to take short, hard breaths to cool down.

They'd sat that way today, groping each other, Tereza trying to be as blasé as Buddy while squeezing tight. Later, at the dining-room table, they went on and on to Dearie about how much they liked the clove-speckled ham, the creamy scalloped potatoes and the peas. Tereza was sure she could hear Buddy's heart laughing as hard as hers at their secret.

Hanky-panky!

How strange love was. She could almost understand how Ma had ended up with Jimmy.

DECEMBER 19, 1956. Dearie stood in the parlor, her breath fogging the window as she watched Ladonna trudge down the sidewalk with the shopping list, any skip in her step long gone, if it had ever been there. Two little girls half a block behind her had stopped to play hopscotch. Dearie could hear their excited laughter. The weather was too mild for Christmas, but school would be out any day now. Buddy'd be working full days at the A&P through New Year's.

The parlor smelled of the Scotch pine he'd lugged home a week ago. The three of them had decorated it with the blue lights and ornaments she and Alfie had collected over the years, including Junior's red and green paper chains, faded now, and angels that Buddy had cut out of black oak tag when he was little. Ladonna seemed to get a kick out of throwing the tinsel any which way. Dearie was surprised Buddy hadn't gotten annoyed at that, him being such a neatnik.

It seemed to make Ladonna feel important to think some truant officer would nab her if she didn't come home by the end of the school kids' lunch break. Dearie didn't think that was likely. Ladonna might have a tiny chassis but her face was older than her years. "If you ask me, Alfie," Dearie said, "the only ones who care about that little girly are me and Buddy. Over a year and nobody's come looking for her." Dearie sent her out with a list every day so that Ladonna would get some sun.

Dearie didn't mind having some time to herself now and then either, for personal things like dusting Junior's picture. It needed attention every few days; even the skimpy winter light coming in from the window right now showed every speck of dust. She studied her son's face, so like Alfie's and Buddy's, especially the long, thin nose. Tried not to think of Junior's bones mixed up with the hundreds of others the Japs had dumped in a mass grave after marching the soldiers to death in the Philippines. At first, the army reported only that Alfred Eldon Jukes, Jr. was missing. Nearly two years later they sent a medal and admitted his unit had been captured.

The Purple Heart had come in a box Dearie kept closed so the fancy ribbon wouldn't fade and the medal wouldn't lose its shine. She opened it and ran a finger lightly over George Washington's face, raised in gold against the purple like a cameo on a fancy brooch. Alfie had made up the story about the shrapnel for Buddy's sake. "Nobody could fault you for that," she said. The prisoners had been starved and beaten, some bayoneted and others beheaded with samurai swords. How could you tell a boy that?

She picked up Junior's picture. Rubbed her cloth slowly in and around the pewter frame's embossed curlicues, imagining as she always did that it comforted Junior. She kissed the cool glass, something she would feel silly doing in front of Buddy or Ladonna. But Alfie understood.

She often pretended that Junior had refused to surrender and was hiding somewhere, not knowing the war was over or that Moira had taken off practically the minute she heard he was missing. Dearie wondered if regret over marrying that fickle girly hadn't driven him to enlist. Alfie built the room in the attic for Moira and Buddy when Junior went overseas. Moira hadn't wasted any time taking advantage, going out togged to the bricks nearly every night, leaving Buddy with Dearie. She'd come home half-lit, her hair and makeup a sight.

Dearie hadn't been able to come up with a good-enough story about his mother's desertion to patch Buddy's torn heart. "Remember that poor boy looking for her every morning, not even over missing his daddy yet?" He was scared to sleep upstairs alone after Moira left. Dearie and Alfie made up a bed for him in the dining room, but he crawled in between them most nights for almost a year, smelling sour from fear and whimpering like a kicked puppy. He wouldn't drop off until he couldn't fight the exhaustion any longer, afraid he'd vanish if he went to sleep.

Moira was a hard one to forgive, even at Christmas.

Dearie wiped off the glass and put Junior back on the radiator cover. If he came home now, he'd be proud of his son overcoming so much. He'd tell Buddy he didn't have to be the he-man he thought his daddy had been, didn't have to prove himself anymore. Junior could help, too, with what the doctors had called Buddy's *condition*. They said it could get worse over the years, but so far he'd only had one serious episode since the first. Oh, he could flare up like a struck match all right and let gloomy thoughts get the best of him, but only at home, it seemed. As far as Dearie knew, his temper hadn't shown up at work or in class, so obviously he could control it if he put his mind to it. Junior could give him some tips on that.

She wondered if she'd been wrong to build up his father so much in the boy's mind. She could have told him Junior had surrendered. But picturing Junior giving up to those murdering Japs shamed her more than she liked to admit. What would it do to Buddy?

She closed the lid on the medal box.

Besides, it might not even be true. Alfie always said you could never see the whole truth, just like you could never see all the stars in the universe.

JANUARY 19, 1957. *When the twilight is gone—wah ah—and no songbirds are singing—wah.*

Linda had set up her record player to repeat the song over and over. The Platters sounded like black butter, an observation she'd never share aloud lest anyone think she was prejudiced which she absolutely was not. For goodness' sake, she'd even begged for and gotten the colored baby doll advertised on *Amos and Andy* when she was little. Normally she could listen to records and do homework at the same time, despite what Daddy claimed. But this night, she struggled with an essay as snow fell like feather dust outside her window.

When the twilight is gone—wah ah—you come into my heart—ah.

Her English class was supposed to look to *Our Town* for inspiration. Miss Firkser had taken them to a community theater production of

the play before Christmas and then assigned them an essay describing
Stony River in a way that would reveal its essential character, whatever
that was. Linda had sat next to Connie Boyle during the play and
they'd both cried. Poor, dead Emily traveling back in time to her
twelfth birthday, only to realize that the living never take time to look
at one another. Linda remembered her own disappointing twelfth
birthday. When the Stage Manager said the dead didn't stay interested
in the living for long, she'd thought of Mother, shut up in her room
across the hall, showing little interest in anyone or anything. It made
her feel hopeless and angry.

And here in my heart you will stay while I pray.

The Platters and groups like the Satins and the Penguins with
their harmonies and high notes gave Linda goose bumps and caused
her to lose her own grip on the earth for a few minutes. Make-out
music. She'd yet to make out with anyone—party kissing games
didn't count—but whenever she heard a *shoo do be shoo be wah* she
thought she knew what it would be like to have your heart all aglow.
Honestly, sometimes it embarrassed her how badly she longed for it.
She practiced kissing on her arm and prayed every day to keep her
feelings for Richie wholesome.

*My prayer is to linger with you, at the end of the day, in a dream that's
divine.*

Should she write about the past like in *Our Town*? Had Stony River
been much different when her father was born in the very house she
lived in now? He was baptized at the same church as she. Had gone to
the same school. She could see him as the Stage Manager:

"Over yonder, two blocks south and three blocks east," he'd say,
sounding more Kansas than New Jersey, "is Mister and Missus Sulo's
house, on a piece of land once deep in blackberries. Ma would send
me out in my knickerbockers to fill buckets of them so we could
enjoy her jelly and jam all winter long. The Sulos came here from
Linden right after Ike took office. Flush enough, I declare, to buy

one of them new houses with the fancy colored stoves and fridges. The missus is a cute little thing, a nurse in the hospital's new maternity ward, and the mister, well, we don't see him much. A travelin' salesman of some sort. Truth be told, neither of 'em is home enough to steer their boy, Richard, down the straight and narrow, though he does keep the lawn mowed all summer, got to give him that."

Miss Firkser said the Russians had banned *Our Town* for making family life appear too attractive. Linda felt sorry for communists with their drab collective-farm existence. But they were screwy if they found family life in Grover's Corners attractive. As for Stony River, it had many more people than Grover's Corners but was just as small in spirit. She could write something scathing—she loved that word—but a good grade might require a flag-waving essay. Ever since Korea, it seemed that criticizing anything American was unpatriotic.

My prayer is a rapture in bloom.

"Write about Bartz Chemicals," Daddy said. "How it's the center of the wheel from which radiate the spokes of Stony River life." And from which spilled the goo that stank up the river. It bugged her that Daddy asked "Father work at Bartz?" whenever she mentioned a new kid at school. Many dads *did* work where he did—the plant employed six thousand, after all—but Linda objected to the implication that if you worked anywhere else you weren't as good.

Stony River sits on the peninsula of I'm Better Than You, she wrote. *White vs. colored. Christian vs. Jew. Catholic vs. Protestant. The married sit in judgment of the divorced. People who live on one side of the highway think they're better than us on the other and those in the big houses near the high school think they're best of all. Patients in private hospital rooms feel superior to those in wards. Some fathers think their jobs are more important than others. Teenagers are no better. Jocks think they're cooler than hoods and nobody wants to be a freshman.*

She struck the last. She was looking forward to being a freshman come September.

Richie was different. He might decide to stop being a hood but he'd never want to be a jock or go to college like Daddy. Why should he? He was going to be an artist. Mother and Daddy didn't like his looks and "the company he kept." They'd told her to stay away from him. They believed she was at the library after school every Wednesday, the only weeknight Daddy "rustled up" dinner, as he liked to joke, giving his legs-apart thumbs-in-belt cowboy impression. But she'd be in Richie's attic studio, posing for a comic strip about a wisecracking husband-and-wife detective team named Glenn and Gilda Daring. The deception pricked her conscience, but her parents' prejudice against Richie bothered her more.

With the world far away and your lips close to mine.

On Wednesdays, she'd stay until the five o'clock blast of the Bartz Chemicals factory whistle. Richie didn't smoke in the studio so she wouldn't have to explain the smell when she got home. He was surprisingly thoughtful like that. She suspected it was her positive influence.

He wanted Gilda to be "zaftig," like Peggy Lee—she loved it when he used a word you wouldn't in a million years think he'd know—and pronounced Linda's figure perfect. He drew Glenn thin as a snake. Linda would have preferred to be less hourglass and more six o'clock, like *Seventeen* model Carol Lynley, but she'd never survive on the single head of lettuce, pound of grapes and three green peppers Lynley claimed was all she ate every day.

Tonight, while our hearts are aglow.

Richie's mother was off shift on Wednesdays. She let Linda wear her trench coat and Richie's father's old fedora when she posed. She took Polaroid pictures of "Glenn and Gilda" for the panels in which they appeared together. She often popped in while Linda was there to ask if they wanted a snack. All on the up-and-up, Linda would tell Daddy if he found out.

Oh tell me the words that I'm longing to know.

Richie sketched Linda leaning against the wall, climbing a step stool he drew as a ladder, and in profile, holding a pistol his father had brought back from the war as a souvenir. "Is it loaded?" she'd asked the first time and he'd said, "Natch. How else you gonna feel authentic?" Palming it made her nervous but a little proud, too, remembering Tereza calling her Goody Two-Shoes. Daddy had a smaller pistol he'd acquired as a volunteer policeman during the war; a hernia saved him from the draft. He kept it, unloaded, in a bedside table. Linda had never even tried to cock it. But Richie's father had taught him how to *fire* their pistol.

My prayer and the answer you give ...

Richie drew her hair a brighter blonde than it really was, with her curls peeking out from under the fedora like fringe. He gave her pointy breasts that made her blush. He did the drawing and she did the speech bubbles. Glenn called men "cats" and women "dolls." Gilda, whom Linda envisioned as an older Nancy Drew—outspoken and fearless—said things like "You big lug" and "Cigarette me." They were working on a story Linda thought they should call "The Case of the Cry in the Night" in which two schoolgirls suspect that a sinister man holds another girl prisoner in a creepy old house, but their parents don't believe them. So they contact Glenn and Gilda, who take the case for free because they're secretly wealthy and on a mission to help the disadvantaged. "Privilege demands social respon-sibility," Gilda tells the mayor in one panel.

May they still be the same for as long as we live.

Linda removed her glasses and stepped to her bedroom window. She cupped her hands and pressed her nose against the chilly pane. She studied the snowflakes that swam in streetlamp light before sinking to the ground. The snow was too fresh for footprints. She thought of Miranda and Tereza. To disappear with so few people caring seemed sadder than to die.

She returned to her desk and wrote: *Stony River is the ground asleep under snow, its secrets imperceptible from behind a thick pane of glass.*

Miss Firkser had begun teaching them about metaphors. Linda didn't know how to extend hers or whether it was even the right one. Maybe it described her own home more than Stony River, with Mother both sleeper and snow. She wished she could tell friends that Mother was terminally ill and she and Daddy were making her last days as comfortable as possible. But Mother wasn't dying. Periodically she'd rise from her bed and take charge with such firm resolve you could hardly believe she'd ever been sick. She'd make beef stew, starch and iron Daddy's shirts, drag Linda out for new shoes. Insert herself into Linda and Daddy's routine as though they were incompetent and needed to be rescued. Eventually Linda or Daddy would say or do something (they were never sure what) to make Mother untie her apron and go back to her room.

That you'll always be there—dadadadadadadadada wah—at the end of my prayer.

"She claims she wanted to go to England during the war and drive an ambulance," Daddy said one night. "She says I wouldn't let her. I don't remember even discussing it." He looked so lost. Linda was confused: Mother didn't even know how to drive, for goodness' sake.

Linda heard a shovel scrape. The snow was falling more thickly, piling in the windowpane corners and turning her room into a cocoon.

In *Our Town,* the Stage Manager said that as far as they knew, nobody remarkable had ever come out of Grover's Corners. Linda intended to be remarkable. She was going to leave big footprints in the snow.

ACROSS THE HALL, Betty Wise sat in bed, propped up with pillows, trying to ease the throb in her neck and shake the dizzy feeling from those dang pills. Over her shoulders, against the room's chill, was a yellow and white afghan she'd knitted back when she felt like knitting.

Roger thought she should be able to "snap out of it," whatever "it" was. When the appendix came out, they'd found scar tissue— the fancy word was *adhesions*—gumming up the works from the hysterectomy the year before. The surgeon claimed that would have accounted for the pain. But Doctor Pierce disagreed. He'd told Roger it was in her head. He and Roger didn't know beans from apple butter. As if she could spunk right up just because they said so.

Linda was across the hall right now, playing her music without a thought that her mother could use some company. The only time she visited Betty's room was after school to ask if she wanted anything. An act of duty, not love. It got Betty's goat that Linda didn't call her Mom. She'd never signed a birthday or Christmas card as Mother. Roger said, "You have a voice. Tell her what you want," but it wasn't the same if you had to ask.

Betty could hear them as they watched their shows at night, their laughter drifting up through the register. Their morning voices were full of hurry. She envied them a place to go each day. She'd stay in bed until she heard Roger backing down the gravel driveway, fix a cup of tea and wander the house picking up after them. She didn't suppose they noticed.

She swung unsteady legs over the side of the bed and shuffled to the window overlooking the backyard. The snow was streaked with light from the house of a woman who came out when the moon was full and ranted in German. Betty steadied herself on the window-sill, fighting nausea. The Bible said a good wife was tolerant and understanding, didn't complain, didn't provoke her husband's anger.

When Betty disagreed with Roger he'd tell her she was wrong but he wouldn't say *wrong*. He'd use words like *emotional, irrational* or *impractical*. He could gnaw an argument to the bone. If Betty went to college she'd learn to argue better, but even if they could afford it, Roger said one family didn't need two degrees.

If he ever raised a hand to Linda, she'd be on the next train home to Mom. But he worshiped her, didn't see her faults. If Robert had lived, Roger would have doted on him and not stolen Linda away from her. Mom had told her countless times to put the boy behind her and love the child God gave her, but three people wasn't much of a family, not like the eight kids her own parents had. The plain truth was that Roger and Linda didn't need her.

She sat back down on the bed and turned her pasty face toward the dressing table mirror. If she had the energy she'd rouge her cheeks. Being with Mom last summer was swell, despite Roger having ruined Linda's birthday by forgetting to get the car serviced beforehand and then spoiling Linda's chance to spend time with a decent boy instead of that hoodlum she seemed to have a crush on. Betty wanted to warn Linda against giving herself away too easily, but she didn't think Linda would listen. She reached for the glass of water on the bedside table and knocked it over. Got down on trembling knees and wiped it up with the afghan.

She was sure she'd get well if they moved closer to Mom and had more land. Betty would plant a vegetable garden and raise a few chickens. She'd tried rhubarb, raspberries, carrots, lettuce and tomatoes over the years, but their postage stamp of a yard didn't yield much.

Roger would never move away from the house he was born in. Betty accepted that. Those first few years she didn't mind sharing a home with Mother Wise, as she insisted Betty call her. She didn't mind taking care of her when she was dying, even though the woman called Betty a hick. After she died, Betty wanted Roger to give some thought to living near *her* mom for a while. But he said, "You're the one who came out here and decided to stay."

True enough. She just wished he'd try to make it more worth her while.

$\mathcal{S}$ THIRTEEN $\mathcal{S}$

MARCH 9, 1957. The air was bitter at two in the morning when Herman drove Tereza home. She let herself in, closing the front door softly so as not to wake Dearie and Buddy. Dearie had begged off work the night before, complaining about her back. She'd planned to take some aspirin and get an early night. Tereza slipped off her shoes, tiptoed across the parlor and turned off the lamp Dearie had left on for her. She was surprised to see light coming from the kitchen and hear Dearie's voice, firmer than usual, fierce even. "Not a word more about it ever again. Ain't nothing to do with us."

Tereza found Dearie and Buddy at the kitchen table, Dearie wrapped in a blanket. Buddy, his leather jacket still zipped up, sat slumped and teary-eyed like a scared little kid.

"What's going on?" Tereza asked.

Dearie jerked a bit then recovered. "Forgot you was still out. Just my bum back. Can't sleep for the aching. Buddy's keeping me company. Ain't he sweet?"

It was the first time Tereza had known Dearie to lie to her.

Dearie didn't go to work the next night either. The ladies' john was full of talk about some cop's murder. One customer showed Tereza a newspaper with the word FALLEN in thick black letters above a picture of the cop. His face looked familiar.

MARCH 11, 1957. The phone ruptured the silence.

Buddy and Ladonna were at work. Dearie had been in bed for two days, wanting nothing more than to sink into a dark lake of sleep. But the same dream kept fishing her out, not letting her rest: Junior with his arms over his head in surrender and Buddy's twelve-year-old face on him, a panicky look in his eyes. She'd wake feeling like a heavy stone was pressing on her chest.

She considered not answering the phone in case it was the cops. She pushed away the memory of Buddy punching himself in the face and banging his head against the wall when she'd visited him in juvenile detention.

Yesterday was the first Sunday in years she hadn't cooked a roast, or anything else. She'd blamed it on her back so that Buddy wouldn't know how poorly she was taking things. She could usually stay cheerful for his sake. She'd told him more than once, "Act like everything's normal and pretty soon you ain't acting anymore." But right now it wasn't working for her. Talking to Alfie didn't help either; she couldn't think of what to say.

The phone wouldn't shut up.

Buddy and Ladonna had hovered around her room all day yesterday. She'd heard them in the kitchen discussing what they might coax her into eating, their cozy voices hinting at something different between them, something more personal. Part of her was relieved—maybe the hormones they'd given the boy hadn't messed him up after all—but being locked up again would. Buddy was too trusting. Later, when he came in with a bowl of chicken noodle soup for her, she couldn't tell if his eyes were wild on account of spooning or fear. On the chance it was spooning, she'd gone ahead and warned him, "Be careful around that little girly. She ain't legal age." He'd frowned at first like he didn't get it then went red-faced and backed out of the room.

Whoever was on the phone wasn't about to give up. Dearie forced her legs over the side of the bed and shuffled to the hallway. Put the cold, black receiver against her ear.

She hadn't heard from her niece in nearly four years. Not since the twit called the cops on Buddy. Irene had made Dearie scrape and bow before she agreed not to press charges, but by then they'd slapped Buddy around and tied him to a chair in a cell.

No question whose sharp, bitter voice it was at the other end. "Don't say a word," Irene said. "I still have a party line."

Bile rose into Dearie's mouth but she swallowed it back. Four years ago Irene had told Buddy he was brain-damaged—a load of hooey; the doctors had ruled that out. She'd told the police Buddy was dangerous. More hooey. The boy just made poor decisions sometimes.

"If anything gets out," Irene said, "I'll know it was you and that'll be it for your little psycho."

Dearie could picture her mousy-haired niece with a holier-than-thou hand on her bony hip. "You threatening me?" she said. "An old lady who ain't done nothing but love you since you was a little girl? If your pa was alive he'd be ashamed of you."

Irene hung up.

Dearie looked at the receiver for a few seconds like it might start talking on its own. She stepped into the kitchen for the Lysol. Came back and wiped down the phone in case Irene's venom had seeped through. She strode into her room, yanked the yeasty-smelling sheets off her bed and turned toward Alfie's urn. "Look at me," she said, "lying around for two days like some dying swan. Forgetting the boy needs me to keep telling him everything's gonna be fine."

◦⟨⟩◦

MARCH 13, 1957. An unexpected snowfall silenced all but the low thud of a bass drum steady as a heartbeat, leading the sixth, seventh and eighth graders out of Millard Fillmore and down the middle of Jackson Boulevard. Even kids you'd expect to sing "Found a Peanut" or do something else just as jerky were respectful. It moved Linda to tears that froze on her eyelashes.

The police had closed the route to cars. The students marched through the colored neighborhood, across Main Street and past the railroad station. One right and one left turn and they were at City Hall, where the doors and windows were draped in black and the flag flew at half-mast.

Inside, the body of Officer William Nolan lay in repose.

Linda could picture those words at the top of a panel for "Another Audacious Adventure with Glenn and Gilda Daring." She'd spring the idea on Richie tomorrow. It might be his big chance to get into True Crime comics.

Officer Nolan was the first Stony River cop ever killed on duty. The story had made the front pages of the three papers Daddy brought home. Linda was drawn to the photos in them: a little boy in a rowboat, a skinny young man graduating from the police academy in 1949, a white-jacketed groom the same year, his wife all lace and pearls and fingerless gloves. The one with his little girl on his shoulders would have been enough to break Gilda's heart.

According to the paper, someone who wouldn't leave his name had called and told the police to check the alley between Jacob's Hardware and Bing's Pharmacy where Officer Nolan lay dying. Linda could see the Darings showing up at the alley, Gilda with her Brownie Hawkeye to record clues the police would miss and Glenn with his magic fingerprint kit. In the comic strip townspeople like Mother would be overreacting, blaming it on hoodlums. Richie could draw their doughnut-shaped mouths wailing, "New Jersey isn't safe anymore. We must move to Kansas." Gilda would say, "Compassionate love is the answer."

After they'd heard about Office Nolan, Mother said, "You're not to be out after dark, Linda, or walk around town on your own." As if Linda had ever been allowed to. Daddy had been shaken by the news, too, especially since he'd been a policeman once. "When we lose one, we all hurt," he said. Linda wanted to say she'd met Officer Nolan but was afraid to admit how, even a year and a half later.

The lineup of students from other schools stretched for blocks. Linda made fists inside her mittens to warm her fingers. Her toes were numb and her kerchief soaked with snow by the time she got into City Hall. She and Connie shuffled with the crowd down a slippery hallway and into a large room where a casket sat on a raised platform, guarded by two policemen standing at attention. The casket was closed.

Connie whispered, "They don't want us to see the bullet hole."

The only other dead person Linda had ever known was Grandmother Wise, who'd looked like a corpse months before she actually died. She'd lain "in repose" in a funeral home, but few had shown up to file past her.

Richie said he didn't believe in life after death; that you lived on only in somebody's memory. As soon as the last person who ever knew you died, you would be gone for good. Linda made it a point to remember Grandmother Wise once in a while, even though she'd been cranky.

Walking to Richie's house after school the next day, Linda built the scene in her mind: a sickly looking woman breaks into the drugstore at night, looking for painkillers. A young police officer, acting on a tip that a runaway teenager is taking shelter in the store, catches the woman sneaking into the alley, her pocketbook full of pills. Little does he know she's lifted her husband's old police revolver out of the bedside table and concealed it in her coat. Gilda would arrive at the crime scene and know exactly where the bullet that killed the officer entered. The story needed some filling out, but it would give Richie a good start.

A weary-eyed Mrs. Sulo answered the door but didn't invite Linda in. She said Richie had gone to help out his grandma in Indiana because she'd cracked a rib. Linda wondered why Mrs. Sulo, a nurse, hadn't gone instead, but it would've been impolite to ask.

"How long will he be gone?"

"Hard to tell."

"May I have the address? I'd like to write to him."

"That wouldn't be a good idea," Mrs. Sulo said and shut the door.

Linda walked home on shaky legs, puzzled why Mrs. Sulo had treated her so rudely. She was more than a little hurt: would it have been too much trouble for Richie to say goodbye?

MARCH 24, 1957. Pulling their coats tightly around them, Miranda and Doris sit on a stone bench before a statue of the Virgin, their backs to the gigantic wooden door Miranda once feared would lock her in forever. All about them, the fresh green of new life pokes through thawing ground. This part of spring is Miranda's favorite: the ground soggy from the last of the melted snow, the air smelling of fermented leaves, the trees raising their arms to receive the rain.

The pigeons that roost in St. Bernadette's eaves do their jerky, head-bobbing dance on the gravel footpath fronting the bench. No matter how far away the birds fly, Sister Theodore said, they find their way home. From the time Miranda arrived at St. Bernadette's the prospect of returning to the home she shared with James has sustained her. She knows now it will never be. Mother Alfreda informed her that the house was sold to pay for Cian's keep and her own, offering it as another reason Miranda should consider convent life. Miranda's tears and protests against the injustice of it had no effect. "Self-pity has never reversed a turn of events," Mother Alfreda said.

How easily all you've known can be taken away.

Miranda hasn't seen Doris in a month. Minutes ago, they embraced awkwardly outside the visitors' lounge. Doris didn't offer her typically broad smile and Miranda held back from what: insecurity, hurt, anger? Sometimes her own feelings are beyond her ken. The bench's damp cold bleeds through the dark brown coat she borrowed from the donation bin. Doris is dressed more warmly in gray trousers and a houndstooth coat but her face is pale as paper, her eyes small with fatigue. A slight breeze—*a faerie wind,* the Voice of James whispers—lifts the back of a red kerchief from her hair.

She tells Miranda it happened on the Saturday before the visitors' day she missed without explanation. She's sorry she didn't call; the pain was too new and tender. Miranda's spine begins to soften and her resistance eases into compassion as what Doris relates unfolds like a scene in a novel. A watery-eyed Frank Dunn appears at the door just after midnight, Father Wolchek, the police chaplain, right behind him. Miranda recalls Officer Dunn at her own door nearly three years ago on that sweltering day, a damp shirt sticking to his back. Although she's never met Father Wolchek, she puts Father Shandley's face on him and garbs him in a priestly cassock.

Doris grips Miranda's arm, infusing it with a gentle current of energy. "All Frank could manage was my name," she says. "Father Wolchek had to ask if they could come in. He asked me to take a seat. Told me Bill was shot interrupting a break-in."

Miranda feels a sharp pain in her chest. She's aware of a siren on the street outside St. Bernadette's as she sees Nolan's legs collapse like a marionette's, then the rest of him drop onto the pavement, the dark blue hat Doris has with her today tumbling off his head.

"I got my coat so I could go wherever he was, take care of him." Doris's hands twist Nolan's hat. "Frank found his voice, then. 'He didn't make it, Doris,' he said." She straightens her back and pastes on a plucky smile. "There, I've told you without crying. I couldn't have, even a week ago. I couldn't tell Bill's folks or mine that night. Father Wolchek had to."

Miranda pictures Nolan on a gurney in the room he called the cooler and shudders.

"Oh, sweetie, are you cold?" Doris asks. Her hands vigorously rub Miranda's arms and shoulders through her coat. "Should we walk around?"

Miranda quickly shakes her head, ashamed of concerning Doris at such a time but annoyed as well. She's not some newly orphaned waif needing to be coddled. "May I?" she asks, reaching for the hat. She remembers Nolan balancing it on his knee the day she met him.

"I brought it hoping you would."

Miranda runs her fingers over the gold braid encircling the brim, the gold feathery shapes on the stiff bill and the bronze eagle on the front. She closes her eyes and draws into the blindness all that her fingers have felt. She inhales deeply for a count of six, exhales for six. Repeats until her body feels light and her mind lifted up and free. She envisions the hat big enough to enter. The lining is cold and slippery, redolent with a gray smell of unwashed hair that pinches her nostrils. Fear and urgency reside within. Swirling colors and shapes behind her eyes give way to images. Her lungs tighten. "Two men running, one falling behind, out of breath."

"Is one Bill?"

"I think not. Neither is tall enough." Miranda hasn't seen Nolan since he and Doris left her at St. Bernadette's, but his height has stayed with her. "One has a gun. There's a car. Three shots. Two wounds." How tragically unnecessary it was. She opens her eyes when she hears Doris weeping. The images vanish.

"Don't stop," Doris says. "I'm okay." She smiles weakly. "Honestly, you'd think I'd be all cried out."

"I'll not be seeing more right now," Miranda says. At times this blind sight feels like a curse. It's as though she's behind heavy panes of warped glass. Did she just see what actually happened or only what Doris thinks happened? Miranda folds Doris's hands into hers and fully absorbs the impact the news had on this woman she loves. She feels no personal loss at Nolan's passing but is fond of Carolyn and wee Mickey. She senses the holes already opening in their hearts.

"I can try another time if you'd like."

"I'd like," Doris says.

Doris has often praised Nolan as a devoted father. Miranda knows only the man who sent Nicholas away. She wouldn't have wanted to be at the funeral even if Doris had invited her, but it wounds her sorely that Doris didn't.

DORIS'S MIND STEWED with emotions: awkwardness at having waited to tell Miranda about Bill's death; guilt over not having been able to rescue Miranda and Cian—a guilt aged nearly two years and implacably linked to anger at Bill; and the grief, of course, the heart-stopping grief. Waking up each morning still feeling the weight of him in her arms.

Now this: Miranda hearing three shots and seeing two men besides Bill.

Having Miranda at the funeral would have been a slap at Bill. Adopting her and Cian was out of the question while he was alive. Now, she dared imagine them living with her, away from the clutches of St. Bernadette's—she'd come to see even the building as evil. She felt its eyes on their backs, sensed its jaws eager to seize and devour them both. Doris blamed St. Bernadette's for Miranda's disturbing ability to go into trances and see things others could not. She prayed every night for Miranda's soul. To see the poor girl in that ratty coat with the missing buttons and those dreary black oxfords! Early on, Doris had borrowed money from her mother and bought the child an adorable fitted red wool coat with a black velvet collar, but it had ended up in some communal wardrobe. Doris was dying to get that trim figure into something spiffy, put some pale pink lipstick on her and enough face powder to smooth out the complexion that had lost its milky purity at St. Bernadette's.

She'd need to go to confession for coveting the girl's share of the proceeds from the house sale, but Bill's life insurance wouldn't hold them for more than a year. She'd met with the mother superior and Miranda's tutor this morning. Mother Alfreda said it was unlikely she'd release a child to a single parent.

A single parent.

The awful truth of those words.

Sister Celine asked Mother Alfreda if an exception couldn't be made; Doris was such a faithful visitor. A faint possibility, the reverend mother said, and only if Miranda returned once a month for religious guidance until ready to enter the convent. Mother Alfreda was worried that secular life would "extinguish the light" of Miranda's soul. Sister Celine said experiencing life outside for a while would ensure that Miranda's choice of a religious vocation was freely made. Doris had kept her tongue but was thinking that, once Miranda got a taste of outside, no way in blazes would she go back. She sensed a sad resignation in Mother Alfreda, who nodded finally and said Miranda would have to agree to it. If she did, Doris would petition the court for an advance on the girl's trust fund. Thank the Blessed Virgin the department had covered Bill's funeral.

"Frank came up to me after we buried Bill, his eyes all red," Doris told Miranda. "He was suffering terribly. He said, 'It should have been me. My kids are grown.' That touched me, sweetie." She pulled a hanky from her coat pocket and wiped her eyes. "It made me feel good to know Frank held him as he died, honestly it did." The walls of her throat closed up; she couldn't stop her voice from going thin and shaky. "Since it couldn't be me."

"Oh, look, I've made you cry," she said as Miranda swiped at her eyes with a sleeve.

Doris's small living room had swelled that night with the police chief, the mayor, the editor of the *Record,* the doctor who'd pronounced Bill dead and the rescue squad volunteers who'd responded after hearing the radio call. She didn't tell Miranda she'd tossed everybody out except Frank and Father Wolchek after the mayor said a guardian would have to be appointed for Carolyn and Mickey. The nerve of anyone deciding a child's mother wasn't guardian enough. Thinking about it enraged her all over again that Miranda had come so close to losing Cian.

"How's my little guy?" she asked now. "I miss him something fierce."

Last summer St. Bernadette's had begun allowing Doris to take the children off the grounds on visiting Sundays. She often brought Carolyn and Mickey along. Cian was a dreamy child, good-natured and affectionate. He called her Dori and gave her little wet kisses. She wanted to clasp him to her bosom every five minutes like some bambino-starved Italian grandmother. She hardly noticed anymore that his head was too small for his body. A sunhat she'd bought him when they went down the shore made him appear almost normal.

"He made a spatter painting yesterday," Miranda said. "Rubbed the toothbrush over the screen, then peered underneath quite seriously and said, 'ooh, ooh,' as the white paint came out on the gray construction paper Sister Cameron gave him."

"What was it like, his painting?"

"Like what the pigeons have left us here, I'm thinking."

Doris laughed. The last time she saw Cian he'd hopped on one foot and counted to two for her. She was sure Carolyn had counted higher when she was three, but being bright wasn't everything. What

Doris saw was a child content with whatever the day brought. If that meant he was retarded, she could think of a worse fate. She suspected he'd be further ahead if he had spent the last two years in her care. And poor sweet Miranda, beset with calluses on her knees and visions she couldn't explain. Doris would be forever atoning for abandoning those children. Why did Bill ask her to take care of them that day and then deliver their souls to an orphanage?

She wanted to ask Miranda, Do you hate me? Instead, she said, "How would you feel about coming to live with me? You and Cian. I'll get a job to support us. You can stay home with the kids. On weekends, we'll take them all over the place. It'll be great fun."

MIRANDA HAS ACHED for these words, imagined her heart thickening in gratitude. She wants to ask, Why now? She's often wondered if, at Doris's house two years ago, she did something so terrible that Doris would never bring her home again, not even for an hour. She studies the pigeons strutting around them, unable to spot two with exactly the same coloring. She admires them for not feeling they have to dress alike as jays, robins and nuns must do.

"Mother Alfreda will send me to librarian school if I enter the convent," she says.

"Why would you want to be a librarian?"

Doris's puzzled look is surprising. Miranda is sure she natters on about the library to the point of tedium. "Did I not tell you I'm in charge of story hour for the kindergartners?" In charge is a bit of a boast. Sister Theodore insists on approving the books Miranda reads aloud to the children. Her dark eyebrows reach their greatest height when she dismisses as lewd or anti-Christian some tales Miranda enjoyed as a child and asks to bring into the library. "Sister Theodore says I have the talent and dedication necessary to succeed."

Doris lets out a shuddering sigh. "Of course you do. But what happens to Cian if you enter the convent?"

Miranda has considered that. It would be good for Cian to have a man in his life, but according to Mother Alfreda, she can never be married in a state of grace, for the "foul stain" of incest has forever derailed the possibility of raising Cian in a true Catholic family. No point trying to explain that, since Danú and Dagda were not blood relatives, it couldn't have been incest.

"Father Shandley says Cian can live with him and his housekeeper," she tells Doris. "I can see him whenever I want."

Doris's face acquires sudden color and her eyes grow alarmingly large. She stands and takes a few steps back on the footpath, frightening a wobbling pigeon. She flails her arms. "That's a horrible idea. I won't have you losing Cian again." The pigeon flaps and climbs until it's wheeling high atop St. Bernadette's.

Miranda recalls the pink-and-green striped towels stacked in Doris's bathroom and a shell-shaped dish holding little round soaps, a big window in the front room to let in the sun. Doris's house has a television. Cian would be able to kiss the screen and say "Snap, Crackle, Pop" as he does in the nursery.

"Could I attend librarian school?"

"I don't see why not. There must be night classes."

If Miranda joins the convent she'll become a bride of Christ and wear a plain silver band. Nuns, like pigeons, mate for life. Mother Alfreda says Miranda's destiny is in the convent. Sister Celine says it's in a world without walls. Their competing visions of her future remind her of James's tale of two swineherds who quarreled over whose power was greater, turning themselves into birds, dragons, sea creatures, worms and ghosts to get the better of each other.

"I need to think on it," she says at last. It won't hurt Doris to wait for a change.

❧ FOURTEEN ❧

MAY 12, 1957. Mother's Day. Linda woke to the clatter of pans, slipped into her robe and opened her door at the same time as her father, in pajamas, opened the one across the hall.

"Your mother must have escaped while I was sleeping," he said with a smile Miss Firkser would have described as "wry."

They stumbled down the stairs to the kitchen. Mother was at the stove slapping bacon into a pan. An apron cinched her pink bathrobe, giving the impression of a giant strawberry cream bon-bon.

"I was going to serve you breakfast in bed," Linda said. Toast and half a grapefruit with a maraschino cherry in the middle. She'd fixed the grapefruit the night before, surgically detaching fruit from membrane, dusting it with sugar.

"Don't bother," Mother said. She hadn't put on makeup and her hair was flat in the back, suggesting she'd been in a hurry to get downstairs and cheat them out of doing something nice for her. She wouldn't be going to church, that was obvious. She was already in a state. Before they knew it she'd need to lie down.

She'd ruin everything.

Every year Linda's parents bought pink carnations for dead Grandmother Wise and the still living Grandma Keynes to appear on the altar with the other tribute carnations. Linda was eager to watch Mother's face as she scanned the church bulletin: *For Betty Wise from her loving daughter.* (Linda had deliberated for some time over whether to say *devoted* or *loving*.) She'd arranged for it secretly with Reverend Judge, paying for it with her allowance. She wanted Daddy to be surprised, too, show him the effort she was making to please Mother and not cause her to be sicker than she already was.

Daddy's voice was husky with puzzlement. "Betty? What gives?"

"What does it look like? I'm cooking bacon. You like bacon, right? And Linda needs her strength if she's going to spend the afternoon with someone else's mother."

She spanked a burner with another pan, dropped Crisco into it.

"Oh, so that's it." Daddy put a hand on Mother's shoulder. She shrugged it off. "Be reasonable, dear. It's not the whole afternoon. Only an hour or so. You knew about this."

The Crisco was spitting. Mother cracked three eggs into the pan.

"Don't treat me like an idiot. Of course I knew about the sale. It was me who rummaged through closets and drawers looking for things to contribute. But until last night I had no idea they'd deliver the money today, of all days." She turned to Linda. "You didn't have the decency to tell me yourself. Your father had to before we went to sleep."

Linda thought she might throw up. The youth choir had held a white elephant sale to raise money for Officer Nolan's widow and kids. They'd taken in two hundred and fifty-six dollars and decided Mother's Day would be the perfect occasion to give it to Mrs. Nolan. Mother had been enthusiastic about the sale, as touched as everyone else in town by the young widow and her small children. She'd gone with Linda and Daddy to stand on a curb with hundreds to watch the funeral procession. For over a week, Linda had anticipated Mrs. Nolan's grateful smile. Linda would tell her she'd met her husband and, if it didn't feel rude, ask if the police had found the gun that killed him.

"I didn't think it would be such a big deal," Linda said, swallowing past the ache in her throat. "I wasn't planning to go till after

Valentino's." Every Mother's Day, Daddy and Linda took Mother to Valentino's where dark-suited waiters would fawn over her, hold out her chair and spread a starched napkin over her lap.

"No, you didn't think, did you? You never think when it comes to me."

Linda wanted Mother to drop dead right on the spot.

Daddy said, "I don't think that's fair, Betty."

"That's right. Take her side. You always do." Mother turned the eggs over, breaking the yolks. Linda detested broken yolks.

"I won't go, Mother. The others can give her the money without me."

"Don't do me any favors. And would it kill you to call me Mom? Mothers are dead people or old ladies who get taken to Valentino's." She slapped one egg and a bacon strip on a plate and handed it to Linda. Slapped two eggs and three bacon strips on another plate and handed it to Daddy. "You can fix your own toast."

"Where's your plate?" Daddy asked.

"The hired help doesn't eat with the family."

"Oh, that's rich." Daddy's voice came out hoarse and unsteady. "It may have escaped your notice but Linda and I do most of whatever gets done around here."

Mother's cheeks flushed deep red as though she'd been slapped. She grabbed the three-pronged fork she'd used to turn the bacon and hurled it to the linoleum floor where it stuck on one of the pattern's hideous thick black zigzags that looked like lightning bolts. It quivered there like an arrow. She took off her apron and climbed the stairs, her footsteps slow at first then quicker and quicker. Linda heard a door slam.

Daddy sat at the kitchen table, a little too straight, staring at his plate. "I'm not hungry. You want mine?"

Linda shook her head. "I hate limp bacon."

She didn't think what she'd said was funny but Daddy laughed and laughed. Finally he wiped his eyes with a napkin, blew his nose and said, "Without you I might end it all, you know." He stood and extracted the fork from the linoleum. "I'll go up and get dressed for church if she hasn't barricaded the door."

Linda scooped the bacon and eggs into the garbage and washed the dishes.

She and Daddy had bought Mother a new robe and a mushy, expensive card with lace on it. Before leaving for church, Linda put the gift box and card on the floor outside her parents' room. She crossed out *Mother* on the envelope and wrote *Mom*.

Daddy canceled the reservation at Valentino's and spent the afternoon behind the closed door with Mother. Mom. Linda sat on the porch eating Fig Newtons, wishing she'd gone to Mrs. Nolan's and thinking about that gun. If it turned out to be the one she'd held as Gilda Daring, it would be wrong not to tell the police. But that would be ratting on Richie. ("You rat on me, I swear I'll kill you," Tereza had said the night she ran away.) She couldn't see Richie shooting anyone, still couldn't believe he was gone. She'd checked with Vinnie, Paul and Vlad for weeks after he left but they hadn't heard from him either. The high-school secretary told Vinnie that Richie's parents had taken him out of school for health reasons. They'd left town a week after Richie and had put their house up for sale.

Over deli sandwiches that night, Daddy said, "Your mother and I have decided I'll rent a room from Mrs. Ernst for a while." Mrs. Ernst sang in the choir and ran a boarding house. "It's really something to learn that, in nineteen years, your wife has never had a happy day."

Linda swallowed hard. "She doesn't mean that." She'd never heard her parents do more than bicker, never heard them shout at each other. Shouldn't you shout at least once before you decide to separate?

"Possibly not, but she thinks she does and that's what's important."

Linda couldn't keep the tears out of her words. "Why do *you* have to leave? Why can't she go to Kansas and stay with Grandma?"

Daddy closed his eyes and sighed. "Her doctor's here. You're here. She wants to have more time with you. This might bring you closer."

"I don't want to be close to her. I hate her."

He stood and crossed to where she sat, knelt beside her and looked up with a pained face. "No, no, no. You mustn't."

She looked past him at the wallpaper teakettles, at a panel where they didn't match. "When will I see you?"

"I'll come by every night if possible. You can call me at work anytime. I have no intention of divorcing your mother, if that's what you're thinking. The three of us will always be a family. I'm just giving her the time she says she needs to get better."

"Does it matter what I want?"

"Not right now."

A drop of sweat crept out of Linda's armpit and ran down her ribs. She could already feel the emptiness of the house without Daddy, the absence of his big voice, her mother's silence behind that loathsome closed door.

JUNE 7, 1957. The room smells of talcum and rubber-faced dolls. The antique desk is open, the scarred surface of its drop-down table exposed. James's scratched ladder-back chair waits before the desk. So loud is the pulse in Miranda's ears, she barely registers the gust of words from Doris explaining how she rescued the desk when the house was sold. It stands now between Carolyn's bed and the one Miranda slept on for twelve years, transformed with new sheets and a pink-and-yellow striped bedspread matching Carolyn's.

Doris wants to know if it's a good surprise: the desk, the chair and her old bed. When Miranda left St. Bernadette's with Cian this morning, she carried only her journal, a high-school diploma, James's red shoes and his billfold.

Doris natters on. She and Bill had no place for the other furnishings. But they saved all the books. Bill had to bring in a ladder to reach the top shelves, something Doris finds heroic, judging from her tone. Miranda wouldn't believe how many books were infested with silverfish. They brought them back, spread them out on the basement floor and set the fan on them before putting them back in the boxes. The records bowled Doris over. She didn't know Miranda's father, of course, but even so she wouldn't have expected him to be a fan of old bands and that baby-voiced flapper. By the way, they found a shotgun in a closet. Bill turned it in at the station.

Doris points out the desk's sprung lock, which Bill suspected was a runaway's doing. The one Doris had brought her the newspaper article about. Would Miranda be able to tell if anything had been taken? Miranda shakes her head. Fortunately, Doris says, the deed to the house was there along with a property tax record; apparently James was paying the taxes in cash once a year. Does Miranda know where he might have gotten that cash? She doesn't; the girls at St. Bernadette's ridiculed the belief in a money tree right out of her.

Doris points out a compartment with sealed envelopes she didn't feel right opening. And what was Miranda's father doing with the creams and dried leaves in the lower drawers? For years James has been Miranda's private property. Even confronted with items so intimately connected to him, she can't begin to explain him and doesn't want to. When Doris says they also lugged over boxes from the basement, Miranda's tongue goes dry. She waits. No mention of the altar or what was on it. Doris says the boxes are in the basement below their feet.

Moments later Miranda perches on a book carton next to the washing machine, under the glare of a naked bulb. Doris has gone to "ride herd" over the three little ones whose wee hooves gallop overhead. Heavy black ink marks boxes of BOOKS, RECORDS, MISCELLANEOUS. In the damp basement air, Miranda's bone-white legs miss their novitiate tights. Doris brought her home in a yellow flowered sundress, brown loafers and white socks folded down into cuffs. She suggested Miranda begin "working on a tan" and shaving her legs.

On the floor to Miranda's right, the oak phonograph winks in the light. She shoves boxes aside to get to it. She squats, opens the lid and fingers the green felt turntable. Spare needles are still in the cup and the crank is stored in the lid. Her eyes fill as she recalls the fire rising and falling on the wall while James announced clarinet, trombone, piano, violin and guitar as each entered a song.

You can discern a culture's traits by observing its deities and music, James told her. He'd reflect on the transportability of both from one culture to another. With a concertina, he said, Miranda's favorite record, "I'm an Old Cowhand," would be indistinguishable in sentiment from a Gaelic piece about a wandering laborer. She didn't have James's knowledge of anthropology. She simply treasured the communion with him that the crackling music offered. She closes her eyes, remembering the feel of his rough trousers against her face and his hand absentmindedly stroking her hair. She's someone's daughter again, touched with love.

The sisters were wrong. She wasn't violated. She was chosen. Danú confirmed that.

She feels a flush of warm air like an oven door opening: the Voice of James urging her to not fear what's in the boxes.

She opens a carton and unleashes a stale smell.

Paradise Regained. The History of Rome. On the Motion of the Head and Blood in Animals. She lifts out each volume cautiously lest it crumble in her fingers. *L'âge de raison. Great Expectations. Parallel Lives. De occulta philosophia.* A few are swollen with damp. *The Prince. Apology. The Elements.* Time has darkened the pages of others around the edges.

Gargantua. The Aeneid. Mathematical Principles of Natural Philosophy. Cuchulain of Muirthemne. She sets each book on the floor. *Beyond Good and Evil. Candide. The Nibelungenlied. Irish Witchcraft and Demonology.* James's penciled notes in the margins of some volumes catch at her heart. *Sex and Repression in Savage Society. Argonauts of the Western Pacific. Sons and Lovers. Critique of Pure Reason.*

Memories like fingers and hands grip her belly and chest.

Such joyous pain.

Heroic Romances of Ireland. The Death-Tales of the Ulster Heroes. The Golden Bough. Brave New World. Tarzan of the Apes. Witchcraft, Oracles and Magic Among the Azande. These would likely be on Sister Theodore's prohibited list. Miranda wants to read them all the more if they are, wants to savor words and ideas so powerful they must be banned.

Quickly now she unpacks the remaining volumes, setting them end to end, alphabetically by author, forming a serpent of books across the floor, her hands agile with purpose. Ah, here are those whose worlds she naively once believed existed outside their pages. *Don Quixote de la Mancha. Ivanhoe. Gulliver's Travels.* And others that befriended her all those lonely years. *Oliver Twist. Emma. Twenty Thousand Leagues Under the Sea. The Hunchback of Notre Dame.* For Cian, Carolyn and Mickey she sets aside *Winnie-the-Pooh, The Wind in the Willows, Through the Looking-Glass, The Jungle Book* and children's versions of the *Iliad* and the *Odyssey.*

James said that if words could be held and tasted and smelled they might be enough to live on. He ferried most of these volumes from Ireland and purchased others later so that she could hear the literary voices of her birth country: *Gone with the Wind, Moby-Dick, The Last of the Mohicans, Of Mice and Men, A Tree Grows in Brooklyn*—she so wanted Francie to be her sister! She knows not how James paid for those books unless by card tricks in pubs. Her favorite was when he changed the colors of the aces.

Over here, the Voice calls. *The cartons from our basement.*

Under rags she finds the altar cloth, chalice, James's cord of knots, the bells, drinking horn, wand and the candle, now soft and misshapen. The candle symbolized awareness, James said. She'd nearly forgotten. She pulls it out and sniffs the soapy smell of the wax.

She wrenches open another box. Hidden beneath a telephone that never rang and lamps that were never lit are the black drapes and the map James drew of their spiritual homeland. Here are the forests and plains, coastline and isles he traversed during meditations and trances, a landscape he said would open up to her in good time.

How careful and methodical he was, journeying in Miranda's eleventh year to the Isle of Labyrinths to seek advice from the magi there. They told him a sacred coupling would bear fruit only if it took place on the thirteenth day before Miranda's thirteenth birthday: Bealtaine, as it happened. For two years they made ready, Miranda prouder and happier than she'd ever been, with James devoted to her preparation. He cast a spell to make her fertile. She recalls holding smooth stones he brought in from the mystical river behind their house and, when she was twelve, drinking a potion to initiate her menses.

Frenetically now she undoes the remaining boxes but can't locate the harp, the blade and the necklace. How could some items have found their way here but not those? The chalice, at least, has not been lost. Winding around its stem is the likeness of a faerie James said protected women from men. Its cloudy pewter surface is cool and smooth in her hands. "Peasant's silver," James called it. The chalice's worth, he explained, was in its emptiness, representing as it did the vagina from which all nature is born. It held the favored position on their altar once Dagda and Danú had called them. James positioned the drinking horn below it to remind them that the wisdom that is Dagda would be prostrate at the feet of the love and compassion that is Danú. Miranda trembles at the realization that her great-grandmother, too, once lifted this very chalice to her lips and felt that first burning sip of wine.

She extracts the wand, a hard, pale brown stick cut from a rowan tree in her great-grandmother's native Donegal, with which James invoked Dagda and Danú. Miranda welcomed them with the tiny jingle bells. Holding the wand in one hand, jingle bells in the other, she closes her eyes and hears James's robe brush the floor like a broom. Breathes in and out until her body is no more than a hum. Behind her eyelids, shapes billow outward—a jingle bell swelling until its keyhole-like openings rise into giant doors. Her feather self floats through one into a vast echoing chamber where James, in black robe and bare feet, lobs a metal ball against the walls, ringing the bell so loudly that Miranda must cover her ears with her hands. Her heart wants to explode with rapture. The chalice magically appears in his hand. He lifts it as to Heaven and chants, "Truly, truly, I say to you, unless you drink the blood of your mother, you have no life in you." When Miranda reaches for the chalice a woman rises from it, naked and sorrowful, her arms holding out a tangerine. As Miranda tries to grasp the fruit, the woman falls from the chalice in a torrent of salt and blood. It carries her and Miranda away, through the giant bell door and into nothingness. Miranda is back in the ocean on that day she thought she might drown until James calls out, "You've always known how to swim!"

She opens her eyes to Doris's stricken face. And finds herself on the cool cement floor.

≷ FIFTEEN ≷

JUNE 22, 1957. Dearie stood up for Tereza and Herman for Buddy. Herman let them use the restaurant before it opened. They could've taken the big room, but Tereza chose the ladies' lounge because it was cozy, plus she and Buddy could face the mirror and be their own audience. The lounge gave off that good clean ammonia stink. The only other person was the Justice of the Peace, a porky man in a light gray suit; you could watch the jacket ride up over his ass in the mirror as he spoke. Tereza wouldn't have minded having Richie there, now that it was safe, but Buddy said Richie and his folks had vamoosed, like Ma, Jimmy and Allen. Tereza wanted Mary Lou, the Polaroid girl from the restaurant, to take pictures, but Dearie said the fewer folks the better so Herman brought his fancy camera from home.

Dearie had made Tereza a sleeveless white linen dress with a scooped neck and a short veil that fell from a little crown of phony pearls. She'd swept Tereza's hair back with fancy little combs. Tereza had bought herself satiny white shoes with four-inch heels so that Buddy wouldn't have to bend down too far to kiss her. Herman showed up with a huge bunch of red carnations for Tereza to hold and one for Buddy's lapel. They smelled like cloves. Buddy was in the same suit he'd worn at high-school graduation the week before. Dearie complained his black boots weren't proper wedding gear, but Buddy said they were like a trademark.

The ceremony was boss. Tereza nearly snorted when she found out Buddy's real name was Eldon. The part she liked best was when he put Dearie's "something old" silver wedding band on her finger. Tereza didn't get to say "with this ring" for him because he said guys who wore wedding bands were sissies. When the JP said "You can now kiss the bride"—their first kiss—Buddy brushed his lips over hers so fast she hardly knew it was happening. Later, Herman popped a bottle of ginger ale.

Tereza had been dumbstruck when Buddy asked her to marry him, especially since he'd been in a funk for a couple months and had stopped going to the movies with her. But then his boss told him A&P was looking for smart, hard-working guys to work their way up and that there was no reason he couldn't manage a store one day; there were over four thousand. Dearie said that would be the ticket to show Buddy was the respectable type, not one to be getting in trouble, and Buddy had bucked up a little. When he found out that A&P liked their managers to be married, Dearie said why wait, do it now, otherwise Tereza was going to have to move out. Dearie wasn't blind: she'd seen her mooning over Buddy and that spelled jailbait. Tereza thought she should become a star first, but Dearie pointed out that A&P had stores in California and Buddy could be transferred to Hollywood someday. In the end, Tereza decided it would be cool to have a husband.

She wasn't old enough to marry, but Dearie knew somebody who made up a phony birth certificate that said Tereza Ladonna Lange had turned sixteen in April. "One year's difference won't make no never mind," Dearie claimed. Even so, she was nervous enough about it to not want a crowd at the wedding. The certificate got the month, day and state right, at least. Ma had told her she'd been born in Broken Arrow, North Dakota. Dearie found out there was no such place and figured Ma had been making a funny, so the certificate said Fargo.

They spent the night in the hotel Tereza had tried to get into on Halloween a couple years ago. Buddy had said, "Where'd you like to go?" and Tereza knew right away. Herman booked it for them. A different guy was at the desk when Buddy signed them in as Mr. and Mrs. Eldon Jukes, both still in their wedding clothes so they'd look legit. The guy didn't ask for their marriage license or any other ID. Just said, "We value Mr. Schottler's business." The room wasn't as big as she expected but nicer than she'd ever seen, with curvy-legged white furniture and a high bed. Buddy called down and asked the color of the carpet, drapes and bedspread because she wanted to know and they said "champagne." He filled the ice bucket with water and put her carnations in it. Red and champagne looked boss together.

They ordered room service: a steak for Buddy and for Tereza chicken à la king that didn't live up to its royal name. Tereza had brought along strawberry-shortcake-scented bath crystals but Buddy said bubble baths weren't manly. He agreed to watch *her* take one (she'd pinched the idea from *True Confessions*), but seeing her naked didn't get him excited. She put on the short black nightie Dearie had bought her and said, "Hold me over your head with one arm like Richie said you could do." He did, stripping down to skivvies first, and she felt dizzy with desire.

They were laughing when he tossed her onto the swanky, satiny bedspread. He straddled her, bent his head and kissed her gently, his lips as soft as Wonder Bread. She pried them open with her tongue. He pulled his mouth away and rolled off her. "The human mouth is a petri dish," he said, whatever the hell that was. He switched on the TV, said, "Look, *Gunsmoke* is on." Propped up the pillows and gestured toward them. "M'lady?"

Tereza was still on her back, staring up at the dangly lamp with bulbs that looked like candles. She took the hand Buddy held out. They sat in bed, hands on each other's crotches, watching TV. Buddy's balls were beanbag squishy even though she was squeezing them half to death. She pulled his limp dick through the opening in his skivvies, ducked down and put it in her mouth. He pushed her head away roughly. "What are you doing?"

"Trying to make you feel good."

"Don't. It's degrading." He pulled away, stood and tromped to the TV. Turned it off.

"What's degrading mean?" Tereza thought about all the guys she'd done at Tony's. Nobody'd ever complained before.

"Shameful. Unbecoming a wife."

"Well, if you don't get stiff, you can't stick it in me."

"What kind of talk is that?" He stood by the TV popping his knuckles.

"So, what do you want me to do?" Buddy was starting to piss her off.

Then it was like somebody had flicked a switch on him that said Act Cool. He hunched his shoulders and stuck his arms straight out in front, hands pointing down. He staggered stiff-legged toward her. "Frankenstein vill show you," he said.

She laughed and screamed in mock fear. In *The Creature Walks Among Us* the horny man-fish monster breaks down a door to get to the blonde actress. Buddy was much better looking.

Frankenstein grabbed her ankles and yanked them till she was flat on the bed, nightie scrunched around her waist. "Don't move," he said in a monster-perfect voice and made his face go blank. He straddled her, put his hands around her neck and squeezed gently. It scared her a little but it felt good, too. His dick rose through his skivvies like a tent pole. She waited for him to rip her nightie off. But he kept squeezing her neck, harder and harder, until she thought her eyes would pop out. When a little strangling sound came from her throat he pulled his hands away. He flopped onto her like a dying fish and rubbed his dick up and down against her leg.

True Confessions had stories about guys who liked doing it crazy

ways. Dearie said her wedding night had been full of surprises. You
had to have an open mind.

JULY 9, 1957. Linda would get to tell tomorrow's flannel-board
story at Summer Vacation Bible School. Eleanor Judge, the minister's
young wife, who had the loveliest honey-colored hair and didn't need
a lick of makeup, had already coached her to focus on the lesson, not
the figures.

"Don't say, 'Look at Noah's bright robe and his big beard.' Say,
'See how Noah obeyed God and went into the ark.'" To Mrs. Judge,
Bible lessons all came down to this: when we get too full of ourselves
and forget God's in charge, it turns out badly.

Today's lesson was about the pitiful Job. Because the Sunday-
school rooms trapped the heat, leaving her charges whiny and listless,
Mrs. Judge had taken the eight boys and twelve girls into the cooler
sanctuary where they sat, cross-legged, on the burgundy-carpeted dais
below the altar. Linda and Mrs. Judge presided on altar chair thrones,
the flannel board on an easel between them. Had Linda known they'd
be entering the sanctuary, she would've worn a dress like Mrs. Judge,
not her irreverent Bermuda shorts and peasant blouse.

As Mrs. Judge recited Job's story, Linda placed the flannel-
backed paper people, animals and objects on the soft cloth board.
Some figures appeared in more than one story. Add paper crown and
sword to Joseph, for example, and he doubled as the clever King
Solomon whose proposal to slice a baby in half made children gasp
in horror. The figure Linda put up now, a kneeling man in a loin-
cloth whose paper face was spotted with boils and whose hands were
raised to Heaven in perpetual anguish, could only be Job.

"Ooh," the children's sad voices said when God let Satan take
away all the animals that had made Job the richest man in the land.

They had to pretend that the single woolly sheep Linda placed on the board was equal to seven thousand, the camel to three thousand, the ox and donkey to five hundred each. "Yay!" they said at the end when God rewarded Job with twice as many animals as he'd lost. All because he finally got it: don't question God. He's the most powerful being in the universe. He gives and takes away because He can.

"Twice as many," Mrs. Judge said with awe in her voice. "Can anyone imagine such a number?" The nine-year-old daughter of Hungarian refugees the church had sponsored last year raised her hand. "Bless your heart," Mrs. Judge said.

Old Mrs. Lambert banged away at the ancient upright's sticking keys—the organ was only for Sundays—as everyone sang "This Is My Father's World." The words *in the rustling grass I hear him pass; he speaks to me everywhere* made Linda tear up because God had never spoken to her and she wanted Him to so badly.

Job's lesson, Mrs. Judge said, was that we should accept suffering with patience, trust and humility. "God lets us suffer because He loves us and wants us to be lovable to others, too," she told the children. "Imagine your mom and dad gave you a puppy."

A boy in the front row clapped.

"Thank you Jeffrey. Now, if you didn't train it to behave, no one but you would love your puppy and want to be near it. So, if you're suffering, it's because God's training you to become more lovable."

Was God training Betty Wise?

The two weeks of Vacation Bible School were up Friday. Linda would be stuck at home listening to things that made her want to cut her ears off:

He seemed happy enough to leave, didn't he?

When you're married, men have certain demands. They don't care if it hurts.

Mom stayed upstairs when Daddy visited, and would later ask, "What did your father have to say for himself tonight?" Linda would shrug, go to her room, eat cookies she'd stashed under the bed and add to her list of those worse off than her: Julius and Ethel Rosenberg's kids, Anne Frank, the Hungarian refugees River Street Methodist *wasn't* able to sponsor, most colored people, lepers, kids with polio. All worse off than Betty Wise, too. Linda had tried to nudge her mother toward more positive thinking with magazine articles about people who'd overcome terrible odds, like the armless woman who painted landscapes holding a brush in her teeth, until Mom had said, "I know what you're doing. You and your father think everyone has to be useful, like a potato peeler. Well, I'm not a potato peeler."

After the flannel-board lesson, Linda herded the kids into the main hall where they drew pictures of Job's animals until their parents arrived to pick them up. Mrs. Judge sent Linda off with Rice Krispies squares left over from the mid-morning snack. Yesterday it had been chocolate chip cookies; the day before, brownies. "For your mom," Mrs. Judge would say, but Linda would gobble them all on the way home.

Today she'd take the longer route past the A&P. They were out of bread and tea bags. She'd rather get Job's boils than shop at Rolf's. The A&P was next to a soda fountain where she planned to sit at the marble counter on a swively red-padded stool and order a cherry Coke. She wasn't in a hurry.

When Linda got home, Mom would be in her room, lying primly on her chenille bedspread, ankles crossed, fanning herself with *The Ladies' Home Journal*. She'd moan about how "boiling hot" it was, as she'd done for the past three days. Linda would have to adjust her eyes to the dim light; the drawn curtains created a permanent dusk. She'd sit on the dressing table bench while her mother went into revolting detail about constipation and stool softeners. She'd count the hours until Daddy stopped by for their nightly chat. He'd hug her as though he hadn't seen her for weeks. They hardly ever ran out of things to say to each other; when they did, they watched TV.

It would take forty minutes to get to her front door.

Forty minutes to remind herself God was in charge.

BETTY SPRAWLED on the sagging couch, one shoeless foot on the floor. She was recovering from taking the bus in boiling heat to and from Lou's office and having talked him into giving her a job. Golly, where she'd gotten the gumption she didn't know. Her heart was still banging around in her chest.

She hadn't gone to her appointment with a job in mind. But while Lou Pierce's nurse, Rose, was taking her blood pressure and complaining about having to work overtime, the idea leaped up and shook hands with Betty's brain. "He pays me for the time," Rose said, "but I'm a nurse, not a bookkeeper. And I need to be home with my kids more."

"Why doesn't he hire someone else?"

"He's tried. Can't find anyone willing to come in the odd hours he needs them."

Betty had worked as church secretary after she came to New Jersey. That was how she'd met Roger. "Why not hire me?" she asked Lou later, quaking inside at her own temerity. "I can type, keep accounts. And I'm free to come in anytime you want, provided the bus is running."

"Heart's good. Lungs are clear," he said, pulling the stethoscope from his fleshy ears. "What about the pain?"

"You told Roger it's all in my head, right? Maybe I just need to be busy. How about it, Lou? Put your money where your mouth is."

She got him good with that one. His wide, normally pale face went strawberry.

She'd start on Thursday. Wouldn't Linda be surprised!

Betty had known Lou for years; he'd seen Mother Wise through her cancer. She'd only come to like him since Roger left. She got so much more out of talking to him without Roger circling about, jumping in to contradict her. As if she didn't know her own pain or how little she slept. She'd convinced Lou to stop giving her pills that made her dopey. She needed to be alert for Linda's sake, get her back to eating better.

When Roger left, a great silence had fallen over the house, awful and swell at the same time. For the first few days, Betty was afraid she'd balled up the works for Linda and herself. But something she couldn't name had been writhing to get out of her. She'd dreaded Roger's footsteps on the stairs to their room when he got home from work, the twist of the doorknob, his infuriating "How's my Sleeping Beauty today?" He knew she rarely slept, even at night. The certainty of pain kept her as vigilant as a new mother. Even now the area around her rib cage was tight, causing her to take baby breaths and pant like a dog. She never knew when the tightness would work its way down to her pelvis and turn into fire.

Reverend Judge had come to pray over her shortly after Roger moved out. He said pain's divine purpose was to shatter the illusion that we were self-sufficient, to remind us we must submit to God's will. His words were no comfort at all.

She checked her wristwatch. Linda would be home soon. She pulled herself up and tried to slow her breathing. Fingered the worn spot on the arm of the drab brown couch that had been Mother Wise's. She'd wanted to replace it for years but Roger always found some sentimental memory stuck behind a cushion. She wouldn't earn much at Lou's but surely enough to buy slipcover material. She hadn't used the Singer in a while, had made most of Linda's clothes until fifth grade when it embarrassed the child to be seen in homemade duds.

Roger stopped in nightly to see Linda. He never came upstairs, which was just fine. It irked Betty to hear him clomping around as if he still lived there, opening the Frigidaire or the cookie jar Linda kept filled, the racket of him rising through the register in Betty's room.

She hadn't told her parents yet or her sister and brothers out in Kansas. They wouldn't approve. But Betty couldn't think anymore with Roger around; she didn't know where he ended and she began. She reckoned she shouldn't have married at all, but what choice did a woman have? Roger phoned each morning to see if she and Linda needed anything. He would have taken her to the doctor's but darned if she'd ask. She had Linda call if the toilet overflowed or anything else went wrong in the house. It was like being sprung from a girdle not having to hear the exasperated patience in Madge Bryson's voice: Are you sure you want me to interrupt him, Mrs. Wise?

She looked at her watch again, a Bulova, a gift from Roger for their fifth anniversary. She'd been hinting for a hope chest. Most girls got one before they were married, but her parents couldn't afford such a thing. She'd asked Roger if what he was getting her needed two people to carry it and he said yes. So didn't he go and carve two men from plywood, nail them to a board and put the watch box between them. She hadn't thought of that in years.

JULY 21, 1957. Buddy's bed was big enough for two people, like he'd known Tereza would share it one day. On this Sunday morning, she sat against the headboard plodding through *The Facts of Married Life,* tracking each word with her finger. She'd borrowed it from the library after asking for a book that would tell you what was normal or not. The librarian gave her one with big words and boring school-book-y stuff but it had a chapter she was keen to struggle through.

Some people do not respond sexually to their lovers.

Buddy was off from Saturday morning until midnight Monday. Sundays they woke up together, Buddy sometimes turning to her wild-eyed, like he was surprised to find her in his bed. Today he'd bounced up and said, as he often did, "Don't dilly-dally." Atlas words.

At the moment he was naked before the full-length mirror, watching himself exercise. Tereza was naked, too, because it was damned hot up there even at eight in the morning. Buddy said it was a scientific fact that heat rose. The fan on his desk going *swish-swish* only shoved around hot air from the open window at the end of the long, narrow room.

The male sex glands are two firm oval bodies about one and a half inches long. They hang between the thighs in a sac called the scrotum.

Was that supposed to mean balls? She looked up from the book. Clasping his hands behind his head, Buddy bent down and touched his elbows to his knees. His leg and back muscles twitched. Compared to his tanned parts, his ass looked like a peeled orange.

"Why are guys' asses higher than girls'?" she asked.

"I'd rather you said *buttocks*." His bent-over voice sounded strangled.

She made a face into the book. Nobody said buttocks.

In its relaxed position, the penis hangs just in front of the scrotum.

"And it's probably biological," Buddy said. "That's the reason for nearly everything."

She looked up again. He was doing squats now, his penis definitely relaxed, sweat beading on the bush around it like dew.

If Buddy's room had been an ice-cream flavor it would've been vanilla: white walls with no pictures, a wood floor, desk, chair and dresser all painted white, no rug. Once a week he scrubbed the walls, floor and furniture with a concoction of ammonia, vinegar, baking soda and water. It didn't smell anything like vanilla.

He had let her hang her Grace Kelly coat and suit, wedding dress, dungarees and uniform next to his jacket, shirts and pants in the open closet. Her pumps, white heels, flats and briefcase sat beside his boots. He'd cleared out a dresser drawer for her. She kept her makeup in her pocketbook because he didn't like anything cluttering the dresser top. An exception was a framed picture from their wedding. Herman had caught Buddy looking off to the right, both arms around Tereza's waist and his chin resting on her head. Buddy liked it because he looked like "a good guy, not me." Herman had caught Tereza laughing right into the camera, looking like somebody you could love, somebody she wouldn't have imagined herself to be.

The clitoris is not unlike a rudimentary penis.

Tereza pulled her knees up and peered down between her legs. Either the book was bull or her body was busted 'cause she didn't have anything like a penis, rudi-whatchamacallit or not.

She slipped into red shorts and a black blouse and went downstairs to pee. Dearie's door was still closed. Tereza made a little noise coming back up the stairs, in case Buddy wanted to scare her. On Sundays, he often hid behind the door and jumped out when she returned from the bathroom. At first he'd only needed her to *act* scared to get hard. Lately he had to believe it was real. Convincing him was good practice. Actresses had to ignore the camera, the director and anybody else watching when they did a scene. Pretend they were going through whatever it was for the first time, even after a hundred takes. Tereza had to forget about Dearie sleeping downstairs and let out her scariest scream, trusting Buddy would put his hand over her mouth. Today when she got back upstairs he was doing push-ups.

She sat on the bed and picked up the book again. *Orgasm in the man is noticeably marked by the ejaculation of semen.* Why couldn't books use words you didn't have to look up?

She hadn't minded being scared when it was a game, but not when it felt real. Like when he'd almost strangled her with a necktie or jumped out at her waving the switchblade he kept in his desk.

Rapid breathing and a series of spasmodic sensations, which reduce her tension, mark the woman's climax.

Tereza reduced her "tension" alone in the bed at night when Buddy was on shift. It was no big deal—she'd been doing it since she was ten. She'd thought it would be different when she got married, that was all. Dearie had given her a hot water bottle with a nozzle and tube to use "after" but so far there hadn't been any after.

The lower end of the vagina has a thin, pliable membrane called the hymen.

She softly tried out the last word. It sounded like Dearie saying Herman.

She stood and peered at the schedule on the wall beside Buddy's desk. He'd be waxing the car this morning. Her morning was free since Dearie fixed breakfast on Sundays. His afternoon was designated for "Tereza." Hers, natch, said "Buddy." She ignored the schedule when it didn't suit her but mostly she went along, hoping it would make Buddy want her more. Plus, she didn't know what might set him off. She didn't want him putting his fist through a wall, sticking his head in a pail of water or something worse.

"Want to go to the show this afternoon?" She enunciated the words, trying not to say wanta. "*I Was a Teenage Werewolf* is playing."

Buddy was ass-down on the floor now, his heels on the bed, doing sit-ups. "We should talk about finances today. I'm not going down the shore tomorrow. I'm taking you to the bank."

Tereza never went to the shore with Buddy on his Mondays off because he couldn't guarantee they'd be back by the time she had to be at Herman's. She'd begun counting on him being away. Mondays before work she was scheduled for laundry, but Dearie did it for her so that she could go to the Linden pool where there was always a herd of boys to tell her she was sexy. Sometimes she let them feel her up.

She straddled the desk chair and stared down at him. "What for?"

"To open a joint account so I can deposit your tips with my pay each week."

Tereza's gut ached watching his long, flat belly muscles lift him from the floor. Up. Down. Ouch. "I don't like the idea of locking up my money. What if I need something?"

Up. Down. "First of all, it's our money now. Same as my pay is our money. Secondly, you can have an allowance. This afternoon we'll talk about how much you need."

"Maybe I need it all."

Up. Down. "That's selfish. It's our turn to look after Dearie."

"Jimmy used to take what Ma made. She couldn't buy nothing without his say so."

"She couldn't buy *anything*. I'm not Jimmy so don't give me your tough look."

He put his hands behind him and lifted his legs and his chest till his body made a V. Lowered and lifted them again.

"Do you love me?"

"I married you, didn't I?" Lower. Lift.

"That don't mean you love me. You never say it."

"Well, I do." Lower. Lift.

"Say it."

"I love you." Lower. Lift.

Tereza twisted her wedding ring around and around. "It ain't right I'm still a virgin."

Buddy took his heels off the bed, brought his knees up and made like riding a bike. He touched his left elbow to his right knee, then right to left.

Tereza got up from the chair and stood over him. "Did you hear me?"

He didn't answer.

"We both had blood tests. You saw mine. It said I don't have a disease."

Elbow to knee. Pedal. Elbow to knee. Pedal.

"Don't you want to feel what it's like inside me?"

Dearie's "Breakfast!" floated up the stairwell.

Buddy leaped up without using his hands, like some Ed Sullivan acrobat act. He toweled off the sweat and put on old bathing trunks and a gray T-shirt, his car-washing clothes.

Tereza blocked his way to the door. "On Mondays I go to the pool, not the bank."

Buddy banged his head on the wall, hard, one, two, three times, leaving an angry blotch on his forehead. He turned to the mirror and said, "Behold. The mark of the devil." Tereza gripped the railing as they went downstairs to the smell of coffee and something sweet.

Dearie flashed them a grin. "How are my little bride and groom today?"

SIXTEEN

JULY 28, 1957. Miranda summons the courage to confront the sealed envelopes Doris has pestered her to open: "Cian's birth certificate could be there. I can't believe you're not curious."

Miranda knows she won't find Cian's birth certificate. It doesn't exist. Lack of a sign, not curiosity, has kept her back: she's not held James's voice in her throat for weeks. If he wanted her to open the envelopes, wouldn't he have spoken?

The priest's homily today—"Expose your fears to God's healing light"—reminded her of Sister Celine's admonition to "face what you don't want to know about your father." Doris has taken the children to visit her parents. How much more of a sign does Miranda need?

She sits at the scarred desk, slides out the compartment containing the envelopes and chooses one at random. Inside: two sheets of thick, soft paper the color of rice pudding. Not the onionskin on which James, concerned about postage, penned letters to his mother before her death. Miranda lifts these indulgent pages to her nose and sniffs the ink: a faintly sharp smell. On them, a missive dated on Miranda's fifteenth birthday. Only weeks before James died.

My darling Eileen, the letter begins in the swirls and delicately shaded letters of James's script—Miranda stifles a gasp. *Am I evil? Will she mourn me? Her fingers are as long and slender as yours. Pallid as the snow she touched only the once, the night I cracked open the back door to the transformed landscape and told her we'd been visited by snow angels. Palsied with fright at the risk I was taking. Jubilant at the wonder in her eyes.*

The trembles come over Miranda's hands and shoulders at the possibility James lied about Eileen dying from food poisoning. She opens the other envelopes, each containing a letter written on an anniversary of Miranda's birth. Allows her eyes only snippets: *Sometimes I think I'm just an old drunk playing with the faeries ... I hold onto her as though there's no gravity ... Have I lost my sense of what is forbidden?* She imagines her mother alone someplace—where, why?—hungry for news of her daughter.

Tucked into one letter is a faded photograph: a young woman, the heels of her white sling-back shoes sinking into a tidy lawn in front of a Hansel and Gretel house. The slender woman wears a long-skirted white suit and clutches three lilies. Her alien face stares back at Miranda, a hint of resignation in its cautious smile, the eyes shaded by a floppy white hat. Written on the photo's underside in James's hand is *Maryland, Sept. 1939.*

Miranda rubs her fingers gently over the slippery surface and senses energy still resident there. She closes her eyes and drinks deeply of air, enlarges the photograph in her mind until it is big enough to enter. She steps briefly into its sunny afternoon, then into the welcome coolness of a long hallway paneled in dark wood. Her inner eyes adjust to the dim light. A different woman with a halo of wispy gray hair appears from around a corner, smiles and waves Miranda forward. "You're just in time. I didn't want to be the only witness."

Three vases of lilies flood the parlor with a cloying scent that constricts Miranda's lungs. The woman in white and two men huddle around a console radio in the middle of the room. Though clean-shaven and impossibly young, the man in the pale blue suit can only be James—the tilt of that head with its unruly ginger curls, the already slouching shoulders. He listens intently, hands shoved in pockets, but when Miranda enters the room he gazes up with a smile so joyous she could swoon.

A crackling voice, full of regret, pulls him back to the radio: "... I have to tell you now that no such undertaking has been received, and that consequently this country is at war with Germany."

The other man, dark-suited and cherry-faced, says, "You're not likely to forget this wedding anniversary."

The woman in white notices Miranda and starts. "This changes everything," she says. Her voice is nasal, harsh.

"Sure and doesn't it," James says. He opens his arms to Miranda in a wide embrace.

The woman glares at him and presses her stomach with both hands. Miranda plunges into a dark, warm pool where the only sound is a steady *lub dub, lub dub*. Her lungs drink a berry-sweet liquid with a bitter aftertaste that suffuses her veins with revelation: the woman wants to flush Miranda from her womb.

"Go back," James says, his voice simultaneously muffled and clear.

Next, the sound of a barking dog. Nicholas?

Miranda opens her eyes, alone once more in the room she shares with Carolyn. She steps to the window: a neighbor's dog, a collie, not a shepherd. She returns to the desk and slides the photograph into its envelope. Kneels beside her bed and whispers, "I cannot do this, Sister."

EVERY DAY BRINGS MUCH to distract her from James's letters: story time with the wee ones; the nightly news from Chet Huntley's sonorous voice; the library she's set up in the living room; the detective who brings her objects to enter; Doris's prodigious Task List.

So many distractions. Yet, here she sits abed with a flashlight casting a pool on the pages in her lap. She has chosen more letters at random and has prayed to Mary and Danú for protection. She keeps a wary eye on Carolyn a few feet away, asleep with her arms flung out, not even a sheet covering her this sweltering night. The child's bubble-bath scent permeates the humid air. Miranda is atop her own sheets, wearing whimsically named shorty pajamas patterned in pink rosebuds on white cotton.

Eileen's shorty pajamas would be silk. Miranda pictures her reclining on a chaise longue in a sanatorium in the Swiss Alps, sipping a tall lemonade laced with mint, each swallow a cruel reminder of her bittersweet exile, necessary to shield her daughter from the pernicious consumption from which she suffers. Despite the mountain height, nary a breeze finds its way through the open window. Eileen fans herself with her dear, brave husband's letters before reading the one written on the seventh birthday of the daughter she sorely misses.

You might rather I'd returned to Ireland with the lass when the university censored my lectures and sent me packing. In my mind I've argued myself dry with you over this. But I would not have been able to keep the Catholics from her no more than my dear mother could keep them from me. I like to think I'm keeping her safe whilst adding to the understanding of how cultural and social forces shape the nascent personality. The contribution we'll make to anthropological knowledge! I was never told the truth as a lad. Think on this: what Miranda will know of what is proper and good, holy and unholy, natural and unnatural will be uncontaminated by the Church or any other institution. Is it wrong to lock her away from a society that sees women as a lower order of being? Wrong to shield her as long as possible from a culture in which goods are the measure of personal achievement? What's wrong with learning for its own sake or simply being?

Eileen leans back in the chaise, closes her eyes and gently shakes her head with a smile. My husband, she thinks: ever the professor, the lecturer. Or perhaps she frowns at the thought of her husband turning their daughter into an academic study. Of his deciding only he knows the truth. It's so hot! Eileen arises from the chaise and paces as Miranda opens another letter, written when she was four, the year after they moved into the house she strains to picture now.

It's been one year, four months and five days since that awful day I stood o'er your corpse and said, "Aye, there was a lass." Wondering who'd stand o'er mine and say, "There was a lad."

Her heart plunges off the Alps. She didn't honestly believe she had a guardian-angel mother languishing in a magic sanatorium kingdom—James would have *sent* the letters—but she wanted to indulge herself awhile longer. The psychiatrist Doris took her to claimed Miranda engages in infantile magical thinking. He suggested she take up painting or writing to channel her fantastical imaginings. He also said she's so anesthetized from a traumatic past she is unable to grasp how "adult–child relations" are viewed in the real world. She told him she did not have a traumatic past.

She forces herself to read on.

Only through Morrigan's intercession have I not been called up here. My volunteer work is all that keeps the widows and gold star mothers from having me drawn and quartered. It terrifies me to leave her alone the nights I must go house to house in white helmet and armband, checking to see the blinds are tightly drawn. I've gotten a guard dog. You'd approve of him, my love. I contemplated naming him Cerberus but settled on Nicholas, after the first, the one with a kind heart who nonetheless brooked no challenge to his authority.

Miranda catches her breath at the dear creature's name. Once she confessed to Father Shandley that she grieved more for Nicholas than she did for James. "Grief is grief" was all he said, assigning her not a single Hail Mary. And grief must have been what James felt for Eileen as he shouldered the weight of Miranda's welfare and, later, Cian's.

She chances a few more letters. *The abilities to charm and heal are passed through the blood,* James wrote on her eighth birthday, *but they must be drawn out else lie fallow. I want her to continue the traditions of her grandmother and great-grandmother before her, to walk the same path, although (no need to point it out, dearest) I'm well aware I'm circumscribing that path.* He wrote of anointing her with cinnamon oil that day and

dedicating her to a life of healing. On her thirteenth birthday—
Cian would have been no bigger than a pencil lead inside her—he
lamented she had little passion for healing. *Books are what inspire her.
She's her mother's child in that. She's read every English language novel and
translation I've allowed her. The small village library has a patriotic fervor for
American novelists. I've overcome my scorn for them for the lass's sake. Pity she
shows little aptitude for French or German.*

Miranda recalls James attempting to interest her in the plants he
grew or scavenged and dried in the basement. She took his knowledge of their healing properties for granted and paid scant attention
to whether it was one pinch or two of this or that. She knew only
that clove set your mouth on fire, mullein was bitter and chamomile
smelled like apples.

*I miss the perilous beauty of Ireland's winter, the trees in their topcoats of
fog. It's hard not to think what I'm doing is completely mad. I need you to say
something handsome to me.*

I have some French, now, she whispers. *Ça ne fait rien.*

Latin, too. *Filia est pars patris.*

Carolyn coughs.

Miranda douses the light.

⚜ SEVENTEEN ⚜

AUGUST 16, 1957. From the day she moved into Buddy's room nearly two months ago, Tereza swore she could hear Miranda's money rustling around in the basement. Yesterday, as if they'd been in a dream together, she woke with the feeling of Miranda's hand on her cheek, the weight of it like guilt.

According to Buddy's schedule, Tereza was supposed to work on grammar this morning. As an A&P wife she needed to stop saying stuff like "ain't" and "I seen." Speak more like Natalie Wood than Sal Mineo, har-dee-har-har. But instead of "conjugating" with a bunch of words Buddy'd give/gave/given her, she'd put on a Popsicle-green circle skirt and a sleeveless white blouse Natalie might wear and snuck out at ten while he and Dearie were still asleep.

The bus ride to Stony River was slow and hot. Already her hair had exploded into frizz and the V between her tits felt wet. She arrived around noon at the stop under the shadowy railway trestle where taxis idled, pigeons crapped and a Crazy Haggerty type on a gray bench drank from a paper bag. The town felt smaller, the trestle not as high as she remembered. Had it really been two years since she and the guys ran around under that trestle shouting *When I'm calling you-oo-oo-oo* into the echo? Stony River felt even stranger to her knowing Richie had been gone for months. He'd left without so much as a goodbye, something that must've pained Buddy awful bad because he never wanted to talk about it.

She'd had breakfast ready as usual this morning when he got home after the midnight to eight-thirty shift he'd been working since they got married. It was nice, just the two of them in the kitchen, arms on the table, leaning into each other to keep their voices low on account of Dearie still sleeping. The sun always rose behind the house and snuck into the kitchen through the back porch. The new light and Buddy's private voice kept her looking for that magic moment when marriage would change them into something cooler than they were alone and make Buddy want to screw her. So far all that had happened was he'd gotten an A&P haircut that looked like a mowed lawn and Tereza had learned to cook oatmeal the way he liked.

Over breakfast, Buddy would beef about how boring it was stocking shelves, making sure every can, jar and box was stamped with a price, scrubbing the floor with a machine that weighed a ton and lugging returned bottles to the basement. He was determined to learn every job because no chore was too lowly for an A&P manager. He had being a bagger down cold. Eventually he'd be a cashier, stock clerk, produce supervisor and so on. He was sure the work would get more interesting and was already dropping words like *merchandise, marketing, inventory* and *stock* on her.

Tereza was just as fired up about becoming an actress, but Buddy wanted her to take over more and more shifts at Herman's so that Dearie could stay home whenever she wanted without "the family" losing income.

Thinking of them as family felt like cheating on Ma.

The Stony River "cop shop," as Vinnie used to call it, was five blocks from the bus stop. Tereza's black flats scuffed the sidewalk as she hustled along. By now Dearie would have found the "went to store" note she'd left by the coffee pot. Tereza would pick up Midol and Kotex before she went back and cook up a story about why it took her so long. Buddy'd never know she was gone; he didn't get up until after she and Dearie left for Herman's.

He slept days when he was on night shift. After breakfast, he'd shower before getting into bed. Tereza would crawl in with him in case he wanted to make out. He never did. But he'd stretch out beside her and hold her for a while, his Lifebuoy smell pinching her nose, before turning onto his stomach and lying frog-kneed like a Dearie miniature. Tereza would get up once his body started sleep-twitching and have a go at whatever he'd put on her schedule.

Not today.

She wanted to find Miranda before Buddy found the money. Every time he carried the vacuum up from the basement for Dearie, Tereza's stomach flipped. If she'd told him right after the wedding, it might've been okay. The longer she kept it to herself, the harder it would be to explain. Not that he'd hurt her if he found out. He wasn't like Jimmy. It was just that he went all funny sometimes, making her swell up with a fear she couldn't name.

The sun was like a hot and heavy hand on her back but Tereza kept her head up and her shoulders back, almost hoping somebody'd recognize her and say what's up so she could say nothing-much-got-married-in-June and see in their eyes she wasn't a loser anymore. She couldn't be sent back to school now. She had a birth certificate that said she was sixteen. Nobody had to know her husband didn't "sexually respond" to her, as the book had put it. Lately she'd been thinking a girlfriend would be a good idea. Not Linda. Somebody who knew something useful. Talking to Dearie about certain stuff would be like ratting on Buddy. Same for the women who worked at Herman's. Miranda was the only teenager Tereza knew of who'd had sex, even if it had been with her geezer father. One guy Tereza picked up at Tony's had wanted her to hum "The Star Spangled Banner" while she blew him. Buddy didn't want her to do anything except look scared while he came on her leg or stomach. Maybe Miranda would say, "Oh, that's normal," or "That's nothing compared to what I had to put up with."

The station was all bustle and dark wood, a few glassed-in offices around a room where several people slumped on wooden benches. Tereza approached a high desk and a cop about twenty-five or so. He had fat earlobes it might be fun to suck.

She made her eyes sappy and her voice all pleading like Debra Paget's in *Love Me Tender,* "Oh please Vance, please, for my sake," the exact line Paget was saying the first time Buddy's hand gripped Tereza's crotch. She introduced herself, lifting her ring hand to the desk. Asked if the cop remembered a Mister Haggerty who'd died and left a daughter. She told him she'd just happened to be near the Haggerty house the day two cops took the girl away, a girl she needed to track down.

"You know the officers' names, Mrs. Jukes?"

"No." She bet this cop wouldn't care about mouth germs.

"You a relative?"

"No."

He leaned over the desk, checked her out. "You here to report her officially missing?"

"No."

"Then I don't think we can help you." He laughed, flashing a gold tooth. "Chances are she's only missing to you."

He probably had bad breath.

"Any idea how I could find her?"

"You could put an ad in the paper."

THE *STONY RIVER RECORD* sat between Dinah's Luncheonette and the Savings Institution in a building with a big glass window, the printing press right up front where everyone could see the guy running it. He probably couldn't goof off for a second.

A bored-looking woman behind a typewriter, wearing glasses

held together with tape, helped Tereza compose the ad. *Miranda Haggerty: I have something that belongs to you. Please write to Ladonna at Stony River Record, Box 42.* Tereza was glad she didn't have to leave an address or phone number; she could call to find out if anybody answered and then come by to pick up the letter.

"How long you want the ad to run?"

"Don't know."

"I can give you four weeks for the price of three."

Tereza paid in cash.

Tereza's ad would run for the first time in a week. Realizing she might hear from Miranda that soon gave her chills. She'd have to come clean about how she'd gotten the money.

EIGHTEEN

SEPTEMBER 5, 1957. Carolyn is braving her third day in kindergarten as Cian lies tummy and elbows down in front of the television. His two-year-old playmate, Mickey, naps on the floor beside him. Doris is at work.

Miranda brews a pot of tea from a recipe in the *grimoire* she found in James's desk. Its early entries are in a language she doesn't know, possibly written by her grandmother and great-grandmother. But James entered various spells and formulas in English. For her sake, she likes to think—needs to think.

At St. Bernadette's he slipped away from her a little at a time, like water in a cupped hand. His letters resurrect someone alien and portray a reality to which she was oblivious. She's read them all now, some more than once, drawn to them like a tongue to an aching tooth. She gets through each day by pretending what's in them is of no consequence. Drawing whatever nourishment she can from the thin gruel of his few tender words about her.

She knows the truth now about the most powerful moment in her life: when a great force overtook her and she floated like a visitor from another realm, convinced with all her being that Danú possessed her womb and was leading Cian through the birth canal. What has brought her heart to its knees is this from James when

Cian was a mere three months old: *I look at the lad and must concede
the experiment failed. What arrogance to believe I had the power to do this,
or the right.*

Not a word of the awe she saw in his face when he first held the
babe.

She pours herself a cup of tea then spreads the letters out on a
square of early afternoon sun lighting the burled maple dining room
table, hoping to make more sense of their meanderings. She's tried
to assess them dispassionately, as a scientist might, noting James's
progression over the years from *I'm the Weaver, spinning my magic* to
I'm the Wanderer, leading you astray. From optimism about his grand
experiment to *drifting through fields of nothingness in search of meaning.*
Miranda knows those fields. She plunges headlong into them on the
edge of sleep and stumbles across them occasionally during the day
when her attention needs to be on the children. Their tall grasses
whisper of annihilation. Insanity.

James could have been wrong about Cian. By the time of that
letter—Miranda was fourteen—he claimed he no longer knew what
he believed, *only what I experience and that is a bewildering madness. I'm
addicted to the feeling of air moving through me when I leave my tortured
mind and go into that dark void. It's not just her isolation I need. It's mine,
away from the well intentioned who would seek to "cure" me.*

Miranda blows on her tea and thinks on this addiction, this
yearning to enter another dimension and leave yourself behind.
How powerful it must have been in James to drive him to lock
her away. She tries to resist when the detective who smells like
cherries and pine needles comes to call, asking her "just one
more time" to enter Bill Nolan's hat, his jacket, shoes or gun.
Will she feel the sudden flush, the chill? Fall into the darkness
vaster than sleep? She fears losing herself there one day, and never
coming back to Cian. Yet she's lured, as James must have been, by

the deeper state of existence she senses beneath her superficial daily tasks.

Mickey flops over on his back, still sucking his thumb, and Cian passes gas.

Nothing James revealed about the preparations for Cian's birth surprises her. He was forthright about what he wanted to do and how. *A notion has made itself known to me, nay, a conviction that it's possible to produce a child that is not of this world,* he wrote on her eleventh birthday. *I've been meditating on the best way to do it. It must not be out of lust.* She agreed they would both walk around the house naked as eels until he could look on her without desire. She never found his body more than an intriguing counterpart to hers. He gave no hint, later, of doubting their success.

The psychiatrist said, "When an adult in a position of trust persuades a child that what the adult wants is also what the child wants, the adult has stolen the child's right to make her own choices." Miranda never questioned the morality of having a divine child, much less the probability. So accepting she was, the *quiet child,* the *good lass* James wrote about to Eileen.

She can picture him at his desk, flask in hand, growing more and more inebriated as he contemplates another lonely year with his tedious daughter and their freak of a son.

I blame myself. I should have waited to woo you. Your grief was too raw, not even a year old, when you faced the prospect of bringing a child into a world that had taken everyone else you'd loved. I was too bloody-minded to understand you couldn't risk another loss. With a longing that wrenches deep inside with fingers of pain I look for you on the dark winding paths of the Isle of Ghosts.

Such dross.

I kneel and call out to my ancestors and yours. Thank their soft Irish hearts for welcoming you. Ask them to forgive you for taking your own life and me for not preventing it.

Miranda draws on the calming oil of bergamot in her tea. That's it then. Eileen could not bear to live any longer for fear she'd lose James and Miranda one day as she had the rest of her family in that dreadful storm. She had not wanted a child for the same reason. She had not wanted Miranda.

❧ NINETEEN ❧

SEPTEMBER 14, 1957. "How goes it, Doris?" Police Detective Enzo
Rotella stood at attention on her front step, crisp as toast in a navy
blue cable-knit sweater vest, white shirt and sharply creased gray
trousers. Under his hands, a book and a newspaper. He'd taken on
Bill's case the moment he heard the call on his walkie-talkie. Gone
straight to the site to collect evidence and was still at it. She hoped he
wasn't here to interrogate Miranda again.

"It goes, Enzo, that's all I can say. What's up?" She couldn't recall
him smelling as strongly of cologne. Bill never wore the stuff. He
reeked, instead, of Frank's cigars.

"Miranda in?"

"Yeah, but we're about to take the kids down the street to the
playground."

"Won't keep you long. I was checking on an ad I placed and
stumbled across her name in yesterday's *Record*. I wondered if she'd
seen it." He handed Doris the paper and pointed to a classified he'd
circled.

She read it quickly. "I'll be darned. C'mon in."

He scraped his brown suede oxfords on the mat and dipped his
head slightly before stepping into the tile patch that served as an
entryway. His hairline was in serious retreat; what hair remained was
trimmed close to the scalp.

"She's getting the kids ready to go out. Hear the ruckus?"

"No."

"Exactly. You hardly hear a chirp when they're with her. Like they're under some spell, especially when she reads to them." Which she did incessantly, wasting time that could have been spent having them scrub their hands and pick up their toys.

He nodded. "She does seem to have stepped from an enchanted forest."

He should try leaving three kids with Miranda each day, not knowing if the fairy princess would be off in Neverland and forget to put the boys down for naps. Doris was as bad as Bill had been, calling a couple of times a day to check on things. She'd come home more than once lately and found Mickey curled up asleep on the floor, sucking his thumb, or both boys wandering around in their birthday suits. Miranda would emerge from the bathroom looking as if she'd been crying, but she'd assure Doris she was fine. Doris had gone back to Children's Aid nearly three months ago, counting on escaping the ache in the house through office work, but anxiety over what might be happening at home kept her on edge.

"Mind if I sit?"

She'd never get rid of him now.

She led him into what had turned into a library, with shelves scaling the living- and dining-room walls. Her father had built them for her. It had been either surrender her walls or put up with books on every available surface, including the floor. Miranda was not content to leave them in boxes in the basement. She'd taped little white labels on each spine according to the Dewey decimal system. Written out a card for every book and arranged the cards alphabetically in a recipe box. With a focus that had amazed Doris, she'd spent weeks deciding what category each book fell into, asking Doris's opinion. *Beowulf:* fiction or folklore? *Myths and Legends of the Celtic Race:* religion or social sciences? Doris asked if there was a category for boring. She'd never been a reader. Neither had her parents, but they'd become sudden converts, borrowing a book or two when they visited, asking Miranda for recommendations. They were captivated by her history. To them she was obviously intelligent, possibly brilliant, but "not quite right," something they attributed to the abuse she'd suffered; Doris had shared the psychiatrist's report with them. They wanted to "encourage" her. Show how broad-minded they were.

Enzo borrowed books, too, perhaps to compensate Miranda for his insistence she tell him time and time again what she saw about that night the unimaginable had happened. While Doris was grateful for the stubborn, painstaking way he followed every possible clue and kept her informed—she now fully appreciated the significance of bloodstain pattern, size, shape and location to crime reconstruction—his persistence in pressuring Miranda to "see" more of the murder scene drained the girl and made her even less dependable.

Doris pushed aside the pink plastic ballerinas and miniature cars to make space for him on the couch. She took a seat in the chair opposite him, feeling frumpy and too warm in old slacks and Bill's red plaid flannel shirt. She told him about the runaway Bill thought had broken into the Haggerty house.

"Two years ago?" he said. "Curious someone would come forth now."

"Could the ad have been running all that time?"

"No. I checked. It's recent. Placed by a young woman described as dark but not Negroid."

Someone might have described Enzo as dark, too. Acne had pitted and stained his angular face the deep purple of plums. It was hard to look at him for long without feeling rude. He'd come to the department with serious credentials—MP experience in Germany and Korea, a degree in criminal justice—but Bill had figured the true secret to the guy's success was that people felt sorry for him and told him whatever he wanted to know.

"You think Ladonna's a real name?" she asked.

"Hard to tell."

He picked up a tiny red double-decker bus and ran it absent-mindedly along his leg, a sensual gesture that made Doris uneasy. "Here, let me get that out of your way," she said, taking it from his hand. "Sorry for the mess. It's a small house for three kids." She set the bus on the floor beside her feet. "For what are you advertising, if you don't mind?"

Enzo stared at the little bus as if it might start moving on its own and then looked up at her with a slight frown. "Witnesses. I run the ad once a month. You never know. Someone might recall a gunshot or a car speeding away. Might have tucked the memory into a cluttered room in his mind, not realizing it mattered."

"It's hopeless, isn't it? Six months and no witnesses, no suspects." The funeral came back to Doris in a rush. The long, somber procession from St. Boniface to the cemetery: hundreds of officers from across the state in full dress, Chief Durmer presenting her with the flag draped over Bill's casket, the melancholy Taps played by the desk sergeant's nephew. She'd had her private moment before the funeral when they opened the casket for her. Had placed her hand over his one last time and kissed his forehead, already picturing the rest of her life without him.

"We have fingerprints and bloodstains." Enzo's tone was patient but weary. "We know the bullet that got Bill came from a German gun. With tenacity and time, every case is solvable."

"That what detective school tells you to say to widows?"

"This is a cop killer, Doris. The department will never give up on it."

Enzo stood abruptly and smiled past her. Miranda was entering the living room, gliding into it, actually, Carolyn, Mickey and Cian trailing behind like ducklings. Mickey waved at Doris and Enzo with both hands. Cian said, "Hi Dori!" Carolyn wore her five-year-old pouty look, Miranda a mint-green shirtwaist that highlighted her eyes. She looked less fragile today, as though she'd resolved something in her mind. The years she'd spent away from the world had stamped her with a certain strangeness Doris suspected would never go away, but she was striking, you had to give her that, especially now that her hair was longer. Doris could see how a man might be smitten, particularly Enzo, who likely didn't have women trampling each other to get to him. But he was old enough to be her father. Thinking of that and the psychiatrist saying Miranda had no context for understanding what James had done to her gave Doris the willies.

A smile lit Miranda's face. "I didn't know you were here."

Cian pulled a tiddlywinks game from under a chair.

"I'm returning Voltaire," Enzo said. "You're right. The shepherd's tale is perfect for me."

Doris plucked three tiddlywinks from Mickey's mouth.

"Was he blind in his right eye?" Miranda said.

Enzo slapped his thigh and laughed. Doris didn't get what was obviously a private joke.

"Gee whiz," Carolyn said, hands on her hips. "Aren't we going to the park?"

"You bet," Doris said. She felt for Carolyn, who missed Bill terribly and had to wait until Doris got home from work before she could roller skate or ride the big-girl bike the department had given her. Doris had arranged for another kindergarten mother on the street to escort Carolyn to and from school. She wouldn't allow Miranda to take the kids farther than the fenced-in backyard in case she got swept away by some vision. Seeing the girl flat on the basement floor barely breathing had shaken Doris. "You want to show Miranda the ad, Enzo? Pronto?"

He did. "Any idea about this person or what of yours she might have?"

"How could I?"

He laughed and squeezed Miranda's arm. "Good response. If you don't mind, I'd like to reply on your behalf and see who crawls out from under this rock."

"I mind," Doris said. "This Ladonna could be a nutcase. Miranda's been through enough."

"I won't let anyone hurt her. She doesn't ever have to meet the woman if she doesn't want to. I'll simply find out what it is she claims to have and let Miranda know."

"I'm not afraid, Doris. Do respond for me, Enzo." She placed a hand on Enzo's arm. "Now, would you be wanting to borrow another book?"

Doris could swear Miranda was flirting. "The library is closed," she said.

SEPTEMBER 30, 1957. Tereza saw herself about to enter a movie scene as Ladonna Lange, described in the script as a movie starlet in black heels, gray coat, poufy black wig and fake pearl earrings as big as silver dollars. In the background you might hear music or traffic. Or a voiceover with her thoughts imagining a grateful Miranda, astounded at how Tereza had stumbled across the money. She'd split it with Tereza and they'd be friends forever.

The director would instruct Ladonna to slow down as she passed the bank and approached the building with a big glass window. The camera would pan to the sign above the window: THE STONY RIVER RECORD. As she got close, she'd glance at the window, like it was no big whoop, like it could have been a blank wall for all she cared. She didn't know that the script called for a guy with a dark face to be standing inside the office with his arms crossed, staring out the window. She spotted him the same time he did her. She saw him jerk to attention. She hurried on by, her heels click-clacking in time with her heart.

A rough voice called out behind her. "Hey! Ladonna?"

She'd picked up the typewritten note the week before. *Meet me at the newspaper office at 10 AM September 30th. If not convenient, please suggest another date and time in writing to Box 56, The Record.* No signature, but "convenient" seemed a word Miranda would use. Tereza should have realized that a robber could spy the ad and show up instead. Good thing she'd left the money at home, bringing only the acorn and shell necklace to prove to Miranda she was legit.

The robber's footsteps sounded closer. The train station was dead ahead one block. She was running now. Her feet didn't feel connected to her legs, but they found the ladies' john behind the ticket seller's cage. A single. Empty. She ducked in and locked the door. A pain chewed through her gut. Her ass met the cold toilet seat just in time, thank God or whoever. She stared at JANET SUCKS COCK on the stall door and wondered if God was like an invisible friend you made up to trick yourself into believing you weren't all alone in the world. Tereza didn't think about God much. She'd been in a church only once when they lived in Florida; Ma couldn't take the heat one Sunday and had dragged her to a cool, dark, high-ceilinged building with whirring fans where people weaved back and forth on their feet, singing and clapping like they'd won on *Beat the Clock*. Dearie wasn't big on church; she'd taken Buddy when he was little but stopped when something scared him. It surprised her when he joined a church in June, but he said that's what A&P managers did. Tereza didn't know if he believed in God. If he were there right now she could ask him. If he were there right now she wouldn't be too chickenshit to leave the john.

The toilet wouldn't flush. She washed her hands in cold, rusty water dribbling from the single tap. She shifted her wig to press her ear against the door but couldn't hear a thing over a rumbling train.

She peered through the crack but couldn't see a soul. The goon might be around the corner, though, waiting to grab her pocketbook. She plucked the necklace from it, slipped it over her head and under the collar of her blouse. He wouldn't get that, at least. Nothing in your pocketbook is worth dying over, Ma said once. Some creep wants it, let it go.

She could smell the day Ma said that, lilacs flowering along the porch railing as they sat thigh-to-thigh on the apartment steps, sharing a smoke, while Allen cycled figure eights on the street in front of them. Ma was full of tips: wipe yourself from front to back, don't knee a guy in the balls unless you can run faster than him after, keep a few bucks tucked away in case your husband drinks up his pay. She'd know what to do if the dark-faced jerk was waiting outside.

"Oh, Ma," Tereza said softly. "Why'd you have to go missing?" She studied her face in the small scratched mirror above the sink. Ma wouldn't recognize her all done up. Hey, maybe the robber wouldn't recognize her as Tereza. Minutes later she had scrubbed off her makeup and ditched the wig and coat in a corner. The Grace Kelly suit she'd worn under the coat would do. She slowly opened the john door and tiptoed out. The creep wasn't there. Eyes straight ahead, she forced herself to walk as normally as possible from the station. She'd make up a story about how she lost the coat. Clutching pocketbook to chest, she put one foot in front of the other, block after block, street after street, until she faced the bullet-shaped, gray cement building housing the Catalog Club. She arrived as the noon whistle belched workers from its doors. Even though it made no sense, Tereza looked for Ma in the pack as it split into small groups claiming scraps of lawn for their asses and lunch pails.

Inside Tereza found a glass-walled office no bigger than the train station john overlooking a long room with shelves of merchandise and two giant conveyor belts, halted for lunch break. A square-jawed, crop-haired woman in trousers and a plaid shirt hunched over a desk in the office, tucking into a sandwich.

Tereza knocked on the doorframe.

The woman looked up. "Yeah?" Tereza could see mushed-up bread in her mouth.

"I'm looking for my mother."

The woman lifted one pale eyebrow. "She on this shift?"

Tereza shook her head. "She don't work here no more. Doesn't. I was wondering if she left an address. You know, for her last pay or something?"

The woman frowned, pursed her lips. "You don't know where your mother is?"

Tereza shook her head, made her hands into hard fists to stop from crying.

The woman narrowed her eyes like she was sizing Tereza up. "Jesus." She swiveled her chair around and slid open a heavy-sounding file cabinet drawer. "How you spell her name?"

"D-o-b-r-a." Tereza wasn't sure how to spell Reenie.

The woman pulled out a file folder and turned papers over. Looked up.

"Renate Dobra?"

"Yeah."

"She hasn't worked here for close to two years. You been looking for her since then?"

Tereza didn't answer. She should have come here as soon as she discovered Ma gone. Somebody might have known something then. "She leave an address?"

"The only one I got is 527 Grove Street here in town. That help?"

The crummy apartment across the street from Linda's.

Tereza sniveled as she trudged to the bus stop. Blubbered all the way to Linden, the tears slipping under her collar, making her neck itch. She'd let herself hope for something and ended up with nothing.

Her mother was who-knew-where, her father was a movie poster and she lived with a pink-haired dingbat who talked to her dead husband and a guy who couldn't get hard unless he scared her half to death.

THE NEXT DAY, she waited until Buddy finished breakfast before telling him she didn't want to play the scared game anymore, that if she couldn't be a real wife she didn't want to be a wife at all. "Maybe you need to see a doctor," she said. "Maybe you need help."

His face turned dark as rain. He slowly pushed his chair back from the table. She was too sapped to care what his scowl meant. She'd pulled herself together long enough yesterday to get through the shift at Herman's and make it to bed where she cried so hard she thought her heart would bust. She'd woken this morning feeling a hundred years old but calmer, too, like somebody had come during the night and sucked the fear right out of her bones. Now she sat at the table and listened to Buddy's slow, heavy footsteps on the stairs to their room, then to wood and glass breaking. Furious sounds that, on another day, might have made her run away. They dragged Dearie from her room, wild-eyed, clutching her robe shut. "What's going on?"

Tereza shrugged.

Dearie rushed from the kitchen. Called up the stairs. "Buddy? You okay up there?" The crashing and breaking sounds continued. "Eldon Joseph Jukes! Come down here this minute!"

Tereza heard a door open and Buddy's boots on the steps. Slow. Heavy. She heard Dearie say, "What's wrong, boy?" Didn't hear if he answered.

He came into the kitchen, eyes in another world, Dearie on his heels like a herd dog. He plucked his leather jacket from his breakfast chair and left the house, letting the porch door bang.

Dearie sighed, sat down heavily at the table and lightly touched Tereza's arm. "Did he hurt you?" Tereza shook her head.

"Your eyes are all puffy."

"I didn't sleep good. That's why." She listened to Buddy's engine turn over and, a minute later, to tires squealing on pavement.

Dearie heaved herself up and filled the coffee pot with water. "I hoped marrying you might save him, but once a boy's been wrecked probably ain't enough love in the world for him."

Tereza thought about that for a minute, about how anxious Dearie had been to marry them off. She'd been too stupid then to ask questions. "Why'd he go to juvie?"

Dearie scooped Eight O'Clock into the basket. "I thought he would've told you."

"Nope." Buddy had said Dearie wouldn't want her to know. Which one was lying?

Dearie snapped the lid onto the coffee pot. "He beat up some girly."

"Why?"

"She called him a fruit. Ain't that a silly word to get upset about? You call me an orange or a banana, even a watermelon and I'll laugh, not beat you up."

"You don't know what fruit means?"

Dearie set the percolator on the stove and turned on the flame. "Sure I do. I also know it's against the law to be one. The girly said Buddy was sweet on another boy. The worst thing was she said it in front of other kids and they laughed. Buddy don't take kindly to being laughed at. He followed her after school and waited until she was alone. Later he said he was only gonna kiss her to prove he wasn't a fruit, but she called him more names."

Tereza stared at the ironing board on the back porch. On Wednesdays she was supposed to iron Buddy's shirts. She didn't think she could muster the energy. "Did he hurt her bad?"

For a few seconds Dearie seemed to study the coffee bubbling up into the glass knob on the lid. Then, "He broke her arm, bruised her up enough to send her to the hospital. I paid the bill. At the prison—they call it reform school but it's still a prison—the doctor said Buddy had no clue all that rage was in him, didn't think it *was* him it came out of. He didn't remember much about it after."The coffee was ready. "Want a cup?"

Tereza nodded. She wondered if the girl had stuck her tongue in his mouth and set him off. "Did he ever have a girlfriend? Before me?"

"Oh, I imagine so. Don't most boys? He was never much for telling me what he was up to the nights he went out. If Alfie hadn't died, Buddy might have talked to him about such things. It hit Buddy hard when he died, like losing a dad all over again."

"How old was he?"

"Seventy-one. Too old to horse around with a boy and help him get that angry energy out."

"I meant Buddy. How old was he when Alfie died?"

"Oh. Eleven. Such a sweet boy when he wanted to be. I ever show you pictures?"

"Uh-uh."

Dearie disappeared into her bedroom and returned with a shoebox. She sat down with it at the table. "I keep meaning to get a scrapbook for these."

Tereza hardly recognized Buddy: a scrawny kid standing on the sidewalk, his hands hanging loose; sitting on a couch; in a wagon holding a grocery bag. Just sitting and standing around like a namby-pamby. "He don't look tough enough to beat up a marshmallow."

"Yeah, I know. That doctor said rage gave him the strength of a fellow twice his size."

"Did the doctor say what was wrong with him?"

"Some big word I don't remember with 'mild' in front of it. He said Buddy imagined things. Well, what child don't? They gave him pills that made him dopey and walk like a robot. He stopped taking them after Charles Atlas told him they were poison. At the time I didn't think that was a good idea, but I gotta admit stopping don't seem to have done him no harm."

"Buddy talked to Charles Atlas?"

"Not in the flesh. But he wrote him a letter. At age twelve. How 'bout that? He's brighter than those doctors gave him credit for. Missed some school along the way, but he always made it up and never failed a course. He don't pussyfoot around when he has a goal."

"Was hurting the girl the only bad thing he ever did?"

"Ain't that enough?" Dearie took a sip of coffee. "Still too hot." She carried her cup to the fridge and dumped some milk into it. "I'm proud of him for settling down with you and doing so good at A&P. His manager has a soft spot for boys who've bumped into the law. He hired Buddy despite his record or maybe because of it—who knows? Alfie used to say if they can pull diamonds out of the ground, anything can happen. Like everybody, Buddy has his goods and bads. He just needs to learn to walk away from his temper, practice walking away till he gets good at it."

"Like swinging a bat? I practiced a long time before I ever hit a home run."

Dearie smiled. "Never thought of it like that." She put her hand over Tereza's. "Ain't gonna leave him are you?"

The sound of the car in the drive stopped Tereza from answering. Buddy walked through the door with the look Jimmy used to get after he'd gone bonkers: ashamed but unapologetic.

"I gotta get some shut-eye," he said. "You coming up, Tereza?"

THE DAMAGE WASN'T AS BAD as it had sounded: only the fancy mirror and the desk chair. Buddy pushed the shards and splintered boards to one corner with his boots. "I'll clean it up tomorrow. You gonna take off your clothes?"

She told him the book said it should go in at a forty-degree angle downward. It hurt when he found the right hole but not as bad as the whiners in *True Confessions* would have you think.

Later, seeing the little boy in his sleeping face, she thought about Alfie and Dearie doing their best to love him but being too old. If she left Buddy, it would be like his ma taking off and Alfie dying all over again. He'd rescued her when she was scared shitless, hadn't thought twice about letting her stay. Tomorrow she'd take some of Miranda's money and buy two gloves, a ball and a bat. She'd write "Tereza, park" on the calendar for Buddy's next day off. Show him what a good hit could do for you.

≶ T W E N T Y ≷

DECEMBER 11, 1957. It starts well, Miranda at the counter by the sink, cracking walnuts, Enzo watching from a kitchen chair, his leg straight out, bouncing Mickey up and down. She asks, Are you not too warm in that jacket and vest? and he says, I need to sweat off a big breakfast. He asks, Are the walnuts for cookies? and she says, No, they're for Cian, don't they look just like brains, they'll make him smarter. She's serious but he laughs. He tells her Mama has been in the kitchen for weeks getting ready to stuff the family with seven kinds of fish and more on Christmas Eve. Even so she'll expect them to waddle to the table the next day for roasted chicken, rice and something-ownee, something-etty and something-enzay. Italian sounds so sure of itself, even when Enzo's voice jiggles from giving horsey rides. He's spoken of this Mama before, confessed he didn't go straight to Bill Nolan's murder site because he called her first; he didn't want her to think it was him if she heard a cop had been shot. He asked Miranda not to tell Doris and she hasn't. She grabs the pencil and paper Doris keeps by the refrigerator and writes down what he's just called Mickey and Cian, would he spell it? R-a-g-a-z-z-i-n-o-s, as in Mama would gobble up these two *ragazzinos*. She likes how he includes Cian with Mickey as though he doesn't see him as different. Enzo says his two sisters and three brothers have produced six grandchildren already but that's not enough for Mama. Miranda

says, You mean she wants them from you? and he says, Yes and that's
when her thinking takes the first wrong turn. Having conversed with
so few men in her life she has little experience decoding their words.
Is Enzo talking about children because he wants a child with her?
Should she come right out and ask him? She can be forthright with
Doris because Doris is forthright with her. Miranda doesn't know
enough about Enzo. When he started coming over he was all business.
It's different now. Doris says that's because he's "sweet" on Miranda
and inappropriately so because of the age difference. Enzo asks about
her Christmas plans. Is he working up to ask her to meet his family?
She tells him she and Doris will get a tree for the children to trim and
they'll go to Mass but they haven't given a thought yet to food. Enzo
pats his stomach, which isn't the least bit stout, and says, A family that
doesn't spend half of each day planning meals for the next is likely
healthier than mine. Is he angling for an invitation from Miranda?
She calls Cian to the table and gives him applesauce into which she's
folded three chopped walnuts, following instructions James left in
the *grimoire*. She sets out a dish without walnuts for Mickey and says,
I've been thinking on that woman who placed the ad, the one who ran
away from you, and wondering if she might have bought my house—
Doris said it was a young couple with a child. Enzo asks what she
thinks they have of hers. She tells him about the harp in the basement
that somehow got missed when Doris packed the boxes—Doris said
she wouldn't have thrown a musical instrument away, it must have
been hidden from view. Miranda doesn't mention the knife and the
necklace, not wanting to explain their purpose. Enzo says I didn't
know you played the harp, but then there's lots I don't know about
you. Miranda hears that as meaning he wants to know. She says, I
don't, it was James who did. Enzo takes a moment to remove Mickey
from his leg before saying, Well then, it might be best if you don't get
it back. James said never ask a question if you're not prepared for the
answer. She plunks Mickey down at the table for his applesauce and

says I'll be calling on the people and inquiring about the harp. He asks, Sure you want to go there again and she says, Aye. She's been thinking on giving James a proper burial—Doris has taken her to the mean plot where his bones lie—and before she does she wants to visit the last place she saw him alive. Cian has finished his apple-sauce. Enzo hoists the lad onto his shoulders. Mickey says, Me next! Cian gives out the deep chuckle he's had since he was a babe that still turns Miranda weak with love. She could be "sweet" on anyone who makes Cian laugh like that. Doris calls Enzo's face "a shame." Miranda admires him for not making excuses for it and not keeping himself away from the world. The Mama he speaks of so fondly must have shown him he had as much right as anyone else to feel the sun and wind and rain on his face. Enzo could help her do that for Cian. She tells him Mama sounds like a wonderful woman with much to teach a young mother and asks if he'll take her for a visit. Enzo sets Cian down and tells the lads to go play with their toys—this old horse needs a rest. When the lads are in the living room he says to Miranda, Come, sit, and pulls out another chair. She removes her apron and wipes her hands on a dishtowel. He gives her a sad smile and says, I want you to know it isn't your fault but Mama would not understand if I brought you to meet her. She would not understand why you're unmarried. She would insist on knowing who Cian's father is. She would make a scene. He touches Miranda's arm with a warm, dry hand and says, Mama is a good Catholic woman who has raised good Catholic children. He gives a short mirthless laugh and says he would have had to become a priest if his younger brother hadn't, he studied theology for a few years, just in case, even though his heart was in crime. Miranda smiles at the image of Enzo's heart robbing a store. Mama would have felt she'd failed the Church had she not produced a priest. Miranda nods and says, Once she meets me she might feel differently about me, as you do. Enzo stands, takes the few steps to the refrigerator, leans against it with his arms crossed and says, You don't seem to understand that what you and your father did was a sin. Mama would not let such a sinner in her house and I would not bring such a sinner to her. Miranda sits for a minute listening to the refrigerator whine—Doris keeps meaning to get someone to look at it. She should ask Enzo to leave but she can't resist petitioning his logical side. She still sees Mother Alfreda once a month and tells Enzo the reverend mother says nothing happens without God's concurrence and to Miranda's way of thinking that means Cian's birth was God's will. Enzo bristles but she continues: If sin is defined as any violation of Divine Providence and if Divine Providence, which is defined as God's will, permitted Cian's conception, then it could not have been a sin. Enzo says, I'm not going to stay and listen to this. His words coil above his head like smoke from a burning pan. Miranda sits at the table as he lets himself out and hears the lads call bye-bye. Mother Alfreda wouldn't be sad to see him go. She says Miranda has the potential to achieve divine communion. She objects to Miranda wasting her gifts on gun-and-bullet parlor games for some detective. It is tempting to surrender and flee this world of appearances. To escape to the deeper, hidden world that beckons. But that would mean abandoning her efforts to give Cian a different childhood than James gave her. She takes a spoonful of Mickey's unfinished applesauce—tartly sweet and hard as a stone to swallow.

✺ TWENTY-ONE ✺

FEBRUARY 14, 1958. The bridal couple sailed past. According to Roger's secretary, Madge, who was also the groom's mother, they'd taken lessons at Arthur Murray for the occasion. The waltzing blur of a bride was a pretty girl from Westfield.

Roger found a recent tendency to be in and out of himself simultaneously curious and disturbing. Take tonight. He was dancing with Linda, maintaining the one-two-three-beat of an old Jolson number. At the same time he was off in some dark corner observing a girl in a luminous blue frock dancing with a blue-suited man. A trifle stiff, she admirably followed his lead while he carefully positioned his hand on her back to avoid her bra strap.

The man was an outsider in her life now, waltzing with a memory: twirling around the living room, his daughter's tiny feet on top of his, a Dorsey tune on the phonograph. Tonight, a live trio: piano, bass and drum.

Roger had insisted Linda attend. The wedding offered the rare opportunity to give her experience in an adult social setting. Even before the separation he'd questioned what she was learning about being a wife.

Take entertaining, for example.

The only people who'd visited their home in several years were from the church, calling on Betty in a charitable capacity. They usually brought something: a coffee cake, a casserole. He couldn't recall Betty offering them so much as a cup of tea. Roger couldn't show Linda how to entertain in his sparsely furnished room, especially with Mrs. Ernst's pungent sauerbraten wafting up through the heat register every other day.

The late afternoon wedding had been overdone: all Valentine's Day hearts and red roses. Afterward, the guests paraded in their cars, puffing out exhaust into the frigid air and honking horns. Linda had slid under the dash, trying not to be seen. They'd ended up here at the Piney Ridge Banquet Hall on Route 22. Not a pine in sight, but at least the place was set far enough back from the road so you didn't hear the trucks air-braking their way to Pennsylvania.

Roger stumbled a bit but recovered by bending Linda back into a dramatic dip. "Lean into it," he said, but she struggled to right herself, neck muscles straining, face flushed.

"Everybody's staring at us."

"Because you're the prettiest girl in the place."

"Yeah, sure."

"You are." Keeping one hand on her back and still one-two-threeing, he dropped her hand and lifted her chin to look into her eyes. His throat tightened; how lovely she'd grown. He didn't mind her roundness as much as Betty did. Nothing wrong with a shapely body.

Linda turned her head away brusquely and placed her hand back into his. Roger's sister, Libby, claimed it was normal for fourteen-going-on-fifteen-year-olds to spurn their parents' attempts at civility. He suspected it was because he hadn't prepared Linda sufficiently for the separation. He hadn't prepared her at all, if truth be told, though it had been a long time coming. Day after day, month after month, for who knows how long, he'd found himself eliminating words and phrases that might set Betty off or send her into retreat. The silence between them had grown like a tumor until that awful Mother's

Day when she'd broken it with the banging of pans and bitter words flung at Linda but intended for him. When, later that day, she said she wanted to be left alone with her pain, he was bereft of words with which to argue.

Two waiters rolled out a table holding an obscenely tall wedding cake.

He hoped Linda wouldn't want to marry some juvenile delinquent. She didn't show particularly good judgment in friends, gravitating toward needy or rebellious types. Take that runaway, Tereza, and the boy who suddenly disappeared about a year ago. Richard? Roger wasn't keen on her newest friend, Arlene, either. Polite enough, but she lived above a tavern with a drunken lout of a father. Roger had never met him but he'd heard the stories from those who had. Not the girl's fault, of course, but she couldn't be the greatest influence.

The number over, Linda turned to leave the dance floor. Roger restrained her, gently he thought, until they had properly applauded the trio. "Whatever happened to Connie?" he asked as he escorted her back to their table. "You and she were such good pals a while back."

Linda winced.

The word *pals*, Roger supposed. Something only a "square" would say, no doubt.

"That was in grade school," she said as if that explained anything.

Roger and Linda were at a table with John Nolte from accounts payable, his wife, Trixie, Madge's younger cousin, Sheila Mulroney, and her husband, Mike. Nolte and his wife didn't inquire about Betty and why would they? She hadn't been to a company event in ages. Waiters had cleared dinner plates away and were pouring coffee and tea. Linda plunked herself down and began crunching an ice cube from her water glass. Roger caught her eye, put a finger to his lips.

Madge's cousin reminded him of a younger Libby, her hair the color of dark rum. Not that Roger drank much rum. He preferred the tart taste of a whiskey sour every so often at a restaurant; Betty didn't allow liquor in the house. A stiff drink might do her good. How could she lie in bed so much and not expire from boredom? Doc Pierce said there was a chance she was allergic to something or had a pernicious form of rheumatism. A clinic in Boston might be able to help, but it took months for an appointment. Roger asked him to get her in line for one.

An amplified male voice announced the cake cutting. Roger pulled Linda's chair around so that she'd be facing the happy couple. She scowled at him. Roger swore he'd never be like his father, who'd flown the coop when Roger was six and Libby eight. Roger stopped by every night to make sure everything was okay. It peeved him to come to the house he'd inherited, sit on his mother's couch and not be able to stay. Wondering what he was missing of Linda's life when he wasn't there consumed his thoughts before sleep each night.

The trio took up another song. Roger asked Sheila to dance.

"Your daughter's lovely," she said on the dance floor.

Sheila felt good in his arms, her chiffon dress soft under his hand, the scent of lilies of the valley rising from her neck. He and Betty had gone dancing when they first met. Betty was flirty, then, in an innocent way. She had this sexy way of pulling her gloves off, slowly tugging at the end of each finger. Lou said the antidepressants he'd prescribed could have made her frigid.

"I think so, too," he said.

"She looks like you except for the coloring. Is her mother fair?"

"Yes." He didn't want to talk to Sheila about Betty. "Madge says you're a teacher."

"Third grade. They're a handful, but I live for Monday mornings. If I had to stay home and clean house all week I'd blow my brains out."

Roger hadn't objected to Betty working before Linda was born, but taking the job at Lou Pierce's office seven months ago was completely unrealistic. She spent more shifts in bed than at work.

Lou said it was a challenging situation and he hadn't ruled out mental illness.

When Roger and Sheila returned, Linda was staring at the floor. She'd eaten his slice of cake—a sickly sweet slab of pink and white—as well as her own.

The bride and groom were making the rounds. Madge's son, Bob, a fit-looking fellow with a crew cut, came up to their table, thanked everyone for coming and asked Linda to dance. She looked down at her lap, shook her head and mumbled no. The young man reddened. Trixie came to his rescue with "*I'd* love a dance."

From his dark corner, Roger saw his jaw stiffen and his face darken. He saw himself whisper into Linda's ear and the two of them make their way to an alcove near the entrance. He saw himself grip her shoulders with his big, square hands. Heard himself trot out his authoritative business voice.

Linda's expression froze as he bit out the words "Don't *ever* turn down a dance, do you hear me?" Ignoring her attempt at an explanation he pressed on, explaining the fragility of the male ego, the courage it took to ask a girl to dance and how humiliating it was to be turned down, especially in front of others. She was to follow along with whatever steps the boy made, laugh if he laughed, reassure him if he apologized for stumbling, treat the dance as though it were the most fun she'd ever had and the boy the most interesting person she'd ever met.

Roger couldn't make himself stop even after Linda's eyes got shimmery with tears and her body rigid as marble. He was that boy and she was Betty, turning away from him night after night, taking her meals in her room, finding any aspect of being his wife repugnant.

They went back into the hall in time for the obligatory tossing of the garter and bouquet. Trixie and Sheila urged Linda to stand with the other unmarried women to catch the bride's flowers. She proceeded to the middle of the floor as though walking a plank.

✦ TWENTY-TWO ✦

APRIL 7, 1958. "Did you know the Dutch bought Manhattan from the Lenape Indians for sixty guilders?" Buddy asked. He gripped her hand so tight it ached, as buildings raced by, the wheels on the track saying *getaway, getaway, getaway*.

"What's that in real money?"Tereza had copped the last window seat. She leaned into her reflection on the cool, dusty-smelling glass, staring out at the remnants of the freak snow two weeks ago. It had started with flakes two inches across and eventually sunk electric wires so low they looked like clotheslines.

"Twenty-four dollars."

"Cheapskates."

She'd been all jumpy inside, anticipating this day. She'd known exactly what she wanted for her birthday when Buddy asked: a day in New York City. She'd wanted to go by herself, but he said there were too many perverts. She could've taken herself almost any day before now but there'd always been reasons not to. For one, being too far away from Ma, even for a day, plus that thing she'd had about finding Miranda. Then not wanting to chance liking New York so much she'd crap out on Buddy for good or be disappointed and have nothing left to dream about.

"You know it's an island, right?" Buddy had said as if perverts hung out only on islands.

At Penn Station she was itching to dive into the crowd as if she lived there. But with one hand on her back and the other cupping her elbow, Buddy steered her to the escalator and all the way to street level where people lined up for taxis and a thousand horns honked. The air was heavy with bus fumes, scorched onions and hot dogs.

"I could do that," she said, pointing to the hot-dog vendor.

"Yeah, but why?" He gripped her hand again, making her wince. "Where to first?"

"The Automat. Herman gave me directions to one near Radio City."

Herman had bought them reserved seats for the show so they wouldn't have to stand in line. Dearie said it was because he was thinking of selling and felt guilty. Businesses had been abandoning Newark. People weren't lining up for the restaurant like they used to. Dearie said she'd retire before any new owners could give her the bum's rush and Tereza should start looking for something else to do. Tereza hoped she'd find that something else in New York.

She'd wanted to eat at an Automat from the time she saw it advertised on *The Horn & Hardart Children's Hour*. Being able to drop coins in a slot, open a little door and take out a baloney sandwich or a slice of huckleberry pie seemed like magic. She wished she'd been a kiddie star on that show, getting to eat at the Automat whenever she wanted. If she ever had a kid she'd make sure it got tap-dancing lessons or learned to play something cool, like the xylophone.

The Automat was twelve blocks away at Broadway and Forty-sixth. Broadway! Seeing it on the map Herman had marked up gave her goose bumps. They took a meandering path there, Tereza carried along by a wild energy. New York was Newark gone mutant. Radioactive with a jillion lights. Exploding with life. A land of glass and metal buildings tall enough for giants to live in. You could get lost here but never feel alone.

It had been seven months since Buddy smashed up the mirror

and desk chair. Right now he was laughing at her bouncing around, twisting her head like a periscope. Where to look first?

Over here: a blind couple with a seeing-eye dog, him squeezing out notes from an accordion, her holding a cup. Down there: a shop window with dead, plucked chickens hanging by their feet. Over here: smoke rings from a painted mouth on a billboard. Down there: a marquee shouting THE MUSIC MAN.

They found the restaurant where actors sat around a big table after opening night, waiting for newspaper reviews. Tereza sized up the doorman under the purple awning and thought *I could do that.* "Go in," Herman had urged. "Order coffee and visit the ladies' room, I'd be interested." But the place wasn't open yet. Even if it had been, Buddy wouldn't have wanted to spend what they'd want for a cup of joe. He had the day all budgeted out: the train ride, lunch at the Automat and a surprise he wouldn't tell her about. She thought about all that money behind the cinder block, not doing them any good.

After the show, they'd check out an A&P not far from Radio City. Tereza pretended to be enthusiastic because managers-in-training needed supportive wives. She almost hadn't gone to the Christmas party, not wanting to hobnob with yoyos that might look down on her for working in a john, but Buddy said his success depended on her going. So she'd bopped around the Legion Hall, a regular Loretta Young, thrusting out her hand and saying, "Ladonna Jukes. Pleased to meet you." Turned out nobody asked what she did. Before the party she'd spent some of Miranda's money on a black chemise and a string of fake pearls, telling Buddy she'd saved for them out of her weekly allowance and the grocery money. At the party, Mr. Hinkley, the fat-cheeked store manager, had said, "You got a real doll here, fella. Hold onto her."

Buddy had said, "Yes, sir."

After that, he started calling her Ladonna all the time, like Dearie had done from the start. She liked it. Ladonna was someone you wanted to screw. Buddy didn't lose himself like the guys in the cars had. She remembered how good it felt to get somebody that horny. Still, it was weird what you could get used to. Buddy said the devil got into people most easily when they were surrendering to passion. When he stuck himself in her he got it over with as soon as possible. She figured it was what most married people did. Lenora from cash at Herman's said sex was overrated and Tereza had to agree.

Tereza was wearing the black Christmas party dress and pearls today underneath her coat in case they went someplace a talent scout might be lurking. Buddy had dressed for work—black pants, white shirt and clip-on bow tie under his leather jacket—to make a good impression at the Manhattan A&P. She'd gotten her hair cut short so it wouldn't be so flyaway. Catching their reflection in a restaurant window, Tereza thought they looked good together. Somewhere along the way the Jukes had seeped into her and worn away the Dobra edges. No more Reenie Dobra's daughter, only Buddy Jukes's wife.

They saw the Automat sign way before they got to it, the neon letters on top of each other like a tower of alphabet blocks. Buddy opened the door for her to the smell of coffee and tomato soup. The place was immense and the Christmas tree sparkly, with light bouncing off a long wall of small glass windows, each holding a plate or dish, like it was a food museum. Not even noon and dozens of people shuffled trays down the counter in front of the little windows.

Buddy went to a glass booth and came back with a fistful of coins.

"I could do that," she said, nodding toward the women in the booth dispensing nickels and quarters with rubber tips on their fingers.

"You'd be better off at the A&P," Buddy said. "Of course you'd have to pass math and English tests and be working on your high-school diploma."

Tereza grabbed two trays, cups, napkins and silverware. Real cups, real silverware. Fancy letters above the windows screamed PIES,

SANDWICHES, SALADS, PASTRIES, CAKES. She dropped three nickels into a slot and turned a chrome-plated knob with a porcelain center— click! A slice of lemon meringue pie. She couldn't find huckleberry. She shuffled down the line and snagged a ham sandwich on a long bun. Buddy got a fruit salad and a Parker House roll.

She poured herself coffee from a spigot in the wall that looked like a dolphin. "I didn't even finish seventh grade, you know that. I'm not gonna sit in a classroom with little kids." She followed Buddy to an empty round table. Marble-topped. A lazy Susan on it with sugar, ketchup, mustard and Worcestershire sauce. The place kept getting better and better.

They sat across from each other.

"You could take a high-school equivalency test. I'd help you study for it."

She took off her coat and hung it over her chair back. "How's that work?"

"You get credit for everything you already know."

"That ain't much." She took a bite of pie and winced.

"Isn't. You okay?"

"Too much lemon. Got me right in the tonsils." She scanned the room, looking for stars dressed like regular schmoes. Buddy tucked into his fruit salad.

"Wouldn't it be cool if you could get transferred here?"

He swallowed, swiped a napkin across his mouth. "What would you do in New York?"

"Are you kidding? Eat here every day. Work at something I love." She shifted into her dahlink accent. "I've gazed into zee crystal ball and see no future in ladies' johns."

Buddy laughed from his gut. To be able to do that for him warmed her insides, like an actor must feel after an audience applauds when it doesn't have to.

"Why can't you find something to love closer to home?"

"Name one star who was discovered in Linden or even Newark."

Buddy leaned over the lazy Susan and spoke softly but sharply. "Ladonna, name one thing you've done to prepare yourself to be discovered."

She gnawed off a piece of ham sandwich and glared at him.

"I wish you'd known my grandfather," he said.

"Alfie?"

"Yeah. He used to say there's no such thing as too prepared." Buddy spun the lazy Susan absentmindedly. "We never ate in the dining room when he was alive. It was his office, stacked high with boxes of old sales receipts. He wanted to be able to look up everything his six hundred customers had ever bought, when and why. It made me mad he spent so much time in there and on the road. I gave Dearie a hard time over it. Didn't understand it was his way of loving me. He didn't want me to go without anything I needed." Buddy's voice went wobbly and tears pooled in his eyes. "He was a good man. My father was, too, and brave. I've got the blood of good men in me, don't I?"

Tereza wanted to make him laugh again but she couldn't come up with anything. She scraped her chair around to his side of the table, patted his arm and said, "Yeah, sure you do."

"God sees I have more good blood than bad, doesn't he?"

Tereza had no idea but she said, "No sweat. He sees everything, right?"

God the Peeping Tom.

THEY APPROACHED Radio City Music Hall from Sixth Avenue. The line for losers without tickets zigzagged along Fiftieth and into Rockefeller Plaza. Tereza couldn't believe it when she was actually under the marquee that wrapped around the building. It gave off heat like a giant chicken incubator.

"The equivalent of the U.S. population has visited Radio City

Music Hall," Buddy said, reading from a brochure Herman had given them. Buddy liked learning shit like that.

She gawked at the bronze-bordered glass display cases, lit from behind, with movie posters and photos of stars. A doorman tore their tickets. They entered a black and gray and glass lobby, the ceiling covered in diamond-shaped lights, white diamonds on the black carpet, and then a bigger lobby that had to have been the most beautiful place in the world, all gold and rusty red, marble, gold foil, cork and wood.

They took the staircase to the first mezzanine, Tereza sliding her hand along the banister's curved polished edge. The windy rumble of an organ vibrated through her body and caught her in the throat. She was finally here!

"It has over four thousand pipes," Buddy said.

"Knock it off."

Months ago Tereza wouldn't have dared say that, but something had shifted between them. She used to think he was better than her; she felt more equal now. He didn't schedule her days anymore and seemed okay with whatever she wanted to do. He used the schedule board for what he called inspirational reminders. Weird stuff, like Make It Stop. Temptation Has Many Guises. He Can Be In Only One Place At One Time. When she asked what *guises* meant he'd stared at the word as if someone else had written it. He'd turned his "Most Improved Charles Atlas Student 1954" trophy to face the wall on the shelf above his desk, he explained, because he was no longer worthy of any award. When she'd asked why he didn't just throw it out he said she was too young to understand penance. That pissed her off; he had only three years on her.

A girl with great posture in black jacket and slacks, white dickey and black bow tie opened the door to a monster stage ("the biggest in the world," Buddy said) under a gold ceiling, arches behind it like sunbursts. They were in a hoity-toity section. Tereza was glad she'd dressed up. The usher led them to their seats. I could do that, Tereza thought, straightening her spine.

"There's night school for adults, you know," Buddy whispered.

"I work at night, remember?" she whispered back.

Thousands oohed as the orchestra emerged from the floor. The giant gold curtain rose in scalloped folds, like a fat lady lifting her skirts, revealing a cathedral with stained-glass windows up to the ceiling. The Glory of Easter, the program called it. So many people on one stage! Priests in sparkly gold robes and skullcaps, nuns in white with tall headdresses bright as the moon, women in gowns holding flowers, the choir forming a cross. So much to take in you could end up seeing nothing, so Tereza focused on a single nun, imagining how hard it would be to keep that headdress from wobbling.

The second half of the show was called "In the Spring." Microphones rose, curtains closed and opened, act after act followed including the Rockettes, at long last, looking kind of goofy as Girly Birds, to be honest. Tereza was thinking there had to be behind-the-scenes jobs up the wazoo at Radio City, and then it struck her like flipping a switch in a dark room: she could do what the people on stage were doing. Buddy was right: she hadn't done a damn thing to be what she wanted to be except daydream. She could learn what she needed to just like Buddy was learning to be a store manager.

THE A&P LOOKED almost exactly like Buddy's, except bigger: the same gray and canned-salmon-colored vinyl tiles on the floor, the same harsh fluorescent lights, the same cigarette display at the checkout counters. After the Automat and Radio City, it was a letdown. The manager, a tall man with a high forehead and big round glasses, pumped her hand and slapped Buddy on the back like they were old friends. "Call me Bert," he said.

"Yes, sir," Buddy said.

"Jack has nothing but good things to say about you, son." Bert led them around the store, pointing out an expanded meats/poultry and cold cuts section. Buddy perked right up at the sight of marshmallows at the end of an aisle. "Exactly where we put ours," he said.

Bert said, "Part of the master plan. Say a man working in a company like Proctor & Gamble gets transferred from Chicago to Manhattan. His wife should be able to come in here, first time, and know exactly where to find her favorite products."

"Genius," Buddy said.

Leaning forward, hands laced behind his back, Bert escorted them up and down the aisles with their displays of canned soup, beans, spaghetti, candy, nuts, tea, coffee, sauces, Chinese food ("much bigger selection than we have in Linden," Buddy said), preserves, jellies, peanut butter, baby food, canned juice. He told them he'd started in a store with one cashier and delivered groceries on a bicycle. He led them through swinging doors to a windowless room with a red Formica-topped table and four metal chairs, a counter with a coffee pot and doors leading to men's and ladies' lounges. "We're here!" Bert sang out, winking at Buddy who winked back.

Two women in hairnets and smocks embroidered with BAKERY emerged from the ladies' lounge carrying a cake ablaze with candles. Bert, Buddy and the two women sang Happy Birthday and not too well. "We didn't know how old you were," Bert said, "so Eleanor and Bernice here used their discretion."

"This is the surprise?" Tereza asked Buddy.

"This is the surprise."

"Your hubby paid for the cake," Bert said. "We threw in the candles. Many happy returns, Ladonna. As you probably know already, A&P is one big family."

Tereza blew out the candles. She counted twenty. Eleanor cut three slices of the fluffy white cake with cherry filling before she and Bernice went back to work. Buddy thanked them and shook their hands. "Don't let us keep you, Mr. Daneke," he said. "We'll eat this real fast and take the rest home." Eleanor and Bernice had left the box.

"I'm not in a hurry. And it's Bert, remember? Take your time and enjoy the cake. We make over a hundred a day, Ladonna."

"No kidding." Buddy would feel at home here. They could go for pizza after her acting class. New York pizza was supposed to be boss. "How can we get transferred here?" she asked.

She felt Buddy stiffen beside her. "Don't embarrass Mr. Daneke."

"It's okay," Bert said. "Good for a wife to be interested in her husband's career. Hers too, right?" He leaned over the table and spoke directly to Tereza. "It's not that simple, Ladonna. You see, transfers come from the regional office. We say what we need and the big brains at regional decide there's someone over here or there that fits the bill. And, until your hubby's ready for assistant manager, he's more likely to get transferred to a store closer to where you live, okay?"

Judging by how gray-haired Bert and Buddy's boss, Mr. Hinkley, was, Tereza would be long past starlet age when Buddy got trans-ferred anywhere. "If we moved here on our own, would you give Buddy a job?" If Tereza couldn't get Miranda's money back to her, they might as well use it for moving and for Tereza's acting, singing and dancing lessons.

Bert smiled and patted her hand. "We do very little hiring here, and when we do, it's low level. If your husband were to come here we couldn't promise to keep him in the management trainee program. You wouldn't want that, would you?"

Buddy stood and held out his hand to Bert. "We need to catch a train. I want to thank you for your hospitality, Mr. Daneke."

"My pleasure. Here, let me help you."

Buddy was struggling to get the cake in the box.

"Yeah, thanks," Tereza said. "It was a real surprise."

"How old are you, if you don't mind my asking?"

"My birth certificate says seventeen."

"Oh my, you've got a lot of living to do."

Bert walked them to the front. "A couple pointers," he said to Buddy. "Get yourself a pair of wingtips. Watch for a Florsheim sale. And when someone asks you to call him by his first name, oblige him, okay? Give my regards to Jack."

Outside, a safe distance from the store, Tereza said, "Bert's a yoyo. Your boots are your trademark. There are other A&Ps in New York."

Buddy kept walking, gripping the box with the cake in it. They'd gone at least six blocks before he spoke, trying to keep his voice calm, Tereza could tell. "If we move to New York it will ruin everything. You don't know how hard it is."

"What?"

"Keeping the bubble in the center."

"What bubble?"

"Ever see a carpenter's level?"

"Yeah. Jimmy had one."

"Pastor Scott told me to imagine a level inside me and try to keep the bubble in the center. He said it's all a matter of balance."

Tereza was sure you could find a carpenter's level in New York. She thrust her arms out to her sides and pretended to walk a tightrope. "Look at me!" she said. "I'm balancing."

TWENTY-THREE

JUNE 14, 1958. Doris waits in the car with the children as Miranda, in flowered sundress and sandals bought for the occasion, climbs the veranda steps, a dream about a dark and fearful manor in her head. Not *her* dream. One from a book she read years ago.

She slept fretfully last night, anticipating she'd find her childhood dwelling as eerie as that manor, the shrubs all about it monsters. But the house she left three years ago appears bright and harmless, garbed now in yellow and white paint, surrounded by grass so green it looks wet. Pansies, petunias and begonias bob their heads in greeting on either side of the steps—young plants with space between them to grow, like the herbs Doris allowed Miranda to sow back of the house on condition she not give Carolyn and Mickey any "funny teas." Miranda created the patch a few weeks ago. Mickey and Cian lay in the hammock watching her, wrapped around each other like vines. So far she's planted only parsley, oregano, mint, thyme, sage and dill, all herbs Doris can find at the grocery store and therefore trusts. Miranda hopes to persuade Doris to drive her down country roads one day in search of chamomile, nettles and mullein.

Mother Alfreda was gracious when Miranda, upon turning eighteen last month, brought in the *grimoire* and shared her decision to forgo convent life in favor of the still-faint whisper of a calling to heal with plants. Mother told her that monks once kept similar books of folklore, using the abundance of God's garden to supplement the healing power of the risen Lord. Should Miranda change her mind Mother would welcome her at the convent. She sent her off with a leather bookmark imprinted with Catherine of Siena's "Whether in the cloister or the world … ever abide in the cell of self-knowledge."

A young woman with raven hair pulled back into a ponytail opens the door. She wears red-and-white checked Bermuda shorts, a white sleeveless blouse, canvas shoes with short white socks and an easy smile on a heart-shaped face. "Miranda?"

Doris has set up this meeting but Miranda insisted on approaching the door alone.

"Mrs. Wilkes?"

"Oh, please, call me Peggy." She has warm brown eyes behind pink-framed spectacles shaped like butterfly wings. "We didn't find the harp, but come on in. Want to look around?"

Miranda hopes Doris hasn't told Peggy too much. She wants to be more to others than some pitiful girl deflowered by her father. She steps into a hallway bathed in light, transformed. The wallpaper is gone, the walls are painted white and a clean-smelling breeze flows through. She once thought the wind, unable to escape, lived in these walls. "If it's no trouble."

"Not at all. I love showing off the place. We've worked on it non-stop for two years. My hubby's a carpenter. He's not here right now. He took our little Cindy to the Flag Day parade."

"Oh, you're missing the parade because of me."

"Happily, yes. Parades bore the pants off me. Want to start in the living room?" She turns left. Miranda follows, her eyes trying to take in everything at once.

"How old is little Cindy?" Doris says it's polite to ask such questions.

"Three."

"My son is four," Miranda says. She can no longer picture Cian in this house with only her and "Da" to amuse him, so at home is he at Doris's. It's Nicholas her heart senses here.

The room she knew as the library has aqua walls, two black leather sofas, a television in a white cabinet and a gold starburst clock above the fireplace. It could be a magazine ad. She can just make out the shadows of the old claw-footed sofa, stuffed chairs and tables that James claimed a short, round, apron-wearing faerie caused to appear before they moved in, a faerie charged with watching over them and the house forever after.

James claimed to see all sorts of faeries: a small, bald man with pointy ears and long teeth who protected the big tree outside their house, walrus people who appeared in the river at dawn and dusk and rat boys who made their home in the river marsh—fat and ugly with dark, hairy skin, long snouts and tails. She smiles to herself: how effective those tales were in keeping her very young self from even wanting to peek at the seductive river that reached out in her dreams, promising freedom and adventure. But who is to say James did not see faeries? That Miranda can't differentiate between the healthy and unhealthy light surrounding people? Or that Cian doesn't enter a story as she does an object, reporting on things the book doesn't? ("Dat river was cold," he'll remark, or "Dat ant bit me.")

Seeing differently might be the truest gift James left them.

"It took weeks to strip the wallpaper before we could paint," Peggy says. "Then we sanded the floors and stained them a lighter shade. Everything was so dark, worse than a funeral parlor." She smothers her mouth with her hand. "Oh, I'm sorry. You lived here a long time, didn't you?"

"Twelve years." The heavy blue drapes are gone. In their place, filmy white curtains. How sunny the room is. Miranda still can't get enough sun. "You kept the bookcases."

"Yeah, but there are more toys on them than books. Cindy's taken over the house."

Peggy leads her through the room in which Miranda and James took their meals. It seems to be another Cindy playroom. Peggy's kitchen is even prettier than Doris's, with white metal cabinets, green countertops and a cat-shaped clock. The wood stove is gone in favor of a gas range with a shelf above it containing small tins of spices from the grocery store. Miranda leans over the stove to read the labels.

"You like to cook?" Peggy asks.

"I like to make different kinds of tea."

"Sticking a bag in hot water is the extent of my tea-making skills."

Miranda describes her garden and her tea experiments: grinding leaves and crushing seeds using a mortar and pestle, carefully recording measurements and each tea's effect on her.

"Gosh," Peggy says. "I thought I was hot stuff for sticking a few posies in the ground."

Miranda peers out the kitchen window at the river—a once-forbidden vista. "Would you mind if I walked along the riverbank behind the house? My father used to gather marshmallows there."

"Come again?"

"Plants with small, pale flowers. If I can find any, I'd like to come back in August for leaves and in October or November to harvest the root."

"What'll you do with them?"

"Dry the leaves for tea to drink for colds or indigestion. And the root's good for sore throats, so they say."

Peggy smiles. "Ah, so they say." She moves through the house with confidence, claiming space that once was Miranda and James's. Miranda thought she'd most want to peer out the attic window again, but she doesn't. The soft spring air in her garden, Mickey and Cian's hammock laughter and the cool, damp earth in her hands are more real to her now than any recollections of this place.

The house has moved on without her. And James is no longer here. She wonders if the voice she heard in her head was really his. If, all along, she hadn't been hearing her own thoughts and replaying memories.

Where James still does reside is in the *grimoire,* in the recounting of his treatments for her and Cian: the weak tea of mashed dill and fennel seeds he fed Cian through an eyedropper when the lad had colic; the clove paste he made when Miranda cut herself with a kitchen knife; the lemon balm tea for her menstrual cramps; the ginger tea for her morning sickness; goldenseal tea to stem her bleeding after Cian's birth; yarrow leaves steeped in water for her sore nipples; thick, salted honey for Cian's teething gums; cod liver oil to make up for lack of sunshine. Once, his remedies seemed like magic. Now they feel like love. By testing the formulas in the *grimoire* she knows she's testing him. If what he said about plants is true, perhaps some of what he taught her about gods and goddesses, rituals and spells, this life and the Other Life is true too.

She doesn't want to keep Doris and the children waiting any longer. She invites Peggy out to the car to meet them. Peggy invites Miranda back for marshmallows, anytime.

A mournful diesel horn on the highway punctuates their words—a sound Miranda used to hear when the World meant "out there" in the parallel universe she's part of now, however shakily. She feels released from the orbit of James's sorrow, at last. Free to turn to the sun.

TWENTY-FOUR

JULY 8, 1958. Linda wasn't thinking right when the pale green
convertible drew up beside her. Even if she had been, she wouldn't
have been able to report the year and make. She was hopeless at
that and wasn't wearing her glasses. They made her look like such
a square. Plus her mind was replaying her disastrous date down the
shore with Lonnie. How babyish she'd looked in her ruffled polka dot
bathing suit next to Arlene and Dee in their two-pieces!

"You didn't bring any money?" Lonnie had asked. He'd grudg-
ingly paid for her boardwalk rides and bought her pizza. Nobody had
told her to bring money. Wasn't the boy supposed to pay? Then in the
fun house he'd pulled her hard against him and grabbed her breast.
She'd pushed him away, of course. He was sullen on the ride back and
didn't offer to see her home, even though it was starting to get dark
when Arlene's date dropped her off at the rec center, in the part of
town where people locked their doors. It was a good half-hour walk
to her house.

Her parents had driven to Boston yesterday and would stay
while a clinic ran tests on Mom. Linda would be free of them for
two more days. She'd practically prostrated herself for permission to
stay alone and agreed to all sorts of conditions she'd already violated.
They wouldn't have allowed her to go down the shore. She'd left
after their daily call this morning and told Mr. Houseman next door

she was spending the day at the library where it was air-conditioned. Now she was hurrying home in time for the nightly calls from people who'd been commandeered to keep an eye out for her when, like sweet manna from heaven, the guy in the convertible called out, "Looks like you could use a ride."

It had to have been ninety degrees all day. Her lavender sundress was wet under the arms and her sweaty feet were stinking up her white sandals. The back of her knees were sunburned and stiffening up. The guy's smile was boyishly sweet and she didn't want to be rude. Besides, she'd never ridden in a convertible. He got out, walked around and opened the passenger door like it was a gift. "They call me Georgie Porgie," he said. He had a crew cut, blue eyes and a big lower lip. He wore a Marlon Brando shirt and tight black pants. His upper arms were bulgy thick. His aftershave had a fine woodsy smell.

"I'm Linda." She dropped the canvas bag with her wet suit and towel in the back seat and climbed in the front. "Nice to meet you, Georgie."

"Where to, sweet Linda?"

"Just a straight shot down this road, not more than a mile. You live around here?" *Just a straight shot*. Where had that come from? Some cornball thing her mother would say.

He didn't answer, just drove, drumming on the steering wheel with his fingers in a calypso-like rhythm: *day, me say day, me say day, me say day-o*. Too bad Lonnie couldn't see her now. When he turned off Grove onto Route 1, she said, "No, no, keep straight," thinking she hadn't given clear directions. He didn't say anything. As they approached the White Castle, she said, "Turn left here. Then a couple blocks, left and left again." He still didn't say anything. When he stopped at a traffic light a few more blocks away she tried to leave the car but the passenger door handle was missing. He reached over and wrenched her to him. Her dress hiked up and the back of her thighs made a sucking sound against the leather seat.

"Where are we going?" she asked. He said nothing but kept his arm around her.

She forced herself to speak calmly. "I'd like to get out, please." He kept driving, steering with his left hand, his right arm painfully tight around her.

She wrestled away and pushed against the car door. He dragged her over again.

Route 1 was busy as usual. She shouted "Help!" but the wind swallowed her words.

He turned off the highway and onto a street with no houses, only a factory and a nearly empty parking lot. Linda had no idea where they were. Georgie looked lost in himself, unaware of her even as he crushed her to his side. She'd never known anyone so strong. Her neck and side felt the strain of trying to twist away from him.

He turned onto a bumpy side road leading to a woody patch, surprising in its sudden appearance. He stopped in a small clearing. Took his hand away to turn off the car. She stood on the seat to climb over the side but he forced her down. He held both her wrists in one hand and with the other scrabbled at her hem, pushing the dress up to her waist. His breath smelled like sour milk. She kicked and pushed. He yanked her dress off over her head, squeezing her ears, pushed her back down on the seat, held her with one hand and unzipped his pants with the other. Then he lay on top of her and rocked back and forth, his weight pressing the air from her lungs. When she felt something sticky on her leg she twisted her head and bit his shoulder hard.

He jerked away. "Fucking bitch. You want to die?" He opened the glove compartment and pulled out a knife. "Beg for your life."

For a moment she thought she'd lose control of her bowels, but an image of Tereza's defiant eyes of all things came to her. She shook her head so hard it made a rattling sound.

"Scream," he said, holding the knife to her throat. "Beg for your life."

She spat in his face and braced for the cut. But he shuddered as though waking from a dream and looked at her with pained blue eyes. He plucked her dress from the car floor and handed it to her. Started the engine while she got dressed. Retraced their route to the corner of the highway and Grove, across from Tony's Garage. He stepped from the car, walked slowly around the front and opened the passenger door from the outside. He reached in the back seat for her canvas bag. Gave her a little bow and that same sweet smile.

She made it across the highway and ran to her house, praying she wouldn't encounter any neighbors, amazed her trembling legs held her upright. The ground beneath her feet heaved like the Staten Island ferry deck. She took a bath, scrubbing herself sore, *day-o* playing in her mind like a stuck record until she had to scream and scream.

TWO DAYS LATER she stepped out the side door that opened onto Mr. Houseman's driveway, keeping one hand on the knob in case she needed to jump back in. She peered left at his garage and then right toward the street. She smelled newly cut grass and saw the clippings on the drive. Minutes ago she'd heard the whooshing slice of his push mower. She couldn't hear it now, but he could be doing the other side of his house, within sprinting distance, if she needed to scream for help.

She hadn't been outside since it happened. But Mom would come home tonight expecting food in the house and Linda had eaten nearly everything in the pantry, including two jars of maraschino cherries, four cans of metallic-tasting green beans and the single can of white asparagus her mother was saving for the company they never had. During her parents' calls yesterday and this morning, she didn't mention she'd shoved the settee against the front door, bumped the kitchen table down four steps and upended it to block the side door. She didn't say she'd shut and locked the windows despite air so hot and humid the saltines had gone soft. Mr. Houseman had knocked

on the side door yesterday. She'd opened a window and told him she
had a sore throat, was staying in until she got better. Sitting cross-
legged in bed, she'd wrapped the phone extension cord around and
around her finger and told her parents everything was fine. She told
Mrs. Judge, Mrs. Ernst and Aunt Libby the same when they called to
check on her.

She locked the side door behind her and crept down the footpath,
her back pressed against the scratchy siding. Once she reached the
stoop, she scanned the street. To the left she could see across the
highway to Tony's, to the right as far as Tereza's old place and Rolf's
store. A car on the highway backfired and she nearly wet her pants,
but nobody drove down Grove Street. There was no sign of Georgie's
car, but he could be waiting anywhere. Maybe he wouldn't recognize
her in glasses, a plaid kerchief and Betty's hideous flowered housecoat.

Even if she could bring herself to venture into Rolf's, he wouldn't
have white asparagus. She'd have to go into town. She darted across
the highway, her mind sprinting ahead. If Georgie suddenly appeared
she'd take refuge in Tony's Garage and use his phone to call the police.
But they might say she'd been asking for it by getting in Georgie's car.
They'd tell her parents, who would have a fit about her going down
the shore. Mom would ask what she'd done to encourage the boy.
Daddy would say she hadn't really gotten hurt.

On the other side of the highway, breathing heavily, she slowed
her pace, still looking left and right. Daddy would have a point about
her not being hurt. It hadn't been as big a deal as it could have been.
Who was Linda Wise compared to all the women in the world who'd
actually been raped? All Georgie had done was threaten her with a
knife, come on her leg and curse at her. His language had shocked
her as much as anything: he'd spoken to her as if she were no more
than lint. Arlene and Dee would probably find the whole thing a riot
if she weren't too embarrassed to tell them. They'd turn it into one
of their stories and spread it all over school, ribbing her for not even

getting a whisker burn out of it. Did Georgie have whiskers? She should have paid more attention. Should have scratched his license plate number in the dirt with a stick. But what if she had? Who would have cared?

It wasn't like anything had really happened.

SEPTEMBER 18, 1958. Betty worked every Tuesday and Thursday from four in the afternoon until eight at night, typing invoices, completing insurance forms and calling patients whose accounts were long overdue. Lou Pierce's office was in a mansion built in the early 1900s by the founder of a music-box company. Lou's late dad, also a doctor, had bought the place sometime in the 30s and turned the downstairs into a medical office. Lou, his wife and their two children lived on the second and third floors. Betty had never been upstairs, but she wasn't bellyaching. It was enough for her to step up on the pillared porch of the grand white building on the elm-lined street and know she had as much right to be there as anyone.

She appreciated the solid feel of the front door and, as she opened it, the scent of furniture wax and rubbing alcohol that greeted her nose. The polished wood floor of the large waiting room, a once-upon-a-time parlor with fireplace and fancy molding, creaked as she crossed to her desk. Her brown leather chair sounded important as it rolled over the Plexiglas that protected an Oriental rug. An adding machine, typewriter, pens and pencils, sheets of vellum, envelopes and stamps waited just for her.

On this Thursday, when Betty arrived, Lou's nurse, Rose, was wrestling her coat on. "Doc's already gone upstairs," she said. "His last patient canceled. Big news in the paper, hey? That's all anybody could talk about when they came in today."

"I didn't see it. What's up?"

Rose crossed to a square coffee table in front of a leather couch and picked up the *Elizabeth Daily Journal*. "Terrible thing," she said. "Such a pretty girl."

Betty scanned the article and sagged like an empty sack. The body of a girl the same age as Linda had been discovered in a pine grove by a couple walking their dog.

"From Avenel," Rose said. "Practically next door. What gets me is the parents reported her missing over a month ago and the police did doodly-squat. They assumed she ran away."

Betty sat at her desk for a few minutes after Rose left, thinking about Linda at home right now by herself. Roger would still be at work. Betty punched the outside line and insisted Madge put him through right away. She told him about the girl from Avenel and was surprised he'd seen the story but hadn't mentioned it when he called her that morning.

"I didn't think we knew the family," he said. "Do we?"

"No, but I don't like the idea of Linda alone while a maniac's on the loose." The girl had died of knife wounds and, judging from the state of her body, the police figured she was already dead by the time her parents reported her missing. "Can you go to the house right now and stay with her until I get home?" Roger ordinarily didn't stop by until after dinner.

"I can, but why the panic? The girl was killed a month ago."

"I know, but the story came out today. They were probably talking about it at school. Linda could be scared silly right now with neither of us to talk to."

"Ah, okay. I'll wrap things up here."

"The paper says her parents had no idea how she'd ended up in those woods. Linda could have been missing all the time we were in Boston and we wouldn't have known."

"We called her every day," he said. "And a number of folks were keeping an eye on her. We would have known pretty quickly."

"Is that supposed to make me feel better?" Betty had wanted her to come with them. Linda wanted to stay with Arlene but Roger had said nothing doing. He'd suggested his place with Mrs. Ernst. Linda cried, said they never trusted her and begged to stay home alone. In the end, guilt about what they'd put Linda through in the past year and her accusation that they were overprotecting her led them to give in.

"Try to calm down. You know how anxiety affects you."

No, she didn't. Unable to find a reason for Betty's pain, the so-called experts in Boston had tried to buffalo her with mumbo jumbo. Considering that both the uterus and appendix cut from her had turned out healthy, they said they couldn't rule out "hysterical neurosis." More judgment than diagnosis if you asked Betty, but of course nobody did.

"I'm calm," she said. "I just think we should make sure one of us is with her at all times when she's not in school." If Linda ever did go missing, the police might assume she'd run away like that ragamuffin Tereza had.

"How are we going to do that?"

"I'll have her come to Lou's office right from school the days I work. You can pick her up here, take her home and stay with her until I get off work."

"You could stop working."

It was hard to put a foot in a closed mouth. Betty counted to five before saying, "Two days a week is all I ask for. They matter to me." They'd talked about it in Boston over dinner one night. Betty had been touched by the way Roger truly listened. "You said you understood."

He sighed. "Yes, I did, and I do." She could hear him shuffling papers. "I'll leave now and drive to the house. And of course I'll pick her up at Lou's on Tuesdays and Thursdays."

"That would be swell. Could you talk to her, too? Make sure she knows what to do if she comes across a thug. The police taught you judo or something, didn't they?" The only advice Betty's father ever had for her was "Never corner something meaner than you."

Roger sniffed out a laugh. "I learned a few self-defense moves. Good thing I never had to use them. Probably would have made matters worse. But sure, I'll talk to her."

"Let me know how you think she is when you do. She's been secretive for weeks. I think she's hiding cookies in her room. I'll bet she's put on a good ten pounds since we got back."

"I thought you were worried about her safety, not her weight."

"I am, but she doesn't eat right when something's bothering her."

Betty heard Roger's briefcase snap.

"She *has* looked tearful lately," he said. "I'll see what I can find out. Do you want me to pick you up tonight? Linda can come with me."

"No, I like taking the bus." She often pretended it was headed for Kansas.

"Hey, listen, why don't I move back home? It would be easier to work out a schedule."

Betty felt herself teetering on the edge of a tall building. If she didn't look down she'd be okay. She counted to five and said, "I suppose we could talk about it."

YOU COULDN'T turn on the TV or walk past a newsstand without seeing a picture of that dead girl. The women who came into Herman's were spooked. They chittered like birds warning each other about a cat stealing up on a nest. Tereza thought the girl was pretty stupid to have gotten herself killed, but Buddy said she and Dearie should be on the lookout for weirdos at bus stops.

"If anybody grabs you from behind," he said, "raise your leg and he'll fall over."

Tereza snorted and said, "I'll tell him I have cooties."

Buddy didn't think that was funny.

NOVEMBER 16, 1958. Enzo calls Doris periodically to say there's no progress on Bill's case but never asks to speak with Miranda. Now doesn't he suddenly appear at the front door for the first time in nearly a year against a backdrop of falling leaves aswirl in a Mary Poppins wind. He looks monochromatically officious in gray overcoat and black fedora, carrying a black briefcase.

"Doris is at work," Miranda says.

"I know. I came to see you." He claps a hand on his hat to hold it down.

"I have chores to finish before Mickey and I collect Cian from nursery school."

"Cian's in nursery school?" From his expression, you would have thought she'd told him the lad had been on the cow's back when it jumped over the moon.

"Why wouldn't he be? He's old enough. Four years and nine months, to be precise." To admit him to the school, Miranda had to swear out a birth affidavit and get it notarized. Provide a father's name. She accepts at last that it's James and wonders how she'll explain it to Cian when the time comes. So far he hasn't asked, perhaps because he lives with two mothers.

"I thought with his, you know, problem, you might hold him back a year or two."

"And not be ready for kindergarten? Be the oldest child in class as I was?" Miranda's words spill out with an intensity that surprises her. "I'll have you know he met the criteria to get in. He can count to eight, bounce a ball and pull up his zipper. He doesn't have as many words as some his age but he's exceptional at one requirement: listening to stories without interrupting."

"That I don't doubt. All those story hours. It's wonderful, Miranda, I truly mean that."

Enzo sounds genuine. She softens to him. She tells him that Doris worked with Cian evenings, teaching him to count, recognize certain words and manage the toilet on his own—"Good shot, Cian!" Miranda used Doris's button box to help him learn to sort by color, size and shape, and she's saturated his brain with cod liver oil, spinach, canned sardines, turnips and walnuts.

Enzo leans forward as if Miranda's words are the most important ever uttered. A habit of his she misread once. She knows now he is simply conscientious at his job. Pride keeps her from telling him that some children in the neighborhood call Cian "pinhead." Carolyn shakes her little fists at them and says, "Get lost!" Cian has always looked adoringly at Carolyn; now he loves her even more. Miranda doesn't think she's jealous, but lately she's been finding Carolyn annoying: the constant nattering, the perfectly straight hair like Bill's, the teeth so big for her face she looks always about to break into laughter.

"How are you?" Enzo asks. "You look good. That color suits you." She's wearing dungarees and a pearl-necked sweater in a shade called persimmon.

"I'm well."

"I mean, how's your life? Are you happy?"

Why does he care? She looks at him for a moment, pondering the question. One might be able to say she's lived happily ever after St. Bernadette's, after James. But she doesn't know what chapter her life is in right now and where this restless yearning she's experiencing will lead. She needs more practice with herbal remedies, but Doris will have none of her special brews. She's read about drugs made from plant extracts and borrows books about botany and pharmacology from the public library. She'll try to learn more once all three children are in school full-time. She hasn't lost all interest in studying library science. But, with James's blood swimming in her, it's unlikely she'll ever be anything as normal as a librarian.

"My days are busy," she tells Enzo. And they are, making the children breakfast, walking Cian and Carolyn to their different schools, playing school with Mickey because he feels left out, fixing his mid-morning snack, doing a load of laundry, collecting Cian from nursery school, making him and Mickey lunch, reading to them, extracting something from the freezer for dinner, greeting Carolyn when she gets home from school, making her a snack, sweeping up and picking up. But for the lack of a husband, hers is a housewife's reality and it doesn't satisfy her.

"You're letting the heat out," Enzo says. "May I step in for a minute?"

She admits him but remains standing in the hallway. He removes his hat. His close-cropped hair is grayer than she remembers but vitality infuses the light surrounding him.

She shuts the door behind him. "Why are you here?"

"I need your help with a case that has the Woodbridge police stumped. An Avenel girl was stabbed to death late in the summer. Barbara Pickens. You might've heard about it; it was in the papers for weeks after they found her body."

"Yes, of course." Doris had been concerned, insisting that Miranda lock the doors at all times and urging her to not speak to strangers.

"I don't want to remind you of too many details," Enzo continues. "I don't want to influence what you might see."

Such presumption. "I haven't tried to see things in a while." If "reading" objects is no longer needed to safeguard a child who isn't divine, why willingly take in another's pain? It seems to make no difference. Murderers and their victims eventually all end up the same: extinguished like candles. There are no saints in Heaven powerful enough to intercede.

"Did you ever consider you might have been chosen for crime work?"

She laughs at his artifice. "By whom?"

"Please. Without you, we wouldn't have thought to look for bloodstains from a second person or a connection to an artist or draftsman." Holding the bullet that killed Nolan, Miranda had seen a slim back bent over a slanted table making bold strokes with a pencil.

"And what good has that done?"

"It'll pay off eventually, I'm sure of it."

"Why do you care about this case if it isn't yours?"

"Cops help each other. You never know, another detective might come across something that solves Bill's case someday." He gives an embarrassed laugh. "Also, to be honest, Stony River gets mostly bicycle thefts and bad checks. It's a chance to put what I studied into practice."

A soldier with no war, a healer with no sick.

Enzo sets his briefcase on the floor gently, almost reverently. He removes his coat and folds it over his arm. "This girl, this Barbara," he says. "She was only fifteen, a good girl, from all accounts. She sang in the choir, did modern dance in school. Talented, you know? Now she's gone and whoever killed her could be getting ready to kill again."

Miranda glances into the living room where she left Mickey building a cushion fort. "I've been saving my energy for healing with plants. I mean to do something important with it one day." She's determined not to be like James, who treated only his family and shut himself off from a world of needs.

"Preventing another girl from being murdered seems pretty darn important to me."

Since leaving St. Bernadette's, Miranda has begun to understand that life is a series of exchanges: her confinement in exchange for

James's freedom to practice his beliefs, the sale of their house in exchange for St. Bernadette's agreement to keep Cian, the prospect of mystic communion in exchange for the facade of normalcy.

"I was wondering if you might find my mother's burial place," she says. "I know where and when she died, but that's all." She has decided to leave James where the city buried him. Eileen's bones call her now.

Enzo's eyes widen for a moment and then he nods. "It's possible." He brings out his notebook. She gives him the details.

"Would you like to sit?" she asks. "I must keep an eye on the lad." He follows her into the living room. Mickey's brown eyes look up at him but the child says nothing, resumes the secret sounds of his play.

Miranda pulls out a chair at the dining-room table. Enzo takes one opposite her. From his briefcase he withdraws a plastic bag containing a petticoat the color of bones. He calls it a "slip," a word that makes her think of falling. He slides the garment from the plastic and pushes it toward her. It gives off a smell like old fish.

She feels hot and cold at the same time. "It's been so long, I don't know how I'll react. Will you watch over Mickey?"

"Of course."

She runs her hand over the petticoat's straps, bodice and skirt, its finely stitched seams. Expensive. A patch of skirt is stiff and faintly stained. She closes her eyes and inhales deeply, one, two, three times. As she begins to lose the edges of physical awareness, panic bubbles in her chest. She opens her eyes to see Enzo staring intently, pencil poised above his notebook.

"I won't let you go too far," he says.

She closes her eyes again and visualizes what she has touched. It's the right size for her mind to slide into, as easily as her body once slid into her mother's petticoat. That one was cotton and rough. This is a softer, thinner fabric, but something scratches her body all the same: sticks, pebbles and pine needles. She lies on her back among trees, the petticoat bunched at her waist, a burning, rusty taste in her throat. Everything hurts: her back, arms, legs, chest. She cannot move for pain and weakness. A tire squeals. She's been abandoned. Left to die. Her thighs are sticky with something that brings back Cian's conception with revulsion and shame. She pushes away the girl's final desperate thoughts, opens her eyes and swallows back a sour taste. "She's not wearing underpants."

Enzo falls back against his chair. "Woodbridge kept that from reporters. What else?"

"She's in the woods."

"That *was* in the news. People walking their dog found her."

"She's alive when a car drives away. I think she was taken to the woods in that car."

"Did you see the car?"

"No."

"Okay, from the top. Tell me exactly what you saw. Every detail you can."

She does, except for her revulsion and something else she can't explain. He writes it down, packs up the petticoat then drives away in the autumn wind.

The rest of the day she's haunted. It's true she didn't see the car, but she had a strong sense the driver was Bill Nolan. That's impossible, of course. Her lingering animosity toward him must have caused a feckless impression. If Enzo visits again, she'll refuse to help further. Who knows what damage she could cause, what person she could unjustly accuse? Prisons are odious places.

❦ TWENTY-FIVE ❦

FEBRUARY 3, 1959. Linda understood three things about herself: one, she didn't know beans about suffering; two, Arlene Varga thought she was wildly funny; three, she could no longer think about some things except in fragments. She often transcribed her shard-like thoughts on baby blue stationery and cut the paper into shivering narrow strips.

Thought: If the Bible is right and God never forgets a single sparrow, He must not have forgotten her. But seeing her and doing something about what He saw were not the same thing because, if He intervened in everything, what would be the point of having free will?

Tuesdays after school, Daddy picked her up at Arlene's apartment instead of Doctor Pierce's—a seemingly major concession from Mom that Linda suspected was meant to somehow annoy Daddy, who'd moved back after the girl from Avenel turned up stabbed to death. With her parents afraid she'd be next and hovering like bats, she felt like a bug in a glass jar with only a few pinholes poked for air. Tuesday afternoons at Arlene's apartment were rare gasps of smoky breath.

Arlene's radiators groaned as if constipated and the air always smelled of whatever Buster's Bar and Grill downstairs was cooking. But Linda could suck on a cigarette and blame Arlene's father for the smell on her clothes. Today, smoke curling above their heads,

Linda and Arlene had watched *American Bandstand* and split a bottle
of beer. Then Arlene insisted they play Jesus Calms the Waves for the
umpteenth time, even though Linda was bored with it and wanted to
do almost anything else. Arlene's mother was dead and her father had
never taken her to Sunday school, so she thought the whole "concept"
of Bible games was wildly funny. Taller by a head, she would sit on her
bed so that Linda could stand over her, wag her finger and say, "Today
we're going to listen to a really scary story about what happened to
Jesus' disciples. And you're going to help me tell it." Arlene would say
"creeeak" and pretend she was pulling hard on oars whenever Linda
said "boat." Count to twelve really fast when Linda said "disciples."
Blow when Linda said "wind" and so forth. Today, as usual, they'd
ended up on the bed laughing their faces off. Arlene had dark wide-set
eyes and a mouth that smiled more on one side than the other. Linda
coveted Arlene's long, black wavy hair and thick bangs. Some girls
at school said Arlene liked her only because Linda was fat and no
competition for boys. They said she mocked Linda behind her back
and only invited her over to get more material to make fun of. They
were lying, jealous because Arlene was so popular.

Thought: Georgie probably wasn't his real name.

For extra credit in social studies, Linda volunteered Saturday
afternoons at the Menlo Park Home for Delinquent Boys, a
disinfectant-smelling, red-brick building to which the county court
sent eight- to twelve-year-old boys when they got in trouble with
the law. They couldn't be held longer than three months. For some it
was the best place they'd ever lived, despite having to be locked into
their rooms at night. Saturday was visiting day and Linda would play
Go Fish and Hangman with the boys who didn't get any visitors. She
sometimes saw Georgie in a delinquent boy's eyes. Maybe, like the
kid whose mother ran a boarding house, he hadn't had a bed to call
his own. Or, if he did have one, he might have been chained to it and
forced to drink his own urine like the skinny boy with cave-like eyes.

It wasn't okay to set fires or torture cats, of course, but you could understand it a little.

This afternoon, after Jesus Calms the Waves, Linda had said, "My mother gripes that I'm getting so fat I'm dee-vel-oping an Oriental look around the eyes. What do you think?" She and Arlene stretched the corners of their eyes and shuffled around Arlene's bedroom, saying "Ah so" over and over in high, squeaky voices.

Some people would say Linda was lucky. She had both a mother and father, even though Daddy slept in the downstairs room in which Grandmother Wise had died. Arlene had only a father who got drunk and sat on the couch scratching his you-know-whats most nights after he got home from his job as a stock boy at Woolworth's. Arlene said he got all his calories from beer. She cooked herself a TV dinner every night and pretended she was eating on an airplane.

On the evenings Mom worked at Doctor Pierce's office, Linda persuaded Daddy to eat TV dinners with her. Tonight it had been fried chicken with mashed potatoes and succotash. One TV dinner was never enough for Linda; she kept a stash of Oreos under her bed.

Thought: Everyone has the potential for good, even Georgie.

On Friday nights Daddy would invite two people over to play canasta with him and Linda: it might be Mrs. Ernst and her hard-of-hearing sister; Daddy's secretary, Madge, and her husband; or the crippled Mr. Klaussner, two blocks away, and his elderly mother. Daddy and Linda made little club, heart, diamond and spade sandwiches filled with cream cheese and pimiento, egg salad, Cheese Whiz and crunchy peanut butter. Linda could make Arlene laugh until she cried just by saying her father served can-a-pees and highballs.

Mom stayed in her room during the canasta games.

Thought: Maybe God *had* intervened; otherwise Linda would've ended up dead, too. When they found the Avenel girl, Daddy said, "You do know better than to go off alone with a stranger, don't you?"

They were studying World War II in history, at last. How, in a world of such horrors, could an insignificant sparrow named Linda Wise have remained safe and warm?

At church camp, over two years ago, Linda had sat under the stars one evening singing "Jacob's Ladder" with a hundred others. So many voices reaching up to the night sky, singing *every rung goes higher, higher*. It had made her ache to believe in the possibility of a world in which everyone was loved and no one suffered.

Tonight she would kneel by her bedroom window and softly sing it before surrendering to sleep and dreams that were nothing but noise; a howling that came from a vast dark place.

MAY 21, 1959. "See you at ten," Tereza said. "Couple minutes after, okay?"

"Till then, my Juliet," Buddy said, inching the car forward as she closed the door. He peeled out of the playhouse parking lot, leaving her in a gust of exhaust that threatened to make her upchuck Dearie's tuna surprise. She pushed open the door to the hundred and fifty–seat playhouse, home to the Union County Dramatic Club. Normally she loved smelling the coffee the director brewed for rehearsals. Tonight it made her queasy. She had two small speaking parts in the production of *A Streetcar Named Desire* that opened in three weeks: a woman relaxing on steps in the first scene and, in the ninth, a Mexican woman who sold tin flowers for funerals.

You had to start somewhere.

Buddy was heading for Bible study to learn more about the big bad devil. He had private sessions with Pastor Scott Mondays and Thursdays when Tereza was in rehearsal. Sometimes he came out feeling good; other times he'd be all twitchy and have to take a long hot bath.

If Tereza had told him tonight, he would've had a few hours for it to sink in before dropping her off and been able to talk to the preacher about it. But it hadn't sunk into her yet and she needed time to come up with the right words. You couldn't count on Buddy's mood. He might have gone weird on her and not given her a ride. And since he wouldn't let her take the bus at night, she would have missed rehearsal.

He'd gotten a promotion but it had come with a transfer to the Stony River store, which Buddy said had an "unbalancing energy," whatever that meant. One night he came home in a state because he'd accidentally touched a woman's hand while at the cash register and she'd pulled back as though he burned her. He said she'd looked into his eyes and seen Satan in him.

The devil thing was getting to be a bit much. When Buddy learned that Satan could appear as a frog, he smashed every one of Dearie's miniatures. Tereza had insisted Buddy clean them up and apologize, but Dearie took to her bed for a full day anyway, refusing to eat anything. Tereza regretted having snuck back the frogs she'd pinched. If she'd left them in Alfie's box of old receipts Dearie still would have had them, at least.

The cast and crew were standing in a clump in the middle of the floor that served as the stage, the audience seats rising on three sides around it. She didn't see Marilyn Shore. Tereza understudied for Marilyn's role as Stella and Stanley Kowalski's upstairs neighbor, Eunice.

The script called for the relaxing woman to be a Negro. Tereza was the darkest in the company. Her other character was supposed to croon "Flowers, flowers for the dead" in Spanish, but since the director didn't expect any Mexicans in the audience, Tereza would say it in English. She'd wear a serape and wide-brimmed straw hat so the audience wouldn't recognize her as the relaxing woman from the first act, although anybody reading the program would find Ladonna Lange listed as both.

Tereza hadn't realized how lonely she'd been for her kind of people, hadn't even known what her kind of people were. The day she showed up for auditions and somebody said "Your hair is just like Dana Wynter's in *The Body Snatchers*," she knew she belonged there.

When she wasn't on stage she helped out with sound effects and props. The sound effects were cool, especially the trains, Stella getting smacked and the jungle sounds. Some props were heavy; she'd have to be more careful from now on when moving Blanche's trunk. She lightly pressed her flat belly. Hard to believe someone was growing in there and would burst out in December. "Don't gain much weight," the doctor had said. "You've got a small pelvis."

She'd gone to see him because a popcorn kernel had scratched her throat and she thought that was why she couldn't stop barfing. His office was close to the theater where she'd gotten a job selling matinee tickets after Herman sold the restaurant. She could eat all the popcorn she wanted for free. "Didn't you wonder when you didn't get your period?" the doctor had asked.

Yeah, she had, but she didn't think you could get knocked up if the sex wasn't fun.

"Hey!" she called out to her fellow actors. Blanche DuBois waved her over. Wouldn't it be something to understudy for that drunken nympho part? Adele Baruch, the director, said Blanche's problem—one, anyway—was that she was "over-civilized." Adele wasn't, with her long, wild-looking gray hair and tight black leather slacks. She was cool.

"Ladonna, you're Eunice tonight," Adele said. "Marilyn's kid sister, Evvy, has been missing all week and Marilyn says her brain's not worth shit right now. Her family is beside themselves. They're all out searching for her."

Tereza felt a sudden stab for her kid brother. "When'd she go missing?" How old would Allen be now? Thirteen? He wouldn't even know when he became an uncle.

"Two, three days ago," said the guy who played Eunice's husband. "Marilyn told me some boys spotted Evvy getting in a car with a man on Monday night. The police are involved finally. At first they thought she might be a runaway."

"I hope they find her," Tereza said. If she wanted to be found.

"Okay, people," Adele said, "let's evict this sad news from our minds for the next two hours. We'll rehearse the first half tonight, special emphasis on Eunice's part for Ladonna's sake. Places all, please, scene one."

Adele was tough: twice a week from eight to ten, no matter what, twenty-one rehearsals in all. If you missed more than a third, you could lose your part. Although Tereza hoped nothing bad had happened to Marilyn's sister, wouldn't it be something if she got to do Eunice after all?

She opened her script and took her place on the prop stairs, kicking herself for not having memorized Eunice's lines. What Buddy had said in New York about not doing anything to prepare herself to be discovered had gotten her off her ass and into the dramatic club. But she still didn't think enough ahead, wasn't ready for opportunity's *thump, thump, thump.*

Luckily she'd heard Marilyn do Eunice many times and could read without having to trace the script with her finger. She stumbled over only a few words.

Eunice wasn't in the second scene. Tereza liked watching the guy who played Stanley rehearse; he could really turn himself into the creep. He was built like Buddy but a few years older with a smoky voice. At the first rehearsal Adele had explained the plot and what the actors were supposed to project. Stanley was a jerk, like Jimmy, but Tereza wouldn't have figured out that he rapes Blanche when he carries her off to the bedroom in scene ten if Adele hadn't said. Some things so obvious to others were thick as paste to Tereza.

Buddy wasn't a drinker or gambler like Stanley and she couldn't imagine him hitting her. But just once she would have liked to have great sex like the Kowalskis—"implied" in the script, Adele said, like the rape. Tereza's mouth was so hungry for a kiss she often pressed Buddy's hand to her lips as he slept. She wouldn't stick around if he ever hit her, but something about him had a hold on her, like something about Stanley did on Stella.

Tereza had to be alert in scene three because, after Stanley hits her, Stella hides in Eunice's apartment, which the audience never sees because it only exists in their minds, like the devil in Buddy's. Eunice tells him to stop yelling "STELL-LAHHHHH!" and tries to keep him away from her friend. But love-stupid Stella comes out and Stanley gets down on his knees and kisses her pregnant stomach. She couldn't picture Buddy doing that, but she hoped he'd be okay with the news once he got over his surprise. A&P liked their managers to be family men.

She tried to imagine their baby's face. Like trying to see a picture before it was painted.

TEREZA WAS HOME before Buddy the next day, so she took a shower and changed into white shorts and a pink-for-girls blouse. Lisa was a nice name. She cleared cobwebs from the chipped white glider in the backyard and waited in it for Buddy. She called out to him as he padlocked the garage door like it was Fort Knox. When he wasn't driving or washing his precious car he kept it locked up. He jumped. Obviously he hadn't noticed her there.

"You look nice. What's up?"

"I need to tell you something."

"Out here?"

"Yeah, Dearie's making us a special meal and the oven is steaming up the house. It got up to eighty today. I felt like a boiled egg in that ticket booth." Tereza had given Dearie the news earlier, Dearie fake-clutching her heart and saying, "I'm too young to be a great-granny." But she'd smiled and cried and squeezed the bejesus out of Tereza.

Buddy ducked his head and climbed into the glider, making it creak and swing. He took a seat across from her. "What's the occasion?"

"Sit beside me, okay? I want us to hold hands."

"If I do, we'll tip over. I need to put weights on the glider."

She sighed. "Okay, stay there but you gotta look at me."

He laughed. "I've never seen you like this. You get the bigger part for certain?"

"No. Marilyn will probably be back. Her sister will turn up."

He laced his fingers behind his neck. "Then what's the word, Thunderbird?"

She grinned at him. "You're gonna be a daddy."

"Is that a line from the play?"

She laughed. "No. I saw a doctor. Santa's bringing us a baby for Christmas."

He dropped his arms. "You're pregnant."

"Yeah."

"What were you thinking?"

"What do you mean, me?"

He got out of the glider and walked around it, cracking his knuckles. He stuck his head in, his face close to hers. "You know there's something wrong with me, don't you?"

"You get moody, if that's what you mean."

"I don't get moody, Ladonna. I'm fucking crazy. The devil lives in me. I've been trying to tell you that for how long. I'm a monster. What kind of life would a kid have with me?"

"You're not a monster." Jimmy was a monster.

He climbed back into the glider, sat and held his head in his hands. "We never talked about a baby. I would've said no."

"We never talked about birth control either."

"That's the wife's job."

"Good time to let me know."

He looked up. "I can see it in your eyes. Why me, you're saying, right? Why'd I get stuck with this maniac?"

She shook her head.

"Pastor Scott says we spend our whole lives trying to get back inside our mothers and Satan spends eternity trying to get inside us. He finds those who don't find God. Some days I can feel God inside me. Other times the devil's winning. I wish I could describe it so you'd understand. I've done terrible things, Ladonna."

"Who hasn't?" She thought about the guys in the cars and about taking Miranda's money.

The porch door squealed open and Dearie yelled, "Supper!"

Buddy covered his face with his hands. "I don't deserve supper."

Tereza wanted to feel sorry for him, but she was tired of his devil talk. Seemed like he was only looking for attention like Stanley Kowalski. She was going to have a baby. She didn't need a whiny husband. She stepped out of the glider and said, "Tough gazzobbies. Dearie went to a lot of trouble, so you're going to eat. And you're going to be a father whether you want to or not. Get used to the idea."

TWENTY-SIX

OCTOBER 20, 1959. Shrouded in a forest-green caftan her mother had stitched, Linda came down to miserly breakfast rations: grapefruit, cottage cheese, toast, orange marmalade and tea with saccharine. She lived for the marmalade. "Where's Daddy?"

"An early meeting." Mom tapped the newspaper with one finger and looked up with a grim smile. "These mothers got lucky, letting their daughters walk home in the dark. Thank heavens one girl had the presence of mind to get the license plate number so the police could arrest this menace." She folded the paper, reached across and set it beside Linda's plate.

Scooping marmalade onto her toast, Linda looked down and sucked in a breath.

"What?" Mom said.

"Nothing." Linda bit into the toast. She'd seen the same police sketch in the newspaper a few months ago: a man spotted giving a ride to a girl the night she disappeared. Mom had flipped over it. Linda hadn't wanted to say anything and risk her parents finding out she'd gotten into a car with a stranger. The sketch could've been of anyone. But here it was again, alongside a mug shot of a man they'd arrested for attempted kidnapping. It had to be him. Those vacant eyes, that simpleton smile. The article said the police were looking for anyone who might have witnessed the attempted kidnapping or had any information about Evelyn Shore's disappearance. It gave a detective's name and a phone number.

Suddenly lightheaded, Linda clutched the seat of her chair.

"What's the matter?" Mom asked. "You've lost your color." She came around and pressed Linda's forehead with cool fingers. "You feel clammy."

"I think I might faint."

"Golly. Here, put your arm around my shoulders. Careful. Slide off the chair onto the floor. Okay. Good. Lie back. I'll get you a pillow and blanket. You'd better stay home today."

Linda was the ambulance Mom had not gotten to drive in the war. It had been six months since she resigned her position with Doc Pierce to take her daughter's fate in hand. She expected Linda to be grateful for her efforts to help her lose weight. But Linda loved her fat. Standing naked before the full-length mirror in her bedroom, she'd caress herself. Knead her stomach rolls like bread dough. Press her jiggly thighs between her hands, admiring the way the skin rippled like a lake's surface. Wasn't skin miraculous, the way it stretched and remolded the body as if it were Silly Putty? In her opinion, she'd become even more *zaftig* than when Richie drew her as Gilda Daring. The kids who called her pig, cow, hippo and whale were ignoramuses who didn't realize that the female was genetically designed with layers of fat for the rigors of child bearing. A round belly symbolized fertility. Linda had no intention of bearing a child if it meant coupling with a man. But the idea of her body swelling with life thrilled her. *Her* life. *Her* flesh. When she could no longer jam herself into her clothes, she took money from her father's wallet and bought a maternity blouse and a black skirt with a panel of stretchy material.

That was when Mom had quit her job and set about making Linda's meals and dishing out stingy portions. She had Daddy padlock the pantry and food cabinets. She raided Linda's room and confiscated every Oreo, Twinkie and Hershey bar. Sent her to school with a brown-bag lunch and no money. She seemed to have boundless energy for the Linda Project. Pain pinched her face from time to time, but she appeared happy. She'd found her calling.

For the first few months of the Project, Linda railed against her mother, hating her—and Daddy, too, for not defending her. She cried at night from hunger. Arlene didn't want to be seen with her anymore, as if being fat was contagious, and the few girls who were still friendly said her mother was right to make her lose weight and her father to cut off her allowance.

When the head of volunteers at the Home for Delinquent Boys told her she wasn't setting a healthy example for the little criminals, the fight left her and she stopped resisting her mother. She was down to two hundred and thirty-six pounds from a high of two sixty. "Slow going," Mom said, but Linda was sad to see herself shrink even a little.

Back with a pillow and two blankets, Mom knelt on the floor and grunted as she rolled Linda to one side to get a blanket under her.

"You don't have to do that. I'm feeling better. I'll get up now."

"Only if you're sure. You can rest down here on your father's bed for a while."

"How long are you two going to have separate rooms?"

Mom puffed out a sigh. "That's not something to talk about right now."

"Why not? If we can talk about my fat, why can't we talk about your marriage?"

"Because it's between your father and me. We'll work it out."

"Then maybe you should leave me alone to work out my weight by myself."

"That's different. I can't stand by and let my daughter eat herself to death."

"So you're starving me instead? No wonder I almost fainted."

"I refuse to argue with you today. I'm not feeling exactly tip-top myself. I'll help you into your father's room, then go up and lie down for a while."

Linda pushed herself up. "I'm fine. I can go to school."

After Mom had gone to her room, Linda sat at the table and stared at the newspaper. She remembered something about the car that might be important—a missing door handle. She shuffled to the wall phone, dialed the number in the paper and made an appointment to see a detective at the Stony River police station after school.

She finished her breakfast and a toast heel Betty had left on her plate.

❦

ROESCH	Detective Arthur Roesch of the Woodbridge Police Department on Tuesday, October 20, 1959, 9:12 AM, interviewing Eldon Joseph Jukes, arrested on October 19, 1959, on suspicion of attempted kidnapping. Also present is Detective Lorenzo Rotella of the Stony River Police Department.
ROESCH	Sorry I can't offer you a more comfortable chair. You okay on that bench?
JUKES	Yes, sir.
ROESCH	Sleep all right last night?
JUKES	Not really.
ROESCH	Well it's a holding cell, isn't it? Nothing special. They give you some breakfast down there?
JUKES	Yes, sir.
ROESCH	Glad to hear it. Mind if I call you Eldon?
JUKES	Most people call me Buddy.
ROESCH	Ah, Buddy then. My friends call me Artie. That's what I'd like you to call me. Yeah?
JUKES	Yes, sir. (Laugh) I mean, Artie.

ROESCH   It's stuffy in here. I hate rooms with no windows. Gotta
          roll up my sleeves. Feel free to remove that nice-looking
          jacket if you get warm. Real leather?

JUKES   Yes, Artie.

ROESCH   Cigarette?

JUKES   I don't smoke.

ROESCH   Oh, good for you. Now, you were arrested yesterday for
          attempted kidnapping on the evening of October 13th. Is
          that right?

JUKES   So they say.

ROESCH   Yeah. So say two young ladies, Susan Jeffers and Nancy
          Pawling. You were arrested at your workplace. At the
          A&P on Main Street, right?

(5-second pause)

          Was that a nod? Yes? Okay. How were you going to
          manage two girls, Buddy? Or did you plan to drop one
          off at her house and take the other somewhere private?

JUKES   · I don't know what you're getting at. I offered them
          a ride, that's all. Just trying to be nice. I like to help
          people. They didn't accept. Nothing happened to them.
          Why are you calling it attempted kidnapping?

ROESCH   Yeah, I can understand your confusion. I guess I should
          tell you we're also investigating a murder and a missing
          girl.

JUKES   What's that got to do with me?

ROESCH   Well, that's what we're trying to find out, yeah? Let me
          show you some pictures.

JUKES   Nobody said anything about murder.

ROESCH   No, you haven't been charged with murder. We'd just

like your help with the case. Look at this photograph,
Buddy, and tell me if you've ever seen these two girls.

(10-second pause)

JUKES   I'm not sure. They look familiar. The girls I offered the
        ride to?

ROESCH   Very good. Yes, we took this Polaroid at the station
        yesterday after they identified you in the lineup.

JUKES   You didn't need a lineup. I would've told you it was me.
        I don't understand. They turned down the ride. They
        didn't get hurt.

ROESCH   Yeah, that was lucky. Here's the thing. When one of the
        girls, Nancy Pawling, gets home and tells her mother
        a man asked her and her friend to get in his car—not
        once, but three times, following them down the street—
        Nancy's mother asks her to describe that man and Nancy's
        description rings a bell with Mrs. Pawling. She saves news-
        papers. Takes them someplace and gets ten cents a pound
        for them. So she goes down to her basement and looks
        through her paper stack. Finds one from five months ago
        with a police artist's sketch of a man three teenaged boys
        saw behind the wheel of a car with a now-missing girl in
        it. She asks Nancy, Is this the man who offered you a ride?
        and Nancy says yes. Let me show you another photo. We
        didn't take this one. You recognize the girl?

(5-second pause)

JUKES   No. That the missing girl?

ROESCH   You're good. Her name's Evelyn Shore. Evvy, for short.
        Pretty, isn't she? Nice smile. Natural blonde, I'd say. I

think they call that hairdo a pageboy. She was last seen
Monday, May 18, around 8:30 at night, getting in a car
those three boys described as looking just like yours. The
police sketch was made from their description of the
driver. See why we're interested?

JUKES   I suppose.

(Unidentified sound)

ROESCH   Cracking your knuckles can lead to arthritis later, I'm
           told, Buddy. Just a thought. Let me show you another
           photograph. We didn't take this one, either. A school
           photo, I believe. They must make all the girls wear black
           sweaters and white pearls. Tell me if you've ever seen
           this one.

(5-second pause)

JUKES   No, sir, I haven't.
ROESCH   It's Artie. Take your time. You don't remember seeing
           this picture in the newspaper last year? On TV?
JUKES   I don't read the news or watch much TV.
ROESCH   Oh, well, that would explain it. The girl's name
           is Barbara Pickens. Her murder is the one we're
           investigating.
JUKES   I just thought of something. You know that missing girl?
ROESCH   Evelyn Shore?
JUKES   Yeah. You said she went missing on a Monday in May. I
           would've taken my wife to her drama club that night.
           She never missed a rehearsal. I would've dropped her
           off around eight then gone to my pastor's office for Bible
           study.

ROESCH   Will your wife and pastor testify to that?

JUKES   I don't see why not.

ROESCH   Okay, good, we'll get statements from them. I want
          to talk about your car for a minute. As you know, we
          impounded it and technicians have been checking it
          over pretty good. They found a pair of women's panties
          stuffed way under the front seat. And want to hear
          something coincidental? The dead girl, Barbara Pickens,
          wasn't wearing panties when they found her. We haven't
          yet asked her mother to take a look at the ones we found
          in your car but we will, we will. What can you tell me
          about those panties?

(20-second pause)

          You're rocking back and forth, Buddy. Do you need to
          go to the can? You're shaking your head no. Okay, let's go
          on. The panties?

JUKES   They must be my wife's.

ROESCH   How long you been married?

JUKES   Two years.

ROESCH   What's your wife's name, Buddy?

JUKES   Ladonna.

ROESCH   Pretty name. Any kids?

JUKES   One on the way in December.

ROESCH   Congratulations. I've got two kids. Lot of work, big
          expense, but I wouldn't trade them for anything. Now,
          your wife, Ladonna. Is she in the habit of taking her
          panties off in the car?

JUKES   I couldn't say.

(Sound of door opening)

OFFICER	Detective Roesch. Got a moment, sir?
ROESCH	Can it wait?
OFFICER	No, sir.
ROESCH	(Sigh) Okay. Good time for a break?
ROTELLA	I can take over. I'd like to press on.
ROESCH	Oh, sure. Good idea.

(Sounds of chair scraping, door closing, chair scraping)

ROTELLA   For the benefit of the recording, my name is Detective Lorenzo Rotella of the Stony River Police Department, continuing the interview of Eldon Jukes at 9:32 AM on October 20, 1959. Pleasure to meet you, Buddy. All right if I shake your hand? Thanks. You've got a strong grip. Call me Enzo, okay?

JUKES   Okay.

ROTELLA   I saw your car earlier this morning. It's a beauty. '53 Bel Air, right?

JUKES   Uh huh.

ROTELLA   What's that color called?

JUKES   Surf green.

ROTELLA   Nice. Dark green top, white walls, fender skirt. Expensive car. Buy it new?

JUKES   No. I wasn't old enough to drive until '55. Got it second-hand that year.

ROTELLA   Still. A pricey car for a teenager.

JUKES   My grandmother paid for it so I could take her places and run errands. She doesn't drive.

ROTELLA   How do you feel when you drive that car, Buddy?

JUKES   What do you mean?

ROTELLA   Take me, for example. I drive a '56 Ford Fairlane Victoria two-door hardtop. Bought it new when I got back from Korea with the money I saved. Not much to spend it on over there, you know? When I drive that car it makes me feel lucky to be alive and blessed to be back in this country. Your car might make you feel more masculine, I don't know. It's a pretty manly car.

JUKES   Why do you care how I feel when I drive my car?

ROTELLA   I'm curious. I like to get to know people.

JUKES   Well, I don't feel like talking about the car. It's transportation, is all.

ROTELLA   Okay, tell me what you like about the A&P.

JUKES   (Laugh) Besides the fact they pay me?

ROTELLA   Yeah.

JUKES   (Sigh. 10-second pause) Everything's in order. You know what to do every day. You're busy. No time for crazy thoughts.

ROTELLA   What kind of crazy thoughts?

JUKES   I shouldn't have said that. I don't have to say anything. I know my rights.

ROTELLA   That's right you don't have to say anything. It's okay to be scared. This is a scary time for you. But, you know, everybody has crazy thoughts. Me, I'm obsessive about my clothes. They have to be clean and pressed, no buttons missing, no loose threads. I think it's because of my face. You noticed my face, right?

JUKES   Yes, sir. What happened?

ROTELLA   Pimples gone berserk. You're lucky you have good skin. Anyway, I think because my face is so ugly I overcompensate with my clothes. What do you think of that theory?

(15-second pause)

JUKES   You know what a carpenter's level is?

ROTELLA   I do.

JUKES   Sometimes the bubble will go way up here, you know?

ROTELLA   For the benefit of the recording, Mr. Jukes is tipping
            an imaginary carpenter's level to show how the bubble
            could drift. Okay, go on.

JUKES   When it goes way up, you have to bring it back.
            Compensate, like you said about your clothes.

ROTELLA   What happens when you don't bring it back?

JUKES   That's not good.

ROTELLA   Not good like in seventh grade when you hurt that girl
            and spent two months in juvenile detention and another
            four in a mental hospital? Sandra Kopec was her name.
            You remember her?

JUKES   Not very well. That was a long time ago. Guess you have
            my records.

ROTELLA   We do. You roughed her up pretty bad. Why was that?

JUKES   I don't remember. I was a stupid kid. I didn't know
            about the bubble then.

ROTELLA   Your records indicate you suffered from hallucinations
            and delusions. You were apparently free of them when
            you were released, but the doctor's report noted that
            stress could trigger a relapse. You under stress these days,
            Buddy?

JUKES   Are you a doctor?

ROTELLA   Nope. Just curious, as I said before. A student of human
            nature.

JUKES   Sometimes what doctors call a delusion isn't.

ROTELLA   Can you give me an example?

JUKES   The devil's as real as God even though you can't see
            either of them. The devil can get into you and take over
            when you're angry. Other times, too.

ROTELLA   What other times?

JUKES   When you have impure thoughts.

ROTELLA   You mean about sex?

JUKES   Yes.

ROTELLA   What do you do when you have impure thoughts, Buddy?

JUKES   Exercise, mostly.

ROTELLA   Yeah, you've got a muscular build. I'm impressed. What else?

JUKES   Just try to keep busy and show the devil he can't own me. Stay away from places he likes. He's supernatural but he can't be in two places at once.

ROTELLA   Where's the devil like to go, Buddy?

JUKES   Bars, card games, parks at night. I stay away from them.

ROTELLA   When you're trying to avoid the devil, Buddy, do you sometimes head out in the car? You know, drive around to clear your thoughts?

JUKES   Yeah, sometimes, but I have to be careful because if the devil got in he'd start driving the car.

ROTELLA   Is it the devil that offers rides to people?

JUKES   Of course not. He doesn't care about people who are tired or shouldn't be out in the dark by themselves.

ROTELLA   Ever given a ride to a guy?

JUKES   No!

ROTELLA   No need to take offense. It was a reasonable question. Why not?

JUKES   They can take care of themselves. It's not dangerous for them. They wouldn't be scared enough.

ROTELLA   Scared enough for what?

(Sound of door opening. Footsteps)

ROESCH   You're free to go now, Buddy. Your wife posted bail, brought a lawyer with her. Somebody will notify you of your trial date. Show up, okay?

ROTELLA   I need more time, Artie. I think we're making progress.

ROESCH   Sorry, no can do.

ROTELLA   I haven't shown him the last picture yet.

ROESCH   Well, that's the way she goes.

FEW PEOPLE telephone Miranda. She recognizes Enzo's voice right away.

"I know he had something to do with the missing girl, Evelyn Shore, if not the dead one, Barbara Pickens," he tells her, recounting an interview the day before with a man he suspects of several crimes. "I was so close to gaining his confidence. And I would have if I'd conducted the whole interview. The other detective hit him too hard at the beginning and put him on his guard. Then we ran out of time before I could ask him how the devil gets into him or show him the dead girl's morgue picture. Twenty puncture wounds that look like leeches, on her chest, shoulders and arms. Made with a double-edged knife. If they've got any soul at all, the morgue shots get to them."

Enzo's disembodied voice is youthful, energetic. His passion for his work helps Miranda turn her mind away from the stinging sensation on her arms and chest. She recalls the sharp pain she'd felt in her chest as soon as Doris said Bill Nolan had been shot. She doesn't always need to enter an object to hear a victim speak to her.

"I wanted to ask if he was on medication," Enzo says, "and if he could go back, what he would change. He's twenty and set to be a father in two months, but he looked like a kid in that bare, intimidating room, all curved in on himself. If he's done what I think he has, he's evil, but I wanted to hug him, tell him he wasn't alone. Is that crazy?"

"I don't think so. I read somewhere that each of us is both killer and killed. Captive and captor, too," she adds, thinking of James. "You saw yourself in him and felt compassion."

"A dangerous trait for a cop," he says. He tells her there's been a promising development. A high-school student claims that this same man, this suspect, assaulted her in a wooded area that might be the one in which Barbara Pickens's body was found. They brought the suspect in for a lineup and she picked him out with no hesitation. The girl is reluctant to testify in court; Enzo will keep working on her. If she backs out, they can always subpoena her.

Enzo hasn't called just to share his day. The suspect's wife's name is Ladonna, he tells Miranda. How's that for a coincidence? They need a statement from the wife, so he's volunteered to take it. And he knows it's an imposition, but if he can get something that belongs to the suspect, would Miranda be willing to tell him what she sees in it?

It's been nearly a year since she entered that poor girl's petticoat and sensed Bill Nolan's presence in error. "I cannot," she says. "I simply cannot."

TWENTY-SEVEN

NOVEMBER 5, 1959. Buddy would be home soon. Tereza struggled to concentrate on cooking his oatmeal. Lately, following her own thoughts was like listening to a TV playing in another room where somebody kept changing the channels.

Buddy's lawyer, Maury Sawicki, said the attempted kidnapping charge wouldn't stick; Buddy's only crime was caring too much about vulnerable girls. Tereza had looked up "vulnerable." *Defenseless.* Like the baby inside her. Growing one was a big whoop. Somebody told Tereza unborn babies feel and hear everything their mothers do and sponge up their emotions. She had to stay cheerful and keep that—ha, ha, thanks, Buddy—bubble in the middle.

She was back to having breakfast ready when Buddy got home from night shift. They'd kept him on at the A&P but moved him to the Cranford store and put him on nights to keep him out of sight. Too many customers would've seen his face in the paper. Dearie was afraid they'd take back the red plastic coffee scoop imprinted "A&P 100 Years," but they didn't.

Tereza was having to learn the meaning of words like *prosecute, indict* and *acquit.* Maury said he might want her to testify at the assault trial about how Buddy had never hurt her. But if she went on the witness stand the prosecution could ask her anything, so Maury said to think about it. He didn't want Dearie to testify for that reason.

Didn't want either of them saying much of anything to anybody before the trial. "You don't know who might be a plant. They need a conviction for political reasons, and if they can railroad Buddy, they will."

Tereza was supposed to trundle off to work as though her life hadn't been thrown into a Mixmaster. She was supposed to say "No comment" to the reporters camped out across the street who shouted rude questions whenever she left the house, but she told them to get stuffed.

She glanced over at the 1960 calendar Dearie had bought and stuck on the fridge. Dearie had marked the dates like birthdays. January 12, Trial #1: attempted kidnapping. February 23, Trial #2: kidnapping, assault with a weapon and uttering death threats. March 23: grand jury.

If the grand jury said the cops had enough on Buddy to try him for Marilyn Shore's still-missing sister, there'd be another date on the calendar. Buddy had taped a Bible verse next to it: "Behold, the devil is about to throw some of you in prison, that you may be tested ... Be faithful to death, and I will give you the crown of life." It made Tereza shiver.

She thought Maury was pulling her leg when he said Trial #2 was about Linda Wise. Buddy humping Linda? Never. He said he recalled asking those two girls if they wanted a ride but not Linda, even though she'd identified him in a lineup. Tereza told him she and Linda had lived on the same street once, but that didn't ring any bells for him.

The door to the porch swung open and Buddy was in the kitchen, making Tereza jump. Somehow she'd missed the sound of his car in the drive and the garage door slamming shut.

She mustered a smile. "How was work?"

He grunted and scraped past her, his boots leaving black marks on the floor. She heard the bathroom door shut. He'd been sulky for the

past week, ever since she'd given the cops a statement about his whereabouts the night Marilyn Shore's sister disappeared. She and Maury
had sat in a room stinking of B.O. and cigarettes. A detective with a
face that looked like somebody had taken an ice pick to it showed her
a pair of baby blue skivvies and asked if they were hers. Maury hadn't
let her answer. He told her later that the cops might be trying to pin
a stabbing murder as well as the Shore girl's disappearance on Buddy.

"Why'd they think those skivvies could be mine?" she'd asked
Maury. He said she should put them out of her mind.

She couldn't. "Why'd they think they were mine?" she'd asked
Buddy the next morning.

"I suppose because they found them in my car."

"You suppose? How'd they get there?"

"I have no idea. My mind isn't mine anymore. Pastor Scott says
if you let your old self die and be reborn, you'll be set free from the
devil's power. I don't know how to do that."

More devil talk. Tereza was sick of it. "Maybe you better get your
mind looked at."

That had seemed to piss him off.

The toilet flushed and he was back in the kitchen. "Dearie still
sleeping?"

"Far as I know."

With any luck Tereza would be out of the house before the old
bat got up. Tereza loved Dearie, but lately she hated everything about
her: her stupid soaps, the stupid funnies she read, the way she said
"Hmm, hmm, good" about her own Sunday roasts. And she acted
like nothing was wrong, hunching over the whirring sewing machine
hour after hour, stitching enough flannel receiving blankets and
sleepers for a herd of babies. Or sitting in the parlor, watching soaps,
knitting tiny things. "I'm done worrying about things I can't change,"
she'd told Tereza. "You got an idea how to make these troubles go
away, I'm all ears."

Two days ago Tereza had blown a gasket at her for not getting help for Buddy when he was a kid, for letting him believe the devil lived in him.

"So you think he's guilty," Dearie had said.

"Well, something's sure not right." Tereza couldn't let go of those blue skivvies. If Buddy had been screwing somebody else after all she put up with, she'd split, even though she couldn't count on Miranda's money anymore to get her someplace.

The day Buddy was arrested, Dearie had contacted Herman, who put them in touch with Maury—"Don't worry about the fee, he owes me a favor." Buddy was supposed to have been at the bail hearing the following morning but the cops kept him for an interview, something Maury raised a stink about. Tereza and Dearie showed up at the hearing with two thousand dollars borrowed from Herman and the eight thousand left of Miranda's money. Dearie had pulled it out from behind the cinder block before Tereza could get to it. She said she'd known it was there from the time Tereza moved in. "I figured you stole it. Didn't want nothing to do with it."

Tereza was more cheesed off than embarrassed: all that worrying for nothing. "If you thought I was a crook, why didn't you kick me out?"

"If you was on the street the cops might've found out about the money, found out you'd been here, put two and two together and got five. Buddy could've got in trouble."

"Sometimes you can be a real yoyo, Dearie. What else you know you aren't telling?"

"If I ain't telling it's because it ain't your business."

Buddy had shrugged and said "Everybody needs a secret" when Tereza confessed she'd hidden the money all that time.

When he was charged with assaulting Linda, his bail was jacked up to fifty thousand. Tereza broke down and cried then and apologized to the baby for making it sad. Dearie pledged the house as collateral and

Herman loaned them the five-thousand-dollar bail bond fee. There wouldn't be much of Miranda's money left after paying him back.

Buddy pulled out a kitchen chair. She set his oatmeal in front of him.

"Where's yours?"

"I ate already." That was a lie. Lately, everything tasted like puke. Her due date was seven weeks away and she was losing weight, not gaining like she was supposed to. The doctor had ordered blood tests and tut-tutted over the deep shadows under her eyes. Tereza didn't point out who she was; maybe he hadn't connected her last name with the man in the news. He'd written her a prescription for milk shakes—a real comedian.

The detective who'd taken her statement asked if she was the Ladonna who placed the ad. She recognized him then as the man at the newspaper office she'd thought was a robber. Maury said she didn't have to answer, but she wanted to meet Miranda. She told the detective only about the necklace, said she'd explain how she got it when she personally handed it over to Miranda. The detective asked her to describe it. A few days later he called to say he'd bring Miranda to a diner a few blocks from where Tereza worked. At eleven o'clock on November 5th.

That was today. Earlier this morning, she'd fished the tiny key out of her pocketbook and picked up the briefcase she hadn't opened for four years. The lock had been sprung. The necklace was there but the black-handled knife was missing.

Tereza looked at Buddy spooning oatmeal into his mouth like nothing was wrong. She thought about how spectacular she'd been as Eunice in *Streetcar*, bringing Dearie to tears at the end when she said Stella had no choice but to assume that Blanche's story about the rape was a lie and continue to live with Stanley.

For the baby's sake she would keep the fear from bubbling into her throat.

MIRANDA HAS NOT BEEN in a diner before, something Enzo finds "astounding." This one is on a loud street. She's let Enzo persuade her to meet the wife of a man he suspects of murder, ostensibly to secure the return of a crude necklace. She knows he hopes for more. She wants to learn how the woman came by the necklace and what she knows about the altar.

Enzo scoops up menus at the front and leads Miranda to a booth with a brown vinyl seat and a red Formica-topped table mounted with a small jukebox. He sits opposite her, facing the door. "Got a favorite?"

"No." She doesn't follow popular music.

The diner isn't busy but the air is congested with grease sizzle, cutlery clatter and the homey smells of coffee, tomato, onion and bacon.

Enzo drops a coin in a slot and presses a few buttons. Music starts right away, bouncy and plaintive at the same time. "I'll sit over there when she gets here," he says, nodding to an empty booth across from them. "She doesn't look dangerous, but no point taking chances."

"It's a wonder I survive the days you're not with me," Miranda says.

He laughs. Stands. "Here she is."

Miranda turns. Hurrying their way is a short, dark woman in a tan raincoat, clutching a purse to her chest. Her face is drawn, her black curls untamed and her eyes anxious. Something about her seems familiar.

Enzo introduces them and offers to buy them whatever they'd like to eat. The menu lists dozens of items Miranda has never tasted, but her eyes and mind are unable to focus. Something about Ladonna has shaken her: a darkness of spirit, an absence of healthy light. It's early for lunch but she asks for a grilled cheese sandwich, what she makes for the children every Saturday.

"Just water for me," Ladonna says, removing her coat. She's bulging with unborn babe under a rust-colored maternity dress that gives her skin a sallow tinge. She slides bulkily into the seat Enzo vacated. He heads off to find a waitress.

"When's the wee one arriving?" Miranda asks.

"Supposed to be Christmas Eve but the doctor says first babies are usually late."

Ladonna's arms are alarmingly thin—not even the kindling to start a fire, James would have said. The skin around her naked eyes is like smudged coal. She sets her bony elbows on the table, leans toward Miranda and says in a rush, "Can't believe I'm finally seeing you again."

"Again?"

"I was near your house the day the cops came and took you and your kid away."

"When my father died."

"Yeah. I didn't know that then. Just saw you leave."

"That's when you found the necklace?"

"No. A couple months later." Ladonna relates how she broke into Miranda's and why. The runaway Doris told her about, the photograph in the newspaper. Ladonna's mouth twitches between sentences, pitiful and appealing at the same time. Would Miranda have had the self-respect and courage to run away if James had beaten her? Would even *she* have known that was going too far? She briefly tells Ladonna about the orphanage and Doris, that Cian is in kindergarten and shows a talent for drawing.

"Kindergarten! Holy moly. Has it been that long? He was so puny."

Miranda smiles at Ladonna's directness. Cian *was* puny. He's almost chubby now, so proud of his little square feet in their Buster Brown shoes, so unbothered by his misshapen head.

The waitress brings their order. Ladonna's hand shakes as she gulps her water. Her fingernails are raggedly bitten down. Miranda would like to take her home and soothe her with lemon balm. "Did you bring the necklace?" she asks.

Ladonna pulls it from her pocketbook. Acorns and seashells that James said Eileen had gathered and strung on wool before Miranda was born. Twenty of each.

Miranda catches her breath, surprised at the sudden longing she has for her younger, undoubting self. "To think you've held onto this for me never knowing if we'd meet. Thank you." She hesitates before saying, "You must have entered the basement."

"Yeah. It was kind of creepy. What was all the stuff on that table?"

"Before I tell you, I must know: did you see a harp?"

"Yeah. I shoved it into a corner."

Miranda nods. Until now, she believed that only she and James had seen the most secret part of their home. What a miracle someone else saw it too. It means she did not imagine it. She takes the necklace from Ladonna. An image of the altar knife rises up before her eyes. She'd forgotten it was missing. Did Ladonna shove that in a corner, too? She blinks the image away.

"The table was an altar," she says, "and the objects on it symbols. The necklace belonged to my mother. My father said it represented the circle of life and death: that when you die in one world you're born anew in another."

"What religion is that?"

"I don't think it *is* one. He claimed to hate religions, especially those whose god denounces all other gods as false. He believed that no one god can express all that's divine."

"What do *you* believe?" Ladonna asks.

"I'm not sure." For some time now, Miranda's prayers have lacked fervor. She questions the value of praying at all. She feels cut off from whatever the word *divine* might mean. Is she so numb, as the psychiatrist said, that no god can reach her?

TRICIA DOWER

"For a while I thought you could count only on yourself. Then I met Buddy and believed in him for a while, but now I don't know." Ladonna's eyes fill.

"Buddy's your husband?"

"Yeah."

"Was believing in him like worshipping him?"

Ladonna barks out a laugh. "That wouldn't be my word for it. But early on, when I looked at him, a feeling would swallow me up that somebody had sent him to save me." She glances sideways at Enzo, leans into Miranda and says softly, "The cops say Buddy done some awful stuff. I don't want to believe it."

Miranda once thought James was as powerful and wise as the gods he told her about. After she discovered he wasn't, she stopped loving him. But she needs to love him, just as Ladonna needs to love her husband. She reaches across and takes Ladonna's bird-boned hand.

It pulses with fear and sadness.

With horror, Miranda sees it transform into a square, powerful one holding the missing knife. The image fades, leaving a sense of peril in its wake.

She leans over the table and whispers. "What happened to the knife on the altar?"

Ladonna pulls her hand away and falls back against the booth, her mouth pressed as thin as a razor. "I don't remember no knife," she says. "If there was one, I packed it in a box with the other shit." She gathers up her coat. "I have to get to work."

"Wait," Miranda says. "I want to help you."

"I don't need your help." Ladonna slides out of the booth. Miranda turns and watches her stumble out of the diner, struggling into her coat.

Across the way, Enzo gives Miranda a quizzical look.

Her chest feels tight and full of ache for the young woman. On the drive home, after weighing the risk of stirring up suspicion where there may be no cause, she tells Enzo she suddenly remembered a knife that went missing from her house. She describes the color and heft of its handle, the length and keenness of its double-edged blade. Leaves him to make the connection between necklace and knife.

❧ TWENTY-EIGHT ❧

FEBRUARY 23, 1960. Linda prayed that God wouldn't let her stumble on her way to the witness stand or stammer once she was sworn in. The man on trial today for assaulting her had been found not guilty of the attempted kidnapping of two other girls last month and the police were relying on Linda to put him away.

Her head was choking with advice from Mr. Krueger, the prosecuting attorney. Look at the jury when swearing on the Bible. Look at the attorney when he asks you a question but the jury when you answer. Speak so the juror farthest away can hear. Don't make jokes, lose your temper, slouch or chew gum. Keep your hands in your lap. Say yes sir, no sir and Your Honor. Stay alert. Listen carefully. Answer only the question asked. Don't say "I think" or "In my opinion"; just the facts, ma'am, as Joe Friday would say. Always tell the truth. Relax, you'll do fine.

Daddy drove to the courthouse in Elizabeth, Mom beside him. Linda sat in the back seat wearing a white-collared black dress Mom had constructed to be "slimming and serious" under a tentlike coat from Montgomery Ward. She'd lost sixty pounds since her mother began the Linda Project, but she was still fodder for blimp jokes. Climbing the steps of the imposing courthouse, she couldn't recall how they'd gotten there. Mom and Daddy went into the courtroom while she sat in a small, airless room with a police officer, feeling like an egg waiting to be cracked.

The officer accompanied her to the courtroom, opened the door and escorted her, as a bride's father might, down the short aisle and through the gated fence separating the audience, like parishioners, from those taking part in the ceremony. He delivered her to a man with a Bible.

Her voice in the hushed room sounded as if it had traveled a great distance.

As she sat in the witness chair, the edges of the room began to blur and she didn't feel fully present in her body. Tall and lean with a high forehead and pale eyebrows, Mr. Krueger had a disapproving set to his mouth. With her parents present because she was not yet eighteen, he'd rehearsed Linda on the questions he would ask. Linda's mother had cried at what she heard and her father had hung his head. They were hurt she hadn't told them before, but when had the three little Wises ever told each other anything that mattered?

Look at the jury. Keep your hands in your lap.

The answers spilled out easily, and although she'd related the events of July 8, 1958, many times in Mr. Krueger's courthouse office, tears still broke and ran down her cheeks as fast as she could wipe them away with the hanky, smelling of roses and lavender, that Mom had taken from her sachet drawer and given her for the day.

Linda took a deep breath before identifying the man who'd attacked her. The audience laughed when she said Georgie Porgie. The judge banged his gavel. The defendant's name was Eldon Jukes, not Georgie. He looked different in his navy blue suit, white shirt and striped tie. When she pointed him out in the courtroom, he gave her that same sweet smile.

The courtroom *did* remind her of church: women in hats and gloves and men in suits on pew-like benches, she at the front bearing witness, an inspirational half-sun window over the double doors that revealed a chandelier throwing off light sparkles brilliant enough to have come from God's fingers. Everything else—walls, floor, tables, chairs, the judge's bench, the railing—was as brown and uninspiring as dirt.

The defense attorney, a Mr. Sawicki, had fat cheeks and a gummy smile. He looked at her sympathetically, said that what had happened to her was terrible, just terrible, the only thing worse would have been if there had been penetration and was he correct in his understanding that there hadn't been penetration? Yes, he was correct. She liked him right away.

Mr. Krueger had said the defense attorney might get nasty and ask her intrusive questions about her sexual history. That wouldn't take long, she'd joked. As it turned out, Mr. Sawicki had only a few questions, his eyes half-closed when he asked them, as though he were thinking of something far away and pleasant. She wanted to close her eyes and bob like a cork in his sea of hypnotic words. She hadn't slept the night before and the room was warm.

Stay alert.

Mr. Sawicki asked whom she sought out after the assault for comfort or medical treatment: her parents, a friend, a doctor? No one, she said, she was too upset and ashamed. Of what would she have had to be ashamed? Getting into a stranger's car. Did she save any ejaculate on a tissue or cloth for later examination? No. Her statement said her assailant picked her up when it was starting to get dark. Exactly what time was that? She didn't know; she hadn't worn a watch that day because she didn't want to lose it at the beach. Was it before dinnertime or after? Oh, after. She and her friends had eaten at the shore before they headed back to Stony River. How long did the attack take, from the time her assailant picked her up to when he dropped her off a few blocks from her home? An hour at least; it had felt longer. Did she look at a clock when she entered her house after the attack? No, but Tony's Garage was closed so it had to have been after seven. Right after seven or much later? She didn't know. Did anyone see her getting in the assailant's car or leaving it? Not that she knew of. Did she have a boyfriend? No.

No further questions.

The judge said she was free to leave the stand and sit in the audience. She felt dismissed, as though she, not Eldon Jukes, had done something wrong. She stood and passed through the gate. She wanted to keep walking out of the courtroom, down the elevator and onto the street, but her father's arm was around her shoulders guiding her to a seat between him and her mother. "You did fine," Daddy whispered. "Just fine." Mom patted Linda's hand.

To show a behavior pattern, Mr. Krueger brought up the recent attempted kidnapping charge against Eldon Jukes and noted that Eldon Jukes had been identified as giving the missing Evelyn Shore a ride. Mr. Sawicki objected on the basis that Eldon Jukes wasn't on trial for those cases. The judge told the jury to ignore Mr. Krueger's comments.

Mr. Krueger entered into evidence Eldon Jukes's A&P timesheet for July 8th, showing he had finished his shift at 4:30 PM. He called in a meteorologist who said sunset on July 8th began at 7:30 PM, when you could reasonably say, as Linda had, that it was "beginning to get dark" and lasted until what was termed "civil twilight" at 8:03. Mr. Jukes would have had sufficient time after work to be where Linda said he picked her up. Mr. Krueger had wanted to subpoena Lonnie, Arlene, Dee and the girls' dates to testify when and where they'd dropped her off, but Linda didn't want them snickering about it at school. She wished now she'd said okay because she couldn't have felt any more humiliated than she did right then.

Mr. Krueger brought in a forensics expert, a detective from the state police examiner's office, to corroborate Linda's testimony about the missing handle on the passenger door of Eldon Jukes's car. The detective said the handle was loose when they examined the car and could easily have been taken off and put back on. Mr. Sawicki asked the detective if Linda's fingerprints had been found in Mr. Jukes's car; the detective said they had not.

Mr. Krueger called up Detective Roesch to tell the jury he'd taken Linda to the pine grove where Barbara Pickens's dead body had been found and Linda had identified it as the same area to which her assailant had taken her. Mr. Sawicki objected and the judge told the jury to ignore Detective Roesch's testimony.

Mr. Sawicki entered into evidence the police report that said Linda Wise was not able to identify the knife allegedly used against her among the knives seized from Mr. Jukes's home. A police detective had spent hours with Linda last November prodding her to describe the knife in detail. She remembered only a black handle. The knives from Eldon's house had brown handles.

Mr. Sawicki called a witness named Ladonna Jukes. As the witness entered the courtroom, Linda clapped her mouth. She wanted to jump up and call out. She'd long ago accepted that Daddy wouldn't have done anything dirty with Tereza. And she realized how scared Tereza must have been to run away. Why had Mr. Sawicki called her Ladonna?

As Tereza settled into the witness chair, Linda smiled and gave her a little wave but Tereza didn't react. She'd gotten softer and grown-up looking. She wore a black-and-white tweed suit and was still tiny. For the first time, Linda felt ashamed about her weight.

Tereza testified that she was married to the defendant, Eldon Joseph Jukes. Linda was more than alert now. Mr. Sawicki asked Tereza to describe her relationship with her husband. After she'd run away from her stepfather's brutality, she said, Eldon Jukes had saved her from a life on the streets when he took her to the house he shared with his grandmother. She'd found a safe, loving home for the first time in her life. Eldon Jukes had been nothing but a gentleman, watching over her, never uttering a cross word, never raising a hand. They'd been married almost three years and had a seven-week-old baby daughter.

Eldon hadn't left her side through thirty-six hours of labor and was so upset to see her in pain he'd nearly fainted. He was a hard-working A&P management trainee, a good husband and father. Tereza sounded like she was reading a script, but even so, she pronounced words a lot better than Linda remembered her ever doing.

Tereza said Eldon had been with her all evening July 8, 1958. That couldn't have been!

Daddy hurriedly wrote a note and reached across the railing to Mr. Krueger, who read it and asked for a ten-minute recess. He took Linda and her parents to a conference room. They told him everything they could about Tereza in the short time they had.

When it was his turn to question Ladonna Jukes, Mr. Krueger asked if she'd ever gone by the name of Tereza Dobra. She looked down at her hands and said yes. Lived on Grove Street in Stony River? Yes. Been friends with Linda Wise? She'd known her, yes. Had her husband, to her knowledge, ever been near Grove Street? He'd driven her there once. So he would have been familiar with Linda Wise's neighborhood, thank you, no further questions.

Linda watched Tereza leave the stand and sit next to a pink-haired lady holding a baby in a yellow blanket. Tereza took the baby and clasped it to her chest. Who would have imagined her capable of such tenderness? Linda was mystified: the tweed-suited wife and mother Tereza had become didn't fit Linda's concept of justice. Tereza hadn't applied herself in school, had hung out with hoods, done vulgar things in cars with men and run away from home.

Mr. Krueger gave the first summation, noting that it took great courage for Linda Wise to come forward as she had with no other motive than to prevent other young women from falling prey to the dangerous Eldon Jukes. He pointed out Linda's positive identification of the defendant in a lineup, her accurate description of his car and the fact that the only person who had testified to Mr. Jukes's whereabouts that night was an understandably biased relative.

In his summary, the defense attorney speculated that Linda Wise
had seen the newspaper account and made up a story so that others
would think she was desirable, given her weight and the pressure on
girls her age to have boyfriends. He said it was hard to imagine such a
heavyset girl going through the gyrations she'd described in the front
seat of a car. No hard evidence placed Miss Wise in the defendant's
car on July 8, 1958, or any other day, for that matter. She was decid-
edly unclear as to the time of the assault. There were no witnesses to
the assault or its aftermath. The make and model of the defendant's
car was described in a newspaper article before Miss Wise contacted
the police and a loose door handle was not surprising in a now-seven-
year-old automobile. He said you'd think someone who'd used his car
for a crime would have disguised that car afterward or sold it. Mr.
Jukes had done neither. Finally, Mr. Jukes was not in possession of any
knife Miss Wise recognized as having been used against her.

The jury deliberated for two hours. It had never occurred to
Linda they wouldn't believe her.

Mr. Krueger said they'd appeal. He'd investigate Ladonna Jukes
and insist that Linda's parents and her doctor testify that Linda's most
dramatic weight gain had occurred after the assault. He'd wanted to
do that today but Linda had objected. What did weight have to do
with integrity? Tereza had lied and they'd believed her. Linda had told
the truth and they hadn't.

Daddy put his arm around Linda and hustled her out. Driving
home, he said the prosecution had done a piss-poor job, and "If they
think they're going to put you through that again, they have another
think coming."

Linda could only say, "They didn't believe me, they didn't believe
me."

"I know how that feels," Mom said.

TWENTY-NINE

MARCH 29, 1960. Not now. Her grief is too raw.

But one day Tereza will remember the four days Buddy gave her as the long, sappy kiss she'd always wanted from him. They were vacation days he'd said would go to waste if a grand jury indicted him for Evelyn Shore's murder.

But how could they have indicted without a body?

The cops only had three teenagers who claimed to have seen Buddy with the girl the night she went missing in a car that looked like his. Maury had said that might be enough along with everything else a grand jury was allowed to consider. They could look at his juvie record. Hear he'd been charged with trying to kidnap two girls, even though he'd been acquitted because the state hadn't proven *intent* to kidnap. They could review Linda's testimony, despite Buddy's not having been found guilty of a single charge related to her. They could fix their beady juror eyes on the pale blue skivvies the cops had found in Buddy's car and be asked to connect the dots between them and the coroner's report that Barbara Pickens had turned up bare-assed even though the dead girl's mother couldn't swear the skivvies were her daughter's. The cops hadn't made any noise about charging Buddy with the Pickens murder, but Maury had advised that another grand jury might be assembled for that since Linda had testified that Buddy had taken her to the same place where they'd found Barbara's body. Tereza had missed Linda's testimony because she was stuck in a windowless room until it was her turn to go on the stand. Maury'd had to point her out after the trial. Tereza could only stare with her yap open. She wasn't sorry she'd said Buddy had been with her the night Linda claimed he humped her. Tereza had trouble recalling what she'd done last week much less on a certain day a year and a half ago. Why not take Dearie's word for it? Maybe she *did* have bad cramps that night and Dearie went to Herman's without her. And even if what Linda said were true, Buddy's going to jail wouldn't change that; it would only rob little Lisa of a father. Tereza knew what that was like. Sometimes you had to make a decision that hurt one person in order to help another. Like Ma deciding not to call the cops on Jimmy. Or weird Miranda ratting about the knife. She'd known it had been Miranda when the cops came with a search warrant even though they said it was because of Linda's statement. Tereza was glad she hadn't told Miranda about the money; she didn't deserve to get it back. Anyway, Maury said the state didn't really care about an assault charge; they'd been waiting to nab Buddy on murder, only using Linda to get her testimony for the grand jury.

Buddy said he wanted to spend his days off with Tereza and Lisa so he could picture what they'd be doing every hour when he went to prison. "Everything will be fine," Tereza said. "Maury will get you off." If she said that enough times, it would come true. She'd decided to believe he was innocent so she could stop wondering where Miranda's knife had gotten to or worrying about leaving Lisa alone with her own pa. Dearie said babies knew the difference between good folks and bad; if Buddy were guilty, would Lisa look at him so sweetly?

Buddy wanted to eat only the kind of food he'd loved before he found Charles Atlas. On day one, Tereza fixed him crispy fried chicken from a recipe on the cornflakes box. Buddy said it was perfect. They stood together over Lisa's cradle, watching her open and close her long fingers, wave her arms and pump her chubby legs. They tried to decide who she looked like more. She had Tereza's black hair (but straight, not kinky), Buddy's blue eyes and long eyelashes, and her own honey-colored skin, lighter than Tereza's. Her mouth looked like Buddy's when she cried. He took tons of photos on the chance he'd catch the devil trying to sneak into her. The film was still waiting to be developed. Tereza asked him how many girls he'd ever given rides to. He wasn't sure, maybe twenty, thirty. He hated to see them walking alone, especially when it got dark. He said most girls didn't know how to defend themselves. Tereza reminded herself how protective he'd been of her when they first met.

He hadn't killed *her*.

Parents magazine said you could raise a baby's IQ just by talking to it. Tereza didn't want Lisa to be dumb like she was so she'd chattered to her until her voice wore thin. On day two she told Buddy, "Let her hear your voice. You're the smart one." He read to Lisa from *Moby-Dick,* said it was his favorite book. "I never knew that," Tereza said as they huddled together on the back porch settee, wrapped in a musty quilt and watching night close in around them.

"Yeah, I love that barnacled old whale, charging around the ocean, pursued by the evil Captain Ahab."

"Does Ahab catch him?"

"No. It's a fairy tale."

"If those two girls had gotten in the car, would you have taken them right home?"

"I hope so. I like that they turned out brave like you."

On day three, Buddy woke up jumpier than usual. He cracked his knuckles so bad all morning that Tereza suggested they go for a walk. He needed the exercise for sure. She hadn't seen him do Atlas in months; the skin of his neck was sitting in folds on his collar. He looked older around the eyes and mouth, too, like time was passing faster for him than anybody else. It didn't help that he hadn't shaved in days. They tried to sneak out the back with Lisa in her carriage, but reporters sprang up out of Dearie's garden beds like weeds.

"How many girls did you kill?"

"Where'd you stash Evvy Shore's body?"

Their questions wound around Tereza like vines, squeezing the breath out of her. Buddy lunged at the reporters, punching the air with his fists, calling them vultures and cussing until they vamoosed.

In air that was beginning to thaw after the cold winter, they pushed Lisa's carriage eight blocks to the cemetery, not a sad place if you didn't come across a kid's grave. Their shoes made sucking sounds on the squishy ground. Buddy said he wanted to be cremated like his grandfather, couldn't see taking up valuable space with his dead bones. Tereza said there was lots of time to think about that. She could picture him one day crouching on a sidewalk tightening Lisa's roller skates with the key, driving her to tap lessons, showing her how to turtle-wax the car. Tereza loved how Buddy's two big mitts could hold all of Lisa. She wanted Lisa Lange Jukes to feel like the most loved child in the world. Her birth had been like winning a prize, a chance to be a better mother than daughter. Tereza still could hear Ma saying, "You was a terror. Didn't sleep through the night, wouldn't go to bed at a regular time, didn't like to be rocked or held." Dearie said she'd never seen a better baby, as if Lisa knew what her folks were going through. "I'm glad you'll have Lisa when I'm gone," Buddy said.

"Everything will be fine. Maury will get you off." That evening, after hamburgers with pickles that made her gums sting, she asked, "Could Linda have been one you gave a ride to?"

"I've asked myself that a hundred times, Ladonna. But when I looked at that girl in court I knew I'd never seen her. You don't forget somebody that fat."

"She wasn't always that fat," Tereza said.

They pushed Lisa to a park on day four and sat on a damp gray bench. Even if the grand jury didn't indict him, Buddy said, his A&P career was over: the others on night shift were nervous around him; he'd be fired before long. The movie theater had replaced Tereza when she went into the hospital to have Lisa. "You should look for something full-time with more money," Buddy said. "Dearie will babysit."

"I've been thinking about waitressing because of the tips. Someplace I could work shifts around acting lessons. I'd like to see food go in, for a change, instead of hearing it come out."

Buddy laughed. "I'll miss you."

"Maury will get you off."

He took her hands in his. "The defense doesn't get to say anything at a grand jury. If they indict me, a judge might not grant bail. I could be stuck in jail a long time before any trial."

Tereza shut her ears to his words, swallowing the urge to puke, as she had for weeks. If Buddy went to prison, she could still see him and ask his advice about stuff, right? It might be better, in a way, because her gut wouldn't churn wondering where he was, what he was up to.

Dearie made her famous garlicky spaghetti for supper with meatballs the size of plums. They turned the dining room into a restaurant, Tereza taking orders from Buddy and Dearie—Salad on the side? Bread? Something to drink? She carried the dishes on a tray. Dearie perked up for the first time in weeks. She said that to get good tips, Tereza would need to "project" more of a personality, like an actress throwing her voice. Tereza saw herself giving impressions of famous actors; pictured people lining up for a table in her section, refusing to sit anywhere else.

That night, Buddy didn't turn his back to her, or curl up into himself and fall asleep as usual. Sitting with his naked back against the headboard, he said, "I need to tell you about something that's been festering in me." His face looked ghostlike in the dim glow of a nightlight they'd bought so they could see their way to Lisa in the dark.

Tereza's gut sat down hard inside her. If he confessed to killing those girls, would he have to kill her to keep her quiet? She parked herself beside him but close enough to her side of the bed to get away. He reached over and gripped her hand. "I know I'm not a normal husband. You deserve better than me."

She let out the breath she'd been holding. Maybe he was just going to tell her he liked boys better than girls. "I never turned you on, did I?" she said.

"If all it took was love," he said, "I'd be your Casanova."

She didn't know what a Casanova was.

He told her that, when he was fourteen, the devil had taken over his body and kicked a hole in Richie's garage. Tereza had nearly forgotten about Richie. How long ago had he moved away to who-knew-where? Buddy said Richie's mom told him that day he was brain-damaged and called the cops. He'd known for sure then that he was crazy because Richie's mom was a nurse. "The cops tied me to a chair and threatened to send me back to the loony bin."

"What do you mean send you back? When were you in a loony bin?"

"For a few months when I was twelve. Dearie said that was a mistake, that cops and doctors didn't understand sensitive kids. But I knew it wasn't a mistake when I saw that it wasn't me they'd tied to the chair. It was the devil. They left me standing in a corner."

"What did the devil look like?"

"Me, of course. That's what he does." He brought her hand to his lips, stretching her arm so much she had to sidle an inch or two closer to him. Her flannel PJs rode up into her crack. She wondered if he was getting ready to break something, wished Dearie wasn't all the way downstairs.

"She made Rich go into hiding," Buddy said.

"Who did? When?"

"Rich's mom. Three years ago. I drove him to his house after the cop shot him, praying to any god that would listen. She went bonkers but had to let me in because I was carrying Rich. She took the bullet out with tweezers, him yelling bloody murder, me crying, scared he was going to die."

"I'm lost, Buddy. Why would a cop shoot Richie?"

Buddy released her hand, drew his knees to his chest and started rocking back and forth. "We're cruising town and he says he wants to break into Bing's Pharmacy. Just to see what could happen. He's making a comic book about twins whose mother is sick and he wants to get it right. We climb in real easy through an alley window and stand there, hardly breathing, waiting for a siren, flashing lights, a Doberman. Nothing. So we pretend we're dropping pill bottles into a bag but we're not touching a thing. Rich is saying stuff like, 'We wouldn't have to do this, Bart, if Ma wasn't so sick and Pop didn't drink away all the money.' I'm laughing. Then the cop rattles the front door. We should've just ducked down. He probably didn't see us. But we panic, climb back out the window and crouch behind a row of garbage cans in the alley. Clumsy me knocks one over. It was freezing that night but I can still feel the sweat coming right through my palms. All I remember, after that, was the cop coming up behind us, Rich running, the cop's gun going off, more shots and the cop falling a few feet away from me. Honest to God, Ladonna, I didn't know Rich had a gun on him. After I left his house I called the police station to tell them where the cop was. I should've seen to him right away, maybe he wouldn't have died, but I was too scared for Rich."

Tereza felt like a bone had leaped into her throat. She clawed back through her memories: the women yakking about it in Herman's ladies' john, Dearie turning the radio off whenever it came on the news. "The cop from Stony River?"

He gave her a quick, sad smile and rocked harder. "Yeah. Dearie said if I didn't talk about it, I'd forget it ever happened. But the devil won't let me forget. He moved into me for good that night. You don't get away with murder without him in charge."

"But you didn't kill him. Richie did."

Buddy was shaking now, his lower lip quivering. "He was my best friend, the only guy who really understood me, and I didn't protect him."

Tereza drew him toward her and he let her hold him until Lisa woke. She brought the baby into bed with them and covered them all with the blanket. Nursed Lisa with Buddy's head on her lap, his thick arms wrapped around her legs, his veins like little blue rivers running under the skin. He fell asleep with a worried look on his face. She was afraid to move in case he rolled away and took his warmth from her. So she lay Lisa down beside her and sat up the rest of the night—a sharp-eyed owl guarding her chicks. She watched the moon paint the far wall with its milky light. Sniffed in Lisa's baby sweetness and Buddy's spaghetti breath. She wondered if he'd loved Richie the way he couldn't love her.

So what if Buddy was crazy? Everyone she'd ever known was nuts in some way. She didn't give a whoop about some cop's murder, either. Or anyone else's when it came down to it because the only people who mattered were those whose breathing you could hear as loud as your own; your mind couldn't take in more than that. That must have been how it was for Ma. Once Tereza ran away, all Ma could've done was think about Allen and Jimmy. People died and went missing every day. Buddy and Lisa were all Tereza's heart could take in at the moment.

On day five, Buddy said, "You gotta get some sleep, Ladonna," and took Lisa downstairs to Dearie. When Tereza woke, Dearie said Buddy had driven to the store for milk and bread.

He didn't come back.

Two days later a reporter found his car at a motel in Irvington and the cops his body in bloody bathwater gone cool. He'd slit his wrists with Miranda's knife—black-handled and double-edged, the papers wrote, like the one that had stabbed Barbara Pickens.

Dearie said the cops and the press had hounded Buddy to death, like dogs on a rabbit. For days she paced the house, wailing, or sat on the back porch with her hands curled in her lap all funny, like her fingers were busted. Complaining to Alfie that it wasn't fair Irene still had Richard and she didn't have Buddy.

Tereza did her crying alone, on the crapper, in the shower or in bed, turned toward the cold, empty spot beside her. She'd cry until she felt empty, like her insides had poured out. Barbara Pickens's and Evelyn Shore's families were pissed off that Buddy hadn't left a note. Pastor Scott said God was angry, too, at the loss of a tortured soul.

Tough gazzobbies.

Tereza had her own feelings to sort out without worrying about God's or anyone else's. At first, she was mad at Buddy for not telling her everything. Then she realized he'd done her a favor. When Lisa got old enough to ask if he'd done those bad things, she could honestly say he'd never said. Lisa wouldn't have reason to ask about the cop. Tereza was pissed off at everyone who hadn't taken care of Buddy the way they should've. Mostly she was scared she wouldn't be smart enough to raise Lisa right without him.

But she was also a little proud.

She wasn't the one who'd split. She hadn't run away this time.

DADDY BOOKED TIME OFF from work to drive Linda and Mom to the Woodbridge police station where Linda would view the knife Eldon Jukes used to kill himself and determine if it was the one he pulled on her. She hadn't been to school since the trial, unwilling to face the inevitable taunts; the trial and her humiliation had been widely reported. So what if she flunked the entire year? It took only ten minutes to arrive in the new turquoise Dodge that was supposed to make them all feel better, a few more minutes to park and climb the steps of the yellow-brick building with tall narrow windows.

Detective Roesch was waiting for them at the entrance in a brown corduroy jacket and tan chinos. In his twenties, Linda figured. He was a big-shouldered guy with a crew cut. He escorted them to a small windowless room that had a table with benches on either side. The detective with the scarred face was there and a young woman who looked familiar. The room was cramped and stuffy with the six people it now held and smelled as if it needed a good clean. Linda fought an impulse to flee.

Detective Roesch said, "You met Detective Rotella before, right?"

Linda and her parents nodded.

Detective Rotella said, "This is Miss Haggerty. She suspects the knife in question was stolen from her house in 1955. Miranda: Mr. and Mrs. Wise, their daughter, Linda."

That name. That wavy hair the color of autumn leaves.

Linda was wrenched back to a summer day a childhood ago when the future was still a sparkly advent calendar, a numbered window concealing a surprise each day. Crazy Haggerty's daughter hadn't died and didn't appear to be a lunatic.

The girl, now a woman, stepped forward and took Linda's hands in her own long-wristed ones. "I asked to meet you," she said, "so I could tell you I admire your courage." Her green eyes felt probing, the press of her palms too intimate. Linda gently extricated her hands.

"Ditto," Detective Rotella said. "Bum luck not finding the knife before the trial. We would've loved to have spared you the ordeal."

Linda could only nod. She was lost in memory. The Miranda of then had been mysterious, even dangerous. This one you wouldn't look twice at in her red plaid skirt and white sweater. Close up, though, something about her was unsettling.

Daddy stepped beside Linda and said, "Was James Haggerty your father?"

Miranda turned to him. "He was. You knew him?"

"Only on neighborhood patrol during the war. Not after that. We live just a few blocks from his old house. Your old house." Daddy dipped his head. "I'm glad you're all right."

"Thank you." Miranda turned toward Linda's mother. "Mrs. Wise, I sense bravery runs in your family." Mom lifted her eyebrows and took the hand Miranda extended. Miranda winced, then leaned in and whispered something to Mom. They sidled to a dark corner and exchanged words Linda couldn't hear until Detective Roesch said, "Can we get started?" Miranda and Mom sat together on one side of the table with Detective Rotella, leaving the other for Linda and Daddy. Linda had never seen her mother take to a stranger so quickly. Detective Roesch stood at the table's end with a plastic bag from which he withdrew a long knife with a black handle. He placed it on the table. Linda noticed Miranda's shoulders sag.

"Do you recognize this, Miss Wise?"

Linda had envisioned a knife stained with Eldon Jukes's blood but this one was clean, its blade glinting under the fluorescent light. She reached beneath the table to still a trembling leg, grateful for Daddy's arm around her shoulders. Her mind flashed to the knife emerging from Georgie's glove compartment. If she'd begged for her life, as he demanded, would she be dead like that other girl? Had the knife been single-bladed or double? Shorter or longer than this one? Was this a test to confirm she was the liar the jury thought her to be? "The handle looks the same"—her voice cracked, making her hot with embarrassment—"but I can't say for sure."

"I understand," Detective Roesch said. "It's tough to register details when your life's in the balance. Miss Haggerty?"

Miranda's face had turned hard. "It looks like mine." She picked up the knife and turned it around in her hand, as though weighing it.

She ran her fingers up and down the handle and the flat part of the blade. Closed her eyes and took deep breaths. So many breaths that, at some point, Daddy cleared his throat and frowned. "Give her a moment," Detective Rotella said.

Miranda was motionless for so long that Linda thought she was asleep or unconscious. Then she shuddered, arched her back and cried out as if she'd been wounded. Linda gasped. Daddy started. Mom laid a hand on Miranda's arm. Detective Rotella stood and gripped Miranda's shoulders. "No more," he said.

Miranda let the knife fall to the table with a thud. She opened her eyes, wet with tears. Rubbed her temples with the heels of her hands and said, "It was never intended to harm anyone."

"What just happened here?" Daddy asked.

Detective Rotella said, "She sees things differently, that's all."

Maybe Miranda *was* a lunatic.

"We'd like to hang onto the knife for a while, if that's okay," Detective Roesch said.

"Do what you like," Miranda said. "I'll not be wanting it back."

In the car, Mom said, "She could be some sort of Jeanne Dixon."

"Why?" Daddy asked. "Did she make a prediction?"

"No, but she asked, 'How long have you had that pain in your pelvis?' I said, 'Seems like forever,' and she said, 'Drink chamomile tea four times a day and take deep breaths while imagining scissors cutting the wires to the pain.' Can you imagine? I've never heard of chamomile, have you, Linda?"

"No." Linda twisted her head to stare at an opportunity for courage disappearing through the rear window. She should've told Miranda she'd seen her before. At seventeen, Linda was still afraid her parents would learn where she'd been that day—nothing brave about her at all.

"She said I should call her at Doris Nolan's house if I'd like to talk more."

"She's living with the widow?" Daddy asked.

"Seems so. She's a strange one, but I don't think she's an unbraked wagon."

Daddy laughed. "A what?"

"You've heard that before, haven't you?"

"Never. You surprise me every day."

Linda lay on the back seat and breathed in the chemical smell of the new upholstery.

❧ THIRTY ❧

OCTOBER 5, 1962. Daddy was home. His briefcase met the floor with a soft plunk. The hanger scraped as he hung up his jacket.

"How are my girls?"

Linda caught the slight stiffening of her mother's spine. "Mom's hand is stuck in the meat grinder and I've melted into a puddle of grease," she called back.

His shoes rattled the furnace grate as he crossed into the dining room. "Very funny." He appeared in the kitchen doorway, rolling up his sleeves, his face flushed from his walk home. "What a gorgeous day. We haven't had the first frost, so technically it's not Indian summer. What would you call it, kiddo?"

"Hot?" Linda was straining spaghetti over the sink, the steam fogging her glasses.

Daddy leaned over the pot Mom was stirring and sniffed. "Hmm, onion? Garlic?"

"Chicken cacciatore," Mom said. "We made it in class yesterday." She'd begun Adventures in Gas-Tronomy at the gas company a month ago. So far she'd come away with recipes for Spanish Rice, Potato Puff Soufflé and Beef Rouladen as well as a red apron exclaiming in fat white letters, NOW YOU'RE COOKING WITH GAS.

Linda slid the spaghetti onto a big platter. She'd go easy on it at dinner. She was down to a hundred and forty-eight and back into clothes with waistbands. According to Doc Pierce's chart she'd be the perfect weight if she grew four inches taller. She didn't care about being somebody else's idea of perfect, but no one would dismiss her or doubt her word again simply because she was fat.

"Car run okay for you today?" Daddy asked.

"Seemed to," Linda said. She'd gotten her license, finally. Took the car to and from County Junior College on Monday, Wednesday and Friday mornings. Daddy walked to work those days. He said he enjoyed the exercise and the chance to smoke his pipe. After Mom read about thugs surrounding a young woman's car at a red light and rolling it over, she'd insisted on riding with Linda. She'd bring a book and wait in the cafeteria until Linda's classes were over, or, if she wasn't feeling well, curl up in the back seat of the car. How she thought she'd be any defense against thugs, Linda couldn't imagine.

On Tuesdays and Thursdays, Daddy drove Linda to and from her part-time job at Quill and Page, a book publisher six blocks from his office. She wouldn't have minded walking, but he said the area had become over-industrialized and unsafe. She'd gotten the position because she had excellent pronunciation. A copyholder, she sat at a book-strewn table in a cavernous, high-ceilinged room, adding her voice to the chant-like hum of dozens of other voices at dozens of other tables. They read aloud from edited manuscripts to better-paid proofreaders whose eyes searched for errors on galley proofs. She'd thought it would be a boon to be paid for reading books all day, but all she ever got were dreary school texts. Plus, she had to read every word and every scrap of punctuation, all without emotion. *Capital T the verb hyphen adverb combination open parenthesis as distinct from the verb hyphen plus hyphen prepositional phrase close parenthesis provides another variation period.*

They took their ritual places at the dining table and bowed their heads. "We thank you for our daily bread and for keeping our precious daughter safe today," Daddy said. The same grace every night, guaranteed to make Linda tear up.

Mom said, "A-men!"

Daddy smiled at Linda. "Split any atoms today, Einstein?"

She made cross-eyes at him. "No, I was too busy recalculating the fulcrum for the George Washington Bridge."

She'd enrolled in remedial algebra and physics in September. Her goal was to attend Angela Brohm's alma mater in Ohio. The sole female social worker assigned to the Home for Delinquent Boys, Angela handled the littlest ones. She called them her "clients." Linda liked how respectful that was, the way it made you think the boys had value and a choice as to how they behaved. Angela usually showed up at the Home at some point during Linda's volunteer shift. She took time to answer Linda's questions about social work and life in general.

Linda took one piece of chicken and filled the rest of her plate with salad.

"As I walked home tonight," Daddy said, "it occurred to me that there are similarities between teaching and social work, especially if you want a career in helping children."

Here it comes, Linda thought: the next volley in his assault against her plans.

"It's not the same," she said.

"How so?"

"It just isn't." A teacher's job was to cram a kid's brain with information. A social worker tried to make sense of what was inside that brain already, maybe stop the kid from turning into a Georgie Porgie. Or a Tereza.

"I'm not keen on your going off to Ohio," Daddy said. "It would be better if you weren't more than a few hours' drive in case of emergency."

"I don't want you living away period," Mom said. "From what I've heard, most campuses aren't safe for women, especially after dark."

Linda suspected they didn't want to be left alone with each other.

"You could live at home if you went to Douglass," Daddy said. "I could get you there in a half-hour or so. Pick you up after work."

When her father drove Linda to work or to the Home, he waited until she entered the building before driving away. He'd be outside when her shift was over, often leaning against the car with his arms crossed, looking left and right like a bodyguard. She'd take her time leaving, refusing to be intimidated by his martyr-like presence.

"Can I get a BSW there?"

"Translation, please."

"Bachelor of Social Work."

"I'd like you to rethink this whole idea," Daddy said. "You might get assigned to Harlem and be murdered. Or end up homeless after giving all your money away. Let's face it: you're gullible, a soft touch." He set his knife and fork down noisily on his plate and looked at her with a hard expression. "I still can't understand why you were so concerned about hurting a stranger's feelings that you got into a car with him."

Mom let out a noisy breath. The Wises had gotten better at discussing some matters, but the assault was still off limits, their individual fortresses of guilt over it impenetrable.

Eldon Jukes's death by his own hand had restored Linda's faith in divine justice. But she'd struggled to forgive him for attacking her and Tereza for lying on the witness stand. Not to mention the jury for not believing her. She struggled to understand why it had happened to her. Punishment for her heedless acts, the times she'd lied to her parents and defied their wishes?

No percentage in playing the what-if game, Angela claimed; some things happened for no reason at all. But after a sermon in which Reverend Judge said all was part of God's plan, it had come to her: Eldon, Tereza, the jury and even Miranda Haggerty had been instruments of God, sent to heal Linda's blindness toward her obesity and her mother's suffering. Angela said that was an interesting theory to which she wasn't inclined to subscribe. But Linda felt sure God had made her suffer so that the scales would fall from her eyes as they had from Saul's.

"I've explained all I'm going to about that day."

Daddy reached over and squeezed her hand. "I know, I forgot. I'm sorry."

"And *Angela* wasn't assigned to Harlem. She isn't homeless, either."

"She's no doubt a fortunate exception." He took a swallow of coffee and put his cup down with a clatter. "You could do worse than working your way up at Quill and Page. With your language skills, you could be a full proofreader before you know it, even an editor someday."

"Saving the world from misplaced commas," Linda said.

"Yes, well we can't all be Flash Gordon or Wonder Woman. Saving Bartz Chemicals from accounting errors has fed this family pretty well, I'd say." He tore off a piece of bread and forcefully rubbed it around the sauce on his plate.

Linda sighed, ready to surrender. She didn't want the rest of the evening to be unpleasant. She had nowhere else to go. Back when she was a kid pretending to have been shipwrecked, Tereza had been so much braver and smarter; she knew there wouldn't be enough on The Island to sustain her. If Tereza were an East German, she'd be tunneling or swimming to freedom. Linda would be one of the others, yearning for deliverance but loath to leave a warm bed.

The rest of the meal passed with little conversation.

"Shall we all do the dishes together?" Mom asked as she did every night.

She became anxious if Linda spent too much time in her room. So, after the dishes, Linda did homework or played solitaire at the kitchen table while her parents watched TV in the living room, taking turns coming into the kitchen on the pretense of needing drinks of water. Before bed, she'd review Mom's daily pain diary with her. It had been crazy Miranda Haggerty's suggestion that Linda's mother record the location, intensity and duration of pains she experienced each day, what she was doing at the time, what she'd eaten, how she'd slept the night before. She gave Mom meditation exercises to "rise above the pain" and little packets of tea leaves to brew if it was especially bad. Supposedly Miranda was studying nights to become a legitimate pharmacist, but she put more store in plant medicine than Linda thought appropriate. Linda was frustrated that a brainstorm hadn't arisen yet out of the data her mother recorded. Mom said it was enough not to feel so alone with her misery. Although Miranda hadn't yet charged for her "consultations," Linda wondered if she wasn't taking Mom for a ride.

October was Halloween month. When Linda was twelve, the first full moon on a Halloween in thirty years had appeared, confirming her deep sense that she'd been born in a special time for a unique purpose. She hoped that was still true. Angela said it was never too late to be what you wanted, to pretend you'd seen into the future and come back to live differently. The application to Ohio State waited in Linda's room, needing only a heaping plate of courage.

THIRTY-ONE

OCTOBER 10, 1962. Miranda stands in a cemetery in Milford, Massachusetts, in the section reserved for suicides. Above her stretches a bellflower-blue sky. Her mother's grave is in sight of a granite tower at the end of the pond: a replica of the stone towers some say Irish monks built as protection from the Vikings and a memorial to the thousands of Irish immigrants buried here. She peers up at its narrow windows and pictures magnificent hair, as long as a summer vine, cascading down through a window at the top. Rapunzel's hair was said to be the color of sunlight, but Miranda always imagined it her own reddish gold.

She places the cushion she's brought on the grass, kneels and studies the engraved words on the polished red-granite marker: EILEEN AGNES REAGAN HAGGERTY, OCTOBER 10, 1918 – JANUARY 7, 1943, AS FLEETING AND DARING AS A THUNDERCLAP. Eileen would have been forty-four today, eleven years older than Doris.

Miranda has taken a train, a bus and a taxi to this spot, imagining this moment ever since Enzo located Eileen's gravesite, wondering whether she'd be overcome with grief or, worse, feel nothing. *She suffers still from the loss of you,* James wrote in the letter on Miranda's fourth birthday. *I say this not to add to your grief but so you'll know how much you're missed.*

She's decided to mark this day with more than her pilgrimage.

She's come looking for her home in the past. "Your entire family may be dead," Sister Celine once said, "but they're still your family." Miranda feels the loving weight of those words and, more keenly, the lack of history to pass on to Cian. James claimed that Miranda's grandmother and great-grandmother had spiritual gifts of healing Mother Alfreda would call "charism." Were they channels of the power that shines light on darkness, brings knowledge to ignorance? Does such power even exist? Miranda is grateful for whatever abilities allow her to intuit the fear and pain at the core of another's illness, but she wants something more transporting. She wants to kneel once more in ecstasy and believe she's been touched by the same magic as her ancestors.

In the *grimoire,* James wrote: *If mystical abilities are to endure, they must be seen to on a regular basis like plants and children. Otherwise they die.*

She's brought a leather satchel containing a white candle in a holder; a metal dish; a small plastic bag with a mixture of aloe, pepper, musk, verbena and saffron; matches; the pewter chalice; the necklace Ladonna Jukes returned; the photograph of the woman in white; a small thermos of red wine; one large envelope with the ashes of James's letters and another with those of her own journal—words as dead as butterflies pinned to velvet in a museum box.

She begins with the spell James used more than once, attempting to contact Eileen's spirit. As far as Miranda knows, it never worked—perhaps because, as James wrote in the *grimoire,* it's meant to be cast in a cemetery on an anniversary of the departed's birthday. Craning to make sure the taxi is still at the gates—too far away for the driver to see her clearly—Miranda places the necklace under the collar of her camel-hair coat. She removes her brown wool gloves and, with her finger, draws an invisible circle around her. She sets the photograph against the headstone. Into the metal dish she pours the contents of the small plastic bag. Striking a match, she sets them alight and says, "Gatekeeper of the Other Life, harken to my plea. When the shrouded sky with crows is rife, bring my mother and father to me. With reason and will summon them both, trailing power and mystery from the Isle of Ghosts." She's had to adapt the spell to accommodate more than one person.

The instructions in the *grimoire* include reciting the incantation three times, then waiting quietly for sign of a presence. She keeps her eyes open in case the sign is visual. Pulls her coat tightly around her. It is nearly noon, yet the sun above emits no more heat than a light bulb. The dark half of the year begins soon, when the dead are supposed to find it easier to walk among the living. Should James or Eileen caress her hair, how will she know it isn't a breeze? She sniffs the air for tangerine but smells only sweet, damp earth beneath grass going dormant.

The next spell, more of a ceremony, is her creation. She sets the candleholder on the ground, lights it and says, "With this candle I honor the flame of my mother's life." She pours the wine into the chalice, takes a sip and says, "With this cup, I honor my mother's blood"—the blood that James in a vision once exhorted her to drink. She stands, opens one envelope and sprinkles the ashes of James's letters atop Eileen's grave while saying, "Dear god of Mother Alfreda, angel of Doris, gods and goddesses of James and all beings of the Other Life, invisible and not, with these ashes unite my mother and father in holy death with an aye, there was a lass and an aye, there was a lad, as it was in the beginning, is now and ever shall be, world without end, amen."

There, she thinks, that ought to do it.

She opens the other envelope and, with a wide sweep of her arm, sends the ashes of her journal into the air where Eileen can catch them and try to make sense of her daughter's childhood should she be so inclined. James can spend eternity fathoming his role in it for all she cares. *I look at the lad and must concede the experiment failed.* She tries not to dwell on those words but they steadily leach through her, like rainwater through layers of shale, swelling the hidden sea of pain inside her. Yet she knows he loved her and Cian. Once, she felt it in every cell. It was a love that held her through the darkest days at St. Bernadette's, assuring her she was worthy of the World and all within it.

"But you were wrong, James," she whispers. Cian is repeating second grade this year because of a tendency to daydream, but doctors find no indication of retardation. Who's to say the lad's small head is not the very mark of his divinity?

She kneels on the cushion again, sips more of the cherry-tasting wine and watches the candle struggle to stay lit in a breath of wind that chills her ears and nose. She slips her gloves back on. What must she look like, kneeling with a string of grubby acorns and seashells around her neck and staring at a candle on an ash-strewn grave? Eccentric, she supposes, even a bit mad.

Rapunzel let loose with a thermos of wine and half a loaf of knowledge.

The wind kicks up with a musical sound and blows the candle out. She throws back her head and laughs, full-throated and free.

❧ AUTHOR'S NOTE ❧

I GREW UP in a town much like Stony River in an age when secrets crouched behind closed doors and it wasn't "polite" to interfere in another family's business. Children were left to decipher the meaning of adult whisperings and come to frightening conclusions.

My recollections of that repressive time informed this novel, as did the murder of a police officer when I was in high school and the subsequent crimes of his killer while I was elsewhere, growing a family and building a career. A *Newark Star-Ledger* account of those crimes in 2008 propelled me back to the era and inspired pivotal events and critical details in *Stony River*.

The novel continues and expands upon "Not Meant to Know," the first in my story collection published in 2008. The story starts, as does the novel, with Linda Wise and Tereza Dobra watching Miranda Haggerty leave her house accompanied by two police officers. But the story focuses on Linda's first steps toward sexual awakening. Tereza runs away as she does in the novel, but Linda doesn't learn where. Linda tries to find out what happened to Miranda, but she isn't successful.

The novel attempts to fill in Linda's blanks. My goal was to produce a "ripping good yarn." But the urge to challenge religious dogma as well as assumptions about right and wrong, sanity and madness, love and abuse crept into the exercise.

Nothing was as it seemed back then. Realizing that has been liberating.

CREDITS

I GOT RHYTHM

Written by George and Ira Gershwin.

Used by Permission of Alfred Music Publishing.

All Rights Reserved. International Copyright Secured.

DAY-O (THE BANANA BOAT SONG)

Words and music by Irving Burgle and William Attaway.

Copyright © 1955; Renewed 1983 BMG Ruby Songs (ASCAP),
  Lord Burgess Music Publishing Company (ASCAP) and Chrysalis
  One Music Publishing (IMRO).

All Rights for Lord Burgess Music Publishing Company in the
  United States and Canada Administered by BMG Chrysalis.

All Rights for Chrysalis One Music Publishing Administered by
  Chrysalis One Music.

International Copyright Secured. All Rights Reserved.

Reprinted by Permission of Alfred Music Publishing and Hal
  Leonard Corporation.

MY PRAYER

Written by Georges Boulanger and Jimmy Kennedy.

Used by Permission of Canadian Shapiro Bernstein–Skidmore Music
  Co., Inc.

All Rights Reserved. International Copyright Secured.

❧ ACKNOWLEDGMENTS ❧

MY HEARTFELT THANKS to those whose wisdom and attention helped shape this book:

Adrienne Kerr, my editor at Penguin Canada, for "getting" what I was trying to say and drawing it out of me with sensitivity and skill. Agent John Pearce of Westwood Creative Artists for his faith, judicious edits and patient guidance. Copy editor Karen Alliston, whose discerning eye and intelligent mind have saved me, no doubt, from post-publication mortification. Critiquers (Is that a word?) *extraordinaire* Diana Jones, Kathryn Lemmon, Marybeth Nelson and Ania Vesenny for soldiering through multiple drafts with patience and good humor. Leanne Baugh, Susan Braley, Hannah Holborn, Susan Mayse and Nancy Swartz for reading early chapters and setting me on the right path. John Metcalf for his professional opinion and encouragement. Carman Lawrick for his unique blend of expertise and perspective. Chuck Sigmund for his knowledge of Catholic liturgy and practices in the 1950s. Lora O'Brien's book *Irish Witchcraft from an Irish Witch* (Career Press, 2005), Eblanna Raven's book *Immrama* (Cafe Press, 2006) and members of an Irish Witchcraft online community for assuring me I couldn't go too wrong with my allusions to the incredibly varied history and practice of Irish paganism. Kathy O'Connell for sharing her experiences at a Catholic orphanage. Walt Waholek, president of the A&P Historical Society, for his enthusiasm and insight into what it was like to work at the A&P in the 1950s and 1960s. Diane P. Jaust, former Radio City Music Hall archivist, for details about the old Radio City Music Hall Easter show and her generosity in reviewing my manuscript. Mike Wolfgang, Katie Wolfgang, Lillian Dobbs and Glenn Dobbs for their continual (and totally unbiased, of course) cheerleading. Colin Dower for the unconditional love that keeps me going.